Unequal Combat

A korshak screen appeared, locked onto a cloudcastle, and paused.

"It's the *Kansas City*," Victor said quietly. Even as he spoke, four more missiles lifted from the cloudcastle.

"Take out the missiles first," Alex suggested.

California nodded. "That's easy," she said. She moved the aiming circle and quickly knocked out all four. Then she turned to the cloudcastle. The aiming circle locked on.

The cloudcastle began to fall, slowly at first, then rapidly, then slowly again as it reached denser air below the clouds. Jets of vapor burst viscously from breaches in the hull and hung like strands of spiders' silk in the thick air. Then the whole structure exploded. Long tentacles of superheated smoke spread from the nucleus, slowly twisting in the thickening atmosphere.

By Crawford Kilian
Published by Ballantine Books:

The Chronoplane Wars
THE EMPIRE OF TIME
THE FALL OF THE REPUBLIC
ROGUE EMPEROR

EYAS

GRYPHON

GRYPHON

Crawford Kilian

A Del Rey Book

BALLANTINE BOOKS • NEW YORK

A Del Rey Book
Published by Ballantine Books

Copyright © 1989 by Crawford Kilian

Library of Congress Catalog Card Number: 89-90749

ISBN 0-345-35730-2

Printed in Canada

First Edition: August 1989

Cover Art by Stephen Hickman

For Scott and Corky McIntyre

Tell the beads of the chromosomes like a rosary,
Love in the genes if it fails

We will produce no sane man again

GEORGE OPPEN, "Route"

One:

Alexander Macintosh, captain and soon to be proprietor of the spacecraft *Wuthering Heights*, felt very ill at ease with himself and his world. The drive had just cut off, and the ship was moving at three hundred kilometers per second; in his present mood it felt like three times that, a headlong acceleration to disaster. Earth glowed bright and welcoming through the skylights in his office, yet he would rather have been out past Jupiter, staring at the cold bright stars.

It was May 10, 2396. In ten hours he would be on Earth, aboard his father's cloudcastle, face to face with people who had come from all over the planet to help celebrate his twenty-fifth birthday. Even his mother was expected—and she hadn't left her property since Alex's departure-day ceremonies five years before. The thought of the reunion made him shudder.

He stepped from his office through tall French doors that opened onto a broad balcony. The air, as always, had the sweet tang of early summer. Four stories below lay the gardens surrounding the main house—lawns, flower beds, and woods, even a shrubbery maze—all well watered by duck ponds and little brooks.

The circular edge of the gardens, a kilometer distant, was marked by an unbroken row of tall hedges that leaned inward a little, an inevitable effect of the curving lines of the kuldi field. Above the hedges rose the delicate fome webwork that supported the airdome over the gardens and the house. Usually the dome projected an artificial sun in a clear blue sky, but just now it showed the fat crescent Earth almost visibly swelling up.

Wuthering Heights had been his twentieth-birthday present, a gift from his father. In it Alex had traveled all over the inner system and twice to Jupiter. Most of it had been grown by molecular machines, which had then grown the robots to assemble it. His father had left much of its design up to him, however, as a kind of finishing touch for his education. "Most people leave that to their molmacs," William Macintosh had said. "But it's too much fun to fool around with a steamship's systems, and you have to show the ship who's boss."

Alex had been disappointed at the time. After his departure day he had had to spend a tedious six months in lunar orbit, getting *Wuthering Heights* into running order, but he knew how wise his father had been. Not many spacecraft proprietors understood their vessels as Alex understood his. And after tomorrow it would truly be his, Alex's own property.

Small consolation. Glumly he paced the wide balcony. Having a wise and generous father was one thing; having to be in his physical presence was another.

In the past five years Alex had been in other people's presence very rarely, and always for sex or dueling. After such a long time alone he was certain that mingling physically with others for ritual socializing would inevitably provoke the wrong reactions. The birthday party was likely to be painful and embarrassing, leaving memories he could neither enjoy nor edit.

Swallows and purple martins darted through the air, hunting mosquitoes raised especially for them. Perhaps, he thought, a rite of passage had to be an ordeal. Departure day had not been much fun, either. Tomorrow, though, he would be a full-fledged citizen, free of parental command and full owner of his own spacecraft. He could journey where he pleased, even out to the Neptune Belt; he could file personal claims on unowned comets and planetoids, go to war to defend those claims, and do anything else he liked.

Not that his parents had been heavy-handed during the transitional period; they had reared him conservatively and well, and he had repaid their efforts by avoiding the temptations of youth. He had no interest in epiphanic drugs and still less in the old-fashioned religions that such drugs had supplanted. His sexual experiences had been enjoyable but discreet. He entered the Database infrequently; he had not lost himself in compulsive efforts to decipher the riddles of the aliens' knowledge. And while he was a fair hand at dueling and enjoyed watching wars, he had not entangled himself in violence as so many eager youths did. Ahead of him stretched centuries of travel, sexual and intellectual amusement, combat and exploration: the proper career of a proper gentleman.

—Wake up, Heathcliff.— The spacecraft's housekeeper, a large and glossy black Labrador, roused himself from a sunny corner of the balcony where he had been napping, shook himself, and padded over. —How are you, Alex?—

—Just fine, thanks!— He wished sarcasm could be properly conveyed by electronic telepathy.

—I think you probably ought to vocalize, you know. Just to get back into practice.—

Alex made a face. —It's stupid.—

—You *know* it's extremely bad manners to communicate with a fellow human over a comlink, especially face to face, and especially your own parents.—

"All right, Heathcliff." Alex sighed. "And I suppose you'll want me wearing clothes as well."

—I can imagine what your father and mother would say to me if I allowed you to turn up for your birthday in your birthday suit.—

Alex involuntarily glanced down at himself. From feet to throat he appeared to have a coat of gleaming, iridescent scales. At that moment they were chiefly red down the center of his torso and along the insides of his muscular legs, turning smoothly to deep blue along his arms and flanks and back to red along his spine and buttocks and the backs of his legs.

"Very funny."

Actually, he was fond of Heathcliff's sense of humor. On long, dull trips the dog was good company. But Heathcliff did have that canine fondness for etiquette, for social rituals, that humanity had largely discarded. Dogs were still unrepentant pack animals. Humans were solitaires.

—Besides, your father is sure to criticize your dermograph.—

Alex decided he would wear a bright white jumpsuit, one with a rakishly high collar. His hands and feet, at least, were colored only by natural melanin.

"I won't argue. Let's go for a walk."

—Wonderful!—

They descended a stairway to the gardens, Heathcliff bounding ahead. Alex found a stick and threw it into a duck pond; the retriever plunged in happily and swam out to get it. The water looked so inviting that Alex dived in as well and spent the next half hour splashing about with Heathcliff. The swim cheered him up.

—You asked me to give you the agenda for the reunion,— Heathcliff said as they finally got out. The heat of the sun began to dry them at once.

"All right."

—We go into Earth orbit in just under ten hours. The shuttle will take you down to *Munshaour*, which is currently moving due east over south China. Rendezvous will be at 5:05 a.m., a little before local dawn on May 11. You'll have time to rest and acclimatize before meeting your parents for breakfast at 8:30. At 10 you'll move into the reception hall to greet your guests.—

"My guests. I don't even know most of these people. Except by reputation, like Mao Jian and Sei Shonagon. And California Moran. I'm going to be a nervous wreck just thinking about them. Listen, Heathcliff, I've been thinking about a journey to Saturn when this nonsense is over. How long would it take?"

The Labrador growled. —We'll ask Emily later, when we have time.—

"All right, all right. I didn't mean to be annoying."

They went back to reviewing the agenda, with Alex cheering up as they reached sundown and his departure from the cloudcastle back to *Wuthering Heights*. He sat on a marble bench and looked up through the dome at Earth.

"Magnify, please, Emily." The image of Earth expanded to a gigantic crescent that filled almost the entire dome. "Thank you."

"You're welcome, dear," the spacecraft's computer replied.

Despite being the home of many dull and annoying people, Earth was certainly pretty enough at a distance. It filled the dome as a fat blue crescent, swirling with clouds. On the nightside, lightning flashed across Asia in regular rhythms—probably some contest of meteorographers, Alex supposed. The Arabian peninsula stood out in sharp detail under a late afternoon sun. The three ice mountains along the Red Sea threw long shadows eastward. They were the nuclei of good-sized comets, landed rather gently on the surface of Earth forty years before and still melting. The green grasslands and blue lakes of Arabia's Empty Quarter were half-veiled by the clouds trailing downwind from the mountains. Here and there sunlight gleamed on the roofs of some citizen's estate; once Alex glimpsed the flash of a bomb. He could have learned whose estate was being attacked, even watched the counterattack, but warfare—even the spectacular sort waged between cloudcastles—was less interesting to him than the slash and parry of individual dueling.

West of Arabia, Africa was lost under clouds that parted here and there to reveal the endless forests of ekata that dominated the continent from the Indian Ocean to the Rift Valley. Not many people lived down there. Ekata was a nuisance, getting into even the securest estate and crowding out the native Earth vegetation. The woman who had first grown the plant from its genome in the Database had been relentlessly warred on by dozens of other citizens until she had moved off the planet altogether.

The Sahara was mostly desert still, though ice mountains softened some of the bleakness of the Sahel. Europe and the Mediterranean lay under cloud, but Alex could imagine the domed palaces on the sea floor of the Aegean, the walled forests of the German estates, and the complicated towers of France and Britain. Out on the Atlantic, the deep blue ocean was mottled with the irregular, multicolored blotches of floating forests—another alien lifeform that should not have been synthesized but which planet dwellers now had to put up with.

Yes, it was pretty and was still the home of most of humanity's twenty million people, yet it seemed to Alex more unfamiliar even than the distant worlds of the Net. After all, in the last ten years he had spent considerably more time studying the other planets of the solar system and those of the trolls, slugs, gryphons, and other species than he had spent studying the world of his birth. With any luck at all, he would not have to set foot on Earth again for a long time—maybe a century or two.

Turning on his bench, he studied the main house with a critical eye. It was all very well for a young man, but perhaps a citizen ought to have something more—tasteful. In its present form the house was a four-story Victorian mansion with a green copper roof and dark-brown wooden siding. Emily said it was not at all like the original Wuthering Heights, but from her description that stone-walled farmhouse would have been quite unsuitable. Perhaps a remodeling could occupy some of the long months of a journey to Saturn. Something more austere, without all the gingerbread: a Chinese pagoda or even a trollish miungaliu.

Well, that could wait until he had the time and energy to quarrel with Emily. And after today he would have all the time and energy in the world.

Getting to the shuttle from the sphere was always a little unsettling. A clear-walled elevator dropped him from the house straight down the shaft to the comet. The focus of the residential kuldi field was of course at the sphere's south pole, and just below it Alex went into free fall. Clinging to a handrail, he watched the mottled black and gray surface of the comet rise up to meet him. Then he was deep within it, and the polished-ice sides of the shaft gleamed in the elevator lights.

The elevator stopped, and its door slid silently open. Alex pulled himself out and floated weightlessly down a long corridor at right angles to the elevator shaft.

The corridor ended in a large maintenance shop full of robots. They puffed little jets of gas to get out of his way and chirped greetings as he passed. Nervous about the reunion, Alex answered them brusquely as he soared across the shop straight to the belly lock of the shuttle. It swung open for him, and he glided into the ship's large dayroom.

Familiar smells filled his nostrils: the rich tang of old leather, the aroma of baking bread. On the floor was a Chinese carpet; the walls were hung with red silk that rippled slightly in the airflow. A cluster of armchairs stood around a coffee table near the back of the dayroom, while at the front a single tall wing chair faced a blank screen. Beside the wing chair was a small table bearing a mug of coffee and a tray of fresh chocolate chip cookies.

—Welcome aboard, Alex.—

"Hello, Charlotte. I hope I haven't kept you waiting."

—Not at all. Would you rather I vocalize also?—

"Might as well. I have to get used to it."

A calm, deep woman's voice came from an unseen speaker. "Of course—Emily told me you were practicing for your party."

"My father's party."

"I'm sure you'll enjoy yourself very much. Please be seated, Alex. Lift-off is in two minutes."

Alex swung himself into the leather-covered wing chair and helped himself to a couple of cookies. As he did, one of the screens suddenly came alive with a view from the nose of the shuttle: the long dark flank of the comet, its antievaporation coat gleaming, and the bright crescent of the residence sphere over a kilometer ahead. Earth was not visible at the moment.

"Here we go," Charlotte said, and Alex felt himself gently pressed back into the rich brown leather upholstery. Acceleration and deceleration were inconvenient sensations in the residence sphere but were amusing to retain in the shuttle. The comet fell away; stars whirled through the screen; the shuttle began to descend.

Landing on Luna was far easier, Alex thought as the shuttle skipped its way around Earth and into the atmosphere. Turbulence over the Himalayas was upsetting, and the planet's horizon put everything into an unfamiliar perspective.

"*Munshaour* is ready to receive us," Charlotte said.

"I should hope so." He studied the cloudcastle's image on the screen before him.

It was about three kilometers long and one kilometer wide, yet its hull was no more than twenty meters thick. From its upper surface, towers and domes—gleaming pink and gold in the light of the rising sun—stood seemingly at random amid parkland and woods. Missile racks and beamers were tucked away on the underside. Near the trailing end of the cloudcastle was a hundred-meter landing strip and a cluster of hangars and maintenance sheds wittily disguised as Greek temples. Alex dourly noted his mother's personal aircraft being towed off the strip into a hangar.

Charlotte pulled the shuttle out of its steep glide in a braking maneuver that slowed it to under one hundred kilometers per hour. The miniature kuldi fields embedded in the landing strip did the rest, bringing the shuttle to a stop almost instantly.

"Home sweet home," Alex muttered.

He had lived there most of his life, from birth until his twentieth birthday, yet *Munshaour* meant oddly little to him. He had played in its woods and fields, explored its engine rooms and warehouses, pestered its robots to entertain him. Sometimes he had even seen his father, though more often in korshak image than in physical presence.

From the shuttle he stepped onto a waiting mobile, a wheeled robot with four seats under a red and yellow striped awning. "Good morning, sir," it said.

"Umph." The air was unpleasantly humid, even at two thousand meters, and Alex's jumpsuit clung stickily. "I presume you're taking me to my father."

"First to your quarters, sir. Then to your parents."

"Of course." He was annoyed at himself for forgetting the agenda; Heathcliff would roll his eyes and whine if he knew how absentminded his master had become.

The mobile carried him down a winding road between palm trees to a grassy clearing where a small stucco house stood beside a pond. Red roof tiles gleamed in the early morning. Welcoming lights burned in the windows. Stepping down from the mobile, Alex walked to the door of the house and stumbled when the door failed to open automatically.

"Of course," he muttered again. His father liked what he called appropriate technology, which meant backward devices like doorknobs and manual switches. He grasped the knob and twisted.

Although the house was no more than ten meters on a side, the interior seemed almost as vast and spacious as a cathedral—a trick of optics. The arched ceiling twenty meters overhead was really a horizontal surface he could touch by extending his hand. Illusions: People were fond of them when they were so easy to create.

A mosaic in the tiled floor led him to another doorway, this one already open. Beyond it was a small, cozy room with a fire crackling before a comfortable chair.

"Welcome to the cabana, sir," the house said in a plummy male voice. "Please make yourself completely at home. It's good to see you back."

Alex grunted and flung himself into the chair.

"I strongly recommend you enjoy a tumbler of molmacs, Alex," the house went on. "We have some new strains of flu on the planet, I'm afraid."

"All right. Be quick about it." Another reason to dislike visiting Earth: all the damn diseases, both native and copied.

A robot glided into the room through another doorway, carrying a silver tray that bore a tall glass of what looked like café au lait. Alex took it and drained it off, finding the taste tart but pleasant.

Waiting for the new molecular machines to do their work, he sprawled onto a bentwood chaise lounge upholstered in some polychromatic material; it cycled, like his dermograph, through a range of hues.

A little drowsily, he asked the house to show him the landscape below the cloudcastle. South China drifted by on the wall opposite an immense desert of eroded hillsides, silt-choked rivers, and scrubby stands of bamboo. Here and there stood the walls and domes of an estate, looking incongruously green amid the dryland scrub. Ruins were visible scattered through the wilderness: a pagoda rising from a swamp, the roofless brick rectangles of a nameless village, an ancient power pylon standing rusty and abandoned on a windswept ridge.

He tried to imagine what it had looked like three centuries earlier, on the eve of Contact, when twenty-first century China had held a billion and a half people. Now not more than a million lived between the ruins of Xianggang and those of Harbin. Only fifteen million lived on the whole planet where almost seven billion had witnessed the first messages from the trolls in 2030.

And only a few thousand of us under the age of seventy-five, Alex reflected. Apart from his parents, not many people believed in producing children or even clones.

While the molmacs did their work, he dozed. The house gently woke him. "Your parents are expecting you, Alex."

"Thank you." Alex stood, took a deep breath, and walked out to the waiting mobile. He sat under the awning and let it glide down the road. The mobile cruised east through a stand of palm trees, then onto a causeway across a pond.

"Stop," Alex commanded hoarsely.

The mobile obeyed. "We're going to be late, sir."

Ignoring it, Alex stepped from the mobile and stood on the roadway, staring in amazement at the eastern sky.

Something was eclipsing the just-risen sun. Beyond the cloudcastle's skyline of trees and towers, a dome of darkness seemed to be rising into a sky that was turning almost purple. The sun was half-obscured already; the rim of the dark dome suddenly turned red-orange, exactly like a planet's atmosphere as seen from the edge of its umbra in space. Then the sun was gone, and the sky glowed with stars. Here and there Alex could see the long, delicate traceries of steamship exhausts stretching hundreds of thousands of kilometers across the sky.

He turned again to the east, where the dome of darkness swelled until it was an almost complete circle of black against the stars. The air turned suddenly chilly.

The mobile spoke again, but this time in his father's voice. "Alex, hurry up. We seem to have a crisis on our hands."

Alex almost used his comlink but caught himself and spoke instead. "What is it, Father?"

"It appears to be a planet, a good-sized one, fifty thousand kilometers from Earth."

Two:

The house, as William Macintosh liked to call it, was a sprawling compound of one-story buildings that formed a kind of labyrinth around a chain of ponds and gardens. At its far end—very close, in fact, to the prow of the cloudcastle—stood the living room, a cathedrallike structure rising thirty meters above the compound with a single tower soaring another fifty meters and ending in the flattened bubble that was William's study.

The living room, like the rest of the compound, was built of fome and exploited that alien material's enormous strength and plasticity. Form followed fancy, not function; walls thinned to transparency where their designer chose or thickened only to bear the weight of the designer's aesthetic judgment.

In the ominous twilight of the new planet's shadow, the rainbow colors of the fome had darkened to a murky purple, and the stained-glass walls of the living room automatically blazed in orange and yellow and green.

The mobile carried Alex down a twisting roadway, past koi ponds and statuary gardens, swimming pools and holaria, until it arrived at the tall front doors of the living room.

"I hope you enjoyed your trip with me, Alex," the mobile said.

"Very much, thank you." Alex stepped down and trotted up the shallow steps to the doors; they swung open silently, spilling yellow light.

Though he had lived on *Munshaour* for most of his life, he still found the living room dauntingly vast. Its multicolored glass walls curved to meet far overhead. Apart from a few clusters of potted palms and overstuffed chairs, its floor was a bare expanse of polished hardwood. On a sunny day it could be quite cheerful and bright, with birds fluttering about and robots briskly cleaning up the birds' messes. That morning, under an unnatural eclipse, it seemed gloomy even where the lights glowed brightest.

"Ah, here he is at last!"

Alex peered about to find his father in the cathedral vastness and then waved self-consciously. William Macintosh was seated at a long table behind an array of ferns; as Alex approached, he saw his mother, Lydia, sitting opposite William. She smiled faintly as their eyes met.

Lydia Korolyeva was a tall woman of 125 or so whose thick blond hair cascaded down over her shoulders to the small of her back. She wore a blue silk blouse, cut rather loosely, and tight white pants that flared into elaborate bell-bottoms. Alex noticed that she had rebuilt her face almost completely since he had last seen her about a month ago, giving herself slightly slanted green eyes and a somewhat longer nose than usual. But the smile was still wryly lopsided, the teeth not quite straight; his mother was vainer about her imperfections than most women were about their beauty.

"Hello, Alex," she said in the deep, musical voice she had had for the last couple of years. "You're looking tired." She gave him her cheek to kiss. The nearness of her prickled his skin and made him feel he was in a dream. He stood up, glad to be out of the aura of her body heat. Yet the presence of his parents was not quite as uncomfortable as he had feared.

"Anxious is more like it," his father said. "Under the circumstances, he's doing very well."

Perhaps in honor of the occasion, or simply because he chose to, William Macintosh wore a navy-blue three-piece suit, a white shirt, and a blue and gray striped tie: very old-fashioned even for a man born in the twentieth century and now close to 450. He had not tampered with his face in centuries: a shock of brown hair falling across a high forehead, humorous blue eyes set under thick brows, an aquiline nose and thin-lipped mouth. Despite his clothing he looked youthful as ever; a stranger might have taken William and Alex for brothers.

William took Alex's hand and shook it firmly and cheerfully. Like most survivors from before the Contact, he was used to physical presence. Yet today he seemed positively glad to see his wife and son.

"Welcome back. Sit down and have some breakfast while we try to find out what's going on up there."

They all looked up through the transparent walls, which curved overhead until they met in a narrow ridge of gold-glinting fome. The new planet was well clear of the horizon, a black sphere partly rimmed in red. Stars and steamship contrails stood out clearly in the darkened sky, and Venus glowed whitely, close to the new world.

"Bliokio!" William called. The central computer of *Munshaour* instantly appeared as a holographic image of the legendary troll philosopher. Alex cheered up a little; Bliokio had been his closest friend in childhood, and he still associated its icon with hide-and-seek and long, quiet conversations that his father had never had time for.

Like all trolls, the icon displayed a powerful forward-curving torso supported by a pair of short hindlimbs and another pair of longer midlimbs. Under the neckless head were trollish arms, slender and multijointed, ending in fingerless disks of muscle that could perform exquisitely delicate manipulations. The icon, like the original Bliokio, was covered in short, feathery fur of a mottled beige and brown. The head was armored in ridges of callused skin and dominated by four eyes—two facing forward and one on either side—above a mobile lipless mouth.

"Yes, sir."

"Would you summarize what you've learned so far? I don't think Alex knows much yet."

"I'll be glad to, Mr. Macintosh." Bliokio projected a hologram of the planet, suspending it a few meters from the table. Alex sat down and absently nibbled a muffin while he watched.

Drawing on monitors as far away as Luna, including a great many whose orbits passed near the intruder, Bliokio quickly set out the known facts and the likely inferences to be drawn from them. The new world was just slightly smaller than Earth and was not one of the thousands listed and described in the Database. It possessed oceans and continents and evidence of a long tectonic history. Its atmosphere was richer in oxygen and nitrogen, poorer in carbon dioxide, and thinner than Earth's. Wherever it had been half an hour earlier, it had orbited a star at a distance permitting extensive glaciation at the poles and in numerous mountain ranges.

Most importantly, the new world exerted no gravitational or tidal influence on Earth or Luna: it was safely enclosed behind a shardana bubble.

"That seems impossible," Lydia protested, and Alex heard a note of professional jealousy in her voice. She had often experimented with bubble generators, creating small and unstable films of the nonspace that the trolls called shardana. None had been more than half a meter across; while she could tune them to be opaque or transparent to most forms of radiation, she had never kept one operating for more than a few minutes. Twice she had built completely spherical bubbles, which had promptly soared into space: Their contents were no longer influenced by any force outside them, including gravity, so they had simply stopped relative to Earth's motion. "Even a perfect tap into the virtual field would scarcely give them enough energy for a bubble that size," Lydia went on. "The trolls themselves can't build a bubble more than eight or ten kilometers across."

"These are not trolls, Ms. Lydia," the computer said. "As you can see, the bubble is transparent to most of the visible spectrum, so we already have a good image of the inhabitants."

The planet hologram vanished, to be replaced with a korshak image: a flat plain, dotted with treelike structures under a deep-blue sky. A wedge-shaped vehicle occupied the foreground. Stepping from it was an alien.

"Gryphons!" William exclaimed. Then, more bemusedly: "*Gryphons?*"

Alex had of course often seen gryphons (who called themselves Chaiar or Sshakta) on korshak. Even so, he felt an odd tremor at the sight of this one. The alien was much more humanoid in appearance than Bliokio: a tall, upright biped with a broad chest, two long arms, and a flat-faced head. The startling crimson oval of the osmotic membrane, extending from collarbone to navel, showed that the alien was male; females' membranes were usually smaller and pale brown. His powerfully muscled frame was sheathed in short, glossy black fur.

The gryphon's face looked like that of a grotesquely masked human. He had a strong, furred jaw and a wide mouth. Above his lips a beaklike brown horn jutted about as far as a human's nose would; the horn extended up across the cheeks and forehead, making his dark-blue eyes seem deeply recessed. The eyes were large, showing no white, and reflected greenly when they caught the light.

Above his horn mask, the gryphon's broad skull was furred in a kind of black mane covering the top and back of his head, his thick neck, and his shoulders. His only garment was a loose network of shimmering threads.

Once he began to move away from the vehicle, the gryphon seemed less human. The joints in hips and knees produced an undulating stride, and the feet—with three long, webbed toes—flexed strangely. One hand reached up to brush the shimmering garment, displaying three fingers and an opposable thumb. Each digit had three joints and ended in a clawlike spur of brown horn like that on his face.

"Bliokio, is this fellow typical?" William asked as the gryphon faded away.

"He seems to be, sir. So far we've counted eighteen million on the surface, and the planet seems to have cities that could house up to a billion more."

All three Macintoshes looked baffled. "Why so many of them? And why cities?" Lydia wondered. "I don't know much about gryphon society, but surely a Net species wouldn't live in *cities*."

"The Chaiar, ma'am, ceased to be a Net species about twelve hundred years ago. They were launching thought bombs against other species and were walled off as a result."

"That's right," William said. "It's somewhere in the Database. The trolls were especially upset about the gryphons. I seem to recall the gryphons were doing some genetic tinkering with themselves and turning out ugly."

"The fellow we saw looked perfectly ordinary," Alex said. His father nodded, a bit abstractedly.

"Don't judge an organism by its phenotype, Alex. After all, we look like pre-Contact humans, but under the skin—"

Aware of the polychrome scales beneath his jumpsuit, Alex nodded. The differences, he knew, went much deeper.

"But if the gryphons were walled off," Lydia said, "what are they doing here?"

"We're working on that, ma'am," Bliokio said. "As I said, the planet itself is not one known to be in the Chaiar solar system—"

"Remind me," William interrupted.

"Xi Puppis, eight hundred light-years from Sol." The hologram of the new planet vanished, replaced by one of the Net: a cloud of stars, well over five thousand light-years across, with about fifty of them—all G-type suns—linked by red lines. Sol lay near the outer edge of the cloud, away from the galactic core, tied to the Net by a single thread to Nu Bootis, thirty-one light-years away. It had been known to the Arabs as Mufrid; now it was known by its trollish name, Kho An. Xi Puppis, called Tayas by the gryphons, lay much farther coreward at the ends of several broken threads.

"How could they travel eight hundred light-years?" Alex asked.

"I assume you're asking me," Bliokio said. "Since the planet appeared without warning of approach and is not one belonging to the Tayas system, I assume the Chaiar have developed some form of spaceflight permitting instantaneous travel between stars. No physics known in the Database could permit such travel. It may be that planetary shardana bubbles are somehow linked to instantaneous travel."

Lydia shook her head irritably. "I think that's inconsistent, Bliokio. We all know why Net species don't bother with interstellar travel. Any ship smaller than a planet would break down en route. But if they can travel instantaneously, why bother with a whole planet and lugging millions of people about?"

"I can't answer that, ma'am."

Alex thought about what his mother had said. It had been one of the bigger shocks of Contact to learn that an interstellar civilization had no interest in interstellar flight. Trade between stars was pointless: Korshak transmission provided all the information one needed, so any alien product could be synthesized from local materials. Exploring the explored was equally meaningless: Any alien locale could be re-created within one's brain while one sat comfortably at home, and even uninhabited systems could be studied in detail from the Net worlds.

The energy costs of an interstellar flight were high but not impossible because the virtual field could be tapped, but the environmental hazards were considerable. To bring a starship up to a quarter of the speed of light—the practical limit, beyond which collisions with dust particles would rapidly destroy the ship—would fill space around its home system with relativistic particles and severely impair korshak communications systems.

Slower travel was possible, but not many troubled to embark on millennia-long voyages. Most species could certainly live long enough to make the trip and could also choose to pause—to go into suspended animation—if they feared boredom. But the thought of being physically in some other solar system simply did not motivate anyone. Furthermore, as Lydia had observed, the support systems of any spacecraft would eventually break down even with constant molmac maintenance unless the craft was as large and complex as a biologically active planet. Bringing along the sun of such a planet was beyond even the technology of the Net.

So each of the species in the Net stayed in the neighborhood of its home sun, content to communicate by korshak at the speed of light. If the news from Juhho or First Stone was five thousand years old, it did not matter; most species' individuals could be immortal if they chose. And if the news was incomprehensible after being filtered through the cultures of several dozen intermediate species, that did not matter, either. Most of the Database was incomprehensible in any case, at least to a novice species like humanity, but thousands of years were available for its decipherment.

Now the Chaiar, after centuries of isolation, had invented a means of faster-than-light travel—and used it to move a whole planet. Why not simply move a comet or two, with a handful of curious explorers? And even if they could travel instantaneously, why not choose to move only information instead, as the rest of the Net did? Moving matter seemed to Alex needlessly redundant.

"It's the cities that worry me," William said. "They imply a social hierarchy." He looked pained. "People giving orders, people taking orders. Like slaves."

Or like young people until they turned twenty-five, Alex thought. But he had to agree. In Net societies individual autonomy was one of the few constants; social pressure on the individual was unheard of, a blunder worse than a crime.

"I'm much more interested in the physics of it all," Lydia answered, her eyes sparkling with animation. "Planet-sized shardana bubbles, instantaneous travel—something new for a change."

"Oh, I doubt that it's really new," William muttered. "It's all probably in the Database somewhere."

Lydia smiled at him. "Really, dear, you put too much stock in the Database."

"Let's recall, *dear*," William snapped, "that we have access to perhaps a millionth of the information in the Database, and we understand perhaps a millionth of that millionth. The trolls are relative newcomers to the Net themselves. They can't be expected to understand everything that the older species have passed on to them, and they certainly don't trouble to explain much of what they do understand."

"Please don't be grumpy, William, especially on Alex's birthday. Let's drop the matter for a while; I'm sure Bliokio will let us know if anything else turns up."

"I'll try to keep you updated without interrupting the party," the computer said, and its icon vanished.

The rest of the morning passed in small talk mixed with more speculation about the new planet. Alex relaxed and began almost to enjoy himself. Watching his father, he felt a mild fondness for the old man; toward his mother, the feeling was one of guarded admiration for her wit and quickness. They were pleasanter people in the flesh than on korshak. Or perhaps everyone was just being sentimental.

After an hour or so the sun reappeared beneath the planet's rim, and the sky brightened. Bliokio said the planet appeared to be moving into a position just ahead of Earth in its orbit.

"I'd dearly love to know how the gryphons are managing that," Lydia said. "Theoretically they aren't even in the universe, yet they're managing to steer their planet very precisely."

A grizzly bear trotted heavily into the living room— William's housekeeper, August. The bear nodded courteously to Lydia and bared his fangs in a smile to Alex, who patted the thick, coarse hair on August's flank. He was as fond of the bear as of Bliokio; he had learned to walk by clinging to August's fur. William and the bear exchanged some brief messages via comlink; then August turned and left.

"Our guests are arriving," William said. "Shall we meet them at the door?"

"Of course," Lydia said. She beamed at Alex. "I can

scarcely believe you're really twenty-five. You've turned out very well, you know. I'm glad your father persuaded me to go through with it."

"Did Heathcliff talk about the guests?" William asked as they walked across the glossy floor to the doorway.

"Not in detail. I've certainly heard about people like Mao Jian and Sei Shonagon, and of course I know Lyell."

William's mouth twisted in an ironic smile. "I've invited people you might enjoy knowing, people who might offer unexpected opportunities."

"I'm sure I'll enjoy meeting them."

William chuckled and winked at Lydia. "If you're typical of your generation, I'm sure you won't. But once you're over the shock of shaking hands, you may find them very useful—especially now."

In rapid succession, a string of aircraft circled *Munshaour* and landed. Then mobiles began arriving at the steps to the living room, each carrying a guest or two.

First to arrive were Sei Shonagon and her daughter, California Moran. Sei affected an ancient Japanese kimono although her features and complexion were currently Scandinavian. Alex knew of her. She was considered an authority on iconography, Database exploration, and sex and had had a string of notable lovers over the past century and a half.

California, as tall as her mother but black-haired and olive-skinned, was the offspring of Sei and the late great duelist Skiudiu Moran. She was about twenty and wore a collar-to-ankle gown of luminar; Alex suspected that she, too, was concealing a dermograph. Her figure, small-breasted and slim-hipped, was deliberately unfashionable when the current craze among young women was the Venus of Willendorf look.

Alex recalled stories about her. She had fought her first buttons-off duel at the age of thirteen and had been Earth champion since the age of sixteen. California had a reputation as an artist as well, specializing in fome sculpture and weaving in pre-Contact fibers. He had seen her at a distance on Luna two or three times but had never found the courage to introduce himself.

He wondered if she ever took lovers, and after meeting her eyes he felt both encouraged and intimidated. She was not the sort of young woman one met in the lupanars on Luna, all coy and concupiscent; California had inherited both her mother's comfortable sexuality and her reputed father's perilousness.

The touch of her hand gripping his felt like an electric shock. He reveled in the strength and smoothness and hesitated to release her.

"Mother said you were shy," she said. "I don't think so."

"Oh, I am."

Her long, slender fingers squeezed his hand a trifle harder. "We'll see about that."

Next came Mao Jian, two meters tall and dressed in a robe resembling live seaweed. He grinned down at Alex, engulfing the younger man's hand in his own enormous paw. Mao was a notable warmaker, remembered for his famous quadruple campaign against four others, all of whom died. Alex was more interested in face-to-face dueling than in the long-distance technological combat of warfare, but like most young people he had followed Mao's career. The thought that Mao would be willing to attend the party made Alex think better of his parents.

They stood on the terrace outside the living room, politely drinking the molmac cocktails William offered them and then switching to tighla or mineral water or coffee. The talk was, of course, about the new planet. Mao Jian speculated that it meant an end to warfare.

"Never fails," he said quietly. His square face was hardened into a frown. "When an advanced civilization takes over a backward one, the new rulers want peace and quiet. We won't be allowed to fight."

"Are you disappointed?" California asked, clearly unimpressed by Mao's reputation.

"If they give us something that's as much fun, I'll be quite content to put away my missiles. If not, perhaps I'll sneak out to the Neptune Belt for an occasional scuffle."

"But are they going to take us over?" Lydia asked. "So far, all they've done is to stand in our light for a little while."

"I don't think they have come just for the weekend," Mao Jian said, which made everyone but Alex laugh. He finally remembered what a weekend was, but the conversation had already gone on.

"... imputing human motives to aliens," William was saying to Mao Jian. "We recall the Euros imposing their culture on other peoples, and we assume that aliens would do the same."

"Haven't they?" Lydia asked, gesturing around the living room and, by extension, the whole cloudcastle.

"No more than you and I have imposed our culture on Alex by bringing him up in it. The trolls gave us what they knew, and we were free to make whatever we liked of it. Just as we gave them our culture."

"Twentieth-century television," California giggled.

"I will *not* be laughed at about this," William said with a grin. "Even by you, California. The difference is that the trolls didn't force us, and the Euros did force their victims under pain of violence to accept Euro culture. Just because the gryphons have actually turned up physically doesn't mean they intend to impose themselves."

"But they were thought-bombing their neighbors in the Net," Mao Jian reminded him. "That's cultural aggression, isn't it? Using your neighbor's own culture to derange him?"

"It may be aggression," William agreed, "but it is certainly ancient history. Five hundred years is a long time."

"*You're* almost that old," Lydia said, "and I'll bet you haven't changed in the slightest, have you, dear?"

William burst out laughing. "Bliokio must be scandalized to hear us speculating on so little evidence. Here comes another guest."

Alex recognized the next guest as soon as he left the mobile and trotted up the steps. Lyell Bradley was the finest molmechanic in the solar system, an artist who had designed whole families of molmacs for hundreds of purposes. Some were prosaic: The air pumps in *Wuthering Heights* had been built by Bradley molmacs. Others were fanciful, like the humming flowers that had been such a fad a couple of years earlier. He was considered eccentric since he had applied almost none of his molmacs to himself; Bradley had stayed with his innate genome and therefore was rather short and wiry, with a prominent nose and close-set brown eyes. He even had a birthmark, a portwine stain on his left cheek that molmacs could have erased in an hour or less.

"Air pumps working all right?" he asked Alex without preamble.

"Yes, sir. Beautifully."

"Ask Heathcliff to call me for an updated version."

"What a practical birthday present," William said. "Good to see you, Lyell. What do you think of this apparition?" He glanced up at the enormous crescent in the sky.

"Interesting," Bradley mumbled, nodding shyly to the other guests and to Lydia. "Y' know, a lot of the Database, the part we can understand, seems to come from the Chaiar. I wonder if that means they think more like us than most species. Their molmacs are really elegant."

"High praise, coming from you," Mao Jian said. Bradley shrugged and looked back up at the planet. It was rising slightly faster than the Sun.

"Bliokio," Alex said, "is the planet still moving ahead of us?"

"Yes, sir. On its present vector it will take up a position about twenty-five thousand kilometers ahead of Earth within seventy-two hours."

"So we'll see it late at night and early in the morning," Lydia said. "Are you picking up any transmissions at all from it?"

"Nothing, but the planet's biosphere shows a great deal of activity." Bliokio presented a rapid montage of scenes: bulky-looking surface vehicles moving along sunken roadways, aircraft of many sizes and designs, and cities built around gleaming lakes and inlets of the sea. Outside one city a fleet of shuttles stood on a vast plain, their white hulls gleaming in the dawn. Alex was struck by how much they looked like his own, which of course had been grown by molmacs derived from the Database. How long ago, and how far away, had the first such shuttle been grown?

Mao Jian rubbed his hands uneasily on the algoid fabric of his jacket. "They transmit nothing, but they know we must be able to monitor them. What conclusions do they expect us to draw?"

"I think they're probably monitoring us," Alex said. Everyone looked at him. "Everyone in the system seems to be chattering away about them, and they're learning a lot just from that."

Mao Jian nodded. "If we had any sense, we'd have gone silent the moment they turned up."

"Good luck," William Macintosh said with a smile. "As soon go into a floating forest and not set the khiudie screaming."

The conversation continued, animated and sometimes argumentative. Alex found himself relaxing a bit, almost as if the people around him were just icons like Bliokio rather than physical presences. Another aircraft landed, and within minutes a mobile brought the last guest.

"Liam McCool!" William bellowed happily, arms outstretched. "I'd begun to think you weren't going to turn up."

Climbing the steps to the front door of the living room was a man in a wrinkled tropical suit. A Panama hat was pushed back from his forehead, revealing a face that Alex recognized at once: long-jawed, deliberately wrinkled, with prominent nose and ears and a broad smile showing slightly yellow teeth.

"Miss a birthday party? Not even for an alien invasion. Isn't it lovely?"

Earth's best-known poet and troublemaker moved with a dancer's grace, though Alex thought McCool looked affected with his wrinkles and white hair. He greeted William with an abrazo, Lydia with a bow and a kiss to her hand. When he turned to Alex, the gleam in the older man's eyes was hard to read: simple pleasure or cheerful malignity? Or was it, Alex wondered, simply the man's reputation?

"Your birthday comes on an auspicious day, Alexander Macintosh." McCool accepted a molmac cocktail and raised it in salute. "Whatever else these gryphons bring," he said, "they bring encounters with divinity."

"Liam, dear, *please* don't proselytize," Lydia said.

"Never, Lydia. But you will allow me to share my pleasure, now, won't you?"

"I only hope they don't give us more encounters with divinity than we can properly enjoy," William said dryly.

McCool laughed. "No more than we deserve," he replied. He was also, after all, a Violent, one of that small but influential religion that believed pain and shock were true epiphanies, experiences of godhead. His conversion had been a systemwide scandal and had inspired a few young duelists to proclaim themselves Violents also.

The party was well under way, and everyone seemed cheerful and at ease despite physical presence and the mysterious new planet. Alex sipped his tighla, a mildly alcoholic drink derived from a trollish plant, and basked in the others' attention. They all seemed like very nice people, especially California.

"Now that we're all here," William went on, clearly

intent on changing the subject, "I want to give Alex his birthday present." He looked a little amused and a little uncomfortable. "We've kept it a secret for a long time now. It seems to be more appropriate than Lydia and I had imagined."

Lydia nodded and smiled, looking equally bemused.

"Bliokio, would you tell Victor he can come out now?"

"Yes, sir."

At the far end of the living room a doorway led to an elevator leading up the tower to William's study. The doorway opened, and a tall form filled it.

"Come in, Victor," William said. "Please don't be shy."

Alex realized his mouth was open and closed it. Coming across the polished hardwood floor with a now-familiar rippling stride was a tall young gryphon. His fur was golden yellow, his eyes black and enigmatic. He wore very ordinary white cotton shorts and a red T-shirt.

The gryphon, a good thirty centimeters taller than Alex, approached him and looked down into his eyes. The impassive beaked face showed nothing. One narrow four-fingered hand reached out to take Alex's; the skin was smooth, hard, and strangely muscled.

"Hello, Alex." The voice was resonant, like an old brass horn. "Happy birthday. My name is Victor."

Three:

Alex had always ascribed his own existence to his parents' sheer conservatism. Almost four centuries after Contact, human reproduction was not only deliberate, it was perverse.

Creating a child, after all, had no economic purpose; nothing did. "Wealth" was a meaningless word when every individual disposed of more matter and energy than whole nations had in the decades before Contact. So one did not produce a child to work, and when one was virtually immortal, one certainly did not produce a child to inherit one's property.

Parental vanity and curiosity? Why bother, when one's computers could project thousands of potential offspring based on minor genetic variations? Ego? The egotists cloned themselves rather than mingling their genes with someone else's.

Loneliness? Millions of happy people had not even spoken to a fellow human being in decades, let alone felt an urge to produce one and rear it to maturity. Computers and housekeepers were far more entertaining than a child, and one could always produce korshak icons of anyone, living or dead, real or imagined, and program them to talk, sing, dance, or behave like clowns. For that matter, one could grow a cuckoo—a troll, gryphon, or any of a score of other alien species whose genomes lay in the Database.

Yet William Macintosh and Lydia Korolyeva had agreed to contribute the genetic materials for a child, and Lydia had even undergone functional intercourse and pregnancy. They had chosen the luck of the draw rather than designing ovum and sperm for some specific outcome. Alex had been a surprise.

Lydia had drawn the line at nurturing him. Alex had been reared by robot nurses on *Munshaour* and then by his father. Only occasionally had Lydia sent an aircraft to bring him to Mordor, her estate in southern California.

He had not much liked it there. Built into the southern slopes of the Santa Monica Mountains, Mordor overlooked the awful wastes of Los Angeles. The estate was a grim and ugly fortress, heavily defended and with few open spaces where a boy could run and play. Lydia spent most of her time doing experiments to try to make sense out of trollish physics and occasionally engaging in a war with some rival scientist; she had little interest in being a mother. As he grew older, she allowed him to explore the region in a sled, but the desert ruins of the ancient city were more depressing than intriguing. Alex was fond of his mother but was always glad when *Munshaour* swung up over the horizon and he returned home.

Not that his father was much more approachable. William was more an engineer than a scientist, exploring the capacities of scores of alien materials. His cloudcastle had been one of the first ever built on Earth, but William's endless improvements had kept it among the most up-to-date. Houseproud, he had had little time to look after his son.

Alex's education, therefore, had been haphazard. Occasionally he would reveal some gulf of ignorance, and his father would angrily set out a curriculum to fill it: the biology of the trolls, the origin myths of the slugs, kuldi physics, the Presidents of pre-Contact imperial America, elementary molmac design. Then Alex was left to himself again to explore the world as he liked.

Usually that meant looking upward and outward, to the delicate webwork of steamship contrails between the planets, to the korshak images of Martian spires and Venusian bastions and the cloudcastles of Jupiter's upper atmosphere. Alex learned the details of the expansion of humanity into space. He dreamed of some day coursing out past Saturn, out into the Neptune Belt to claim comets and fight wars over points of honor. Earth seemed dull and crowded by comparison, and he yearned for the day when he could break free.

Sometimes, out of boredom more than curiosity, he explored the records of the pre-Contact world his father had been born into. Much of it was unintelligible, and the rest was both fascinating and disgusting. Molmac technology had been confined in those days to planting natural seeds

—the clumsy and inefficient survivors of millions of centuries of random evolution—and then parasitizing them. People actually *ate* plants and animals, turning all that beautiful complexity into heat and protein in an awkward, immoral, and ultimately doomed attempt to stay alive.

Wild molmacs—bacteria and viruses—in turn had parasitized humans. Almost everyone got sick repeatedly and took it for granted. Molmacs got into cells defended only by crude antibodies. Molmac waste products polluted the cells to death, or else the molmacs subverted them into producing new molmacs of no use to the person.

Natural antibodies, utterly lacking in intelligence, had often caused more trouble than they were worth by reacting against harmless foreign substances like dust or pollen or organ transplants. Many people had even died thanks to the stupidity of their microscopic guardians.

Still, the pre-Contact world held a kind of gaudy attraction. The crowdedness, the squalor, the willingness of people to rule and be ruled, the cheerful squandering of life for mysterious economic and superstitious motives—Alex felt a slightly unhealthy fascination for it. Sometimes he thought it was simply the pleasure of feeling superior to them all, of watching them reenact their little lives and futile passions as unintended farce.

Then, as he grew older, he had begun to feel envious of the holographic ghosts of that ancient age. They had enjoyed a certainty, a confidence, that modern humanity had lost forever. For centuries they had thought themselves the center of the universe. Their later learning had somewhat humbled them, but it was only abstractly chastening to know that Sol was a minor star on the fringe of a typical galaxy. Until Contact, humanity had remained at the center of its own universe, not even aware that DNA was one of the commonest molecules in most solar systems and that intelligence was one of DNA's inevitable accomplishments.

As a little boy Alex had laughed at the images of humanity's hysterical response to Contact. As a youth he had looked more pensively on those famous scenes following that Sunday in 2030, when Earth's television sets had suddenly filled with images of nightmare creatures somehow speaking English:

"Hello to Earth! We like your radio. We like your television, too. Electromagnetism is cute! We have a different way to communicate, so we're sending it to you. More after these messages."

The moment had been anticipated so many times, especially in the premillennarian culture of the twentieth century, that humanity had been initially skeptical. Then, after a few days of nonstop, unstoppable information, hysteria erupted. In Iran, Brazil, and Australia the authorities tried to black out the alien broadcasts by sabotaging their own TV systems; their citizens, fearing an invasion was imminent, rioted or fled to the hills. The French detonated hydrogen bombs in the upper atmosphere, trying to drown the broadcasts in electromagnetic pulses, but succeeded only in crippling the economies of the northern hemisphere.

Within weeks it did not matter. Korshak receivers were easy to build, if not to understand, and scores of countries were soon competing to absorb the exponentially greater flood of data that korshak could carry. Each country was terrified of losing some advantage to the others, even if it meant committing all its scientific and engineering resources to trying to understand the aliens.

They called themselves Pirid or Brith, using a vocal apparatus very much like humans', but almost at once they acquired the nickname of trolls. They had begun receiving human broadcasts around 1930, and a few trolls had been curious enough to pay intermittent attention as radio was supplemented with television. By 1999 two or three trolls understood human languages and culture well enough to launch Contact. Earth was drawn into the Net not by the collective decision of some wiser race but by the whim and curiosity of a few individuals.

So into the computer networks of Earth had come the Database. At first it had contained only some basics: korshak theory and applications, elementary molmac technology, and information on how to build archives for the rest of the Database, a mass of information acquired by the trolls in the fifty thousand years of their membership in the three-million-year-old Net.

The information was absolutely free of noise; that was one of the benefits of korshak. Every korshak transmission was broadcast, freely available to anyone with a receiver. It travelled at the speed of light but suffered no attenuation or degradation of signal within galactic distances.

Most of it, however, was incomprehensible. The trolls did not seem to care; they themselves still did not understand most of what had come to them from older species. Like the other members of the Net, humanity had thousands of years to study the Database, which would of course continue to grow; they would master it eventually. Meanwhile the trolls asked only for korshak transmissions from Earth to expand the Database.

Something like a conversation developed between humans and trolls. The trolls wanted the human genome and showed where their own genome was in the Database. Inevitably, someone grew a troll and then other alien lifeforms. The trolls who grew humans then asked questions: "Why don't you protect yourselves better against infection?"; "Why do you band together under insane males?"; "Why do you think the appendix has no function?" They were content to wait sixty years for an answer.

Sometimes the wait was much longer because not many people were in a position to reply. By the middle of the twenty-first century human society was breaking down under the stress of Contact. Cultural values failed. Religions vanished, sometimes after a last frenzy of faith and bloodshed. Industries collapsed. Alien organisms like ekata and floating forests spread chaos through Earth's ecosystem. A few countries tried out troll technology in wars; the results fascinated the trolls but left few human survivors.

The survivors, if they could master enough troll technology, became almost invulnerable. An estate of a few hundred hectares could supply all the raw material needed to maintain a couple of dozen people in comfortable and secure independence. Defending it was sometimes difficult; if korshak was by nature open, the technology of defense—and especially of defense molmacs—was a closely held secret on each estate. Most wars soon became ritualized exchanges of token violence rather than struggles to the death.

The nation-states were dead by 2085. Communities died with them, leaving the family as the largest social unit. By the middle of the twenty-second century the family, too, had vanished, except for a few sentimentalists like William and Lydia. Genuine anarchy prevailed, a condition of purer freedom than anyone had ever dreamed of. Anyone could do anything, and did, with no deterrent except the rarely exercised power of an annoyed neighbor to blow one into gamma rays. In that freedom, at least, humanity was on a par with the godlike species of the Net.

"He's beautiful, William," Sei Shonagon said, stroking the gryphon's golden-furred arm. "You've outdone yourself."

Beaming, William held up his hands modestly. "The compliments should go to Lydia. Once I told her what I wanted, she came up with most of the formulas."

Lydia laughed. "The formulas are easy. William put in the time to grow him and teach him, like Alex. How do you like him, dear?"

Alex stood beside the gryphon, looking up into his enigmatic and intelligent eyes. "He's magnificent. I never expected—Thank you both."

"We thought you'd find him more interesting than some icon," William said. "Actually, I'm going to miss you, Victor. You've been good company."

"I'm going to miss you, too, William." The gryphon's deep voice resonated hollowly behind his beaked mask. "But I think it'll be fun on *Wuthering Heights*, too. And maybe I can come back sometimes."

"Of course, of course. Whenever you like. Might even get Alex visiting more often."

"Come with me, Victor," Alex said. Unlike people, the gryphon's physical presence was completely unthreatening. Alex was eager to get acquainted. In his elation he caught California's eye, and before he could stop himself he smiled at her. "Want to come too?"

"Love to."

Liam McCool converged on them. "May I join you young people as well? I feel the need for a walk."

"By all means, Mr. McCool." But Alex wished the man had stayed behind.

"Fragrant Harbor," Liam McCool said, walking with Alex and California and Victor along a glassed-in gallery overlooking the ruins of Xianggang a thousand meters below.

"Fragrant Harbor," McCool said again, "haven of opium dealers and taipans and commissars. First the Chinese drove the Euros out of Guangzhou to protect Chinese culture. The Euros built Xianggang, and the Chinese risked their lives by swimming those waters to reach it. Five million people, living in warrens, working in sweat and misery and glad of it. And now it's all one with Nineveh and Tyre."

Alex presumed he was referring to persons or cultures in the Database and said nothing. Within moments of his arrival on the cloudcastle McCool had allowed himself to become drunk, saying it aided the literary sensibility; it had certainly made him more entertaining than the rest of the party, who were still back in the living room pestering Bliokio for updates and speculating aimlessly about the gryphons' purpose.

"What do *you* think of gryphons coming to Earth?" McCool demanded suddenly, turning to face Victor. The gryphon looked down at McCool and smiled beneath his mask of horn. Small, sharp brown teeth showed for a moment.

"I don't know, Liam. I would be interested to know your opinion."

"Diplomatic, isn't he?" McCool said out of the corner of his mouth.

Alex gestured to a broad, curving bench. "Come and sit down with us, Victor. Tell us about yourself."

Seated, the gryphon seemed no taller than the humans. He put his hands on his upthrust knees and looked down at the burned-out wasteland of Kowloon.

"I don't know where to start. I'm five years old, but William says I'm fully mature. He's trained me to help run the cloudcastle, but mostly I just study."

"And what do you study?" Alex asked. Seated next to Victor, he enjoyed the gryphon's physical beauty and pungent scent.

"Human history and some science."

"Human history? Why not Chaiar history or trollish history?" McCool demanded.

Victor looked past Alex and California to meet McCool's gaze. "William says I'll be living among humans, so I should know them."

"Read human history and you'll only feel as baffled as humans do," McCool said. "That's why most of us prefer to stay ignorant of our sordid past. Tell me this, Victor: Do you feel at home on Earth? Do you ever wish you could see your home world?"

"I feel at home here. I don't know anything else. I

would be interested to see Makhshuar, yes, but I am a cuckoo, Liam, not an ugly duckling."

McCool roared with laughter and then calmed himself enough to explain the allusion to California and Alex. Alex felt mildly embarrassed that a gryphon should know human folklore better than he himself did. Well, it was all in the Database; he would simply follow the leads Victor gave him.

"Won't you be homesick leaving the cloudcastle?" California asked.

"Gryphons are homesick only for their birthpond."

"Ah, yes," McCool said thickly. "You hibernate or something of the sort."

"We did, long ago. In the winters on Makhshuar, we went into the waters of our birthponds to sleep until spring. Sometimes I feel the wish, when *Munshaour* enters cold weather."

McCool was chuckling. "Do you like being given away, Victor, like a piece of property?"

"I don't have a choice, Liam. Besides, I think it would be interesting to live on a steamship."

"I think we'll get along, Victor," Alex said. "It'll be fun showing you around the place. And I can certainly use some help running it."

The cloudcastle was slowly turning south; looking up, they saw the new planet looming overhead. Reflected Earthlight made its nightside a blue-gray swirl set off by patches of light: gryphon cities.

"Maybe we'll visit your cousins over there," Alex said with a smile. "If we can figure out the resonance of the shardana bubble."

The gryphon said nothing, but Alex could hear him snapping his nasal cartilage. Wasn't that supposed to mean anxiety in gryphons? Probably just as well not to push it.

"Lunch will be ready soon. Let's start back," Alex suggested. They rose and strolled back down the gallery, out into a little garden full of splashing water and lily pads. The open air was abruptly cool. The long passage of the new world's shadow had chilled the air across the Pacific.

California took Alex's arm. "I don't like the cold," she muttered. "Least of all when it's caused by . . . that."

The urge to pull himself free was brief and weak; he actually began to enjoy her presence. "It's very unsettling," he agreed. "I'll be happier when I'm back in *Wuthering Heights*. Cloudcastles seem awfully vulnerable, somehow."

"So does a reefhouse. Sei's built me a lovely place in Bikini, eight meters down. It's wonderful, but somehow I think I'd like something more solid. Or more mobile."

Alex was surprised. A young woman with her reputation for physical courage should not have been worried about being hurt.

"Do you actually think something violent might come out of this?" McCool asked.

"Maybe not intentionally," California said, "but if they can move planets around, even a little mistake could hurt a lot of people."

McCool suddenly looked sad. "I promised your mother I wouldn't proselytize," he said, "and I won't, but I truly think you had both better prepare yourselves for some kind of violence."

Alex frowned. "How could we prepare ourselves for a—a tsunami or Earth breaking up if that shardana bubble pops?"

"Not that. Not that. More subtle violence. The imposition of will and the test of self."

"You're probably right," California said. "If we have to fight them, we'd better be ready to do it on our own terms."

That's why she feels insecure, Alex thought, his respect restored. But how could you fight a species like the gryphons?

He was impressed also by her calm acceptance of McCool's religion. Violence had a disquieting authority to it even to those who did not believe. The old faiths had crumpled within a generation of Contact. Others had arisen—Xenolatry, Humanism, Piridism—but only Violence had survived the centuries since then. Perhaps the Violents did not entirely understand the Net, but they certainly understood something in human nature.

And what if he's right? Alex wondered. Are they really going to impose their wills on us? That's ridiculous. But he thought about the ruins of Xianggang. When a technically advanced culture met one less advanced, did they ever—*could* they ever—treat each other with respect and forbearance?

They entered the living room again, where one area

was brightly lit and tables stood heaped with food and drink. William and Lydia beckoned.

"About time," William said impatiently. "I was about to send for you. We've got the birthday cake all ready."

Just as they were sitting down and a robot was bringing out the cake on a platinum tray, Bliokio's icon abruptly appeared at William's elbow.

"Please excuse my interruption, everyone—and especially Alex. We have a transmission from the new planet. Shall I continue recording it, or would you wish to see it at once?"

William glanced at his son. "As you wish, Alex."

"Let's see it, Bliokio."

A korshak image formed instantly a couple of meters away from the table. It was a young man with unruly brown hair falling across his forehead. He wore an old-fashioned white shirt and a navy-blue suit cut like William's.

"I bring greetings to the people of Earth from the planet Habrakha," he said in good if slightly old-fashioned English with an accent that flattened his r's.

"We have come to bring you into the Pattern. My name is John F. Kennedy."

Four:

Alex was impressed by the technology backing up John F. Kennedy; from the image of a single individual, really just an icon, the korshak transmission expanded into a hemisphere over ten meters across that blanked out the living room behind it. Kennedy stood in a large office of the kind people had used before Contact. It was cluttered: bookshelves, curtains, an ornamental cloth of red and white stripes with a blue and white patch. Yet with sunlight streaming through its windows, the office looked comfortable and amusing; Alex made a mental note to consider redoing his study on *Wuthering Heights* in a similar style.

Kennedy leaned against the edge of a desk and slipped a hand into a pocket in his suit coat. He seemed to be smiling directly into Alex's eyes, a simple korshak illusion.

"Now, ah, we realize that the appearance of Habrakha has alarmed many people, and that's why I'm addressing you now. And we want to assure you that you are in no danger whatsoever. Habrakha will remain safely behind its shardana bubble for as long as it remains in the solar system.

"Perhaps you're wondering what human beings are doing on a planet from another system." Kennedy grinned. "It's a long story, but I'll try to keep it brief. Three hundred Earth years ago the Chaiar philosopher Durung defined the nature of reality with a new science called the Pattern. Durung showed his people that the Pattern required them to take it to all the intelligent species in the galaxy. Thanks to the inspiration of the Pattern, Chaiar scientists discovered the secrets of instant travel between the stars and took up the philosopher's command.

"Three species besides the Chaiar are now part of the

35

Pattern, including the Pirid. The Chaiar learned about the existence of Earth from the Pirid and decided to bring humanity into the Pattern also."

He shifted his weight, yet his eyes still seemed locked on Alex's. "Here's where we come in. The Pirid had grown some humans, but the Chaiar expanded our population so that we could serve to help explain the Pattern to you, our brothers and sisters."

Kennedy paused, and tears seemed to glisten in his blue eyes. "I wish I could tell you what it means to us to look on the home world of humanity, at the most important moment in human history, and to know that soon all of our species will be safe and happy in the Pattern.

"I don't have time to explain everything now. But please don't be afraid. Some of us will be landing on Earth soon, and those emissaries will show you what the Pattern means. When you understand it, you'll never be afraid again. You'll have your place in the Pattern, and—" He shrugged and smiled. "When you have your place, you have everything. Until we talk again, I want to wish you joy and peace."

The korshak image was gone.

"Didn't look *that* much like Kennedy," William said. "The voice was pretty close, though."

"Who is Kennedy?" California asked.

"He was an American President," Alex said, amazed that his father's drills in ancient history had suddenly become relevant. "His assassination was the start of the American Decline."

"He's also been a cult figure off and on," McCool said. He no longer seemed drunk, but Alex did not like the light in the poet's eyes. "William, wasn't there a bunch back just before Contact that claimed he was the Second Savior?"

William nodded. "I remember them well. Mostly leftover chiliasts from the turn of the millennium. They said his next return would bring the rule of God."

"Surely the trolls didn't have Kennedy's genome," Sei Shonagon said.

"No," Lydia agreed. "But they'd have had plenty of images of him. Retroplanning wouldn't be hard."

"Maybe not," Lyell Bradley said, "but I'd certainly like to know how they did it. We're still working with off-the-shelf genomes, and when we tinker with 'em, we usually screw up." He glanced at Victor, who stood silently beside Alex. "No offense, Victor."

"Not at all, Lyell. William didn't tinker much with me, except to adapt me to an oxygen-rich atmosphere. He tells me I'm based on a Chaiar scientist named Bhrukang. I'm proud to be grown from such a template."

"Well," Bradley went on cheerfully, "I'm looking forward to learning from these people. Imagine—actual physical access to a species that's learned about us, that understands our culture."

Mao Jian and McCool laughed together without humor. "They understand us too well," Mao barked. "Using a human cult figure for their first communication. We're lucky they didn't use Jesus or the Buddha. They're trying to put us off guard."

"Exactly!" McCool said. "I smell real trouble here, William. Think: Why would they travel on a planet, in their millions, with a population of human cuckoos? To trade? To pay a friendly little visit? No, they've come to invade us. To conquer us."

William and Bradley winced as if embarrassed, and Sei Shonagon looked baffled. "Liam," William said patiently, "if trade is pointless, so is conquest. What would they do if they conquered us—put us to work mining salt?"

McCool gave him an unpleasant grin. "They don't want our labor, William—they want our *souls*. They want us to be part of this pattern of theirs. He said they've taken over the trolls and a couple of other species. That's the only motive anyone could have for interstellar conquest—winning souls."

Lydia stood up and paced about restlessly, her blond hair like a halo around her angry face. "Bliokio," she commanded. "Would you please rerun that transmission, with a subtext analysis."

"Of course."

The computer was not able to reproduce the whole transmission, but the image of Kennedy was sharp. He spoke and moved in short segments, then froze as Bliokio analyzed the data in each segment.

"Kennedy is a force-grown adult like Victor," he said. "His physical age is about twenty-five Earth years. His actual age is probably between ten and eleven . . . He is in good health . . . not a clone—retroplanned . . . with some modifications I don't understand . . . His intelligence matrix is 9469799 . . . Very close congruence between speech content and emotional charge."

"Hold it there," Alex said. "You're telling us this person has a matrix with four nines in it? They must be able to force-grow intelligence as well as bodies."

"Yes," Bliokio agreed, waving his gripper pads. "He is a highly improved version of a human."

"This pattern must be something extraordinary," Bradley said. "Bliokio says Kennedy wasn't lying, so we already have one supergenius vouching for the Chaiar."

McCool growled. "I don't care if they give us a million cuckoos singing the praises of the Chaiar. Kennedy seems altogether too confident. He means to take us over."

"No," Mao Jian said. "The Chaiar do. He's merely their Judas goat."

Alex felt baffled again. What was a Judas goat? Never mind. The warmaker and the poet obviously did not like Kennedy or the forces behind him. Bradley was eager to learn what the Chaiar could teach, William and Lydia were suspicious but uncertain, and Sei Shonagon was already looking bored about the whole thing.

"Bliokio," he asked, "are you monitoring any reactions to Kennedy's speech?"

"Thousands, Alex. Would you like a quantification?"

"Just a general sense."

"Most people seem relieved that Habrakha isn't a physical threat. A large minority are trying to communicate directly with Habrakha, but no one is receiving a reply. Opinion about the Chaiar's intentions is divided. A few people approve of the Chaiar. A very small number think this is the first stage of an invasion. Most are uncertain."

"What's *your* opinion?"

"I tend to concur with Mr. Mao and Mr. McCool."

"Come on, Bliokio, get a grip on yourself," William said. "We don't have anywhere near enough evidence. And here *you* are, of all people, jumping to conclusions."

"I said I tended to concur, not that I agreed wholeheartedly," Bliokio said peevishly. "I'm still open to new evidence. As a precaution, however, I'm arming the cloudcastle's defenses."

"What a fussbudget," William growled, pleased to have annoyed the computer. "Well, while you're manning the battlements, perhaps we can finally have lunch."

He led the way out of the living room to a terrace

shaded by grape arbors and overlooking a koi pond. Small tables had been arranged in a U shape so that everyone could see one another and enjoy the view as well: From the nearby edge of the cloudcastle, the South China Sea extended to a misty horizon.

Alex sat between his parents, who had dropped the subject of the Chaiar and were chatting instead about the mugginess of the south China climate. Victor sat just behind Alex; California was a couple of tables to the right, smiling and gossiping with Mao and Bradley.

She interested him. Partly, he admitted to himself, because of her reputation and partly because of her unusual slenderness. But more because she was alert and attentive, listening and watching without saying much. Those dark eyes, beneath thick, straight brows, revealed an intelligence he wanted to explore. He had been shy about speaking to her on Luna, but he was about to become a citizen, able to do as he pleased. It would be pleasant to do things with California Moran. He saw her smile at Bradley and felt himself cheered by it.

A small mobile glided out bearing trays of food and drink on its broad back. Everyone seemed hungry except for McCool, who continued to drink whiskey. Alex found some of his favorite childhood dishes set before him: cabbage soup, sausage and fried potatoes, a brittle salad of radishes and onion and snap beans. He ate with enjoyment, even bantering a little with William and Lydia.

The wind had settled into the southwest, and as *Munshaour* turned onto a northeast course, Alex saw the new planet Habrakha sinking almost perceptibly toward the western horizon. The crescent of its dayside looked like a great curved horn; the oval of night was dark blue against the paler blue of the sky. A patch of cloud drifted across the face of Habrakha, making the planet seem at once both farther away and frighteningly close.

We're trapped here, he thought detachedly. Bliokio and McCool and Mao are right. They're going to take over Earth, the other planets—everything. And then we'll have to do whatever they want us to.

A sudden painful sense of loss and anguish gripped him. All the adventures he had planned, the journeys far across the system and back, the duels and couplings and amusements: A whole life had vanished just as it was about to begin. His father and mother, the guests—they chattered easily with one another, ignoring the portent in the sky.

As he looked at them, Alex felt an unfamiliar emotion and finally decided it must be pity. They looked so delicate, so fragile. John F. Kennedy and the gryphons would sweep them all away: the combative Mao Jian and McCool, the uninterested Sei Shonagon, William and Lydia and Lyell and California.

But they won't sweep me away, he promised himself. Triggering his comlink, he called his shuttle. Charlotte answered at once.

—Prepare for an early launch,— he ordered.

—Where to, Alex?—

—Straight back to *Wuthering Heights*. Tell Emily I want a course that'll take us out to the Neptune Belt as fast as we can go.—

—Very good, Alex.—

He turned back to the conversation just as a mobile brought out his birthday cake, its top blazing with falsefire, and everyone began to sing. He smiled dutifully, but when he caught California's eye, she did not smile back.

"Make a wish, Alex," Lydia said.

The falsefire glowed red and orange on the table before him. Alex ignored it. He looked at his parents, then at each guest in turn.

"We all have to get out of here," he said. "Off the planet, out as far as we can go."

His own words startled him. Why had he said "we"? Everyone looked surprised, too, and then embarrassed—except for McCool, who grinned evilly and raised his empty glass in salute.

"You can smell it, can you?" McCool chuckled. "Smell divinity at your neck? Think you can outrun it?"

"Oh, shut up, Liam." Lydia looked cross. "Alex, dear, there's no need to *panic*. We'll all be keeping an eye on the gryphons and their cuckoos. Won't we, dear?" she added to William.

"On very little else, I'm afraid. Alex, let's talk about this a little later, shall we? Come on, enjoy your cake."

Alex stood up. "I appreciate what you've done, Father —and Mother. I'm grateful for everything you've given me. But I'm not panicking. It's just that I'm the only one here with a working spacecraft. Please, if you like, come with me on *Wuthering Heights*, and I'll grow you some new spacecraft of your own once we're out in the Cloud. But if you stay here, they're going to take you over or kill you."

Uncomfortable silence fell. Alex was beginning to feel foolish when California left her chair and walked over to him.

"I'll go with you, Alex."

Surprise and delight filled him and then faded as he saw how serious she was.

Sei Shonagon's perfect Scandinavian features darkened. "You'll do no such thing, young lady. Just remember you're still under twenty-five. You're going straight home to Bikini."

"Yes, but just to pick up a few things." California looked at her mother with calm defiance. "Come on, Alex, blow out your falsefire and let's have our cake."

A puff of carbon dioxide turned the falsefire into nothingness, revealing a large chocolate cake frosted with the Roman numerals XXV. Trying to smooth over the dispute between Sei and California, Lydia gave them the first slices and set up a cloud of small talk that Alex found embarrassingly out of character.

William seemed to feel the same way, and as soon as the cake had been ritually tasted, he put his slice aside.

"We are met here, as a family and friends, to confer full adult rights on Alexander Macintosh. I hereby do so, proudly and happily." He handed Alex a small chip of platinum; installed in Emily's circuitry, it would free *Wuthering Heights* of any control by William or Lydia. Everyone applauded as Alex accepted it, then shook his father's hand and awkwardly embraced his mother.

William cleared his throat. "Now that the official ritual is over, I'd like to say a few personal words. Alex, you put me in an interesting position. I'm your father, and I wish you well. You're an intelligent and resourceful young man; I'm especially proud of what you've done with *Wuthering Heights*. You have centuries of self-actualization before you, and so far you have struck interesting themes that your life will develop. But as your first adult decision, the first major theme, you've chosen to run away from something we still can't pretend to understand. That imposes a decision on me both in my old role as your father and in my new role as your fellow adult. Do I admire your decisiveness and quick understanding, or do I condemn your hysterical impulsiveness?"

"Or do you mind your own damned business?" Alex snapped. He cooled almost at once. "I'm sorry, Father. This has been a stressful day. I'm as worried for you and Mother, and the rest of you, as I am for myself. My offer stands—you're all welcome to come aboard *Wuthering Heights*. I'm planning to head out to the Neptune Belt. Maybe the gryphons don't mean us any harm and we can return happily in a few months. But if they're truly dangerous, we'll at least be at a safe distance."

William nodded, his youthful face unreadable. "Perhaps so, although I suspect that the Neptune Belt is well within the gryphons' reach. And if that's the case, I would sooner be conquered with my dignity intact—here, on *Munshaour*, with my friends and attendants around me."

"Well spoken," Mao Jian said thoughtfully. "Not that you're wrong to go, Alex. But I think I could fight a better war from my own estate than from yours."

"And I," McCool said. "After all, with korshak we're as close as we need be."

"There's *not* going to be a *war*," Sei Shonagon snapped. "We're all going to get on with our lives. If the gryphons want to go on and on about some pattern or what have you, all we have to do is detune the korshak. California, I think it's time we said good-bye."

"You're right, Mother. Good-bye. I'll talk to you soon, if you don't detune *me*."

The older woman's exquisite features cooled to a mask of serenity. "As you wish. You're still a minor, but it would be vulgar to tyrannize you. Good-bye, my dear. William, Lydia." She turned to Alex, smiling but with a cold glint in her eyes. "Alex. Enjoy your tour of the Neptune Belt, dear. I'm sure California will enjoy every moment. We'll keep you posted on what's happening here in the real world."

Silks rustling and teklets clattering, Sei Shonagon swept off the terrace toward a waiting mobile.

The party had turned into a disaster, though not, Alex consoled himself, the disaster he had imagined. At least he had not challenged anyone to a duel or propositioned anyone. His parents kept up their blind cheerfulness, though they must have been appalled by his behavior.

He was appalled by it himself. His concern for the others was uncomfortably out of character and very bad manners, the next thing to trying to dominate a fellow citizen. Coming from a brand new citizen, it was almost too absurd to be insulting. Yet embarrassed though he was, he still worried about what would become of his parents and the guests.

Still, the party went on. Lyell Bradley ignored everything except his cake and coffee, and Mao and McCool muttered together. California seemed pleased to have her mother gone and chattered happily about life in space and the accommodations that *Wuthering Heights* could provide. Alex was impressed with her casual display of strength; he would never have challenged his parents like that, even at California's age of twenty-two. And while Sei Shonagon seemed flighty and trivial, she was a tough and experienced woman who had survived and prospered through two centuries and more of disaster and confusion. Her daughter had evidently inherited that toughness and more as well from her father.

As conversation droned around him, Alex turned on his comlink again. —Charlotte, change of route. We're going to Bikini first to pick up some luggage for California. She's joining us for the trip to the Belt. So is Victor.—

—That'll make a nice change.—

—I think so, too. We'll have fun.—

If that was an appropriate term for a headlong flight. But it would be fun, and they might well be back in a few weeks or months with nothing to fear but the teasing of their friends. But somehow Alex suspected that the arrival of the gryphons and their human cuckoos was not just a passing scare.

He looked out at the view. Over everything hung the misty white, dark blue threat of Habrakha, looming like a hallucination in the sky above China.

Five:

"Welcome aboard, dear!" Charlotte said. Normally she was just a disembodied voice, but with guests aboard she manifested herself as a hologram of Charlotte Brontë, complete with ringlets and an early Victorian gown and shawl, though with a very different personality.

"Thank you, Charlotte. I'm delighted to meet you." California looked around the dayroom with interest, evidently pleased with the period furnishings.

"We'll be launching in just a moment. Please make yourselves comfortable. Victor, I *think* this chair will be all right for you. Bliokio told me it would."

"Yes, ma'am. It'll be fine," Victor answered. He settled himself into an overstuffed chair with a rippling movement of his legs. If he was curious or excited about his surroundings, he gave no sign of it. Alex wondered how gryphons, with their immobile faces, communicated nonverbally. Perhaps he would begin to pick up signals as he got to know Victor better.

"I hope you won't have to stay at Bikini too long, dear," Charlotte went on. "If we can lift to orbit within an hour and a quarter, we'll be back on *Wuthering Heights* by suppertime. Otherwise you'll have to make do with my cooking, which is not as good as Emily's, I'm afraid."

"I'll be as quick as I can, Charlotte. Don't worry."

The hologram nodded, smiled, and vanished. California, sitting beside Alex and crossing her long legs, went on: "What a nice lady."

"She's sweet," Alex agreed. "Emily's a bit of a crab, but she has more responsibilities. And she means well. I think you'll like everyone on the ship."

"Well, if I don't—" California paused, and her smile faded. "I was going to say I could just ask you to grow me a shuttle and send me back home. I guess it won't be that easy, will it?"

"No."

Alex began to feel the seriousness of what they were about to do: embark on a journey of several months, perhaps years, with a young woman he had met only hours before and with a gryphon. It could be very unpleasant if he and California did not get along.

Well—he looked at the gryphons' world in one of the screens—nothing was the same as before. The sooner they got out, away from the gryphons, the sooner they could return to a civilized style of life. And if California did turn out to be difficult, he would be happy to find her a comet and grow her a spacecraft of her own.

Almost as if she had read his mind, California said; "We're going to be stuck with each other, Alex. Maybe to the death." She looked into his eyes, and he saw something feral glinting there, some spark of Skiudiu Moran's combativeness. Alex felt he should have been repelled by it, but instead he felt attracted.

The shuttle's kuldi field lifted it off the cloudcastle; for a moment the screens showed only the glittering blue of the South China Sea. Then the images blurred as the shuttle hurled itself upward and eastward across the Pacific.

"Charlotte, would you please patch us in to some of the bulletins?" Alex asked. The ship's computer did not bother to reply. Instead, a screen suddenly filled with the hologram of an Arabian-looking woman's face.

"This is Fahzia. Tonight's Database dive is still on, people, gryphons or no gryphons. Be ready to link up at 1700 universal time." An idle effort, Alex thought: Team dives accomplished no more than solos and pairs. Most team divers were more interested in the hallucinatory experience of the Database and the postdive dizziness than in actually retrieving new data.

A man with high cheekbones and tiger-striped skin replaced her. "Everyone who wants to invite the gryphons to land, register with me, please. We want to set up a reception area and throw a party. I *can't* do it all my*self*."

A beautiful black woman with falsefire hair said, "All you meteorographers, we're putting on a display for the Chaiar that's going to cover South America and about half the south Pacific. We're going for a six-hurricane chain and pulsed lightning, so we need all the people we can get. Let's give 'em a real show!"

A round-faced man in armor announced, "Combatants! I'm claiming priority in challenging the first cuckoo that lands. Anyone goes for that sucker before me will be *gezera ta oue*."

Alex snorted amusedly. *Gezera ta oue* was a cultural cliché that translated from trollish as "held in memory." Anything that had to be destroyed would be held in the destroyers' memory: for the trolls, such preservation justified all change. The round-faced man was a fairly well known minor duelist of the Starway School, which counted status by the number of victims held in one's memory.

"Idiot," California said. Alex grunted agreement. He did not have much respect for Starways; quantity was meaningless without quality, without a display of genuine dueling style and intelligence. California, as Skiudiu Moran's daughter, would feel the same. He felt a ripple of camaraderie. They had something in common, a rapport that would make it easier to spend the coming months together.

A woman with an archaic bouffant hairdo appeared next on the screen, breathily announcing the formation of something called the JFK Fan Club. "Anyone who gives any trouble to our hero and his friends will get an immediate declaration of war from all club members," she said with a sweet smile.

The bulletins went on, displaying the concerns of various individuals and groups on Earth and in near space. Only a bare majority referred in any way to the gryphons and Habrakha. Most simply passed on their usual gossip and information. Milo Heller, a popular stand-up and one of Alex's favorite entertainers, was running a new routine that did not even mention Habrakha.

"Everyone sounds an awful lot like our parents," Alex observed as the shuttle began to decelerate. "Maybe we're overreacting."

California shook her head. "You know we're not. Most people are taking it easy because they're too set in their ways. They don't want to change, even when they know they have to. We're young enough to jump."

"Do you always jump into strange men's spacecraft?"

"Only when alien invaders turn up. Actually, I was

thinking about going into space myself when I turned twenty-five. Bikini's nice, but it's getting awfully crowded. I've got five estates within a hundred kilometers. Sometimes you can't even go for a swim without running into somebody."

"On *Wuthering Heights* you can't go for a swim without running into Heathcliff."

"I think I'll like him. He's your housekeeper, isn't he?"

"Yes. A good one. The molmacs seem to like him. Sometimes I'll communicate directly with them, but Heathcliff's got more patience."

"I know. I've got a sweet little seal, Belinda, who looks after mine. She'll be lonely while we're gone."

"You're welcome to bring her along."

"Oh, she likes the lagoon too much. Besides, if this is all a false alarm and we come back, I'd like to see the place kept up."

Alex was quietly relieved. Heathcliff and Emily would be gracious to his guests, but it would be asking a lot to impose another housekeeper.

The shuttle banked, slowing, and descended to within a couple of meters of the surface of Bikini's vast lagoon. The screens showed distant coral atolls, furry with palms. Below, the water was blue and clear; California's estate, eight meters down, was a green patchwork of gardens under a flattened dome.

"Coming down?" California asked.

"Of course. Will you need help? Victor—"

"Victor can stay here." She glanced at him. "Or he can go for a swim."

The gryphon leaned forward a little. "I would enjoy a swim, California. I don't get many chances to swim in water this deep."

"You'll be all right?" Alex asked. "Would you like Charlotte to look after you?"

Victor uttered a metallic noise like a small gong being struck: gryphon laughter. "I'll be fine, Alex."

While the shuttle hovered on its kuldi field, Alex and California stepped through the doorway onto the deck of a small marine mobile. It greeted them cheerfully, folded a transparent glass hemisphere over them, and submerged. Five minutes later the sub docked inside California's estate.

Alex was entranced by the quality of the light inside the dome. Shifting blues, ranging from aquamarine to turquoise and lapis lazuli, seemed to swirl around it. The sun was bright in the shallow water, and schools of fish gleamed in scores of colors. Just beyond the restless ripple of the surface was the narrow triangular shadow of the shuttle. The underwater light gave a surprising richness to the plants and statuary of the garden: red-leaf palms looked almost purple, and cypresses were black.

"That's a beautiful statue," Alex said, pointing to a life-size bronze in the garden.

"It's Apollo. I found it in a Syracusan shipwreck in the Tyrrhenian Sea."

As they stepped through the air lock into the garden, a seal's head lifted from a narrow canal beside the footpath.

"Hello, Belinda!" California sang out, and then switched to comlink. Belinda kept pace with them as they made their way to the main house; Alex saw that the canals ran everywhere under the dome, giving the housekeeper easy access to the estate's gardens, storage areas, and factories.

The reefhouse itself was two stories high, roofed in transparent fome, faced with white stucco, and built in an angular U around a swimming pool. Mobiles were already scuttling in and out, piling small and large boxes on a transporter standing beside the pool. Belinda glided into the pool from her communication canal and uttered a loud bark.

"You don't know what you're talking about!" California said. "It'll be fine, Belinda. You just have to look after things the same way you do when I'm at Mother's. I'll be seeing you on korshak probably every day. You will *not* be lonely. You'll get some peace and quiet for a change."

She turned and rolled her eyes at Alex. "Really, Belinda does go on sometimes. I don't know who's worse, her or Mother. Come on inside and I'll give you the quick tour."

Alex thought it was a very tastefully designed and furnished estate, though its manufacturing capacity seemed a bit limited. California had simply not bothered to install more than the essential programs, while Alex had taken pains to make *Wuthering Heights* as versatile as possible.

California led him through living rooms, the kitchen, and any number of amusement areas: a painting studio, a ceramics workshop, a holarium, a well-used dueling pit. They came at last to an upstairs room with a transparent roof and walls overlooking the pool. Bright blue light shimmered down through the dome, which was not far overhead. A waterfall spilled down one wall of rock and moss and then vanished beneath the floor. The carpeting was soft and dense; the room was furnished with a low bed and a table or two.

"This is where I sleep."

"Very nice."

She turned to look at him, her dark eyes gleaming. "This is why I really wanted to come back to Bikini, Alex. If I'm going to live on your estate for God knows how long, we'd better be compatible. So come and lie down and let's make love."

Alex felt a moment's anxiety, a mixture of nerves at her proximity and at Charlotte's impatience to get into orbit. "Couldn't it wait until we're back on *Wuthering Heights*?"

She shook her head as she peeled her gown away. "I'm sentimental. I always begin my affairs right here in this room."

Her only dermograph was a small one that made her left breast look like a red chrysanthemum. But she liked Alex's glowing scales and made love with a good humor and energy that he had rarely encountered in the lupanars of Luna. He enjoyed her heat and the sleek hardness of the muscles under her glowing gold-brown skin.

Afterward she pulled him under the waterfall, kissed him happily, and said; "Well, we're certainly good lovers. Think our molmacs will get along?"

"They'd better." He kissed her back, wondering why he felt so oddly about her. It was not just the respect due a good duelist and coupler or aesthetic admiration for a well-kept body. It was something like the fondness he had felt for his parents and the guests, an unusual and slightly alarming emotion. He worried about her, about all of them, and he had never felt that kind of worry before.

As they dried off, Alex looked up through the glass roof and saw Victor swimming powerfully just above the dome. He was looking down and waved. Alex waved back, wondering how long the gryphon had been out there. Gryphons were amphibious, after all, capable of drawing oxygen through their chest membranes as well as their lungs. Victor could have watched the lovemaking from start to finish if the sight of copulating humans had interested him at all. Even if it had not, it was faintly annoying to think that one's intimate behavior had been performed in sight of an alien.

California was now all business, pulling on a tightsuit that glowed in changing shades of sunset: red, orange, pink, and black. She hurried Alex downstairs with her. They climbed aboard the transport mobile and returned to the air lock, with Belinda pacing them in the canal. Smaller mobiles transferred California's luggage to the sub, then rolled aside to make way. California turned to look one last time at her reefhouse.

"Good-bye, Belinda. See you soon. Be a good girl."

The seal barked and submerged. California turned and gave Alex a slightly unhappy smile. She was on the edge of tears. He understood.

"If you like, we can rig up *Wuthering Heights* so it looks just like this place."

"That would be sweet, but don't bother. I told you I'm just an old sentimentalist." And she kissed his cheek as they climbed into the sub.

Victor rode up with them, one powerful four-fingered hand gripping a mooring cable. He looked in through the bubble, his face an unreadable mask, but Alex felt the gryphon was having fun. Back on the surface, Victor shook himself like a dog and then followed them up the ramp into the shuttle.

Charlotte was very tactful about having a dripping-wet gryphon forming puddles on her carpet. But just as the launch was about to begin, she called an abort over Alex's comlink.

—I've picked up a message from the Chaiar, dear. They say they're sending some of their shuttles to Earth, and they want all air-to-space traffic to cease for the time being.—

Alex laughed and then repeated the message to California and Victor. "Have you ever heard of such a thing? They *can't* be afraid we'll collide with them."

"Would it hurt to wait?" California asked.

"As a matter of fact it would," Alex said. "We'd be delayed for some time. But it's the principle of the thing. I'm not about to change my plans because of someone who's barged in without even an invitation. I'm an adult; I don't have to take orders from anyone now, least of all a bunch of aliens. Charlotte, go ahead with the launch."

"Shall I keep you up to date on the Chaiar?"

"Yes, you might as well."

The shuttle's nose tilted up. A moment later they were accelerating eastward into an empty blue sky. On one screen the Chaiar planet hung as a fat crescent; it was already below Bikini's western horizon, but Charlotte was drawing on images from space and central Asia. At a com-link command, she expanded the view so that a portion of a nightside continent was enormously magnified and light-enhanced.

Scores—no, hundreds—of shuttles were lifting off from a field that must have covered thousands of square kilometers. The ships were delta-winged, perhaps five times the size of Alex's shuttle, and moving with surprising speed. Charlotte estimated that the first of them would enter Earth's atmosphere within an hour.

"I don't like the look of that," Alex said. "Charlotte, get us out of here. I want to be home and accelerating out of orbit by the time those ships land."

"Yes, Alex."

"And while we're lifting, call my mother and father, please."

A double korshak image appeared in the middle of the cabin, showing William in his tower study and Lydia in her aircraft.

"Father, Mother, you know about the ships coming from Habrakha. This could be your last chance to get out. Would you reconsider and join us?"

Lydia shook her head grimly. "I'm halfway home to Mordor, Alex."

"And I'm certainly staying on *Munshaour*," William added. "I must say, we think you're overreacting. But do stay in touch, will you?"

"Of course." Alex felt abruptly tired. "Take care of yourselves."

"And you do the same," Lydia said. "We'll worry about you. California, I hope you enjoy your time with Alex."

"I already am, Lydia. But I do think Alex is right. You should really get off Earth for a while."

They smiled and shook their heads.

"Thank you for the party," Alex said. "I'm sorry it turned out the way it did."

"Not at all," William said with a bland smile. "I hope you two will call Sei before you leave."

"She's next on our list," California said.

But Sei Shonagon refused their signal, and did so through the korshak image of a robot rather than one of herself.

"She's really angry," California said as the image vanished. "Usually she saves the robot for lovers she's bored with."

"We'll try her again in a day or two, when she's calmed down," Alex promised. "Charlotte, how are we doing? What's our ETA?"

"We're nearing orbit. But I'm getting a signal from the Chaiar ships to return to Earth at once."

"Let's see it."

A human materialized where Alex's parents had just been. She was a sleek black woman wearing a kind of chiton that had been in style on Earth about thirty years before. Her eyes met Alex's, though he knew she could not really see him.

"All ships heading for Earth orbit or farther into space!" she said in a musical voice. "Abort your trajectories and return to the surface at once. The Freedom Fleet will be entering the atmosphere within the next ninety minutes, and you are a hazard to navigation. You have thirty seconds to abort. Any ships ignoring this order will be shot down. I repeat: Any ships ignoring this order will be shot down."

Alex laughed as the black cuckoo disappeared. "Shot down, indeed! Carry on, Charlotte."

"Could they really do that?" California asked.

"Dear, I have no idea of their weaponry," Charlotte answered. "The nearest Chaiar ships are now about eight thousand kilometers from the surface and braking. I see no signs of hostile preparations." She gave them an image of one of the ships. Its pearly, iridescent surface was featureless. Alex saw nothing like the missile racks or beamers with which *Wuthering Heights* was armed.

The shuttle trembled slightly, as if it had encountered a turbulence impossible at over a hundred kilometers above the surface. Alex swore as acceleration suddenly ceased and everything in the cabin went into free fall.

"We've been hit," Charlotte said, clutching her shawl closer about her narrow shoulders. Her image remained fixed to the floor while Alex, California, and Victor rose into the air. "It's some kind of beamer, and it's cut right through our drive unit. I'm afraid we're going to reenter the atmosphere."

The screens showed faintly curved horizon tilting, then tilting back and drifting upward. The shuttle was already descending and yawing as it did so.

"Can you glide us in, Charlotte?" California asked.

"Of course, dear. I'm not sure just where. We'll be coming down somewhere in the eastern Pacific, about a thousand kilometers west of the Oregon coast. If they attack us again, however, you'd better prepare to eject. That beam weapon of theirs is dreadful. Dreadful."

The computer's tone made Alex shiver. Charlotte was not easily disturbed, but the Chaiar beamer had clearly alarmed her.

"We're not ejecting, Charlotte. Don't be silly. We wouldn't leave you."

"If they hit us again, dear, I wouldn't give you the choice. I'd just blow the cabin free. And if you wanted me back, you could always build me a new mainframe."

"Just worry about getting us down safely," Alex said. "And would you let our parents know what's happened?"

"Of course." Charlotte paused for a second. "They're informed. Your mother's housekeeper is sending out a sled to rendezvous with us."

"A sled?" Alex yelped. "That means we'll have to go back to Mordor, and I want to get *home*. Patch me through to her."

Lydia, still aboard her aircraft, appeared on one of the screens. She smiled wryly at her son and California.

"So they're not going to let you run away," she said. "That makes me think the Chaiar really do mean to take us over."

"That's why I wanted you to leave," Alex answered with fraying patience. "Now we're all stuck here."

"Oh, I have no intention of leaving Earth just now. I'd rather dig in and meet them on my own ground."

"That's all very well, Mother, but they've just shown us what they can do at a range of eight thousand kilometers." He pulled himself down into a chair and gripped its arms to keep himself from floating out of it again. "Once they're knocking on your door, you may find it hard to ignore them."

Lydia smiled again. "I'm about to land, dear, and then

I'm going to be very busy for a while. The sled's locked on to your shuttle, but it's not very fast, so you may have to wait a few hours. I'll have a room set up for you here. California, will you want to share Alex's room?"

California looked scandalized. "I should hope not! If you haven't got enough space, I'll just go back home."

"Oh, no, we have plenty of room. I just thought you might want to . . . stay close to Alex." Her image vanished.

Malicious old woman! Alex thought. Well, they would have to put up with her for a time, until he could repair the shuttle and get back home. Surely the Chaiar would not— could not—enforce a permanent ban on spaceflight.

"Dears, please pull yourselves into a chair and I'll strap you in. I'm going to start decelerating, and it may be a bit bumpy."

The ship shuddered heavily as it fell toward the cloud-masked ocean. Alex and California gripped their armrests tightly, half-amused and half-alarmed. Victor seemed undisturbed; he watched the screens with his long legs oddly crossed.

Charlotte was doing a wonderful job of flying with no drive, Alex thought, but what would they do when she finally hit the water? The shuttle could not float, least of all if it had had a hole drilled right through its hull. Hadn't the ancients kept spare boats for that sort of thing? He considered asking her but decided it would be tactless.

"Touchdown in thirty seconds," Charlotte said. "I'm afraid it's going to be even rougher, but at least we won't sink."

"Why not?" California asked.

"I'm landing us on a floating forest, dear."

Six:

Through patchy cloud, the floating forest looked like an archipelago. An organic mass, it sprawled across a hundred kilometers of ocean. In many places it lay deep beneath the surface, creating bays and channels, while in others it extended for twenty or thirty kilometers at an average height of forty meters above sea level.

From the air, Alex thought the forest looked amazingly like his dermograph: a scaly, multicolored surface that rippled and glowed in complicated patterns shaped by the wind. The "trees" of the forest had close-packed trunks, some as tall as fifty meters. They had neither leaves nor branches but were capped by heliotropic organs that looked like ancient radio telescopes, shallow bowls up to three meters across. Most of the tree trunks were green or yellow, but the caps were red, blue, black, orange, and brown.

"Hold on, dears," Charlotte said, and the chairs extruded safety belts. A last strip of cloud whirled past. The forest rushed up beneath them on the screens, then seemed to fall away as Charlotte brought the shuttle's nose up in a last braking maneuver. The forest looked like a flower bed of enormous mutated poppies.

Alex had expected a cracking noise; instead, the trunks yielded with a kind of hiss to the impact of the shuttle's hull. The shuttle swayed and bumped, sometimes hard enough to throw the passengers against their straps. After half a minute the shuttle's forward momentum was gone and it settled heavily toward the forest's matrix—a vast, tangled mass of roots and bulbs. With a last thump, the spacecraft came to rest.

"Is everyone all right?" Charlotte asked worriedly.

"We're fine," Alex said after a quick glance at California and Victor. "But now what, Charlotte? This is a dangerous place. Can you keep us sealed off until the sled gets here?"

"If you like, dear."

California laughed. "Alex, you've been away from Earth too long. Floating forests have been mutating for years. Some of the plants are pretty nasty, but you'd have to impale yourself on a spikeweed to hurt yourself."

"Beyond repair, you mean."

"Of course."

Alex still felt a little anxious. A popular theme in some of the cruder entertainments was the threat of liquefaction into a greasy froth through the use of gierzhi or some other alien toxin produced by floating forests.

Still, he realized that California was right: he had indeed heard that the forests were losing their toxicity. But it was hard to overcome the fears instilled by all those horror shows he'd watched as a child.

"We should stay here until the sled reaches us," he said.

"You can go outside if you like," said Charlotte. "There's a channel about a hundred meters south of us; that's probably where the sled will come. You can walk down there and meet it."

California smiled, her eyes on the screens and their images of smashed yellow trunks and torn caps of red and blue. "Really, Charlotte? That sounds like fun. Come on, Alex—and Victor."

"I'd like to go out," Victor said. "I've seen floating forests from the air, but it would be interesting to walk in one."

"I don't know," Alex said, feeling embarrassed that California and the gryphon were evidently braver than he was. Then, after an uncomfortable pause, he added, "All right. Charlotte, keep in touch. We should be back soon."

The hatch slid back, and they looked down at a tangled ruin of tree trunks and smaller plants. The landing board extended and angled down until it rested on the debris two meters below the hatch. Irritated by his earlier caution, Alex led the others down onto the tree trunks. They looked back at the swath, a good twenty meters wide, that the shuttle had cut. It extended westward for what must have been several kilometers.

Sunshine glared down on them; the air had the tang of salt and a stranger, richer perfume as well. To Alex it smelled like a mixture of musk and blood. A deep silence lay over the forest, broken abruptly by the shrill piping of a khiudie, a batlike creature native to First Stone, that had been popular as a pet a couple of hundred years ago. Disease had wiped out the domestic varieties, but wild ones still flourished in the floating forests.

"Come on," Alex said. "Let's find the channel."

Footing was awkward at first as they stepped from one narrow, slippery trunk to the next and detoured around the heliotropic organs. Then they reached the edge of the swath; beyond it the matrix was a soft, resilient mosslike surface, a mottled gray-green out of which trees rose every couple of meters. Underbrush flourished: spikeweed, tilki, and a dozen other alien plants lifted strange fronds toward the light filtering down from the caps.

"It's like one of the old cathedrals," California said as she looked up. The translucent caps glowed in a dozen colors like ancient stained glass. Alex thought of the living room on *Munshaour*, with the ever-changing colors of its glass roof.

Though the matrix went down many meters, they could feel it rise and fall a little beneath their feet; that close to the edge of the forest, the ocean swell had some effect. Alex wondered what creatures might have found homes in the bulbs and roots of the matrix: many alien species besides the khiudie had escaped from their human creators and found their way to habitats like that one.

Victor soon found the easiest way south through the forest, leading them past spikeweed clumps toward the brightness of open air ahead. They reached the shoreline and Alex paused, astonished.

"I can't believe it," he said.

Rising from the matrix at the edge of the water were clumps of moss and patches of ordinary beach grass, evidently untroubled by the alien ecosystem around them. That seemed impossible: terrestrial plant DNA was as subject to dissolution as that of animals. California had been right—the floating forests were no longer as hostile to terrestrial life as they once had been. He wondered why.

"This is beautiful," Victor said. "I wish we could stay longer."

Alex and California paused and looked around. "Well, I suppose it is pretty," said Alex. "But I'll be glad to go. I don't know what worries me more, the alien plants or the familiar ones."

She patted his shoulder. "Don't be such a fretter, Alex."

A breeze ran through the forest, causing the trees to whisper as they brushed against one another. Alex looked at the underbrush and then up at the seed cases swelling under the caps. Never mind the apparent harmlessness of the island—let one of those cases burst or a spikeweed fire its needles, and it would be all over. His father and Sei Shonagon would have to clone new offspring from their children's cell banks.

Odd, the thought of actually dying and staying dead. Most people chose such death after two or three centuries, or in the most serious kind of dueling and warmaking. There, death was a statement, an expression of personal style. Being digested by a floating forest was something else altogether.

Sunlight blazed on Victor's golden fur as he stepped out of the forest onto the edge of the channel. There the matrix sloped away into deep water and then climbed up above the surface thirty or forty meters away. Fish swam in the clear, pale blue water.

"See?" California said. "They don't even kill fish anymore." They walked along the channel while little waves splashed near their feet.

"Has someone been experimenting with the forests?" Alex asked.

"Some people think so," California answered. "It's been going on for two or three years now, but it's affected all the floating forests, all over the world."

Alex shook his head. "Anyone who did change the forests would have to know a lot of alien botany."

"And anyone who experiments with alien plants usually has to fight a lot of wars," California agreed. "I don't think anyone's fought a war about the forests."

"Nevertheless," said Victor, "Earth plants are living here, and Earth fish are thriving in the water."

A shadow flicked across the matrix, and Alex looked up to see a bald eagle glide overhead. It flapped its enormous wings and settled onto the edge of a cap, where it looked down at them.

"Bird life, too," Victor said. "This is very interesting, Alex." He paused, and they heard his nasal cartilage snap.

"That's the answer," the gryphon said. "Molmacs."

"What?" Alex said.

"I'm in communication with wild molmacs." He paused for a moment. "They inhabit most of the plants and animals on this forest. Apparently they arrived a year ago in a dolphin, from another forest. The molmacs have been spreading across the ocean for several years, colonizing the forests. They've learned how to modify the plants' chemistry; that's why the palms can grow."

"And the eagle is inhabited by molmacs also?" Alex asked.

"He's part of the colony." The gryphon said nothing for a few moments. Then: "I've told them about the invasion. They're curious. They would like to know if we would take that eagle with us as an observer."

Alex looked up again. The eagle seemed oblivious to them. With a lazy flap to his wings he lifted from his perch, then plunged toward the water with talons extended. Foam sprayed around him as he soared upward again, a small red snapper wriggling in his grip.

"Alex, I'm not sure I want to invite wild molmacs to join us," California said.

He nodded. One's own molmacs could sometimes be a nuisance, and mingling different strains of them—as he and California had done while making love—could make their hosts mildly ill if the molmacs did not get along. Wild ones were notoriously independent, rarely interested even in communicating with humans let alone helping them. It made sense that they would seek out regions avoided by humans, like the floating forests. They had never knowingly harmed a human, but accidents sometimes happened when domestic molmacs reacted violently to their wild cousins.

"Even so, California, they must be pretty smart if they survived here, and they've learned a lot. Besides, he's a good-looking bird."

She rolled her eyes and sighed. "This is the strangest day I've ever been through. I try to please my mother by going to your birthday party, and gryphons invade, and my mother gets mad at me, and I decide to run away to space with you, and we get shot down, and now we're on a floating forest talking to wild molmacs in a bald eagle."

Alex guffawed, his anxiety gone. "Come on, California, aren't you having fun?"

"It's certainly more fun than your birthday party, but I just hope we can get up to *Wuthering Heights* without being shot down again."

His smile faded. California was right. The Chaiar might well post a permanent ban on leaving Earth, and they seemed fully capable of enforcing it. For that matter, even if he and California could get back into space, the Chaiar might put another beam through *Wuthering Heights* and leave it a powerless lump of ice tumbling in a doomed orbit.

Well, worry about that in good time. He turned back to Victor, who seemed to be staring south across the water to some outlying islets. The gryphon's nasal cartilage was snapping, but if Victor was excited his voice did not betray it:

"The molmacs are glad you're taking the eagle. They say he needs lots of fish."

"We'll try to keep him happy. Can he come down and get acquainted?"

"Of course."

The eagle abandoned the red snapper and glided out into the sun before descending. He landed gracefully on the spongy matrix, not far from Alex and California, and looked at them with a powerful yet uninterested gaze.

"Would you like to communicate directly with his molmacs?" Victor asked Alex.

"I'd rather not, thanks." Animals like Heathcliff—and, apparently, aliens like Victor—were better than humans at dealing with the microscopic computers that served as brains for molmacs. Using a comlink to talk to an animal or a normal computer was one thing; dealing with the roaring cacophony of thousands of molecule-size intelligences was another. It could be done, but most people did it only when no animal or computer was available as a buffer.

"Does the eagle have a name?" California asked.

"Several, but none that translate into human language. He's quite willing to accept whatever name you give him."

California grinned. "We'll call him Lord Whitehead, then."

"Why?" Alex asked.

"He was one of the old philosopher-kings, you know, like Marcus Aurelius and Lord Russell. This fellow looks quite regal, too." She held out her hand. "Come and say hello, Lord Whitehead."

The eagle rose and settled on her forearm, his talons just pressing the fabric of her tightsuit sleeve. His yellow eyes blazed at her.

"He's beautiful," she crooned. "But I can't believe how light he is."

"Victor," Alex asked, "does Lord Whitehead have a comlink for himself or is he just a vehicle for the molmacs?"

"He has a very distinct personality. His molmacs are already working on developing his intelligence a bit, and improving his language skills. His comlink operates on channel 1245."

Tentatively, Alex tuned his own comlink to that channel.

—Hello, Lord Whitehead.—

—Hello, Strange Male Waddler.—

"I see what you mean," Alex said, tuning out at once. "We'd better wait until his language skills are better. I'm surprised he speaks English at all."

"The wild molmacs all speak it. Apparently they originate from a crew of dolphin workers who lived near Harold Muir's reefhouse. The dolphins escaped when the dome blew in."

Alex and California nodded. Harold Muir had been a nasty old man and an accomplished warmaker. His death at the hands of Mao Jian, fourteen years before, had been widely celebrated. Alex recalled that Muir had also been a first-rate molmechanic, one of the few Lyell Bradley had ever respected. Evidently his work had not only outlived him but flourished.

California began to walk along the springy matrix shoreline with Lord Whitehead on her arm. Suddenly she paused.

"Alex—look!"

Beyond her, in the deep blue sky above the western horizon, scores of contrails fine as spiderwebs were extending eastward. The ships of the Chaiar invasion fleet had entered the atmosphere.

—Charlotte,—Alex called on his comlink. —Where's the sled?—

—Two of them are approaching. The nearer one will be here in about ten minutes.—

Trust Lydia to send a backup. —Can you direct the sleds to us?—

—Of course, dear. Now, don't worry about me. I should have a new kuldi generator grown within a day or so. Then I'll come to collect you. Meanwhile, you enjoy yourselves. I'll let Heathcliff and Emily know where you are.—

—You're a sweetie. We'll miss you.—

—I'll miss you, too.—

While Lord Whitehead went back to finish his fish, they watched the contrails lengthen and thicken. After a few minutes a distant rumble filled the air. The Chaiar ships were deep within the atmosphere, on courses that would bring them down at various points in North America.

"That cuckoo called it the Freedom Fleet," California said quietly. "I didn't like the sound of that."

"Neither did I," Alex answered. "I just hope they're too busy landing to notice a couple of sleds."

She looked at him, her dark eyes large and amused. "Just because we got shot in the ass, d' you think they can do *anything*?"

He felt uncomfortable: California had a disagreeable ability to understand him. "Well, they can shoot me, and I can't shoot them. That's why we're trying to get away, isn't it?"

"Sure, but I don't think they're going to shoot every little sled they see, and I'm certainly not interested in running away forever."

"What's that supposed to mean?"

She turned a cartwheel on the spongy matrix, then a backflip, and turned a brilliant smile on him. "We go out and figure out a way to shoot *them* in the ass. And then we come back and do it."

Alex looked up again at the contrails. More of them were appearing, and the thunder of their passage was growing louder. He admired California's attitude, but how the gryphons could be shot in the ass remained unclear.

"I can see we're going to have a wonderful time together," he said.

She threw her arms around his neck and kissed him. "I think so too!"

The rumble in the sky changed pitch. Without letting go of California, Alex turned and looked across the lagoon.

The silvery gleam of a sled had appeared between two of the outlying "islands" of the floating forest, making directly for them. It was hovering just a meter or so above the water, its kuldi field kicking up a halo of spray.

"Your mother's certainly quick," California said as the sled came to a halt above the matrix. It was a small one, about five meters long and two wide, with a narrow cabin mounted above the platform. A transparent canopy protected four chairs in the cabin.

"Good afternoon, everyone," the sled said, lifting its canopy. "Please get on board whenever you're ready."

"I'm ready right now," Alex said. He stepped onto the platform, helped California up, and then stepped over the rim of the cabin. Victor followed silently and settled himself in one of the chairs. His legs folded a little awkwardly, but he seemed comfortable enough. Lord Whitehead flapped in and perched on the back of the seat next to Victor. The gryphon extended a three-fingered hand and stroked the eagle's feathers.

"He's very excited to be travelling," Victor said.

"Aren't you?" California asked with a grin.

"Yes, I am," he answered in his deep, metallic voice.

"It's always exciting to be shot out of the sky," Alex growled.

"We have been very lucky," Victor replied. "Perhaps luckier than we realize."

Alex gave the gryphon a sidelong glance. Sometimes Victor's unemotional voice made him sound as if he were speaking like one of the ancient oracles, with a hidden meaning. If they were all going to be cooped up on *Wuthering Heights* together for years, he would have to train Victor to speak more naturally.

The sled lowered the canopy and swung silently back across the lagoon. It accelerated rapidly, pushing its passengers back into their seats. The plume of spray blocked the rear view, and the floating forest soon disappeared in the glare of the westering sun.

"Wait a minute," Alex said. "Sled, you're on the wrong course. We should be heading southeast, not northeast."

"The course is correct, Mr. Alex. We're heading for Jasper House."

"Where? We should be going to Mordor, in southern California."

"I'm afraid you may have misunderstood, sir," the sled

answered. "I'm the property of Mr. Liam McCool, and we're returning to his estate in the Giuliu Tuo. He's delighted to be able to offer you his hospitality."

The sled lifted to ten meters above the sea and surged forward. Within a minute and a half it was at cruising speed, two thousand kilometers per hour. Overhead, the Chaiar contrails were widening and blurring.

Seven:

The sled flew northeast, just a few meters above the sea, at supersonic speed. Victor and Lord Whitehead seemed interested by the dizzy rush of water below them, but Alex and California ignored it.

So did the korshak images of Lydia and McCool that appeared to hang suspended just outside the sled's cabin, unruffled by the shock wave.

"Liam, this is atrocious behavior," Lydia said. She had reached Mordor and changed into working clothes: loose khaki trousers and a cotton blouse. She was sitting in a rather elegant version of a Barcelona chair cast in fome. "I *insist* that your sled change course and transfer Alex and California and Victor to my sled."

The korshak image of Liam McCool on the opposite side of the sled shrugged and grinned. He was still dressed in his wrinkled tropical suit, and his seamed face was crumpled into a grin. "I'm only trying to be helpful, Lydia. And the best help your boy could ever hope for now is the right frame of mind. I want to warwire him. And California, too, of course."

"Warwire them! Turn them into Violents, you mean."

"Don't we have any say in this?" Alex interrupted. "I'm a duelist, not a warmaker. War doesn't interest me. Least of all against the Chaiar."

"Remember what I said about kicking the Chaiar?" California said. "How are we going to do it if we're not equipped?"

McCool's image, half-obscured by flying spray, turned to look in at them. "Well said, California. By God, your father may have been a duelist, but he could fight a war when he had to. Warwiring doesn't *compel* you to make war; you two know that. But if the Chaiar force war upon you, then at least you have a chance. And of course I

65

wouldn't force you to undergo warwiring. Good lord, Alex, your dear mother and father would be raining missiles on my head. Mao Jian, too. He takes war too seriously to let people fool around with it. I expect to have enough problems with the Chaiar; I don't need my friends trying to kill me as well."

Lydia looked unimpressed. "Turn your sled around, Liam."

"A compromise?" McCool asked Alex and California. "You two finish your journey to Jasper House. I'll give you my argument for warwiring, and you'll be free to turn me down. Whatever you choose, I'll have you on your way to Mordor at once. Your shuttle will be ready to fly again in a few days, and off you'll go—back to *Wuthering Heights* and any destination you choose. Mm?"

Alex frowned and turned to his mother. "He's right about one thing, Mother: We can't afford to fight each other. I'm willing to hear his pitch, on those terms."

"So am I," California said. "But I'm not afraid of being warwired, anyway."

Lydia smiled without much pleasure. "All right, dear," she said to Alex. "You're a citizen now. Do as you please. I'll keep in touch." She vanished.

"Liam, what's happening up there?" California asked. She pointed to the smearing contrails that were turning pink in the early evening.

"John F. Kennedy has been, mm, very eloquent. Would you like to hear what he's had to say?"

"No," Alex said. "Just give us the news."

Where Lydia had been, just off the right side of the sled, new korshak images formed: pearly-iridescent shuttles landing in meadows, salt flats, beaches, even long-abandoned old highways. Human cuckoos soared out of their hatches, evidently equipped with some kind of Chaiar levitation device. Some headed for estates, but most simply cruised, seemingly aimlessly, in widening spirals around their ships.

Local humans were gathering around some of the cuckoo ships; Alex was glad to see that aircraft were not being attacked. A few cuckoos met the locals with open arms, but most continued their spiral flights.

"What are they up to?" California asked.

A korshak image expanded, locked onto a female cuckoo who looked like a teenager. She wore a kind of tightsuit striped in orange and red. A shoulder harness supported a thick rod about a meter long: the levitation device, Alex supposed. It jutted out beyond her shoulders like atrophied wings. In one hand the cuckoo held a smaller rod pointed toward the ground. The girl's pale features were calm but alert, her blue eyes observant behind a transparent shield. Red hair fluttered below the rim of her helmet.

"She's shooting something into the ground with that gadget," McCool said. "My guess is it's some kind of molmac plant. Or several kinds, more likely."

"If they are growing new molmacs," Victor said, "we should find out what their properties are. They may be dangerous."

"Ah, Victor, you've been well educated." McCool nodded. "I intend to find out as soon as possible. This young woman isn't too far from me, a couple of hundred kilometers east. As soon as she's gone back to her ship, I'll nip out and see what I can find."

Another image replaced the redheaded girl: a tall young Asian-looking cuckoo, in identical uniform, falling dead from the sky with his face and chest drenched red. Beyond him a sled curved up toward a rampart of cumulus clouds. A few seconds passed. The cuckoo dropped out of sight while the sled dwindled into the distance. Then it exploded in a yellow flare.

"And that happened ten minutes ago in India," McCool reported. "The Chaiar are rebroadcasting it with a tedious narration. A show of force to discourage interference."

Alex slumped back in his seat. "They can move planets, they can shoot down shuttles, they can retaliate even for a hit and run. How are we supposed to fight them?"

McCool's image rubbed its hands together. "Not by feeling sorry for ourselves. God be praised, we've been granted a new dimension of Violence. I only hope we're worthy of it."

"Worthy of it?" Alex repeated sourly. "I don't feel worthy at all. You'd waste your time warwiring me. It'd just make me feel better about being vaporized like that sled."

"Well, that would be some consolation, wouldn't it?" McCool chuckled. "I promised your mother I wouldn't proselytize, Alex, but let me just suggest this to you: God loves entropy. That's why he makes so much more of it all the time. He reverses it sometimes, creates order out of chaos, but that's to make the return to chaos more interesting. Most people don't understand that simple point, so they struggle against the inevitable triumph of entropy, and all they do is make themselves miserable in the process. If they would only go with the flow, relax and enjoy it, they'd know the real purpose of life.

"Now, the Chaiar have come to bring a new kind of entropy to us—and they'll experience it too, believe me. As soon as John F. Kennedy started yelling about the Pattern, I knew we were dealing with limited minds, antientropic minds—" His voice rose almost into a cheer. "—solid-gold *losers*, Alex! They're doing God's will by trying to impose order, and we'll do God's will by resisting. And the universe being what it is, we'll win."

"By getting blown to shreds."

"And joining God quicker than we would otherwise. But we join him inevitably. Why shouldn't we put on a little show for him in the meantime?"

California stirred restlessly. "It's a great philosophy for an old fart, but I'm too young to appreciate it. Liam, is there anything to eat on this sled? We're starving."

"Oh, of course! I'm sorry. I'm a bit old-fashioned in my culinary tastes. I hope you like Italian food."

"That'll be fine," Alex said. He was glad California had deflected the old man from his religious tirade. When the galley under the dashboard popped open, he gaped at two large disks of meat, cheese, and vegetables.

"What's that?" California asked.

"Pizza," McCool said. "I think you'll like it. And now, if you'll excuse me, I'm going to pop out and see what that cute redhead's been planting out on the prairie."

His image vanished. The sky was darkening overhead, and the sun had sunk behind a bank of clouds on the western horizon. Up ahead loomed the coast of West America. The sled gained altitude and thoughtfully turned up the light enhancement so its passengers could enjoy the view.

They crossed the Olympic Peninsula, a wasteland of eroded hillsides and dead, rotted tree trunks, and descended dizzily again over Puget Sound. Within a few minutes the sled raced over the broad delta of the Fraser River and the ruins of Vancouver.

"Looks just like Hong Kong down there," California

remarked. They glanced down at the ancient towers of Vancouver, scorched and stained by centuries of fire, rain, and sun. Much of the city had turned to swamp, but little grew except a few scrubby bushes. To the north, across the city's old harbor, rose mountains even more eroded than those of the Olympic Peninsula. The slopes were gouged by deep gullies pumping yellow mud into the harbor.

"Sure looks like West America," Alex said. "Just like the country around Mordor. I wonder why anyone thought this was country worth living in."

"It was all forest a few hundred years ago," Victor said. "It's died away since Contact."

Alex and California shrugged. "You sound like my father," Alex said. "Always going on about the good old days."

The gryphon looked at him with gleaming, unreadable eyes. "Your father taught me just as he taught you, Alex."

"I suspect you were a better student." Alex finished the pizza, thinking he should remember to get the recipe for Emily.

The sled flew on over the snow-capped peaks of the coast range and across the great plateaus beyond. Here and there gleamed the lights of some lonely estate. Not many people chose to live in West America.

They crossed the Fraser again, hundreds of kilometers north of Vancouver and close to its origins in the Giuliu Tuo, the splendid mountains once called the Rockies. Seen in light enhancement through the canopy of the sled, their peaks glowed blue and purple beneath a lavender sky. The sled rose, following a pass marked by long lakes, and then they were in the great valley of the Athabasca, with the ramparts of the mountains all around him beneath the moon.

Jasper House, Alex knew, had been McCool's estate for more than a century, and the old poet had done a great deal to its surroundings. For scores of kilometers in all directions forests stood green and dense on the mountainsides as they had long before. The lakes that dotted the valley were clear, and careful microclimatology had restored glaciers to many of the mountains.

The main buildings of Jasper House stood above the braided courses of the Athabasca, on a high shelf of land where the ancient town of Jasper had been before Con-

tact, but his auxiliaries—factories, stores, transports—
were concealed below ground. From the air, all that could
be seen was a small compound of two-story log cabins in a
patch of grass and shrubs overlooking the river.

The sled banked, dropped, and slowed to a landing in
the middle of McCool's compound. The canopy popped
open, and Alex shivered a little. The night air that far
north had a sharp chill.

"Doesn't the air smell good?" California said, springing
from the sled to the ground. The sky was dark, of course,
but the estate itself was bathed in warm yellow light. They
found themselves in an open area dotted with tussocks of
coarse grass and lichen-crusted stones. The forest, mostly
lodgepole pines and aspen, grew thickly along the bounda-
ries of the clearing.

"It smells wonderful, but let's get inside." Alex saw his
breath fluttering white and wondered why McCool allowed such uncomfortable conditions on his own property. The estate did not even have a proper dome. Victor
sighed, fluffing out his golden fur, while Lord Whitehead
squeaked, perhaps in response to the cold or perhaps simply for the pleasure of it. The eagle flapped his wings and
rose to Victor's shoulder.

McCool, wearing a parka and plaid trousers, came
striding from the largest of the cabins. "Welcome to
Jasper House! Come on in and have something hot to
drink. We have a lot to talk over."

As they followed McCool into the cabin, Alex felt inexplicably tired. Usually his molmacs kept him free of such
feelings; it had to be some psychological reaction to the
events of the day. Even walking into the home of a Violent
could not rouse him to full alertness. Alex suspected he
would need actual sleep, hours of it, when usually he had
no more than a few minutes' nap every night or so.

The interior of the cabin was like a museum of pre-
Contact life. The varnished log walls were adorned with
real paintings, not holographic imitations, and the furniture reminded Alex of old twentieth-century movies: plaid
fabrics stretched over frames of wood or iron with cush-
ions of some springy material that had to be genuine foam
rubber. A real fire burned in the fireplace, and an enormous dog, warming himself on the hearth, wagged his tail
in welcome.

"My housekeeper, Brian Boru," McCool said, introducing them. "An Irish wolfhound, of course."

"Of course," California said. "He's beautiful."

—And so are you, California,— the wolfhound replied via comlink. —Please, come and sit down. The robot will be here with a drink in just a moment. Lord Whitehead, would you like a perch for the night?— Brian Boru pointed with his whiskery muzzle at a moose head hanging on the wall opposite the fireplace, and Lord Whitehead abandoned Victor to settle himself on one of the moose's antlers.

An ambulant robot, looking out of place in the old-fashioned setting, strode into the living room bearing a tray with coffee, mugs, and cookies. McCool, beaming, served each of them before sinking into an armchair and crossing his legs.

"When I overheard your messages to your parents," he said, "I saw my opportunity and took it. The invasion's proceeding rapidly, and we'll have to act fast ourselves. Brian, an update, please."

—Six hundred and eighty-two shuttles have landed so far,— the wolfhound replied. —Another hundred and twenty are en route, and at least four hundred more are launch-ready on Habrakha. Most of the shuttles carry crews of cuckoos who are seeding several kinds of unknown plants. About a hundred gryphons have arrived as well, but they haven't been active. The cuckoos are also transmitting propaganda on several korshak bands. Would you like to see what it's like?—

"Spare us for now," McCool said. "What about the human reactions?"

—Most landings have been peacefully met by local people. Some cuckoos have been invited onto estates. In a few cases the proprietors have threatened the cuckoos. The cuckoos haven't responded, but in six cases where they've been physically attacked, the cuckoos have destroyed the attackers.—

"I'm surprised that there are six vertebrates left on this planet," McCool growled. "No, I'm unfair. More people will think of resistance once they see what the Chaiar and the cuckoos are up to. But it'll be a sad and sorry attempt."

"How can we do better?" California asked.

"Warwiring, for a start. Then we've got to get you two off the planet and set you to finding allies."

"Allies?" Alex repeated. "What have allies got to do with it?"

"You're still thinking like a duelist." McCool's smile had no humor in it. "All you care about is the test of the individual, mm? Hand to hand, may the best fighter win, may the loser be kept in memory."

"I'm not expecting to win against the Chaiar. I just want to get some breathing space."

"You'll get none. The Chaiar have managed this invasion by cooperating, and they'll win if we don't cooperate, too."

"You mean with other people? Like the old days?"

McCool shook his head sadly. "Alex, *dueling* is now the old days. Individual warmaking is the old days. Modern warfare is what the gryphons are doing to us. So you're going to have to get as many spacers as possible working together. No, it's not going to be easy."

"It's going to be impossible. Besides, what's the point? Suppose, we, we—organize an armada and try to counterattack. They'll just shoot us down again."

"Oh, I'm not thinking about a frontal attack, Alex. Not at all. I'm thinking about creating a supermind."

"What does that mean?"

"A merger of molmacs on a grand scale. Trillions of those little computers, linked up and thinking hard, figuring out ways to make the Chaiar wish they'd never come here."

Alex lifted his hands in frustration and let them fall in his lap. "It's bad enough sharing molmacs with family, but sharing strangers' molmacs—I don't know if I'm ready for that, Liam." The idea was almost perverted. Every citizen developed his or her own molmac technology and kept most of it secret. After all, one's defenses were based on it. A few geniuses like Lyell Bradley might give away some of their technology, but only because they were supremely confident of what they had kept for themselves.

"Besides," Alex went on, "I can barely communicate with my own molmacs, and you want to form some kind of merger of thousands of people's?"

"With millions of people's." McCool stood up. "Come with me for a moment, everyone."

He led them down a flight of creaking wooden stairs to a basement that was considerably larger than the house above it. It had been outfitted as a laboratory, and on one illuminated table in a corner stood a sealed hemisphere of clear fome. Inside was a small pot with a single plant growing in it. Its leaves were dark and almost perfectly circular; they grew in pairs, tilted up to the light. At its tip was a small pink bulb.

"Four pairs of leaves," McCool muttered. "When I brought it in from the prairie, there were only two. It likes the warmth and light."

"What is it?" California asked.

"A Chaiar molmac factory. The prairie's covered with them, all the way to Edmonton."

"And it's going to grow until it bursts," Alex said.

"Exactly." McCool nodded somberly. "Brian Boru estimates it's still a couple of days from maturity."

"And you've brought it into your own house?" California said incredulously. "What if Brian's wrong and it bursts right now?"

The old poet looked at her with a faint smile and shrugged. "We don't even know what kind of molmacs it's producing, my dear. For all I know, they're designed to build highways or plastic knives and forks. Anyway, it would take them a while to figure out how to escape from the dome."

Alex controlled an urge to bolt back up the stairs. "Doesn't it seem more likely, Liam, that they're growing molmacs to invade us and take us over?"

"It certainly does. And if we're going to defend ourselves, we'll have to learn as much as we can about them. Brian Boru and my computer, Sanjuro, are monitoring the plant very closely. Very closely. And passing the data on to my molmacs. They'll be working out countermeasures."

The old man knew how to take a calculated risk, Alex thought. But the flower under the lamps filled him with horror. Incompatible molmacs were one thing, an avoidable nuisance; the alien object was nothing but infection, a weapon designed to subvert its targets at the level of the nucleus itself. Even the toxins of the floating forests were trivial compared to the potential catastrophe in that simple finger-sized plant.

"If the prairies are covered with these things," he said, "putting a dome over this one doesn't help much. You'd need a dome over the whole estate."

"I don't think domes will be of much use against these

things. We'll have to fight them on their own terms."

"In our own bloodstreams, you mean," California said.

"Among many other battlefields. We won't have much time."

"Let's go back upstairs," Alex said. "I want to get some rest."

"Of course."

McCool led them back to the living room, where Brian Boru thumped his tail and whined a little. He was indeed worried about the little plant in the basement.

"The bedrooms are another flight up," McCool said. "Take any one you like. I'll call you in a few hours."

"Do you want some company first, Alex?" California asked.

"Very much."

McCool extended a hand to the broad wooden staircase and patted each one's shoulder. "Good night; good love. We'll talk in the morning."

"Thank you, Liam." Alex shook the old man's hand and climbed the stairs with California beside him. They found a room sparely furnished, with a simple bed and a wide window that showed the Athabasca and the mountains beyond it. Their forested slopes and glacier-mantled peaks glowed in light enhancement.

Alex turned the window to normal, and it darkened to show only a reflection of the room. California peeled off her tightsuit with a sigh of relief. A few seconds later he was as naked as she, and the only light in the room came from the moon shining high above Mount Tekarra.

He clung to her with unexpected fierceness, finding consolation in the smooth heat of her skin and the strength of her limbs. When they were done, she kissed him lightly and rose from the bed. Moonlight glowed on her hips and breasts as she stepped lightly away toward a room of her own. Alex felt a brief pang of longing, of wanting her to stay with him while they slept. The desire embarrassed him with its perversity. Then it passed, and he turned over to sleep.

Later in the night he stirred, blinked, and looked out the window. The sky was brighter, almost a predawn blue. The moon was gone, and in its place Habrakha rode high over the mountains. It was smaller than it had seemed yesterday when it had first risen above the horizon, yet it was still immense: a sphere half blinding white and half Earthlit blue.

Alex closed his eyes again, trying to find sleep, when his comlink roused him with a silent howl. It was Heathcliff, calling from *Wuthering Heights*.

—Alex. Alex, they've killed your father.—

Eight:

Sitting in that log-walled bedroom overlooking the Athabasca, Alex watched his childhood home explode in pulses of black and orange and yellow. He watched it from satellites and from the cameras of *Wuthering Heights*, in slow motion because it had happened in less than a second.

The cloudcastle had been cruising east-northeast across the Pacific, and a Chaiar shuttle had overtaken it. A cuckoo had left the shuttle to descend through the humid afternoon air, a young white man in a black tightsuit.

William Macintosh had been in his study, watching the shuttle hover not far above. He had looked out from that spherical room atop his tower, the room Alex remembered as the most interesting in all of *Munshaour*. He had been wearing spotless white cotton trousers and a pale blue shirt. A korshak image had appeared beside him, the image of a woman.

"We are here to sow the seeds of the Pattern on your cloudcastle," she had told him.

"Are you, indeed? I'll thank you to wait until you're invited."

The woman, brown-skinned with very white teeth, had smiled. "Please invite us, then."

"Not in this century. Get out of my airspace, you and your flying friend out there."

"We are serving the Pattern. When you understand, you will obey gladly."

"All the more reason not to understand. If your levitating friend isn't back inside your ship in one minute, I will open fire on him and you."

Her face had hardened. "I will not argue with you. We offer death or the everlasting joy of the Pattern."

76

"A false dilemma if ever I heard one. You have forty-five seconds."

"I must warn you. We will destroy your cloudcastle and everything in it."

"Your manners are atrocious, young woman. Please remove your korshak image, your companion, and your ship."

Her image had vanished from the study, but the ship had still hovered overhead and the young white man had dropped closer. As he swooped down over a lawn, his planter poised, William had fired simultaneously at him and at the ship.

The white man had vanished in a burst of smoke, his body carbonized by a beam. A flare of white fire had erupted from the belly of the ship as it reflected a second beam; then its pearly hull had darkened—

At that point the transmissions from *Munshaour* had ceased. Magnified images from satellites had shown the alien shuttle unscathed as an explosion blew the prow off the cloudcastle and three more explosions wrapped it in fire. The towers fell, the ponds and streams vaporized, the rhododendrons and eucalyptus trees exploded and burned. Bliokio and the grizzly housekeeper August and all the household robots had vanished. Out of the bottom of the expanding cloud, with dreamy slowness, the remnants of *Munshaour* had trailed streams of smoke and fire as they tumbled to the sea below.

The Chaiar ship, undamaged, had circled the cloud until all the debris had fallen from the air. Then it had accelerated southeastward, to some new target.

Wuthering Heights had been overhead at the time, and Emily had recorded the destruction of *Munshaour* in great detail. She had kept the spacecraft's cameras focused on the sea for half an hour while the smoking wreckage burned or sank.

—I'm very sorry, Alex. I always admired your father.—

—Thank you, Emily.— He pulled a blanket around his naked body, feeling cold though the room was warm. Habrakha's blue light poured through the window where the korshak images had been a moment before.

He drew a long, slow breath and then, surprised, began to cry. After a minute or two he stood up and went to the window. He stared up at the swirling whiteness of the alien planet's dayside and smashed the side of his fist against the unbreakable glass.

"Liam! Liam McCool!"

He and California and Victor watched the sun rise. They were in a small room looking north and east across the river valley to a long range of jagged peaks standing against a reddening sky. Habrakha was not visible from there: It had already begun to sink in the west. Alex had given up his jumpsuit for a pair of shorts and a T-shirt much like Victor's; his dermograph glowed red and orange and yellow in the light of the just-risen sun. California wore a black tightsuit set off by a single white epaulet.

McCool walked into the room, dressed austerely in a dark suit and a white turtleneck. "Alex, will you go first?" he asked quietly.

"Yes." Without hesitating, Alex sat in an old-fashioned armchair. California held his hand while McCool took something from a cabinet: a small, metallic-looking disk. It fit easily in the palm of his hand, reflecting the ceiling lamps on its glossy blue surface.

"Some of the young fellows like a bit of ceremony," McCool said. "They miss the whole point of Violence. And I think you've already undergone your ceremony, mm?"

"Yes."

"Then take this and hold it in your hand." McCool gripped Alex's right wrist, pulled his hand up, and pressed the disk into his palm.

It felt slightly warm but of course caused no pain or even numbness. The injection mechanism was a needle too fine to see, let alone feel. Alex knew the molmacs were coming down the needle, entering his bloodstream, negotiating with his native molmacs, and moving swiftly to his brain. They were not like the antibody molmacs he had been served a day before, which induced a mild fever; these were more businesslike, too specialized to cause even the faintest malaise.

"Of course you won't feel different," McCool murmured, "but you'll tend to think a little more, mm, aggressively. Strategically. The idea of running won't seem so interesting."

"We'd better not want to commit suicide against them," California said.

He took the disk from Alex's palm and pressed it into hers. "Of course not, dear. As one of our prophets once said, the whole idea is to make some other poor son of a bitch die for *his* country."

Alex frowned, not understanding. "Countries don't have anything to do with it. They killed my *father*."

And was that adequate grounds for grief, for revenge? His father had been a hard, egocentric man, indifferent to others' feelings and perhaps to his own as well. William Macintosh had chosen to sire Alex to prove some ideological point, to demonstrate his conservatism with a living symbol. He had chosen the time and manner of his death as consciously as he had chosen the guest list for the birthday party; the cuckoos had really been only the instruments of his vanity. His death was no different from that of a duelist who called for unbuttoning the foils or a warmaker arming his missiles with live explosives. And yet Alex grieved and felt a sense of injustice that both enraged and surprised him.

"Never mind," McCool said. "Let's sit and watch the sun rise and then go have some breakfast. We won't have many moments this peaceful again for a long time."

Victor sat silently by the window, his massive chest rising and falling as he breathed.

Fluffy white clouds hung in the spring morning sky, occasionally drifting across the face of Habrakha. Sunshine gleamed on the snowcaps of the Colin and Maligne ranges across the river. More contrails appeared high up.

Alex clapped his hands together. "That's enough," he said. "Liam, I want a conference: my mother, Mao Jian, Lyell Bradley, Sei Shonagon, and us."

McCool nodded. "Sanjuro!" His household computer appeared in the korshak image of a twenty-first-century Japanese bureaucrat: tall, balding, in a sober blue suit and Paisley ascot. "Arrange a conference, please. We'll take it on the sun deck."

"Very good, sir. Please accept my condolences, Mr. Macintosh, and let me know if I can do anything more for you."

Alex was already on his feet and heading for the sun deck. "Thanks, Sanjuro. Hurry up, California—Victor."

McCool chuckled. "Doesn't take long once the molmacs get to work."

Squirrels scampered over the sun deck and leapt up into nearby lodgepole pines, shrilling. Five or six elk browsed nearby, occasionally lifting their heads to regard without curiosity the group on the deck.

The korshak images were vivid, detectable more by their incongruous light and shadow than anything else. Mao Jian, though his image was in full sunlight, looked dark and shadowy. He was wearing a khaki many-pockets vest over a white cotton shirt and baggy olive-drab trousers. To Mao's right sat Lyell Bradley in a glossy silk smoking jacket—not that he ever smoked; on the war-maker's left was Lydia, looking both austere and beautiful in a plain black turtleneck over white leotards. Sei Shona-gon, gloriously naked, appeared to recline on a pale yel-low chaise that nicely set off her tan. She seemed to Alex to have forgotten her sulk. She greeted him cheerfully and sympathized with California's account of being shot down without betraying a hint of maternal disapproval.

"A lot has happened since yesterday," Alex said when the greetings were over. "I thought then that we'd have to run for it and just hope we could get out to the Neptune Belt or somewhere else away from the gryphons. Now I'm not sure that's possible, and even if it was, I think I'd rather stand and fight."

"Well said," Mao grunted.

Lyell Bradley frowned. "What would we fight with, Alex? And where? They're already established all over the planet." He gestured awkwardly to a dataframe that appeared to hang suspended in the air at one end of the sun deck. Its constantly shifting numbers and images summarized the extent of the invasion: 1,620 shuttles landed, 167 en route, 18 returning to Habrakha, 148 cuckoos killed, 3,609 humans killed, 2,769 estates de-stroyed, 6,349,367 humans officially welcoming the Chaiar, 9,020,533 humans taking no position, 30,840 offi-cially opposing them and threatening force. The dataframe changed too fast for the eye to follow: 4,102 estates de-stroyed, 6,245 humans killed, 28,204 officially opposing.

"What's more," Bradley continued, "a lot of those neu-trals are recluses. Most of them probably haven't popped their domes in fifty years. They're so fugued out, they don't even know the invasion's on, and they won't care when they do. Over a third of the people on Earth have accepted the gryphons. Anyone who publicly resists is being killed." The number of pro-Chaiar humans jumped as he spoke to 6,467,110. "So we're not going to find very many allies."

"Not on Earth," Alex agreed. "I want to get the spacers on our side. Liam thinks we can get them to merge their molmac computers with ours and form a kind of super-mind that could outsmart the gryphons."

The initial reaction was much as Alex's had been: em-barrassment. Physically sharing ordinary molmacs was in-timate enough; sharing molmac computers, linking them into a single unit, seemed an outrageous abandonment of individuality. He argued the case as strongly as he could, with McCool chiming in from time to time, and the lis-teners eventually accepted the idea, at least in theory.

"The spacers are all being very quiet," Lydia said, "even by their standards."

Alex nodded. "I think they're just watching. We need to make contact with them and get them involved in devel-oping Liam's supermind. After all, there are almost five million people out there. If they all linked up and put their molmacs on the problem, we'd get somewhere in a hurry."

California spoke up. "Fair enough, but what if the gry-phons get out there as well?"

Alex was struck by a glint in her eye that had not been there before—the result of warwiring, he suspected, won-dering if he had it also. "So far they haven't even bothered the ships in Earth orbit. I think they want to make sure Earth is safe before they take over the rest of the system. That gives us some time. Liam, can you get out an APB?"

McCool nodded. "We'd better agree on what we want to tell them."

Mao Jian frowned. "The gryphons are likely to monitor the APB, just the way our computers are monitoring their broadcasts. Korshak is open to everyone, after all. Do we want to reveal ourselves to them?"

"Don't worry." McCool chuckled. "We can phrase it as a bulletin in slang. The gryphons can't know much about our history and culture for the last thirty years, so they're not likely to catch the meaning."

Lyell Bradley cleared his throat. "We're asking the spacers to join forces and link up their molmacs. Are they likely to do that, even with an invasion on their screens? Spacers are pretty individualistic."

"If even ten percent agree, we'll be the biggest organization in centuries," Alex answered. "And if we can get some results in a hurry, we'll attract more people."

"Always assuming," Bradley said quietly, "that a few hundred million molmac computers can equal a whole planetful of advanced aliens."

Victor, sitting beside Alex, raised his hand. "All they have to do," he said, "is find a Chaiar weakness and a way to exploit it. It seems likely to me that a molmac merge would enable us to explore the Database and find some weapon or technique that will work against them."

Bradley nodded. "Well, I'm in. I'm giving you all my access codes."

The others, predictably, were less eager to agree. To link one's molmacs and databases with those of others was an act of self-exposure requiring enormous trust. Alex realized he had not thought that through. He knew it would be hard to share his own resources, and even harder for spacers still remote from the invasion.

"Well—" He sent a comlink message to Emily, who responded with slightly scandalized agreement. "You have my access codes, too, now."

Each in turn did the same. In the process, Alex thought, they had created a germ of the supermind McCool wanted. What would it be like when it could draw on the unimaginable power of billions of molmac computers and private databases? Perhaps, as Victor had suggested, even the Database itself would yield its secrets to such a mind.

They spoke rapidly, framing the message for the APB. Phrased in duelists' slang, it sounded like an invitation to a round-robin tournament; that alone would tip people off that it was no innocent message, since dueling was never that organized.

"All right," McCool said, looking at the message glowing on the dataframe. "'Come one, come all, knifers and gunners, to the biggest round-robin of them all. Pull yourselves together, ninja, and gather your little bitty wits. No crotch plates, just a good friendly scrum between hosts and guests, special prizes for winners. First rounds with your neighbors, semifinals announced later.'"

"Sounds good," Mao Jian grunted. "Get it out."

McCool nodded, then looked shocked.

Mao Jian had vanished. So had the others, and the dataframe.

The four of them were alone on the sun deck, with Lord Whitehead perched a hundred meters away in a lightning-blasted snag overlooking the river.

"Sanjuro!" McCool bellowed. The computer image did not appear. The old man opened his mouth to shout again, but Sanjuro's voice sounded in their minds through their comlinks.

—Excuse me for invading your thoughts,— the computer said. —I am unable to project an image of myself. The gryphons have jammed all korshak bands beyond the short-range neurotropic. So comlinks work over a couple of kilometers, but nothing else except the gryphons' own transmissions. I can give you a sample, if you like.—

The sun deck filled with a blue-green haze, shimmering rapidly as Sanjuro ran through the bands; then the haze vanished, replaced by John F. Kennedy standing side by side with a small, wizened old man in rags.

"Mahatma Gandhi," McCool snorted. "We'll be getting the Buddha and L. Ron Hubbard next."

"Yes, John, the whole world has welcomed the Pattern," Gandhi was saying. He was speaking clear standard English, much like Kennedy. Alex reminded himself that the Gandhi cuckoo, despite his appearance, was probably only a few years old. "Apart from a very few unhappy people," Gandhi went on, "the rejoicing is universal. For a little while we are preempting the korshak bands to make sure no one misses the good news."

"What's next, Mahatma?" Kennedy asked, grinning.

"At our present rate, all of humanity on Earth will be gathered into the Pattern within three or four weeks. Then we will turn to the moon and planets. By the end of the year we expect to have just about everyone in the solar system working within the Pattern."

"That's very good news indeed. And we're all grateful that so few people have been sacrificed to achieving our goals."

"John, I think humanity has been crying out for this. When you look at how people have lived since Contact, it's clear that they had no more purpose in their lives than the trolls did until they joined the Pattern." He pursed his wrinkled lips and shook his head. "Empty, empty lives. People have spent their lives in foolish games, dueling, fighting, sexual promiscuity, idleness. And always alone. A corruption, a perversion of human nature."

"How so, Mahatma?"

"The Pattern has made us social animals, John. We want to belong; we want to know the rules and live by them. All the knowledge that came to Earth with Contact has corrupted humanity. And look—only twenty million humans, where once we numbered in the billions! Isn't that a clear sign that we weren't made for the empty knowledge of the Net?"

"It certainly is," Kennedy agreed.

"But now we can put that knowledge to proper use by disseminating the wisdom of the Pattern. Once humanity is joined to itself again, and joined to the Chaiar and the other species in the Pattern, we will take our rightful place."

"Thousands of people are calling us, Mahatma." Kennedy looked out, seemingly into Alex's eyes. "If you want to join us, your computer can reach us at these band values." Trollish symbols glowed briefly in the air before the two korshak images. "If you need more time, please think over what we've said. We realize that joining the Pattern is a big step. If you'd like to talk to someone face to face, we'll be glad to send an adviser to meet with you and explain what the Pattern means to you personally. Now, Mahatma, I'd like to thank you for your time. My next guest is Karl Marx, who has some important information for all of us about the benefits of the Pattern."

McCool guffawed and ordered Sanjuro to shut off the korshak. "Well, what now, children?"

Alex paced to the edge of the deck and looked down at the river gleaming in its braided channels. "We've been cut off from korshak contact with each other," he said, turning around, "but what about radio or television?"

"What about smoke signals?" California snapped.

"No, he's right," Victor said. "Electromagnetism is crude, yes, but it could work well enough for our purposes."

"That's silly, Victor," she protested. "The whole idea of linking up our molmacs means korshak. Good heavens, we just gave each other our access codes, but they're meaningless now. We can reach our own molmacs, but not other people's. The electromagnetic spectrum isn't wide enough, even if you could get the molmacs to build little TV transmitters and receivers."

"Of course." Alex nodded. "But we can at least keep in

touch with one another and pass some information back and forth."

"Assuming anyone's listening."

"That's not quite fair, my dear," McCool said. "Household computers routinely monitor the EM spectrum, just the way the trolls did when they first picked up human broadcasts. Trouble is, we'll have to build a TV transmitter." He paused. "Sanjuro tells me he can have one up and running in about twenty minutes."

"That'll help," Alex said. "But California's right. We can follow what people are doing, but we can't really link up with them. Even assuming we can hold out for any length of time here, we'll still be operating on our own. We've *got* to use korshak."

"But we can't," California answered impatiently.

"Not here. But from what those cuckoos were saying, they're saving the rest of the system for later. I'll bet korshak is still running fine off Earth."

"A fat lot of good that does us."

"Emily will have the shuttle fixed within a day or two."

"And they'll just shoot us down again."

Alex chewed his lip. "We'll think of something." He looked at Lord Whitehead, who seemed to be dozing on his snag overlooking the river. "Or the molmacs will." He switched his comlink to the eagle's channel.

—Lord Whitehead. I want to talk to your molmacs.—

The eagle did not even trouble to reply; instead, Alex's head filled with a crackling roar that seemed to go on forever before a clear signal emerged.

—We are here.—

—You are linked to our molmacs?—

—Yes, we are here, yes, here, here.—

—Think how we can return to our ship and launch for Venus without being attacked.— It would have to be Venus, if only because at that point in their orbits, Venus was five or six days closer than Mars. Besides, the population of Venus was half a million, and another hundred thousand spacers were in the vicinity at any given moment.

—It can be done, done, yes, launch, Venus, launch. First you need protection, guard, protection, first, danger.—

—Protection against what?—

—Molmacs, molmacs, gryphons and molmacs, the

plants, good invaders, slavewires, molmacs.—

—The plants are creating molmacs to enslave us?—

—Yes, yes, smart molmacs, they find the receptor sites, find, smart, we work on resistance, resist, defend our people.—

—How can they enslave us?—

Not words but images answered him: molecular images, each transformed as new molecules—the gryphon molmacs?—hooked onto them. Alex recognized some of the molecules as epiphanics. That made sense. They were powerful hallucinogens, capable of creating intense religious experiences. Some people were addicted to them, living in a state of ecstasy. The Chaiar must have found the epiphanic receptors in the trolls' human cuckoos and designed molmacs expressly for those receptors.

He thought of the plant growing in McCool's basement and shuddered.

—Can you protect us from slavewiring?—

—Soon, soon, protect, soon.—

—Can you free us from slavewiring if the Chaiar molmacs invade us?—

—Maybe, we hope so, maybe, yes, maybe.—

The enormous valley, with its vast sky and endless mountains, seemed almost claustrophobically constrained. Alex looked around as if some escape hatch might present itself. His warwiring made him feel good when he thought of combat, but when he could see no plausible defense against the Chaiar molmacs, he felt a furious aimlessness.

—Can we help you? Can we give you anything?—

—Time, yes, time, hours? days? more data, a cuckoo? good, cuckoo, full of molmacs, study closely, closely, examine, molmacs, molmacs.—

—Thank you. I'll talk to you again soon.—

He broke the link with a gasp of relief. It had been like trying to conduct a conversation with a stadium full of maniacs. He wondered how Heathcliff did it.

"Well?" California demanded.

Alex held up a hand. "Liam, would you ask Sanjuro to call one of those numbers Kennedy was giving? We need a cuckoo, in a hurry."

Nine:

Somehow he had expected California to worry and McCool to welcome the idea of luring a cuckoo to Jasper House; instead, California laughed while the old man frowned.

"The plant in the basement is sealed off," he said. "But the cuckoos are obviously in close touch with their masters. If we bring them here and something goes wrong, we won't have much chance to escape."

California grinned, showing lovely white teeth. "If something goes wrong, we'll be slavewired and glad to be part of the Pattern."

"On the contrary, dear," McCool said quietly. "If something goes wrong, Jasper House and everyone in it will be vaporized. I can assure you of that."

She seemed unimpressed, and Alex thought again of her duelist father. "It'll blow up too fast to tell, won't it?" she said. "Well, then. Anyway, nothing's going to go wrong. I think it's a wonderful idea, Alex."

"What do *you* think, Victor?" Alex asked.

The gryphon had been sitting immobile ever since the korshak images had vanished; he might have been a purely decorative icon. But he responded at once.

"From what I have seen so far, the idea isn't likely to work, Alex."

"Why not?"

"Bliokio was able to gauge John F. Kennedy's intelligence matrix from a few seconds of analysis. Chaiar computers will certainly be able to do a deep analysis of anyone here who sends a message, and they're certain to detect a lie. Therefore, they're not likely to come anywhere near us. They might simply dust us with molmacs or let the molmac plants do the job. They might even destroy the estate as they destroyed *Munshaour*. They certainly won't send cuckoos here and allow us to capture them."

Alex shoved his hands in the pockets of his shorts. His arms and legs gleamed red and gold, the dermograph scales glittering in the sunshine. "Well, what would *you* do, then? Wait for them to come and get us?"

"Of course not, Alex. Simply have Sanjuro send the message."

McCool chuckled, reconciled to the risk by the quality of the deception. A computer's lie, after all, could not be exposed by nonverbal signals. "Very *good*, Victor. Should have thought of it myself. I'll get right on it. Before we send the message, though, what will we do when the cuckoos arrive?"

"Good question," California said. "They have at least two people on each shuttle, don't they? One to pilot and one to plant."

"Probably a lot more than two," Alex said, nodding. "And the pilot at least is sure to stay in the shuttle. They'll be in touch with each other, so anything that happens to one is known to the others—and to the gryphons. We can't simply lure a cuckoo into the basement and cut his head off."

"All we need is a small blood sample," Victor said. "If we can obtain it painlessly, the cuckoos won't realize what's happened."

"The cuckoo's molmacs might," McCool said. "And if they set off an alarm, we're as bad off as if we'd slugged him with a hammer."

Alex looked at Victor, who looked back impassively.

"That is a chance we will have to take," the gryphon said.

First they coded an innocuous message for Sanjuro's TV transceiver, which the computer had set up in the living room. The message was a plaintive bulletin about a fictitious birthday party for California, asking the invited guests to reply electromagnetically. Sanjuro bounced it off an ancient satellite, using himself as the speaker, as Victor had suggested.

Replies came in almost at once in quaintly two-dimensional images: Lydia said she was sorry she could not attend but invited California and her guests to drop by in a day or two. Mao Jian said he was looking forward to the party and had some interesting new games they could play. Sei Shonagon and Lyell Bradley replied together from her estate in Japan, saying they could not wait to see California's face when she opened her presents.

"What's Lyell doing at Mother's?" California wondered. "I wouldn't have thought he's her type."

"Or she his," McCool said. "I'd be happier if they were at Lyell's. He's away from his resources, and I doubt if your mother's labs and molmacs are as good as his."

"All we've really learned," Alex said, "is that people are working on the problem, but we're still going to have to get together to do anything."

"And we *can't* get together," California said. "Not without korshak."

"We'll have to see what the molmacs can do once they've studied a cuckoo." Alex shrugged. "This is a lot like dueling. You don't know what to do until your opponent does something."

McCool nodded. "It's also very much like an old sport called fly-fishing. We cast the lure and see who bites. Sanjuro, send the message to the gryphons, please."

Sanjuro obeyed and received an immediate acknowledgment from an icon of John F. Kennedy that materialized near the fireplace: "We will send a team to visit you as soon as possible. Please be patient. The demand for visits has been extremely high. Thank you for your interest in the Pattern."

"I've just had an awful thought," Alex said. "What if the cuckoos can detect lies too? We can't use Sanjuro when we're talking face to face with them."

California looked angry for a moment. Then she asked Sanjuro to run an analysis of all recorded human/cuckoo interactions so far to judge whether any reflected such an ability in the cuckoos. The image on the TV screen blinked a couple of times.

"Several teams appeared to distrust messages they received," he said, his voice sounding flat and unnatural coming out of a speaker, "but it looks as if they requested backup analysis. In fourteen cases they didn't do anything to harm their suspects. In thirty-nine they killed their suspects. Would you like to look at the raw data? It will take some time to go through, I'm afraid."

"Never mind," McCool said. "No, wait. Show us the nonviolent interactions."

The recordings had of course been picked up from kor-shak, and it took Sanjuro several seconds to translate them into electromagnetic signals that could be observed on a TV screen. To save time he split the screen into six frames, each portraying a different interaction. Most had been recorded and broadcast by the humans involved, although a few had been broadcast by the cuckoos as part of their propaganda programming.

Different people had responded differently to the arrival of a cuckoo shuttle. Some had stood at the gates of their estates with bouquets; others had received their guests in what looked like throne rooms. Most betrayed considerable nervousness.

"They're not used to physical presence," Alex said.

"Are you?" California asked.

"Not entirely, even now. But it doesn't seem to bother the cuckoos. They just don't like jumpy people."

"That one isn't jumpy," Victor said, extending a long finger toward one of the frames. "He seems to be on epiphanics."

"You're right," McCool muttered. "Isn't it embarrassing, watching a human being on his knees?"

"*That's* what'll do it," California said. She hugged Alex's arm. "Just before they get here, we bomb ourselves with epiphanics. We'll be just another gang of bliss-outs."

Alex felt himself shiver. California's touch was pleasant, but old habits died hard. And the thought of taking epiphanics was alarming. If warmaking inspired that kind of behavior, he preferred the honest malevolence of dueling. "How—how do we get the molmac sample?"

"Each of us will have microneedles embedded in our hands," McCool said with a smile. "One way or another, we'll shake hands with them or touch them. That should be all it takes."

"And if we can't touch them?" Alex insisted.

"Brian Boru will be bristling like a porcupine, won't you, old boy?"

The wolfhound grinned and thumped his tail.

The day wore on in anticlimactic tranquillity. Habrakha sank into the west behind the black snow-streaked bulk of Whistlers Mountain. The sky was clear except for an occasional contrail. While everyone had a light snack of pastries and coffee, Sanjuro took a few minutes to grow the needles and synthesize the epiphanics.

"I'm sorry to have to make you wait," the computer apologized over the TV. "Mr. McCool never keeps them in stock. And I want to be sure that the dosages are just right. A milligram too much and you might never come back to your senses."

McCool growled and glared at the TV image. "Ignore him when he talks like that. It's just his way of bullying."

Alex smiled tightly, trying to remind himself that Emily tended to bully him the same way on *Wuthering Heights.*

The epiphanics appeared at last, three small white lozenges on a bronze plate borne by a house robot. Alex looked at Victor.

"Isn't he going to get one, too?"

"I'm afraid I don't know how to induce religious ecstasy in a gryphon," Sanjuro said. "In any case, I don't think Victor should even be here when the cuckoos arrive."

"Very wise, Sanjuro," McCool said. "Victor, when they do come, would you mind going to your room?"

"I'll be glad to."

"Perhaps this would be as good a time as any, then," Sanjuro said. "A shuttle just passed overhead, and a cuckoo is descending toward the house."

"Ah!" McCool's eyes lighted up. He took the bronze plate from the small table where the robot had left it and offered it solemnly to California. "Since it was your idea, dear, please take the first one."

She hesitated for a moment, then took a lozenge, looked hard at Alex, and popped it into her mouth. Alex reached out and took another. Victor walked out of the living room without a word.

McCool took the last epiphanic, muttering something about communion. All three sat back in their chairs, waiting for the drug to take effect. Alex was beginning to wonder how long the wait would be when the front doors swung open and a young woman strode in. She wore a green tightsuit, and her flying harness was tucked under one arm.

"Good afternoon," she said.

Alex stood up and gasped. She was the most intensely real being he had ever encountered; the noon sunshine behind her seemed pale in comparison.

"My name is Fredrika Aalstrom. Call me Rik. May I come in?"

A cuckoo namesake of the great twenty-second-century singer did not seem at all absurd, even if the cuckoo was a tall, radiant blonde and Aalstrom had been black. Alex put out his hands to her and felt tears start down his cheeks.

"Please—oh, please come in. We're so glad you could come."

She smiled. "I'm glad to be here to serve the Pattern."

"Yes, the Pattern," California said. "We've been waiting so long, so long. And now—now—you're *here*."

"Dear child of heaven," McCool murmured, smiling beatifically. "Come and sit with us, honor us with your words. Tell us about the Pattern."

Rik walked confidently across the floor to the cluster of chairs and couches where the three of them stood. She paused just a moment at the sight of Brian Boru, who was sitting on his haunches beside McCool. The wolfhound wagged his tail and held out a paw for her to shake. She did so, smiling.

"He's a good dog, and he's glad to see you," McCool crooned. "Please, dear Rik, come and sit." He took her hand in one of his and gently touched her upper arm with the other. She allowed herself to be guided onto a couch. Alex sat on one side of her, and California on the other. Each clasped hands with her.

The young woman was patient with them; she seemed to understand their feelings. They babbled about the Pattern, asked questions, and did not wait for answers but babbled some more. Alex was sure she would suddenly grow wings. Somewhere far back in his mind he wondered if Rik's fellow cuckoos were monitoring the conversation, analyzing it, judging its validity. It hardly mattered; the universe made joyous sense as it never had before, and he thanked Rik for making him see that.

"...the Pattern fills the universe," she was saying at some point. "Sometimes you can't tell it's there, but it is. A drop of water looks chaotic, but freeze it and its pattern appears. Everything in it falls into place. Our work is to help the Pattern appear here on Earth and among all humanity."

"Yes, yes!" California whispered. "Among *all* humanity, here and everywhere."

Rik smiled affectionately. "The planets will have to wait, I'm afraid. First we have to fit this world into the Pattern, and we have so few people—hardly one for every thousand Earthborns. Eventually we'll turn to the others."

"Why wait?" Alex demanded. "Rik, why wait? Send us to go before you. I have a spacecraft in orbit. We could be talking to the Venusians in ten days."

She patted his arm. "It's a sweet thought, Alex. But the Chaiar would have to decide that, not a simple girl like me."

"Then let's ask them," Alex insisted. "Oh, I can't wait, Rik. It could be so exciting."

"I can ask, Alex. I can't promise."

"That's enough," he said hoarsely, almost on the edge of tears.

"Before I do, I have a gift for you." From a pouch on the belt of her tightsuit she drew a small yellow rod. "Come close and look at this."

They crowded close to her. "What is it?" California asked.

Rik waved it before their faces. "Molmac spray," she said. "They'll help strengthen your conversion to the Pattern."

Even in the intensity of his epiphany, Alex realized what that meant. He turned to stare at Liam McCool, then at California, while he waited for Jasper House to blow itself into vapor.

Ten:

The spray in Alex's nostrils smelled like roses and hashish. Suddenly he slumped back in his seat, vaguely aware that McCool and California were sagging also. From the corner of his eye he saw Brian Boru galloping for the front door, which opened obediently before him. Must really have to go, Alex thought.

He tried to raise a hand and failed. The sense of helplessness did not bother him much, thanks perhaps to the euphoria induced by the epiphanic, yet he was painfully aware that all his newfound joy would vanish within seconds as Jasper House exploded. Just on the edge of this wonderful moment—

Another part of his mind calmly analyzed the reason for the paralysis induced by the spray: It would take time for the Chaiar molmacs to genuinely convert them to the Pattern, and immobilizing the convert would forestall suicide or some other rash action.

Pointless in this case. As soon as Sanjuro realized that they were slavewired, he would carry out McCool's standing order and detonate whatever device had been prepared for the purpose. Jasper House and much of the Athabasca Valley would disappear in a nuclear fireball, and the conversion of humanity would go on without them.

"Don't be frightened," Rik said with a comforting smile. "The paralysis will be gone in a couple of minutes. And then you'll understand everything."

—Alex. California.— It was McCool, transmitting directly to them through their comlinks. Despite his paralysis and religious ecstasy, Alex felt himself blushing at the undignified intimacy of it. He saw California's hands twitch as if she were trying to raise them to push McCool

94

away. McCool himself sat on her far side, apparently staring at the ceiling.

—Forgive this intrusion. I've just talked to Sanjuro to urge him not to detonate the house. We all have too much to live for now.—

—What did he say?— Alex asked. That kind of communication between humans was worse, in its way, than being in physical presence all the time.

—He's holding off. He says he'll keep us under observation.—

—So he might still do it,— California said.

—I don't know. In a way I don't care. I'm beginning to understand what the Pattern really means, after all.—

—So am I,— Alex answered. —It's beautiful, isn't it?—

The Chaiar molmacs worked fast, he thought, even faster than the ones that had warwired him and California that morning. They were neutralizing the epiphanic and pouring undreamed of data into his mind.

Already he saw himself and the others in the room in a different light. Jasper House looked like a pathetic hovel, a shabby little cabin fit only for savages. California and McCool and he himself were those savages, wretched, ignorant, and blind. By comparison Rik was almost angelic, a being in harmony with herself and the universe. She knew her place in the Pattern; they did not. Yet.

He began also to see how the Pattern worked, at all levels of the universe, from the virtual field to the galaxy clusters. At most of the levels physical law ensured the integrity of the Pattern; only at the quantum level and where conscious, symbol-manipulating life arose was it threatened. Intelligence meant that instead of inevitability, uncertainty ruled. DNA itself was immensely stable and obedient to the Pattern. It could replicate itself identically, inevitably, for millions of years. But when DNA built itself into organisms of sufficient complexity, chaos broke out, disrupting the Pattern and destroying itself.

Most organisms, even the most advanced of the species in the Net, felt the need for the Pattern but associated it with the primitive religions or other social-bonding customs of their remote ancestors. Thus they turned away from the only understanding that could give meaning to their existence. Even the Chaiar had done so until Durung had achieved his brilliant insight and shared it with the rest of his species.

Like personal memories, Alex saw what had happened: Isolated from the Net, the Chaiar had turned in upon themselves, exploring new concepts, rejecting the poisoned, chaotic wisdom of the Database. Realizing at last what the Pattern was, they had realized also that it must be restored to all intelligent life; the entire Net, and other species as well, deserved to rejoin and advance the Pattern.

The epiphanic's effect was gone, but Alex felt a burst of gratitude to the Chaiar. Now he saw what countless philosophers had only dreamed of seeing: the universe as a whole, purposeful, intelligible. Trillions of molecular complexities made him what he was; individually and collectively they were meaningful, unless he acted to make them otherwise. And he had been pursuing futile goals, amusing himself with less than trivia, squandering the mind that could play a part in restoring the universe.

He felt a sudden awful surge of guilt and shame, none the less painful for knowing it had been induced by Rik's molmacs, and its memory stayed with him even after they dissolved it in a bath of pleasure and relief. He felt strength return to his limbs and raised a hand experimentally.

"Thank you, Rik."

"You're welcome, Alex." She smiled at him, serenely beautiful, intimidatingly simple.

"We have some things to tell you." Alex looked at California and McCool, who nodded silently at him. "We invited you here to deceive you, to try to learn more about you and the gryphons so we could resist you."

"I'm not surprised. Many people have done the same thing."

"But—we may be blown up, Rik. Liam told his computer to destroy this whole area if we were converted. Now he's told it not to, but the computer's still trying to decide."

She sat back, crossing her long legs. "If that's our pattern, so be it."

McCool cleared his throat. "My dear, I think Sanjuro —my computer—understands our changed circumstances. Otherwise he would have destroyed us as soon as you brought out that sprayer. I think, therefore, that we have time to discuss what should happen next."

"What do you think?" Rik asked with an encouraging smile.

"We invited you here to deceive the gryphons into letting us return to my spacecraft," Alex said. "We wanted to get out to Venus or Mars, or beyond, and unite the spacers in a network to oppose you."

She laughed musically. "Form a pattern to fight the Pattern?"

"Well, we weren't very original, I admit. But now I see that we really should go into space—and prepare the spacers for you, just as I suggested when you arrived. Venus has the most people, and I know it fairly well. I'd love to take the Pattern to the Venusians."

Rik stopped smiling and nodded. "It's a good thought, Alex. What do you think?" she asked California

"I'd love to go. Just give us a few thousand of those sprayers of yours, and we'll get the whole solar system behind you."

"I think you would, too. You three strike me as unusual, much more socially oriented than most Earthborns. You couldn't escape your cultural background altogether, of course. That's why you wanted to resist. But you did it by looking for a pattern, didn't you? And you're aggressive, which is always helpful. I'll notify my superiors and see what they think of your idea."

The thought of anyone being superior to Rik filled Alex with awe. "I hope they say yes," he mumbled.

"Something's bothering me, Rik," California said. "Why have your people killed so many of us? Even Alex's father was killed."

The cuckoo sat up, her eyes filled with sympathy. "It seems hard, I know. But sometimes the Pattern demands urgent action and a clear space to grow in. It isn't static, is it? We can tell very quickly when we find someone who just doesn't fit the Pattern at all—people who just shouldn't exist. We could convert them, but they'd recognize their own superfluity and take their own lives. Just because something exists doesn't mean the Pattern needs it. Least of all when it opposes the Pattern."

Alex nodded. It seemed embarrassingly clear. His father had drifted, literally drifted, aimlessly about the world for centuries. He had outlived any purpose he once might have had. The cuckoos in the shuttle over *Mun-*

shaour had recognized that within seconds and removed him from the Pattern.

"We need to talk to some of our friends and relatives," he said. "My mother is still resisting the Pattern, and California's mother."

"That will be hard to do with the korshak blackout still on."

"We've got an electromagnetic communications set-up," Alex explained. "It's crude, but it works."

Rik seemed interested. "Go ahead and try it. I'd like to see what it's like."

"Sanjuro," McCool said, "bring the TV in here, please."

A mobile rolled into the living room with the communications rig on its back. Sanjuro signaled Mordor and got a prompt response. Lydia's head filled the screen.

"Alex, you've called at just the right time," she said with a gleam in her eyes. "Listen, I've made more progress than I ever could have imagined. I've got a shardana bubble over the *whole estate*! Can you believe it? It's fifty kilometers in diameter! Fifty!"

Alex gaped at her. "A complete bubble?"

"Well, about three-fourths of one. Enough to keep the cuckoos out. I could make it a complete sphere, but then I'd go whizzing off into space, wouldn't I? Don't want to do that until I know how to steer."

That made a horrifying kind of sense to Alex. A shardana bubble did not really exist in ordinary space, so anything it enclosed was unaffected by the outside world.

Rik, who was sitting out of Lydia's sight, seemed as surprised as everyone else. She stood up and moved in front of the camera. Lydia looked at her in startled dismay.

"How did you manage this?" Rik demanded. "No one on Earth has ever built a shardana bubble more than a hundred meters across. You don't have the technology for a larger one."

Lydia's eyes narrowed. "Alex, what's this person doing with you?"

"Mother, this is Rik. She's our contact with the Chaiar. We understand what the Pattern is now. We understand why Father had to die. Resisting is stupid. We see that now, even Liam McCool."

"True, Lydia," McCool said. "I know you don't like

proselytizers, but this isn't a religion. It's the simple truth."

Lydia's expression turned from surprise to horror to cold impassivity.

"Simple truth appeals to simple minds. I wish you zombies joy of it. Good-bye."

The screen went blank. Rik shook her head.

"I think your mother has a definite place in the Pattern, Alex. But if she hides under that bubble, she'll only harm herself and disrupt other people."

Alex stood up and walked nervously about the room. Lydia's refusal even to listen was a painful breach of the Pattern. He would have to call her again soon, when she had had time to reflect.

"I want to try reaching my mother," California said. Sanjuro obligingly tuned in Sei Shonagon's estate. A robot again answered; this one, at least, was humanoid in appearance.

"My mistress is not receiving calls," it said quietly. "She has decided to pause. She does not intend to resume life for at least one hundred years. If you would like to leave a message, I will notify her when she awakes."

"Pause—she's gone into suspended animation?" Rik said. Alex and California nodded. "Well, in good time we'll wake her, but we won't wait a century."

"Poor Mother," California said. "I guess Lyell wasn't enough to keep her conscious. It was all too much for her."

"Many Earthborns have done the same thing," Rik said. "They've run from the Pattern."

"I have a feeling we're not going to do any better with Mao Jian and Lyell Bradley," California said. "They'll either reject us or run away."

"Lyell and Mao will fight," Alex said, and McCool nodded.

"It's unfortunate," Rik said. "Actually, that's not the right word. Fortune doesn't happen in the Pattern. But I see that you still have affection for your old friends and family, and I regret the distress you feel. As you become more comfortable with the Pattern, you won't feel bad at all about death—other people's or your own."

"Will they all have to die?" California asked. "Can't you revive my mother and convert her?"

"Oh, I'm sure we'll try. But as I said, not everyone fits

the Pattern. Alex's mother almost certainly would fit, but she's resisting. Unless she changes soon, she'll lose her place." Rik paused. "I certainly didn't expect an Earth-born could build a bubble that big, and only a day after we arrived. Was your mother working on shardana physics before?"

"She's always done a lot of experimenting," Alex said. "I never paid much attention. But I don't think she's done anything with shardana bubbles before now; she's been using her molmacs as a kind of supercomputer."

"I see. That's a clever kind of improvisation. Our computers are so powerful, we don't need to form linkups. We didn't realize your molmacs were so advanced. All the more reason to make sure Earth joins the Pattern."

California laughed. "Make sure? Is there any doubt?"

Rik laughed, too, and a moment later the men joined in. The front door opened, and Brian Boru entered. He was panting, and blood ran down his gray fur from a wound on his neck. Whimpering, he came across the floor to where they were sitting. His comlink went on, using a broad channel they could all pick up.

—Hurt myself.—

"Poor old boy," McCool said, patting him. "What happened?"

The wolfhound licked McCool's hand, then turned and rubbed himself against Alex and California. They petted him, too, while he licked their hands and bare legs. He shoved his wet nose against Rik's leg. She patted him a little cautiously.

"What happened, Brian Boru?" McCool asked again. The dog repeated his simple complaint as he went on nuzzling them and demanding attention.

"Sanjuro," McCool called out. "What's happened to Brian Boru? Did he fall or something?"

"I couldn't say, sir. He went into the woods, out of sight of my monitors, and then came back as you see him. Shall I have the robots clean him up?"

"Please. Go on, old boy." McCool gave him one last pat, and the dog ran out. The old man chuckled.

"You know, Rik, we probably could have saved you a trip," he said. "I've got a molmac plant downstairs. One of your people planted it out on the prairie, and I brought it home yesterday. I presume it would've had the same effect as your spray."

"Among other things. Each of those plants produces a great many different kinds of molmacs. What color is the head?"

"Pink."

She nodded. "Mostly converters. But the pink ones also produce soil catalysts and killers."

"What does that mean?" Alex asked.

"We're going to make the ecosystem more compatible with the Chaiar," Rik said. "That means changing the soil chemistry and getting rid of a lot of microscopic life-forms. It's a slow process, but in a decade or two you won't recognize this world. It'll be like Habrakha and the home world, Makhshuar."

"Where were you born?" California asked.

"Oh, on Habrakha."

"And how do they move a whole planet through space?"

"That's completely beyond me, I'm afraid. They tell me that Habrakha was originally in a system about four hundred light-years from here. The Chaiar settled it about a hundred years ago, changed its ecosystem, and then moved it into the Tayas system about five years ago."

Tayas, Alex knew, was the sun of Makhshuar. "Why?" he asked.

"We were a big colony, Alex, but not that big. The Chaiar had to move millions of themselves to Habrakha before we could come here. We'd built cities for all the newcomers, and then we had to build our shuttles and—" She gestured gracefully. "—countless other things."

Alex felt a sudden surge of excitement. "I'll bet Earth will be like Habrakha, won't it? The whole planet will go on to the next system."

"I think so. Each world we bring into the Pattern is given more worlds to convert. The trolls are preparing to do that with their planet, but it'll take them a long time. Their chemistry is so different from Makhshuar's. But I think the Chaiar are planning to use Earth, Venus, and Mars—and maybe Titan as well."

Alex reached out and gripped California's hand. "I can hardly believe it. Three or four planets, travelling to the stars."

"All the more reason to hurry the conversion of the rest of the system," McCool said, pacing up and down the living room. "If the Chaiar want comfortable planets, they'll need to do a lot. Rik, can you approach them and get their permission for us to leave Earth?"

"I've already done so, Liam. The answer is yes. They agree you should go to Venus."

Alex bounded to his feet. "We're going! Rik, can you come with us? We need you."

She looked taken aback for a moment. Then she nodded. "They agree. I don't want to leave Earth so soon, but they see a quick advance for the Pattern. How will we get to your spaceship, Alex?"

"My shuttle's repairing itself on a floating forest in the Pacific. It should be ready very soon. Sanjuro, can you contact Emily and ask her how it's going?"

The computer's voice replied almost instantly. "She says she needs only some last minute tests. She can launch tonight and pick you up here. That would put you back on *Wuthering Heights* within twelve hours."

"Very good. Tell her we'll be waiting."

The rest of the afternoon was a kind of party. They ate, drank, laughed, and played games. Rik learned about their lives, but they learned little about hers. From time to time they tuned in the korshak broadcasts from the Chaiar: John F. Kennedy had been replaced by Winston Churchill and Mikhail Gorbachev, who spoke cheerfully and naturally about the success of the Pattern so far.

"At this point," Churchill said, "the overwhelming majority of humanity has turned decisively to the Pattern. I am pleased to say that our emissaries are being welcomed with a degree of enthusiasm impossible to calculate or to deny. On all sides, the people of Earth have accepted the Pattern as the self-evident truth that it is. I believe this shows the close affinity of humanity and the Chaiar; our minds work similarly for all our physical differences."

"This is so," Gorbachev agreed. The port-wine stain on his bald scalp reminded Alex of Lyell Bradley. "I see it as a sign that humanity will hold a special position in the conversion of other species, a position second only to the Chaiar themselves."

"That would be a signal honor indeed, Mikhail. And a proof that even a backward species like our own can leap to the front once it recognizes the Pattern and carries it out."

Alex found the thought both exhilarating and obvious.

Of course they were like the gryphons, so of course they would understand gryphon thought better than most. He realized that the korshak broadcasts, which had seemed so inane a few hours before, were intended for converts rather than resisters.

Sanjuro laid on a splendid dinner, served by robots sheathed in silver and gold. Everyone ate and drank happily, talking eagerly about the conversion of Venus and Mars. Near the end of the meal Sanjuro announced that the shuttle had left the floating island and would arrive at Jasper House in about thirty minutes.

"Very good, Sanjuro. Thank you," McCool said. Then he paused. "Good heavens! Victor, how could we have forgotten you!"

The gryphon stood in the doorway of the dining room, his fur gleaming as golden as the flanks of the serving robots.

"I have been resting," Victor said. "Please don't let me disturb your meal."

Rik rose from her seat, extended her arms out from her sides, and bowed her head. She spoke briefly: deep, resonant words in Chaiar.

"Thank you," Victor said. "I speak very little of my species' languages, but I recognize your greeting. Please sit down."

Without taking her eyes from Victor, Rik obeyed. "You didn't tell me a Chaiar was here."

Alex felt a mixture of amusement and embarrassment. "I—thought you must know somehow. You know so much. And so much has happened since you arrived, I just didn't think about him. He's a cuckoo, of course, born right here on Earth. I guess you could say my father gave him to me as a kind of present."

"You understand now that no human can own a Chaiar." Rik seemed pained even to say such a thing. "Least of all this one. He is a clone of Bhrukang, the greatest Chaiar scientist of the ages before the Pattern."

"Indeed." Alex felt a ripple of surprise on the surface of his euphoria. He had not realized what template Victor had been taken from. "He'll serve the Pattern with us. Won't you, Victor?"

"I must tell my superiors," Rik said, but Victor raised a hand to forbid it.

104 / Crawford Kilian

"It will be seen to," he said. "Of course I will come with you. I look forward to learning from Rik." He pulled up a chair and joined them at the table. "Sanjuro, may I have a cup of tea? Thank you."

Alex and California glanced at each other and then at Victor. Rik's behavior had changed dramatically with his arrival. She seemed in awe of him; he might have been a cuckoo, but he was still a Chaiar and, genetically, a great one. That in turn made Alex feel he had underestimated the gryphon. The journey to Venus could not help but succeed if Victor was part of it.

The shuttle announced its arrival with a long, rolling sonic boom. At close range, Charlotte's comlink sounded in Alex's head

—Hello, dear. I understand we're taking another young lady as well as California.—

—That's right. You'll like her.—

—I'm sure I shall. Well, I'm parked just outside. Let me know when you're all ready. If it's no inconvenience, I'd like to launch sometime in the next hour and a half, or we'll have to chase *Wuthering Heights* halfway around the world.—

—We'll be aboard before you realize it.—

The house was suddenly full of mobiles scuttling back and forth with luggage. McCool went downstairs to bring his plant back outside—"No sense wasting it on an empty house," he said—and spent some time discussing household matters with Sanjuro. California and Rik went outside to watch the mobiles loading gear into the shuttle; Alex joined them.

"It's a lovely ship," Rik said. "Not really a Pirid design, though."

"Most people find troll shuttles ugly," Alex said. "They'd rather design their own. Mine is based on the old Soviet shuttle. I like the classic style."

"And how do you like ours?" she asked.

"They're beautiful. I'd love to ride in one some day."

"I'm sure you will."

McCool finally emerged from the house, pulling on a white raw-silk jacket. His wrinkled face was creased with smiles.

"Just making sure Sanjuro looks after Brian Boru. Ugly

wound he picked up, wasn't it? He didn't want to talk
about it."

"What about Lord Whitehead?" California asked suddenly as they were climbing the ramp into the shuttle.

Alex and McCool looked around. The late afternoon
sky was clear and empty, and the trees nearby showed no
sign of the eagle.

"Don't worry, dear," McCool said. "I don't think Lord
Whitehead would really fit in with the Pattern."

"You're right." California shrugged and grinned and
turned to the shuttle doorway. "I can hardly wait to see
Venus."

"And Mars as well, perhaps," Alex said.

The dayroom was just as they had left it, though it
looked to Alex as if Charlotte had touched up the Chinese
carpet a little. With no korshak images on the screens, the
room looked a little dull.

"Please strap yourselves in, everyone," Charlotte said
over a loudspeaker. Her voice sounded odd to Alex; then
he realized she was speaking via electromagnetism. "We'll
rendezvous with *Wuthering Heights* in an hour and thirty-
one minutes."

The screens lighted up with electromagnetic images,
sharp and clear but no match for korshak. They watched
the mountains tilt and fall away as the shuttle soared
steeply away.

The climb out of atmosphere was rapid. As they curved
eastward over the continent, the stars emerged in the
darkening sky. Steamship contrails shimmered in the
blackness like strands of spiderweb. Eventually Habrakha
rose over the curved horizon, a vast glowing crescent that
drowned out stars and contrails alike.

"Someday we'll go there, too," California said. "A
whole world, living in the Pattern." She looked affectionately at Alex. "Aren't we lucky, Alex?"

"There's no luck in the Pattern, silly," Rik said. "We're
in it because we're in it."

"I see," California answered a little uncertainly.

An odd, feathery flapping sound came from the corridor back of the cabin. Alex heard the shrill cry of an
eagle. As he turned his head to look for it, he saw California, Rik, and McCool all convulse in their chairs. At the
same moment he felt himself heaving up against his straps.

His whole body felt as if it had caught fire. Victor, seated beside him, seemed very far away; the gryphon looked at him without expression.

Alex screamed. He was faintly aware that the others were screaming also. Then he passed out.

Eleven:

Alex slipped in and out of consciousness. Occasionally he heard Charlotte over his comlink, along with responses that might have come from Victor or some stranger. The words meant nothing; perhaps they were in some alien language, yet they were familiar.

His own thoughts scarcely made sense. Images crowded upon one another: memories of long ago on *Munshaour*, a duel on Luna, Heathcliff leaping for a stick, Victor swimming through the clear blue water over California's reefhouse. He wondered if that was how one's life flashed before one's eyes at the moment of death, but the ideas of life and death, eyes and moment and self, lost their meaning even as he thought of them.

Once or twice he felt achingly cold, but most of the time he was hot. He was distantly aware of hurting. Sweat coated his skin, trickled into his eyes, salted his lips. He thought about opening his eyes but could not remember how to do it.

After a long time he felt powerful arms lifting him from his chair, strange hands gripping him. His eyes opened, and he saw a red and gold blur that turned into Victor's chest. The gryphon was carrying him like a baby; Alex's cheek lay against Victor's pebbly osmotic membrane, and he could hear the strong-weak-strong rhythm of Victor's heartbeat. Alex closed his eyes again and dozed off.

He dreamed of flying and woke to find himself in free fall, floating through the access corridor from the shuttle hangar to the living quarters of *Wuthering Heights*. The tentacles of a mobile held him. The walls of the corridor slid past. He waited serenely for the passage through the south pole doorway and the return of kuldi-field gravity; it came uneventfully, and the mobile entered an elevator to the residential level.

Gravity was the pleasant .9g of home. The elevator hummed upward, level after level, and stopped. Doors slid open, and there was the second floor of the house, its windows full of sunlight. Heathcliff stood in the wide hallway, wagging his tail anxiously.

—You're awake, Alex. Are you feeling all right now?—

—I'm tired. Where are the others?—

—They're coming up next. I'm putting California in the guest room next to yours, and Liam McCool next to her, and Fredrika next to him. Will that be all right?—

—What about Victor?—

—He wants to stay on the main floor. And Lord Whitehead wants to be outside, of course.—

—Lord Whitehead?—Alex felt stupid and blurry.— He's back on earth.—

—He came aboard the shuttle before you did. He triggered your deconversion.—

—My what? You're not making any sense, Heathcliff.—

The mobile was rolling across the hallway into his room. It pulled back the coverlet on the bed and lowered him gently onto it. The sheets felt smooth and comfortingly familiar.

—Get some sleep, Alex. I'll explain when you're rested.—

He wanted to object, but it was easier to curl up first and think about how to phrase the objection. In what seemed like an instant he was wide awake and the room was in darkness.

A word or a comlink command would have turned on the lights, but Alex preferred to roll out of bed and walk in the dark to the windows.

The gardens below were moonlit. Overhead, through the dome, Earth's nightside made a vast arc of blackness, relieved only by pale streaks of cloud, flickers of lightning, and the pinpoint lights of widely scattered estates. Beyond the curve of the planet, the stars and moon shone brilliantly, but they paled even as he watched. Habrakha rose, eclipsing the moon.

Until that moment the normality of *Wuthering Heights* had made him forget the events of the last two days. Now they rushed back with the unreal intensity of a well-remembered dream. Down there on Earth, the blasted ruins of *Munshaour* lay at the bottom of the South China Sea.

Mordor lay under a gigantic shardana bubble. Thousands of people had been killed, and hundreds of thousands—millions—had been converted to the Pattern. He had been among them.

But not any more! he thought.

He was about to leave the room when he realized he was naked and had guests aboard. Fumbling in a closet, he found shorts. When he pulled them on, he saw that his dermograph—the beautiful, changing multicolored scales he was so proud of—was gone. His skin was its normal pale brown.

The doors to the guest rooms were closed; Alex ignored them and went down the broad flight of stairs to the living room. Lights burned there, and a pleasant fire crackled on the hearth. Icons of Fred Astaire and Ginger Rogers danced across the floor to unheard music: proof that korshak worked here. Heathcliff was dozing in front of the fire while Victor sat nearby reading a book. The gryphon looked up and nodded.

"Good morning, Alex."

—Morning, Alex,— Heathcliff echoed.

"Good morning, dear," said Emily's disembodied voice. Unlike Charlotte, she rarely projected an image of herself.

"Good morning, everybody. Heathcliff, would you order me some breakfast? And then tell me what's been going on."

"I can do that," Victor answered. "You and the others had to be deconverted."

"Wait a minute." Alex sagged into a chair and held up a hand. "We were blasted on epiphanics to fool the cuckoos. Then Rik sprayed us with molmacs, and we converted for real. How could we be deconverted? And if we were, why did the Chaiar let us leave?"

Victor laced his fingers together in an oddly professorial gesture. "Lord Whitehead's molmacs recognized what had happened to you when Rik sprayed you. They asked Brian Boru to get a sample of Rik's blood and molmacs. He went outside, and Lord Whitehead picked the sample up. The wild molmacs analyzed Rik's molmacs and then transferred some of themselves back to Brian Boru. That was the wound you saw on him."

"And then he came in and licked us!"

"So the molmacs penetrated your skin. They spent

some more time analyzing the qualities of the Chaiar molmacs, and then, once the shuttle was launched, Lord Whitehead gave the signal and they attacked. It looked very unpleasant for you."

"It was awful. I thought I was dying."

A mobile rolled up beside him and extended a tray over his lap; on the tray were plates of eggs, bacon, tofu, and hash-brown potatoes. Alex took a mug of coffee first.

"The molmacs knew it would be hard on you, but they decided that a sudden, complete attack was the only way to make sure the Chaiar molmacs couldn't resist."

"That's a very Chaiar kind of strategy," Alex grunted.

"Yes, I suppose so. In any case, the deconversions went well and no one suffered serious harm. I think it would be impossible to convert you again; your systems are full of antibodies now."

The gryphon's calm, resonant voice stirred a feeling in Alex that he had rarely known; he could compare it only to the emotions he had felt watching his father's cloudcastle explode. He suspected it was what people had formerly called anguish. Without realizing it, he had loved his father; without willing it, he had loved the Pattern. Both were gone, and he could scarcely tell which was the sharper loss.

After a few seconds the constriction left his throat, and he could trust himself to speak. "Do you understand what I've gone through, Victor?"

"Yes, I think I do. It must be very painful. Would you like to return to the Pattern?"

"No. But it . . . seemed so clear. It made so much sense. Now it just seems silly."

"Gryphons and humans are very similar. We both use symbol-analog communication systems, and they naturally tend toward universality. We're predisposed to prefer order to chaos, or what we perceive as chaos. If our systems aren't complex enough to form analogs adequate to our surroundings, we look for patterns or we impose them. When the Chaiar were expelled from the Net, they needed a pattern very much. Humans need a pattern to make sense of the Net."

"And you don't?" Alex asked with a little bitterness.

"I'm a Chaiar. I look for patterns all the time. If Rik had sprayed me with the right kind of molmacs, I would have accepted the Chaiar pattern. I'm glad she didn't, because the Pattern seems too simple to be a useful analog."

"What we have now is even simpler," Alex said softly. "Nothing but a desire for revenge."

"That's your immediate motivation, perhaps. In the long term we're trying to make enough room and time for humanity to create its own patterns. And for me to create mine." Victor rubbed his beak. "The Chaiar pattern comes out of a desire for revenge also, you know."

Alex nodded. A little absently, he realized that Victor was no longer a pet or accessory, if he ever had been. The gryphon had assumed a new role, not quite a leader but certainly not a follower.

"Please have something to eat before it gets cold," the mobile murmured in Alex's ear. He sighed, dug his fork into the mound of scrambled eggs, and forgot about Victor. The food tasted good, and he realized how hungry he was.

Sunlight broke suddenly as *Wuthering Heights* came around the curve of Earth. The curtains in the tall windows, the carpets on the floor, the icons dancing across the room all seemed to burst with color. Habrakha was still out there, a blue and white hemisphere, but it seemed pale in the unscreened glare of the sun.

The others were all silent and depressed as, one by one, they came downstairs. California refused to eat anything, and so did Rik; McCool munched a slice of toast and then went out into the gardens without a word to anyone. Alex sat on a terrace and watched the old man prowling restlessly around the grounds. Overhead, the face of Earth filled the dome.

After a time California came out and sat in Alex's lap. Her physical presence still made him a little uncomfortable, but already he associated that response with the long ago times of three days earlier. They were lovers, companions. He talked quietly with her, hugged her when she cried, and cried a little himself.

"I almost wish Sanjuro had blown us up, after all," she murmured in his ear. "Do you know what I remember feeling while we were converted?"

"Happy?"

"Dangerous. Didn't you? We were still warwired—the molmacs didn't change that. We were going to go out to Venus and convert those people or wipe them out. If Lord

Whitehead hadn't rescued us, we'd have done it, too."

"Well, now we're dangerous to the Chaiar. More than we were before."

"I sure hope so. But how could it feel so good to be in the Pattern? It was like—something had been filled up in me. Something empty I hadn't even known about."

He nodded. Now they were empty again. They might fight the Chaiar, but not with the calm certitude of cuckoos blowing up cloudcastles. They were going to risk their lives, and probably lose them, for a negative: for freedom from domination. If somehow they lived to regain that freedom, he had no idea what they might do with it. Somehow a life of dueling, Database diving, and aimless interplanetary travel no longer seemed that interesting.

McCool walked back up from the gardens. He was wearing a blue silk shirt and an ancient pair of jeans. His wrinkled face was creased with a grin, but Alex saw something like pain in his eyes.

"Since we've been denied gryphon salvation," McCool said, "we'll have to go back to our own superstitions, won't we? Is the war on again? Of course! And you're still warwired? Good! Can an old man get a cup of coffee around here?"

Rik eventually came out onto the terrace also. Her face was gray and slack, as if she had had no sleep in days. She wore some old robe of Alex's, and her blond hair hung messily over her shoulders. She sat in a chair holding a mug of tea and watching the swallows swoop down from their nests under the eaves.

"Are we still going to Venus?" she asked after a long time.

"Yes," Alex answered. "Ignition is in three hours."

"I don't belong to them anymore. It's a strange sensation, not belonging. I used to have it in my dreams sometimes, and now it's come true. Do I belong to you?"

"No one belongs to anyone," California sad gently. "You just belong to yourself."

She smiled uncertainly. "I hoped you would say that. I used to love those dreams, but I didn't dare admit it. So now I belong to myself." She paused and looked at them, her blue eyes calm and sad. "We can't beat them, you know. They're too powerful."

Alex glanced at California, who had moved from his lap to a nearby chair. He was surprised at the compassion in

California's smile. Somehow he had not thought of her as a person with any empathy for others, least of all for a deconverted cuckoo. Perhaps all the psychological upheaval they had gone through had changed them more than they realized. He wondered uncomfortably what unnoticed changes he might have undergone.

"A few wild molmacs broke us out of the Pattern," California said. "If we can link up a whole lot of molmacs, maybe they can break the Pattern altogether."

"It doesn't matter. I don't care if we win or lose." Rik's eyes—large, blue, slightly slanted—were hard. "The gryphons *grew* us, like the hukhung plants we were sowing. We're just tools to them."

"What are you to yourself?" California asked.

She shook her head. "I don't know yet. I feel—foolish. Angry."

California touched her shoulder. "Do you know how to duel?"

"No."

"I'm going to teach you."

Feeling restless, Alex left them on the terrace and went upstairs to his office.

"Emily, give me an image of Mordor, please."

"Of course." One wall of the office disappeared, and he seemed to be looking down on southern California from an altitude of perhaps two thousand meters. The image compensated for the inevitable haze over the Los Angeles basin. Populated or not, the area's atmospheric inversions were a permanent feature.

Mordor stood on the southern flanks of the Santa Monica Mountains overlooking Beverly Hills and the sea. It was a vast complex of structures, some of them rising in three-hundred-meter spires above the eroded brown slopes. The visible part of the estate was the least of it: Alex recalled endless tunnels and shafts deep beneath the surface, where his mother had set up labs and factories.

The shardana bubble was not directly visible. Lydia had tuned it to be transparent to infrared, visible light, and a little ultraviolet. But weather broke around its curved surface like surf around a stone. A band of cloud had drifted in from the west, encountered the bubble, and split into two ragged streamers that clung to its lower reaches. No weather could cover the bubble; it was fifty kilometers in diameter, which meant its highest point was twenty-five kilometers above the surface.

Looking closer, Alex could see other signs of the bubble's edge. In many places it had intersected standing buildings; the buildings had collapsed. A few small streams, suddenly dammed, had formed ponds against the inside of the bubble.

As he watched, four missiles struck the bubble in rapid succession. Matter-shardana interactions were intrinsically unpredictable; one missile ricocheted off the bubble at a sharp angle and detonated over eighty kilometers away, while the others hit the interface and disintegrated. Bits and scraps of smoking junk trailed away down the unseen curving surface of the bubble toward the ground far below.

"Emily, who fired those?"

"I don't know, Alex. I can't compute their trajectories. They were cruise missiles, not ballistics."

"But clearly human."

"Oh, of course. Nothing like whatever it was that shot down Charlotte or that beam that killed your poor father."

"So humans are already working for the Chaiar, fighting their own species."

Emily said nothing. Alex glowered at the curving arcs of smoke and debris falling toward the ruins of Los Angeles. He thought of the molmac plants, the pink-budded hukhung, and understood the reason for the attack. Even so, to turn against the handful of resisters, to do the Chaiar's dirty work for them, only made the surrender of Earth that much more abject.

"Show me Mao Jian's estate, and Lyell Bradley's."

Mao's was a sprawling array of low buildings and gardens in the cone of an extinct Mexican volcano. Like Mordor, Mao's estate was surrounded by a huge shardana bubble, but this one was perfectly reflective, a vast hemispherical mirror. The mountainous terrain around it was black and smoking, as if an eruption were under way, but Emily recognized the aftermath of a nuclear attack.

"Nuclear!" Alex shouted. "These people have no decency at all. He'll have to keep that bubble up for years before the radiation dies down. At least he's still alive, I hope. Show me Lyell's place."

Another shardana bubble, this one transparent, hung high over Lyell Bradley's estate in the Maldive Islands south of India. It was visible as a circle of tranquil water, sixty kilometers wide, surrounded by a narrow line of white surf. The bubble must have formed at high tide, because sea level within it was over a meter above the surface outside. Within the circle, Bradley's eight little islands gleamed like emeralds. If the estate had been attacked, Alex saw no sign.

"And Sei Shonagon's."

The gaudy palace where California's mother lived stood on the shores of Japan's Inland Sea. No bubble protected the estate. A Chaiar shuttle hovered nearby, and on extreme magnification Alex could see cuckoos moving about the grounds on mobiles.

"Poor Sei," he muttered. "Still no chance to communicate with anyone?"

"We can get korshak only from satellites more than a thousand kilometers above the surface," Emily said. "No one on the surface except the Chaiar can transmit in korshak, and all three shardana bubbles are currently opaque to radio and television. If they're being attacked with nuclear weapons, that makes sense. An electromagnetic pulse would destroy most of their EM equipment."

So their three allies were safe behind their enormous shardana bubbles but incommunicado. Belatedly, he realized that if Lydia had developed the secret of giant shardana bubbles, she had been able to send it to Mao and Bradley via radio or television rather than korshak.

"Did my mother send us the data on shardana bubbles?"

"Oh, yes. The principles are amazingly simple, but detuning a bubble is impossible unless you know the precise resonance scale. And the potential scales are virtually infinite. That means the Chaiar won't be able to penetrate them."

"So we could put a bubble around ourselves."

"I suppose so, but we'd go out of control. Your mother still hasn't figured out how to steer a bubble."

Alex nodded. "Well, you'd better get the machine shop working on a bubble generator."

"I already have. It should be operational in about a day."

"Good." If *Wuthering Heights* came under attack, a bubble would at least save them from annihilation. But the ship would instantly cease to travel along its trajectory; in effect it would stop dead relative to the solar system. That was why Lydia had created only a partial bubble, to anchor Mordor firmly to the Earth. And a complete bubble would also be completely opaque to korshak; with a partial one, Lydia could at least pick up the gryphons' transmissions. If the blackout ever ended, she could be back in touch with *Wuthering Heights* within minutes.

"Are you monitoring the Chaiar korshak?"

"Yes. Would you like a summary?"

"Later, maybe. What about spacer korshak?"

"Very busy. Some of them are already asking the Chaiar to send them more information about the Pattern."

"Idiots. Anyone talking about resistance?"

She answered by presenting a map of the inner solar system on the screen, from the sun out to Mars. Space around Mercury, Venus, and Mars was thick with steamship contrails, all on courses that would take them to the outer system and the Neptune Belt.

Just before lunch, Emily ignited the ship's engines and a jet of superheated steam spurted from the stern of the comet. *Wuthering Heights* accelerated at 1g for a little under nine hours, achieving a velocity of 320 kilometers per second before the kuldi-field ignition cut off. It was a reckless squandering of ice but one that would put the ship in Venus orbit in less than ten days.

Within the living quarters, of course, the kuldi field remained at .9g. Nothing gave the impression of movement. If the dome had been clear, during maneuvers the transit of stars across the sky would have been obvious, but Alex kept the dome an opaque sky-blue, with a false image of the sun moving from an arbitrary east to west. When he or his passengers wanted to see outside, they used a smaller korshak field.

"We've got to arrange a deception for the Chaiar," California said when they gathered for drinks before dinner in the living room. "They'll be expecting reports from Rik every few days."

"I'll ask Emily to design an icon of her," Alex said. "And then Emily can answer for her. They can't spot a lie from a computer."

Rik herself looked expressionlessly into her glass of tighla.

"What do you think of the idea?" Alex asked her.

"It makes sense. Emily, can you do that?"

"Of course, dear. How does this look?"

An image formed on the carpet: Rik in her tightsuit, looking as confident and poised as she had the previous day in Jasper House.

"I'm going to need whatever language you use with the Chaiar," the computer went on. "Perhaps you'd like to join me for a downloading session after dinner."

"Of course." But she seemed to Alex to be only polite, a guest obliging her hosts. He wondered what her real thoughts were about resisting her former masters.

No matter. Draining a stein of beer, Alex felt hopeful for the first time since his deconversion. If the Chaiar could be fooled by a computer-generated korshak image and could not penetrate one of their own giant shardana bubbles, they were a little more vulnerable than he had imagined.

For a day or two everyone tried to forget what was happening outside. They ate, slept, played games, and went for walks with Heathcliff. When Emily offered summaries of gryphon and spacer broadcasts, Alex told her to save them for later. Even Victor seemed to retreat; he spent almost a full day at the bottom of a pond.

"It's strange to be on the same spacecraft with Bhru-kang," Rik said as she and Alex sat by the pond. The gryphon's body was dimly visible three meters below the surface. "I keep thinking I should treat him like an Old Guide—the most important gryphons. But he doesn't act anything like them."

"He's still a little boy," Alex said. "He's just six."

"I'm only five. And the first two years I didn't do anything except grow and learn."

"What did they teach you?"

"The Pattern, the Pattern, the Pattern. And a little about Earth and human beings. Now I know just how little."

"When you came into Jasper House, I thought you were the most perfect human being I'd ever seen."

She laughed without amusement. "Those epiphanics must have been really powerful. I feel more like the most perfectly exploited human being. If those molmacs from Lord Whitehead could only get into every cuckoo's bloodstream, the Chaiar would have to do their own dirty work." Rik watched a family of wood ducks paddle across the pond. "Maybe we could manage that. I should talk to the molmacs."

"Get Heathcliff or Victor to do it for you. Talking to molmacs is like going crazy."

"I like going crazy. I've been crazy ever since we left Jasper House, and it's wonderful."

"And you're crazy enough to want to fight the gryphons?"

"That's how I know I'm crazy. Because we're sure to lose."

Alex sighed and rubbed his bare legs, as if that could bring back his dermograph. Hearing her say it made it seem far more certain; it was no consolation to think, like McCool, that being blown to bits would only reunite them with God in the blissful chaos of entropy.

He thought about his father, seated in his tower study watching the cuckoos' shuttle in the final moments of his life. The old man had not even had the decency to leave a last message for Alex or Lydia.

Only then, as he recalled the image of *Munshaour*'s crashing into the sea, did he realize that William Macintosh had left a message, after all.

Twelve:

"Are the Chaiar still talking to you?" Alex asked Rik when they were two days out from Earth. Lunch was just over; Liam McCool and Victor had gone for a walk in the gardens with Heathcliff. The others were sitting in the living room.

"They're talking to Emily. She's telling them what they want to hear: Everything's just wonderful, and we're already talking to some interested people on Venus and Mercury."

"We are?"

"Of course," California said. "If they can monitor korshak as well as we can, they'd better hear us communicating with our intended converts, right?"

"Poor Emily," Alex sighed.

"Nonsense," Emily said, her voice emanating from an empty armchair. "It's quite a challenge to create this deception. I'm enjoying it immensely."

"Then poor us," California said. "If you're communicating with people who want to convert to the Pattern, how are we going to make anyone believe us when we ask for help to *fight* the Chaiar?"

"Especially if the Chaiar are still monitoring our korshak," Alex added.

"The same way you're talking now," the computer replied. "Face to face."

Alex groaned. "Great. The people we want to talk to will consider us insane or traitors, and the people who want to talk to us really *are* insane or traitors."

"I'm sure you'll figure something out," Emily replied.

Rik and California talked about going for a swim. Alex slumped in his favorite armchair and brooded.

Face-to-face contact with the Venusians would indeed be essential; the gryphons could monitor all korshak

119

broadcasts at least as easily as humans could, and they might well be able to black out korshak around Venus if they wanted to. Deceiving them was not too difficult: In three and a half centuries, humans and their computers had become highly proficient in false imaging. But communicating at a distance with potential allies would be impossible. Maybe a high-speed electromagnetic burst or something in a clear code that Venusians would understand and gryphons would miss? That had worked with Lydia, Mao, and Lyell, but Venusians were different.

The Mercurians were a lesser problem. Most were recluses, anyway, uninterested in events outside their estates. A few were involved in bulletins or entertainments; they tended to visit the platforms on Venus, and no doubt he could meet some of them there.

If he could match orbits with one of the Venus platforms—Xanadu or Joituinio or Eros—and go aboard it, face to face would be relatively easy. For the grounders and floaters of Venus and the burrowers of Mercury, the platforms served the same function as the cities of Luna. They were places where people could meet for sex and fighting. But if the platform owner did not approve of *Wuthering Heights*'s ostensible missionary purpose, he or she might well try to blow the ship to pieces.

Even if they were allowed aboard a platform, Alex reflected, they would have to avoid would-be converts to the Pattern. He did not want the gryphons to learn that their emissaries were betraying them. Alex remembered how easily his shuttle had been shot down; he suspected that the gryphons could do the same thing at interplanetary distances.

With a silent comlink command to Emily, he asked for an update on the invasion. New images appeared where the fireplace had been; California and Rik broke off their chat to watch.

Emily had edited hundreds of hours into brief sequences that portrayed an almost painless takeover. One clip showed John F. Kennedy himself landing at a new city in the Sahara, Ektunghar, built within hours of the first shuttles' arrival. His welcomers were mostly cuckoos, but several hundred Earthborns had turned up also and agreed to settle in Ektunghar rather than return to their estates.

Other settlements were rising elsewhere, sometimes on the sites of pre-Contact cities like Nanjing and Dar es Salaam. Converts and their robots were doing most of the work; the converts, at least, seemed to be enjoying it.

"I hate them," California said after a few minutes spent watching the construction of a new city in the Andes. "They look so . . . stupid-cheerful. It's like having a good time building your own coffin. I can hardly believe people actually used to *want* to live like that, cooped up together in cities."

Telescopic scanning of Earth showed a less attractive picture than the gryphons portrayed. Emily counted over four hundred estates blasted into rubble; most had tried to seal themselves off against the hukhung plants and their molmacs. A few proprietors had blown themselves up rather than convert.

The hukhung plants were spreading faster than ekata ever had. Across India and Arabia they already formed a waist-high jungle, and large patches were spreading over South American and southern Europe. Rik said the purpose of most of the plants was to boost the Earth's atmospheric oxygen by about four percent while reducing nitrogen by ten percent. A thinner, oxygen-rich atmosphere would be more congenial for the Chaiar.

Victor was surprised. "William Macintosh adjusted my metabolism slightly to handle the atmosphere and some of the proteins. That was all it took," he said.

Rik smiled crookedly. "You changed your pattern. The Chaiar don't do that. On Habrakha we used to get sick sometimes from anoxia at high altitude, and from molmac allergies." The smile disappeared. "A lot of people died from allergies. They didn't bother to adjust our metabolisms or our immune systems."

The three estates under shardana bubbles appeared unchanged. All three were opaque to visible light and all but narrow segments of the electromagnetic spectrum; obviously they did not want to suffer the effects of a photon probe or a nuclear weapon.

"I wonder how long they can last," Alex said. "They need some kind of source for heat and light as well as their bubbles."

"A kuldi generator," California said, stating the self-evident.

Alex nodded. "Probably two or three of them. "I can't imagine a generator that could run an estate's system *and* a fifty-kilometer shardana bubble."

"The gryphons use V-taps," Rik said.

"We still can't handle them very well," Alex answered. V-taps could give theoretically unlimited power from the virtual field, but they could be unstable: An imploding tap would leave a kilometer-wide crater where an estate had been. That was why few people used them, and then only in short bursts to strengthen their shield fields during beamer attacks. "Besides," Alex went on, "even if a tap worked perfectly, what about the waste heat? Eventually the inside of the bubble would be hotter than Venus."

Rik shrugged. "I don't know how the gryphons do it. I know that if anyone fired a beam or a photon probe at Habrakha, the bubble would turn opaque just under the probe."

"The gryphons can do anything," Alex muttered.

A few other Earthborn spacecraft left orbit for Mars and the outer planets; they exchanged messages with *Wuthering Heights* and turned out to be on the same mission of conversion. Alex left the conversations to Emily, who created icons of everyone aboard and put outrageous words in their mouths.

"I wonder if they're lying to us the same way," Alex said to her after listening to the captain of a ship bound for Saturn.

"It's possible, but I wouldn't bet on it. You were very lucky to have Lord Whitehead around."

"If we'd been really lucky, we'd have stayed converted and happy instead of going off to make the Venusians believe us."

"Don't feel sorry for yourself, Alex," Emily said sharply. "You're a grown man now."

On the fourth day Victor spoke privately to Emily for a few minutes and then went into his favorite pond, where he had been spending much of his time. When he emerged just after lunch, a mobile was waiting at the edge of the water. It gave Victor a small gray object, something like a twenty-first-century computer plate. The gryphon walked dripping up to the terrace, where Alex and California were practicing with epees.

"Your workshops are very good," Victor said.

Alex put down his sword and wiped sweat from his face. "What's that?"

The gryphon handed him the plate. It was square,

about thirty centimeters on a side, and quite thin. The material was a metallic-looking kind of fome that Alex had not seen before.

"It's a tight-beam transceiver. It uses korshak, but it can't be monitored outside the beam."

"I never heard of such a thing! Where'd you hear about it?"

"I invented it. It's a very rough analogue of a laser."

"What's a laser? Never mind. And this is how we contact the Venusians?"

"Yes. First we have to tell them how to build one of their own."

"That figures." Alex pondered the implications of korshak narrowcasting. Ordinary korshak permitted everyone to eavesdrop on everyone else; one could live alone and yet share in society. Now one could seal oneself off with just a select few and make information a kind of private property, as it had been before Contact. He was not sure he liked the idea, though the narrowcaster could be invaluable for his purposes.

"But how do we tell the Venusians about it without using regular korshak?" California asked.

"We'll use the Database. The Venusians are good drivers. I'll position the information where they're sure to find it. Since the Chaiar don't like to use the Database, they're not likely to notice. I'll tag the narrowcaster with an image of Heathcliff. If your mother or Mao or Bradley go diving, they may find the narrowcaster, too, and recognize its source."

That night Alex switched the dome imaging system to show them Earth and Habrakha. The two worlds were already far distant, twin ovals of light with the smaller oval of Luna to one side. Combined, they gave the illumination of a full moon to the gardens.

Listening to the crickets and frogs, Alex sat on the terrace with California and Rik. "How much longer before the conquest is all over?" he asked the cuckoo.

"Just a few weeks. The Chaiar took over the trolls in a month and a half."

"The same way?"

"Yes. Troll cuckoos, a planet moved into place, and then the landings and conversions."

"It doesn't seem possible," California said. "We're a

bunch of primitives compared to the trolls. How could the gryphons just walk in?"

Rik smiled without humor. "The Chaiar were in touch with the trolls for thousands of years. They knew everything about them. By comparison, humans are hardly known at all. Sometimes, when I was growing up, I got the feeling the Chaiar don't respect us very much. They think we're stupid."

"Compared to them we are," Alex muttered, slapping at a mosquito whining in his ear. The swallows were not doing their job well enough, he thought.

"But the gryphons don't link up their molmacs, do they?" California asked.

"No. They don't need to. Their molmac computers trade information all the time, but they don't form permanent links because any one of them has all the power they need."

Alex thought for a moment and began to cheer up. Arrogance had been his father's downfall; that had been the message William Macintosh had left behind. Maybe it would be the gryphons' also.

"It feels wonderful to be in the Pattern," Alex was saying. "Sort of like—remembering a word that's been on the tip of your tongue. You just recognize that it's the right one, the one you've been looking for."

"That's right," California chimed in. "And you feel so self-confident—you know you can do anything!"

Their listener was an overmuscled Venusian floater dressed in a loincloth and a loose white shirt. He smiled and nodded.

"Sounds great. Tell me more."

"That's enough, Emily," Alex growled. The korshak icons went on talking animatedly but silently.

Alex and California were in Alex's bedroom. McCool had taken Rik on her first Database dive; they were tranced out in the dive room on the main floor. Victor was somewhere in the gardens.

"You've really got the deception down cold," California told the computer.

A disembodied chuckle answered her. "I told you it was fun. Also instructive. Most of the believers aren't very bright. The intelligence matrix of that fellow is really dreadful."

"We don't sound very smart ourselves," Alex said. "I

just hope we don't ruin our credibility with the people we want to reach. And I wish someone would find Victor's narrowcaster in the Database and get in touch with us."

. With Venus on the far side of the Sun from Earth, the trip was a long one. They had been en route for a week and had two more days to orbit. Nothing much had happened. Space between Mercury and Mars was full of steamship contrails as spacers headed outward for the presumed safety of the Neptune Belt and beyond. More than a hundred proprietors in the outer solar system were actually launching into interstellar space and then pausing themselves; they hoped to wake up in a different system centuries later. Emily doubted whether more than two or three would survive the journey. Too many systems would break down, and eventually the maintenance systems themselves.

That thought sent Alex out of the residence sphere and down into the machine shops and drive systems. In space suits, he and California inspected the molmac growth vats, the kuldi generator, and the scores of systems that kept the ship running and secure.

"Can you explain to me," she asked, "how a kuldi generator can drive a ship *and* keep gravity on in the sphere?"

They were riding through the heart of the comet in a little car on rails down the main tunnel to the drive unit.

"If I could do it in detail, I'd be the greatest scientist in history. All I know is how to set the field, not why it works. Set it one way, and you get artificial gravity. Set it another, and the artificial gravity is so intense that it accelerates matter to hundreds of kilometers a second. It's something like the old mass drivers they used just before Contact, but the drive unit's only about half a meter long. Some of the energy goes back into melting the ice and pumping steam into the drive, but most goes into ejecting the steam and moving the ship."

"My mother used to tell me about the days when they used rock instead of ice. Can you believe they were ever that stupid?"

Alex nodded, watching the smooth reddish-black walls slide by. "No environmental awareness at all then. A few idiots filled so much space with rock dust, you couldn't even get up to a decent speed without blowing holes in your ship. There are still places in the outer system where you can't get up over fifty, sixty kilometers a second.

With ice crystals the problem isn't so bad, especially since we learned how to keep the crystals small and disperse them."

She smiled at him through her transparent helmet. "Ever cross somebody's contrail?"

"I'm not that stupid."

After inspecting the drive unit, he took her down a narrow tunnel that led to the surface of the comet. It was easier to see as an absence than as a presence. The sky was full of stars and the distant triple spark of Earth, Habrakha, and Luna, but the surface was simply black and featureless.

A few meters away, a tower rose toward the stars. It was perhaps ten meters in diameter and thirty high, and it glinted metallically in the starlight.

"That's one of the ejection tubes," Alex said. "It looks just the same when it's running full blast." He hooked them both to a railing and pointed up into the sky.

"Look at all the contrails. The whole system looks like a spiderweb. Everyone running for cover, except us."

She looked up at the twin blue sparks and their smaller white companions. "Are you ever sorry we were deconverted?"

He thought for a moment. "Sometimes. Sometimes I miss the happiness. What about you?"

"It was wonderful being in the Pattern, I guess. Maybe it was that sense of belonging. Then I think about how dull it must really be, going on and on feeling like that. Here we are having this adventure, risking our fool necks—and it's a lot more fun, isn't it?"

"It's fun, yes. But the real fun is having you here with me."

"What a sweet man you are. Aren't you scared they'll probably win?"

"That doesn't matter. We'll make a point."

She smiled beautifully in the starlight, and her gloved hand slapped his shoulder. "Talking like a duelist! I'm getting fond of you, Alex. Let's go back and get out the foils."

They passed the time in dueling, making love, and designing new combat systems for *Wuthering Heights*. He had always understood his spacecraft better than most proprietors did, and now that he and California were warwired, they could devise some highly effective weaponry.

A simply modification to *Wuthering Heights*'s beamers increased their range from two thousand kilometers to five thousand. Improving the education of the ship's missiles gave them greater evasive powers and more ability to calculate target trajectories.

But Alex knew that such improvements were merely cosmetic; they would be almost useless against the Chaiar. Until the Venusians found the narrowcaster, *Wuthering Heights* would be isolated and ineffective.

"They're out of the dive," Emily told them.

"Good," Alex said. "Let's go see if they found anything."

McCool and Rik lay side by side in the dive room, a small cubicle furnished with little more than a wide, soft bed and a couple of chairs. They were sitting up on the bed when Alex and California entered. McCool looked older than usual; Rik seemed oddly cheerful. Shiny red circles were stuck to their foreheads: dive patches, linking them to the Database and to Emily's databanks. Alex peeled them off and placed them on the reader beside the bed; Emily would transcribe the data into her own memory.

"That was fun," Rik said, rolling off the bed and collapsing on the carpet. She burst into giggles as Alex helped her back to her feet. California put an arm around McCool and led him to a chair.

"I'm much too old for that kind of thing," he muttered.

"Did you find anything useful?" California asked.

"Someone's picked up Victor's narrowcaster." McCool rubbed his face. "But that was all I could learn. The Database seems to get stranger all the time."

"I thought it was beautiful," Rik crooned. Alex thought she looked a little drunk: Many divers entered the Database simply for the postdive disorientation. "No wonder the gryphons don't like it. You could get lost in there and never think about the Pattern again."

"Were you looking for anything special?" Alex asked her.

"Ancient history. Chaiar history. But I couldn't find it. I left a blaze—a yellow flower."

Alex nodded. Once the original Database archives had been built, an endless stream of information had poured into them from the Net as well as from humans. Some of the Database could be tapped like an ordinary computer, even down to printouts on paper, but the quantity and organization of information made that pointless. And the original designers for some reason had not made it accessible to any mechanical computer. Instead people patched directly into the Database; then they fumbled about looking for whatever might be both intelligible and useful, leaving crude blazes to mark their paths and returning with information that their mechanical computers tried to make sense of.

The experience of diving was often nightmarish. Many of the Net species organized information in utterly baffling and sometimes frightening ways. Diving was far from efficient; Alex recalled his father once commenting that humanity had so far gained useful access to perhaps a millionth of the material in the Database.

"You'll do better next time," he told Rik. "If you know what you want, sometimes it turns up right where it ought to be. Most people don't bother—they just go serendipping."

He and California helped them out of the dive room and down the hall to the living room. Victor was just outside on the terrace, tossing pieces of fish to Lord Whitehead. The eagle caught each one easily, circled, and swooped down for the next morsel. Heathcliff sat watching; he obviously wanted to snap up a bite or two, but Lord Whitehead had evidently warned the Labrador to keep his distance.

"Victor, would you come in for a minute?" Alex called. The gryphon put down his bucket and walked in through the open French doors. Lord Whitehead promptly glided down, knocked the bucket over, and finished the rest of the fish.

"Liam and Rik have been diving," Alex explained, "looking for some kind of information we might be able to use against the Chaiar. You seemed to do really well on that dive the other day. Can you give us any suggestions?"

"I wish I could. Most of the Database is as strange to me as it is to you. I can understand much of the Chaiar data, or at least the way they're organized. But I can't tell you how I understand. The analysis happens on a subconscious level, and I don't think you share the same mental process."

"Are the molmacs making any sense out of what you've learned?" McCool asked.

"They seem a little frustrated," Victor answered. "I think the Database is beyond their resources. They very much want to link up with the Venusian and Mercurian molmacs so they can analyze the Database more effectively."

"Why haven't they done so already?" Rik demanded. "They can use korshak, too, can't they?"

The other humans laughed. "Don't forget that molmacs are very private property," Alex said. "They're designed with an immune response so they can't communicate except with their owner's permission."

"Otherwise everyone would know everything about everybody," California added. "Remember that horror show a couple of years ago, about the mutant molmacs that communicated with the other man's molmacs while the two men were dueling? So the other man could tell what was coming next, and killed him?"

"I thought it was stupid," Alex said. "It could never happen like that. Anyway," he went on, turning back to Rik, "we can't form the molmac network until we get the spacers' permission. And when you monitor korshak it sounds as if half the spacers want to join the Pattern, not fight it, so we're going to have problems."

Victor smiled, showing his small brown teeth below the hawklike point of his beak. "We've survived so far. I'm sure we'll do all right. As for the Database, Rik and I should go diving together."

"An alien-human dive?" Alex was surprised to find himself shocked. "Well—"

"If she's interested in ancient Chaiar history, perhaps I can help her find it."

Rik seemed hardly to be listening. Alex saw the gleam in her eye and realized that she was already thinking about the indescribable colors and shapes and sounds within the Database.

Thirteen:

The missile attack came when the steamship was a day out from Venus orbit.

Wuthering Heights was decelerating hard behind a dense plume of steam. The missiles, from Eros platform, were smart and vicious. They came out of the glare of the sun, aiming themselves straight at the ship's vent and using the plume as a shield.

On korshak in the living room, both the sun and the steam were invisible and the missiles resembled spiders: shiny black hemispheres a meter wide, trailing ten leglike sensors. Alex swore but found himself much less frightened than he had expected. His warwiring made him eager for combat; he felt both exhilarated and intensely focused. For a moment he considered turning on a shardana bubble around the ship, but he rejected the idea at once. It would be inconvenient to fall out of normal space even for a few minutes and then be forced to alter the ship's trajectory to reach Venus orbit. Revealing the existence of the shardana generator might be tactically unwise. And hiding inside a bubble would not be any fun.

"Emily, stern beamers on!" he commanded. "Full power."

Liam McCool stood beside him, grinning happily. "Don't forget the plume will attenuate your beams," he said. "So let 'em get in close."

Alex nodded but said nothing, concentrating on the korshak images. Beside each of the missiles, numbers glowed yellow and red, changing with range, speed, and vector. Otherwise, the images were so sharp and real that the living room seemed to open directly into space.

The missiles were closing at a little over 13,000 kilometers per minute, 220 kilometers per second. The plume would shield them from the beamers at maximum range, so he could not expect a kill at over 2,500 kilometers. That would give him just over ten seconds to lock on and kill four smart and evasive missiles.

The missiles, however, would expect to face beamers with the standard 2,000-km range; they would probably not commence evasive action until then. That gave Alex a two-second opportunity.

He took it. Looking at the nearest missile, he gave Emily a comlink order to fire a quarter-second beam, then glanced instantly to the next one and fired again. The third target was actually the most remote of the four; it had hung back to observe the fate of its companions and to take unusual action if needed. Alex destroyed it at a range of 2,350 kilometers, then beamed the last one at 1,800. *Wuthering Heights* continued to decelerate through a mist of vaporized metal and fome, some of which condensed onto the ice of the ship's stern.

"Praise God!" McCool murmured while Rik and California cheered. Then Rik frowned.

"It was lovely shooting, Alex, but why didn't you let Emily do it? She'd be much faster."

Alex guffawed in surprise. "Let *Emily* do it? Rik, I'm the proprietor. It's my *job* to defend the ship. Fighting's a human job."

Rik did not look persuaded. "The missiles were not human, but they were fighting."

"Somebody had to educate them and tell them what to go after, just the way I do with my own missiles. And whoever fired them must feel pretty bad now. You get really fond of them."

California smiled at Rik. "I know it sounds funny, but that's the way it is. The machines can do all kinds of things, but we're the bosses, so we're the fighters."

"What if you came up against someone who did let computers do the fighting?" Rik asked.

The Earthborns all looked scandalized. "They'd probably all eat animals, too," California said scornfully.

Rik looked really baffled. "We eat meat. We had veal for lunch and bacon for breakfast."

"All synthetic," Alex explained. "The molmacs grow it from templates. It's genetically derived from the animals, but it was never alive the way an animal is alive."

"Lord Whitehead eats fish right out of the pond," Rik persisted.

"He's an *animal*," California said. "It's all right for animals to eat each other, and for molmacs. But ... we're human, after all." She looked at Rik with uncertainty. "When you were on Habrakha—did you—"

"Eat animals? Of course. The gryphons have the genomes for all kinds of Earth species. Most gryphon foods are poisonous to humans, so they grew the animals for us."

Alex avoided California's gaze. Rik might have been human, but her cuckoo upbringing made her seem to Alex more alien than Victor in some ways.

"Emily," he said, eager to change the subject, "get me the platform master, please."

"Remember that the Chaiar are listening, dear."

"Yes, yes!" Alex snapped. He was feeling a postcombat high intensified by his warwiring.

The link with Eros took a few minutes. At last a man's image appeared on korshak: Balthasar Uiliu, platform master of Eros. He was a slender and graceful black man in a baggy gold robe sitting on a Chippendale chair in an elegantly furnished Georgian drawing room.

"I'm Alex Macintosh. We've met before."

"About two years ago, wasn't it? Good to see you again."

"Please don't fire any more missiles at us. All we're trying to do is meet peacefully with Venusians and Mercurians who want to hear what we have to say."

Balthasar's smile was white and predatory. "You're about as welcome as a heat wave in Beta Regio, Alex. Surely you must realize that."

"I think more people support us than you'd like to admit. Anyway, you've made your opinion perfectly clear. I'd retaliate, but too many people depend on your platform. I'm here to make friends, not enemies."

Uiliu studied him with distaste. "Just stay away from Eros, Alex. And I reserve the right to resume hostilities if I don't like what you're doing."

"Understood." Alex rudely broke off contact without a farewell and then chuckled. "That went pretty well," he said to Rik and California.

"You mean he's willing to let us go into orbit even after he tried to kill us?" Rik said.

California patted her shoulder. "We really haven't explained some things to you. Fighting is—well, sometimes it's deadly serious and sometimes it's for show. Sometimes both. Balthasar was showing everybody he doesn't like the invasion and people coming to convert Venus. If he'd killed us, fine. But the important point was to show his opinion. And Alex could've fought back. We're tougher than we look, and we might even be able to blow Eros out of orbit. But then we'd get all the floaters and grounders mad at us, and they'd declare war to express their opinion, and maybe somebody would actually put a missile or two into us."

"And ducling is the same kind of thing," Alex added. "Usually it's buttons on, but sometimes we fight to the death just to show we're willing to. It's called making a point."

Rik shook her head. "But your molmacs revive you, don't they?"

"After a duel? Sure. Of course, after a war there's not much left to revive."

"The Chaiar don't fight that way. They're organized, and they don't play games."

"I know," Alex said. "Sometimes it really worries me. My father used to say that changing a cultural value is the hardest thing anyone can try to do." He shrugged. "I don't see how we'll get humans to stop fighting the way they're used to unless the molmacs come up with something."

Victor came into the living room carrying the narrowcaster. He extended it to Alex.

"I think you'd better try to contact someone," the gryphon said. "The Venusians are clearly getting nervous."

Alex shrugged and accepted the flat metallic plate. He turned it on with a comlink command and found himself staring at Balthasar Uiliu again. The platform master looked surprised.

"What's this, then?" he demanded. "How did you know about—about this?"

"Emily, give Balthasar's computer our story."

After a three-second pause, Balthasar nodded; his computer had evidently judged the story valid.

Alex went on. "Now, I have to take a big chance with you, Balthasar. If the gryphons find out we're trying to fight back, they might be able to wipe us out even at this distance from Habrakha. If you or anybody else tells them, we're finished."

Balthasar listened attentively. His inner eyes, like a wolf's, reflected a luminous green.

"You look like good luck, Alex. We got the narrowcaster a couple of days ago. Dwuliu Carson found it in the Database, right where your computer said it was. Dwuliu passed it on. We figured it'd be useful if the gryphons tried to black us out, but it also lets us talk without the sellouts listening in."

"Sellouts?"

"You know, people who want to surrender to the gryphons."

Alex sent a quick comlink query to Emily, who explained that "sellout" referred to a pre-Contact practice of giving political support in exchange for money, privilege, and enhanced social status. The archaic term reminded Alex that he was dealing with relatively backward people. Even his father, born before Contact, had rarely behaved as if ancient values meant anything Alex had never been much interested in money and the other old religions, but he reminded himself that the Venusians—and other spacers—were all he had to work with. He would have to tolerate their quirks.

"We have a more effective use for narrowcasting," Alex said slowly. "But I think we'd better talk some more before I explain what it is."

Balthasar leaned back and grinned amiably. "I have all the time in the world."

"I mean face to face."

The platform master sat up, frowning. "Something too private even for the narrowcaster?"

"Something we need to discuss very privately before we go to your friends."

Balthasar rubbed his chin. "You go into orbit—"

"About 0330 tomorrow morning. We can sled over to Eros about six hours later."

"Make it eight hours. I'm not up before 1100."

"Very good." Alex tried not to show his distaste for someone who chose to sleep for hour after hour each day.

With the contact broken, he turned to the others. "If we can persuade him, we can persuade his friends as well, all at once."

"And if we can't?" McCool asked.

Alex hesitated for a moment. "Where's Lord White-head?"

—Here—

"What do you and the molmacs suggest we do if we can't persuade Balthasar and his friends to link up with us?"

—Molmacs say stay in orbit, look in Database, try again. I say kill him.—

Wuthering Heights entered Venus polar orbit on schedule. The steamship was the same distance from the surface as Eros, about eighteen thousand kilometers; it would take a few hours to catch up with the platform and match orbits more precisely.

California and Victor went down to the shuttle dock to make sure Charlotte's defenses were running properly; other Venusians might want to register an opinion while the shuttle was en route to Eros. Meanwhile, Alex, Rik, and McCool went up to Alex's office to plan the approach to Balthasar.

Looking up through his office skylight and the dome beyond, Alex could see Venus as an oval of yellow cloud, mottled here and there by turbulence. The Great Y was clearly visible where the equatorial jet stream split to northwest and southwest. Just beyond the terminator, nightside lightning flickered constantly.

Here and there Alex caught a glint of sunlight reflecting from the clouds or from the Zone of Venus, a man-made ring of comet nuclei and asteroids used by the Venusians as a source of water and other volatiles. The zone was attenuated but potentially dangerous; Emily had already changed course slightly to avoid a hundred-meter lump of rock.

Rik and McCool looked upward at the planet. "You'd think they could terraform it into something more comfortable," Rik remarked.

McCool nodded, smiling. "A few people tried, a hundred years ago. They got some comets onto the surface, so the atmosphere still has a little water vapor, but the grounders blew up four or five more nuclei and a couple of steamships as well. The floaters backed them up."

"But why?"

"Venusians like to do things the hard way," Alex said. "The grounders like living under ninety atmospheres, and the floaters like swimming around in the smog belt. It makes them feel tough. Emily, can you show us the surface and pinpoint the estates and cloudcastles?"

The image in the dome abruptly changed. They saw a yellow-gray surface pocked with ancient craters and volcanic cones, with the highlands of Ishtar and Aphrodite rising black above the plains.

The twenty thousand grounder estates were gleaming green sparks, mostly clustered in the highlands, where temperatures and pressures were slightly lower than on the plains. The cloudcastles of the floaters, twenty-five times as numerous, were blue sparks moving on the winds from east to west.

"I've only been on the surface once," Alex said. "That was a visit to the north pole. A man I'd been dueling with on Eros invited me down to his place."

"Did you enjoy it?" McCool asked.

"It made me nervous. He was like a lot of grounders, showing how brave he was by letting his systems run down. The temperature in most of his estate was around fifty degrees Celsius. His house was the only place you could be comfortable."

"Can we use him as part of the molmac network, or is he a sellout?" Rik said.

"He's dead. His dome collapsed about six months after I was there." Rik looked appalled. "Well, I said he was a show-off."

"Is Balthasar a show-off also?" McCool asked Alex. "Will he and his friends want to do things the hard way?"

"They'll want to keep things the way they are. Merging molmacs sounds pretty radical."

"As radical as terraforming Venus?" Rik said. The two men looked at her. "That's what the Chaiar would be sure to do. Then they'd get an extra planet out of this system."

"But it would take centuries," McCool objected.

"You don't know them. Fifty years at most. Look at what they've done to Earth in just a few weeks. The atmosphere's already changed."

"Rik's right," Alex said. "The Venusians are watching what's happening on Earth. The gryphons could easily design a molmac plant to convert carbon dioxide into carbonates. That would bury the existing surface, thin the atmosphere, and start cooling things off."

"They could cool it off even faster by putting a shardana bubble around it for a few years," Rik said. "One that would let infrared pass through from the surface but block it from the sun."

"Add a few more comets," said McCool, "and you're on your way to a new Earth. Well, Alex?"

Alex grinned. "I think the Venusians'll hate the very thought of it."

"It looks like a blister on a potato," California said as the shuttle neared Eros. Alex nodded. The residential sphere of the platform was built into the end of a roughly cylindrical asteroid about five kilometers long. The sphere itself was over three kilometers in distance. Unlike *Wuthering Heights*, Eros had several residential levels and an opaque, windowless white exterior. People went to platforms to look at one another, not to admire the view.

At the moment, the platform was curving around Venus's nightside. Far below, lightning flickered under the clouds; Eros itself glittered with hundreds of lights. On all sides, other shuttles kept pace. Most were Venusian, but Alex was glad to see that several Mercurian spacecraft were there as well, both shuttles and steamships.

Charlotte announced that she had permission to dock, and a few minutes later the shuttle moored smoothly to an umbilicus four meters wide. From the shuttle air lock, Alex and California glided two hundred meters in free fall down the umbilicus. At the far end they slipped easily through the boundary of the platform's kuldi field into a .8 gravity.

In the reception foyer a humanoid robot was waiting, a rosy-pink blond Willendorf type with heavy breasts and bulging belly ill concealed beneath a stylish synthetic rawhide tunic. Dermographs made her bare arms and legs glitter; when she smiled in greeting, other dermographs in her forehead and cheeks emitted sparkles of light.

If the robot disapproved of California's slenderness, she gave no sign of it but ushered them onto a sleek green mobile and waved farewell. The mobile accelerated smoothly down a wide corridor lined with marble and adorned with both statuary and holograms. All had something to do with sex or violence or both; Alex was especially struck by one holo showing two naked duelists running each other through and embracing in a passionate kiss before falling dead.

"Is that what goes on here?" California muttered.

"Not when I was here before. I think Balthasar likes to romanticize things a little. It's usually buttons on, and most people are more interested in sex than dueling, anyway."

The mobile slid into a large, clear-walled elevator that lifted them quickly to the top level of the platform. On the way they glimpsed three lower levels of narrow-laned villages, grassy meadows, small groves of oak, pine, or palms, and plenty of ponds and streams. Each level created the illusion of being outdoors under a clear blue sky. Several hundred people were copulating in the fields, swimming in the ponds, or brawling in the villages.

"Just like Luna," Alex said.

"Too crowded," California complained. "On Luna you might have twenty or thirty people under a dome. This is as bad as a city."

"Well, not many Venusians want to be platform masters." It took a certain kind of personality, Alex reflected: someone willing to build a social center with no reward but thanks and the entertainment the guests provided. Luna had several dozen; Venus had three.

The elevator deposited them in Balthasar's private suite, furnished in the Georgian style they had seen during their first conversation with him. Balthasar, dressed in a red plaid kilt and tweed jacket, greeted them with handshakes and smiles.

"Please, make yourselves at home." He gestured grandly to a cluster of chairs and lounges that appeared to overlook an English garden on a misty day. A humanoid robot in black tie and tails glided up with a tray and offered sherry.

They spent some time in small talk: the number of guests on Eros, amusing incidents involving them, a dueling contest that Balthasar hoped California would take part in. At last, after two or three sherries, Balthasar leaned forward.

"Now, just what is it that you don't want to entrust to the narrowcaster?"

"It's something we need your advice on before we go further," Alex said. "We think the only way to fight the gryphons is to build a supermind by merging molmac computers."

Balthasar looked disappointed. "Well, go right ahead, then. Don't need my permission."

"Not out of brand-new molmacs," California said. "That would take too long, and the molmacs wouldn't be any smarter than the ones we started with. We want to link up people's existing molmacs."

Balthasar smiled dismissively. "Absurd. Be asking people to put their lives and freedom in other people's hands. Maybe they'd do it on Earth, but we value our freedom too much."

"This is why we wanted to talk to you personally," Alex said. "I'm a spacer, too, remember. I don't like the idea of losing control over my molmacs and giving away my defense secrets. But I can see that if we don't merge, we're never going to find a way to beat the gryphons."

"Out of the question."

"Do you have an alternative?" California asked.

"Don't like the gryphons and don't like what they're doing on Earth. But——" Balthasar shrugged. "We have a lot of smart people on Venus. Good divers, good fighters. Grounders, floaters, everybody here knows how to survive. Don't tell me we can't fight the gryphons without merging our molmacs."

"Of course you can," Alex agreed. "But you're certain to lose. And then you're not part of the Pattern, and they blow you up. You'd be better off converting now."

Balthasar nodded and brushed at his kilt. "Suppose you're right, and we do surrender. What happens next?"

California looked at him solemnly. "They squirt their own molmacs up your nose, and you're a happy part of the Pattern. You won't mind when they take away Eros and when they terraform Venus."

"Take away—why would they do that?"

"Eros has nothing to do with the Pattern, Balthasar." Alex spoke quietly. "All the people enjoying themselves here ought to be working for the Chaiar. And if they terraform Venus, they can use it like Habrakha, to go conquer some other world."

"That's outrageous. But merge molmacs—I hardly *know* you."

"And I hardly know you. I don't like this, either. I didn't like it when I was going to merge with my mother and Mao Jian and Lyell Bradley."

It was name-dropping, but it worked. "*They're* merged?"

"Not really. They started to. The korshak blackout screwed everything up for us. So far the merge is pretty small—my molmacs, Liam McCool's, and California's internals. Plus a few from a human cuckoo, a gryphon cuckoo, and some wild ones."

Balthasar seemed not to be listening. After a while he said, "And some wild ones. This is crazy."

"Your computer must be monitoring us," California said. "Ask it if we're lying."

He stared out into his holographic English garden for a moment, then turned back. "No, you're not lying. And that's one reason why you wanted this face to face, isn't it? So I couldn't write you off as a computer deception. Well, you may not have all the answers. Maybe there's still some way to beat the gryphons without giving up our souls."

"What do we have to do," California murmured, "put a sword to your throat?"

"No...It's all so sudden. Wish I had some time to think, consult my molmacs, talk to friends. Dwuliu."

"What about him?" Alex asked.

"He's more or less the leader of the grounders. Persuade him to merge with you, I'll go along. So will a lot of other people. Thousands."

"I'm ready to talk to him anytime," Alex said. He settled back in his chair just slightly, beginning to feel they were making progress.

"I'll call him. You'll have to go down to see him."

Alex sat up again. "On the surface?"

Balthasar nodded. "Diana Chasma. *Beautiful* place."

Fourteen:

Balthasar himself piloted them down from Eros. His shuttle was a thick-walled sphere about twenty meters in diameter, with surprisingly little room inside for his Georgian furniture.

"Insulation and cooling," he explained when California commented. "Down where Dwuliu lives, the temperature's around 475 degrees Celsius. Actually a little higher just now, because it's been noon at Diana Chasma for the last couple of weeks. And he's at ninety atmospheres. Likes to say no one can get any lower than he does, but that's not true. He's up on a cliff overlooking the Chasma, and if he wanted to, he could go another four-five kilometers down."

"Why doesn't he?" Alex asked.

"He'd lose his view."

The shuttle detached itself from Eros; on the korshak screens, Alex saw *Wuthering Heights*'s green and gold running lights gleaming among the stars.

—Heathcliff, tell everyone we're fine,—he called.

—Sure will. Have fun.—

The shuttle lost velocity, and the platform seemed to race away. They were falling toward Venus; since Balthasar had not bothered to use light enhancement, the screens showed only darkness broken by constant flashes of distant lightning.

"Lightning's pretty from up here," Balthasar said, "but wait till we're down on it. You can expect to get hit two or three times, minimum. But then you're at least out of the worst of the wind."

"It wasn't very pleasant when I was down before," Alex said, though he realized Balthasar was deliberately trying to make them nervous. Venusians got a laugh out of scaring newcomers.

141

California, at least, seemed unfrightened. She watched the forward screen, which showed only a curve of grayness below a sprinkling of stars, and nudged Alex when the curve suddenly acquired a pink rim that widened, brightened, and turned yellow.

Sunrise on Venus was surprisingly gradual even at that height. Light diffused through the sulfuric acid haze of the upper atmosphere, growing stronger without giving much definition. Flickering numbers, suspended in the korshak images, showed altitude, temperature, and other data.

"If we're headed for Diana Chasma," Alex said, "aren't we bearing too far east?"

Balthasar shook his head. "We're coming in over the south pole and then up to the equator. The wind's always blowing from the east, from our right, at about 360 kilometers per hour. So we have to compensate."

"With a kuldi field?" California asked, surprised. "Why not just barge on through?"

Balthasar grinned at her. "Need a really big generator then, and the whole shuttle would have to be about half again as big, and that would give us too big a cross section for the wind, so I'd need a bigger generator—see what I mean?"

She nodded, obviously surprised to be in an environment that even troll technology could not quite handle.

At a hundred kilometers above the surface the korshak screens began to display the presence of relatively dense atmosphere. As the shuttle fell, temperatures rose: minus one hundred degrees Celsius at ninety kilometers, minus fifty degrees at seventy kilometers. Then they were down in the upper haze level, a bright yellow mist of sulfuric acid that rapidly thickened into the upper cloud layer. The temperature rose to plus thirteen degrees like a fine autumn day at Jasper House, and the atmospheric pressure at fifty kilometers was the same as Earth's at the surface.

As Balthasar had predicted, the winds were intense. The shuttle swayed and heaved, sometimes rising abruptly or falling like a stone. Visibility was poor, the yellow haze swirled past, giving no sense of distance except when the shuttle dropped through a narrow clear zone. Near the bottom of the lowest cloud layer the winds began to die, but there the clouds flared with lightning, and twice the screens went blinding white as bolts hit the shuttle.

At thirty kilometers they fell through the bottom of the

clouds in a short-lived shower of sulfur particles that evaporated in the intensifying heat. The sulfur zone yielded to a superheated ocean of carbon dioxide.

The clarity of the atmosphere was surprisingly good, and Balthasar was using light enhancement as well. The shuttle was dropping from a yellow-orange overcast toward a yellow-gray surface still too distant to show much detail. The temperature was 220 degrees, and the pressure was over eight atmospheres.

A new kind of turbulence rocked the shuttle. "Air's getting thick enough to drink outside," Balthasar explained. "We start behaving more like a sinking stone than a flying object."

That was the altitude where most floaters kept their cloudcastles, Alex knew, and when he looked for them, he could see a couple in the far distance. Their running lights twinkled in the thick air as he watched, one took a lightning bolt with no ill effects.

The shuttle's curving flight was carrying them across a vast plain, the Helena Planitia. Here and there it glowed red where a volcanic vent was active, but for the most part it was a featureless basaltic wasteland. The deeper they sank, the slower their progress, the superheated carbon dioxide outside was already at a pressure of twenty atmospheres.

The terrain began to break up into foothills, slopes, and actual mountains. The eroded remains of ancient craters looked like atolls without an ocean. Lightning strobed constantly, and Balthasar let his passengers listen to the endless rumble of thunder.

"Southern edges of Aphrodite Terra," he said, pointing ahead. "Pretty, isn't it?"

The mountains seemed very close below. Despite the stillness of the atmosphere at the surface and the lack of water, the peaks looked weathered. Millions of years of lightning strikes, acid, and sluggish winds had worn away most sharp edges. The slopes were scarred in places by avalanche chutes, and the valleys were choked with stony debris. Yet they lacked any trace of streambeds. Several of the peaks were clearly extinct volcanoes; others still fumed from glowing calderas.

The last hundred kilometers of the journey took as long as all the rest of it. Balthasar forced the shuttle through the thickening atmosphere while constantly checking the external temperature. "We're at the equivalent of nine hundred meters beneath the sea on Earth," he said. "Does anybody live at that depth?"

"No," California said. "They could, I suppose, but why bother?"

"Ah." Balthasar smiled. "There's the difference between us and Earthers."

Alex reflected that Balthasar himself had chosen to live thousands of kilometers above this awful place but said nothing. He watched the gray mountains slide by below, growing closer all the time. Then the mountains fell away.

The shuttle was gliding along the eastern lip of an immense gray-walled canyon whose near side plunged steeply for over five kilometers to a fringe of talus slopes and whose far side looked like a mirage in a smoggy, rippling haze. They had reached Diana Chasma, a rift valley even larger than Valles Marineris on Mars. The valley stretched north, its cliffs more visible than its floor.

Looking down, Alex gasped. "Something's moving there!"

"Where?" Balthasar followed Alex's pointing finger. Off in the valley, something dull red was indeed moving. "Lava. Sometimes it takes centuries to cool down, turn solid. You should see the lava bogs in Maxwell Montes. Ah, here's Khanshoiar."

It was a trollish name; Alex snorted at the irony of naming such a place "Green and Tranquil Ponds." Then again, *Munshaour* meant "Firmly Rooted." And Dwuliu meant "Explorer." Perhaps that meant Carson would be willing to consider Alex's plan.

A flattened dome, mottled white and gray and about half a kilometer across, perched just at the edge of the cliffs. Alex looked again and realized that the dome was actually the top of a kilometer-high cylinder set into the cliff so that a narrow wall of fome was exposed. Light gleamed from a vertical row of wide windows in the wall: Dwuliu Carson must indeed have treasured his view.

Balthasar's shuttle computer had been in constant touch with the household computer at Khanshoiar, and the ship glided down to a perfect docking beside the dome. A folding roof rose over the shuttle and sealed itself, becoming a hangar. Pumps vented the carbon dioxide, replacing it with a slightly thinner and cooler atmosphere.

"By the time we're ready to leave," Balthasar said, "the shuttle skin will be down to about a hundred degrees. And with the pressure down, the shuttle molmacs can do any repairs." He waved them toward the air lock.

"You mean even this ship could be damaged if it stayed down here too long?" California said.

"It's damaged already. If we just sat on the surface for a day or two, we'd be sure to spring a leak or overheat. Old saying: Don't land if you can't drydock."

The air lock cycled, and the outer door opened onto a tunnel much like the one that had linked *Wuthering Heights* and Eros. This one, however, was rigid and had been designed for walking rather than floating. A fine, intricately woven carpet muffled their footsteps as they walked fifty meters down the tunnel to a door of solid gold.

"Welcome to Khanshoiar," said a mobile robot waiting for them by the door. "Please step aboard. Mr. Carson is waiting for you in the orchard."

It was certainly a better maintained estate than the dump he had visited at the north pole, Alex reflected as the mobile rolled through the golden door. They had come onto a wide concourse just under the edge of the dome. The floor and walls were faced with unfamiliar minerals, green, black, and red, all doubtless natural to Venus and polished to a high sheen. Like a tiger's eye, the stones reflected light with the shifting glitter of chatoyancy. A constant rumble and boom came from somewhere in the distance.

As the mobile traveled along the edge of the concourse, Alex looked down and felt dizzy: The mobile and its passengers were on the brink of a thousand-meter vertical drop. At the bottom of the estate was a miniature forest, a stand of trees with snow on their branches.

In between, the vast hollow cylinder was ringed by balconies at intervals of about a hundred meters. The inner surface of the cylinder was faced with rough-cut Venusian stone resembling agate, and from each balcony a small waterfall plunged in spray to a pool in the balcony below. To the west, the windows to the outside looked dauntingly large.

Alex leaned next to California and muttered. "He must have the best insulation and cooling of anyone in the system."

"I hope so. I really hope so," she murmured back.

The mobile entered an open-sided elevator, and they began a gentle descent down the wall. Seen at closer range, each balcony/concourse turned out to be a mansion in itself, with lavish rooms opening onto the great atrium. The balconies were also gardens, each with plants, animals, and birds of a different Earth ecosystem. Those at the top were tropical, changing to temperate ones near the bottom. In several of the concourses trolls were visible, but it was impossible to tell whether they were icons or cuckoos. Each concourse, on its western side, had access to a window twenty meters wide and five meters high, overlooking the fumaroles and talus slopes of Diana Chasma.

"Are all grounder estates like this?" California asked Balthasar.

"The highlanders' places are a little bigger, but most of them don't have windows. Dwijin's very proud of his windows."

The air took on a perceptible chill as the elevator descended, and when it reached the bottom, its passengers could see their breath in frosty flutters. The last waterfall, designed to break into a fine mist, provided steady snow for the forest at the bottom of the atrium. It was a stand of firs and pines, almost a meter deep in snow; some had blown onto the concourse that ringed it. Looking up, Alex saw the small white circle of the dome a kilometer above. It would be hard to suffer claustrophobia in this place, he thought, and equally hard to avoid vertigo.

"I hope you're not too cold," the mobile said. "The forest is in its winter cycle at the moment. The orchard should be more comfortable."

The concourse divided the forest from subgardens of bog and tundra set into niches forty meters deep. The mobile hummed swiftly down the glossy stone pavement and made a sharp right turn toward a pair of high glass doors that parted to let it pass. Warm, moist air from within turned to a puff of mist. Then the door closed, and the mobile was rolling through a small orchard of apple and cherry trees. Ahead was a sullen glow of yellow-orange light; when the mobile cleared the last of the trees, its passengers could look across a well-trimmed lawn to a swimming pool set just below the window.

The light from the window was like that under an impending thunderstorm on Earth. Outside and far below, the floor of Diana Chasma was still except for the flicker of moving lava. Lightning flashed every few seconds, the source of the rumbles they had heard since entering the estate.

"Welcome," Dwuliu Carson said, rising from a deck chair beside the pool.

He was a tall man with a wide, cheerful face and curly blond hair cut short. In black shorts and T-shirt he looked both casual and dramatic. Something in his graceful, long-legged stride reminded Alex of Victor. If he felt uncomfortable in the physical presence of others, he gave no sign of it.

When introductions were over, the three guests joined Carson by the pool. California complimented him on the view.

"Some people find it monotonous at first," he said. "After a while, though, you begin to look for the little changes. Sometimes the mirages let you see hundreds of kilometers, or they distort the view. The light changes, the lava moves, a little buckshot falls."

"Buckshot?" she repeated.

"Not really. But lead's a liquid out there, and so are cadmium and tin and zinc. They smelt out, especially when a volcano erupts, and we get rains of liquid metal droplets. They're quite pretty. Nuisance to get it off the windows when it freezes, though. Sulfur rains are even worse. At ground temperature sulfur ought to be a vapor, but it stays liquid under pressure. Slides around on the windows, and the molmacs have trouble absorbing the droplets." He smiled as a robot glided through the trees with an ample lunch on its back. "I'm sorry. We grounders are very boring about the weather."

"What happens during the night?" California asked. "Do you use light enhancement?"

"Very rarely. The lightning keeps going, and you can see the lava even better in the darkness. It adds to the variety. All right, now, we have some very nice sandwiches here—some good elivikio; I've got a troll gardener who really knows how to grow it. And we have tofu—some salads—and a very nice white wine from the grapes I grow up on Deck Six."

Alex took his cue from his host. If Carson wanted small talk and gossip, that was fine. He vaguely recalled that

Carson was a little over three hundred years old, virtually a contemporary of Alex's father and similarly fond of surface ritual. With the possible exception of Liam McCool, those old people could not be rushed.

"Mr. Carson," California asked, "if Balthasar's ship needs to be repaired every time he comes down to the surface, how do you keep this whole beautiful estate functioning?"

"With a great deal of difficulty." Carson laughed. "What you've seen is a small fraction of the place. The factories, generators, cooling equipment—all that sort of thing is buried under the cliffs. Go down a couple of hundred meters and the temperature's only about eighty degrees Celsius. A lot of the technology I've invented myself, and I guess most other grounders have done the same or they wouldn't be down here. I've got at least two hundred varieties of molmacs that can function at temperatures up to five hundred degrees and pressures up to two hundred atmospheres. I've got factories producing high-temperature fome. The exterior of this estate is completely replaced every six months—the windows are replaced every hundred hours."

He gestured toward the window behind the pool. "It looks like a single sheet of glass, but it's really made up of fome panes less than a millimeter on a side, and it's quadruple-glazed. The molmacs work on it constantly, eating the old panes and excreting new ones. Some grounders like to let their systems run down, but I try to keep them functioning perfectly. Otherwise I'm likely to wake up dead."

"A lot of work," Alex said.

"My household computer has more capacity than forty estate computers on Earth, and I'm still adding more." He grinned, obviously proud of his ability to survive and flourish in that impossible place.

At last the conversation turned to the invasion.

"The news is bad," Carson said calmly. "We haven't seen so many deaths since the last of the post-Contact wars, when I was a boy. The Chaiar aren't even bothering to conceal the death rate."

"But everyone seems to have accepted the Chaiar," Alex said. "Why would they bother to kill anyone now?"

"Look," Carson said. "This was on a gryphon broadcast yesterday."

In an estate in northern Madagascar a woman with golden skin coughed blood onto her hands and stared at it in surprise.

On a cloudcastle over the Amazon River a man crawled on his belly across the polished hardwood floor of his living room while beside him his gorilla housekeeper grunted in anguish. The man's skin was erupting in blisters that tore and bled; he left a trail of blood and lymph.

In one of the new Chaiar cities a woman with falsefire hair sat on a bench in harsh sunlight, gasping for breath. Thick white mucus streamed from her nostrils, eyes, and mouth.

"Some of the gryphons' plants are producing toxins that human molmacs don't know how to handle," Carson said. "A lot of people are sensitive to them. A lot."

Alex felt something like the anguish he had known when his father died.

"They're getting *sick*," he whispered. "Those are sick people." It was one thing to see disease on old tapes from pre-Contact or the first terrible century after it; it was quite another to see modern, living people suffering from disease.

"Worse than sick, Alex. They're dying. I can hardly believe it myself, and I can still remember the last of the great plagues."

"Why—why would the gryphons allow it? Surely they must realize what their plants are doing."

California laughed harshly. When her eyes met his, he realized she had been just as shocked by the korshak images. "Come on, Alex. We've been close enough to the way they think to know why. If people die, they're not meant to be in the Pattern anyway. Anyway, according to Dwuliu's figures—" She nodded at glowing numbers in the korshak images. "—it's affecting only about fifteen percent of the population. Less than two million people."

Carson's images also showed other humans still trying to resist and being destroyed. But there was nothing like coherent fighting. Each human fought an ordinary individual war against some cuckoo shuttle or settlement, launching missiles or firing beamers and then being blasted to vapor in reprisal. A few, by blowing themselves up, saved the Chaiar a little time and weaponry.

Alex stood up and walked up and down beside the

pool. The sinister yellow-orange light outside made Carson and California look like golden statues.

"You're a long way from Earth here," he said. "What do you think about what's going on?"

"I have old friends on Earth. I'm sorry for them."

"Sorry enough to fight the Chaiar?"

"Not sorry enough to fight them the way some Earthers are."

"Neither are we. We think the only way to do it is to create a kind of supercomputer out of linked molmacs— ours, yours, Balthasar's, as many as possible here on Venus and anywhere else."

Carson's handsome features revealed nothing. "What specific results do you expect to gain?"

"We don't know. But we expect a supermind would be able to use the Database better and figure out the physics the gryphons are using."

"But anyone who had access to the supermind would also have access to people's personal records and technology."

"Yes."

"Alex, that's not acceptable. I get into wars sometimes. If my enemies understood how my defense systems run and how I keep this estate functioning, they could turn this place into a puff of steam."

"Surely no one would dream of that, not when the gryphons are about to take over."

Carson smiled a little. "Tell me when any human society has united against an outside threat. The Spaniards didn't beat the Aztecs—the other Mexican tribes did that. The Ukrainians were glad to see the Germans invade the Soviet Union. Contact with the trolls led to the worst wars in human history. Someone's always more willing to settle scores with old enemies than to fight with new ones."

Balthasar nodded in agreement. "True. Half my guests hate the other half."

"But we can't afford that now," California protested. "We'll all be destroyed like those poor people if we don't join together."

"Abstractly, no doubt you're right. But no one's going to be the first to expose himself to harm."

"They're going to terraform Venus, you know," Alex said, feeling a little desperate. "They'll strip away the sulfur clouds and precipitate the carbon dioxide and drop a few thousand comets on the surface to give it some water and oxygen."

"I hope not. But if they do, what of it? I can either fight them to the death or leave Venus for the outer system."

"Where they'll eventually catch up with you," California said.

Carson shrugged. "At least I'll have lived longer than if I'd revealed all my secrets to my neighbors."

Alex saw lightning reflected on the surface of the pool. "Ask your computer," he said slowly, "if there are any estates still holding out against the gryphons."

"I don't have to," Carson said instantly. "Three estates are under the biggest shardana bubbles I've ever heard of. One of them's your mother's place, isn't it? Mordor?"

"And Mao Jian's Castillo Paricutín and Lyell Bradley's Free Acres," Alex shot back. "My mother's molmacs worked out the physics for those bubbles, and she sent the data to us while we were on our way to Venus. Join us and you get the data. Then you can put a bubble around this place that no one's going to get through."

Carson's gray eyes focused on Alex with a new intensity. "A bubble would keep the heat out as well, wouldn't it?"

"Heat, missiles, beamers, gryphons." Alex waved a negligent hand. "It wouldn't matter what you shared with other people, because they still couldn't detune your bubble without knowing the bubble's resonance. That's why the gryphons still haven't been able to get at Lydia and Mao and Lyell."

Carson rubbed his chin. "Fifty kilometers. That would take me out to Lead Creek. Plenty of room for mining inside the bubble."

"Plenty of room for anything you want to do, Dwuliu," Alex said.

"What would I get out of this?" Balthasar demanded.

"Freedom to go on running Eros," Alex said. "You could also put a partial bubble around your platform. And of course you get access to whatever the supermind comes up with. Whoever has a narrowcaster gets everything."

Carson was looking at the orchard, where apples glinted among the leaves. "All right," he said. "I accept your terms. Let's work out the details."

Fifteen:

The return to Eros seemed short: Alex was constantly on the narrowcaster, linking Dwuliu's molmacs with Balthasar's and those of *Wuthering Heights*.

Emily broke in not long before the shuttle docked again. "The deception is getting more difficult, dear. Now I have to deal with the Venusians and Mercurians as well as the gryphons. You would be *appalled* to know how many of these people are ready to convert. Projecting from inquiries, I'd say we have forty-five to fifty thousand converts just on Venus, plus another ten thousand who might tilt that way. On Mercury it's harder to tell because most of them are recluses, but certainly no fewer than four thousand converts and almost five hundred potentials. I've had to put together a potted message, just like the one you got from John F. Kennedy when you told them you wanted to convert."

"At least you're able to send the gryphons a lot of good news," Alex said.

"Yes, but at some point they're going to wonder why we haven't run into more trouble than we have. Or one of our new friends is going to be tactless."

"I know." She was right. Dwuliu and Balthasar would be spreading the news about narrowcasting and molmac merging to people they trusted; eventually they would choose the wrong person, or someone would accidentally reveal what was going on. "All we can do is hope to build up the biggest merge possible before the gryphons learn what's up."

He felt grateful for his warwiring; without it he would probably have been horribly depressed. He and his friends were involving thousands of people in a gamble: that enough molmac computers, linked together, could find some weakness in the gryphons and drive them out of the solar system. He did not want to ask Emily what the odds might be on such a gamble.

Balthasar was in good spirits as they returned to his private quarters on the back of a mobile. "My own computer is assessing the current visitors," he said. "A lot of sellouts, but a lot of resisters too. By this time tomorrow you should have a couple of hundred new people in your merge."

"You'd better plan to put up a bubble as soon as possible," Alex told him. "I'd give us maybe forty-eight hours before the gryphons realize they've been tricked."

"Then we'll make it a busy forty-eight hours."

While Balthasar supervised the contacts with his Venusian visitors, California and Alex called *Wuthering Heights*. Victor replied from the dive room.

"Rik is in the Database again," he told them. "Lord Whitehead's molmacs are very happy with the merge so far. They've suggested some new places to go diving."

"Where's Liam?" Alex asked.

"Somewhere on Eros. He said he needed some rest and recreation."

"Well, we'll look him up in a little while. Victor, have you and Lord Whitehead thought about getting in touch with the Martians and Jovians? Without the Chaiar eavesdropping?"

The gryphon shook his head. "They would be as likely as the Venusians to spot the narrowcaster in the Database. I think for now we can simply wait for them to call us."

"I wish my mother had a narrowcaster. I worry about her and the others."

"I understand. If the Chaiar would lift the korshak blackout from Earth, we might even try a clear-code send. But for now we can only wait."

Alex grunted. Victor's calm could sometimes be annoying.

Viewed from Balthasar's quarters, the life of the platform acquired a slightly unreal quality. Alex and California watched revelers copulating in the gardens, drinking and fighting in the villages, and dueling in the fields. Most seemed to be having a good time, but a large minority had withdrawn from participation: They watched the duels and lovemaking but accepted no challenges or invitations. Instead they sat in the village inns, talking quietly and drawing others into their conversations.

"Sellouts," California said as they studied one group. "Look—that one talked to our false images. Balthasar, can you pick up what they're saying?"

The korshak images of a trio of drinkers suddenly began to speak:

"I've talked to Alex Macintosh three times now," one of them was saying, "and he makes a lot of sense about this Pattern thing. The gryphons are hundreds of thousands of years ahead of us. If we cooperate, we'll be in on the biggest thing anyone ever dreamed of. If we try to fight, they'll roll over us like an Atalanta breeze."

"Looks like old Balthasar himself must think so," a woman agreed. "He gave them a couple of shots, but he let them link orbits. I understand he even took them down to see Dwuliu and try to talk some sense into him."

"And Dwuliu didn't shoot them down," said the third, the overmuscled man who had talked with Emily's false images a few days before. "If that son of a bitch is going over to the gryphons, we might as well get on the bandwagon."

"What's a bandwagon?" Alex asked.

"They mean join the fashion," California said. "That's something we hadn't figured on, that they'd be watching us and drawing conclusions. Balthasar, is that going to make it harder to recruit people?"

"We'll see." At an unheard comlink command, the korshak image changed to present a naked couple rolling about on a bed in one of the platform inns. Judging from their spectacular dermographs, both were young; the man had ostentatiously neglected to repair a number of dueling scars on his face and chest. When they paused for breath, Balthasar spoke.

"Excuse me, Freddy, Corazón—it's me. Talk for a minute?"

The lovers, evidently seeing a korshak projection of their host, nodded and smiled. Balthasar gave them a quick, serious explanation of what was going on. Freddy seemed to like the idea out of sheer perversity: He was a grounder from Maxwell Montes who had started several wars in the last year. Corazón, a Mercurian, seemed a little dubious at first, but the prospect of a giant shardana bubble over her Caloris Basin estate won her over.

"Don't use your comlinks to contact your computers," Balthasar warned them. "Wait till you get home, and then have them each build a narrowcaster. We'll put the merge together after that."

"When do we get our bubbles?" Freddy asked.

"First thing we'll send you, after the linkup."

"Haw! Let's get out of here," Freddy brayed, hopping out of bed and yanking on a shimmery lace tunic. The image of the bedroom vanished.

Back in his elegant living room, Balthasar smiled at Alex and California. "I think we have the answer to your question. We just have to talk faster than the sellouts."

His butler arrived and said softly, "If I could interrupt, sir, we seem to have a little trouble at the Troubadours' Tavern."

"What kind of trouble?"

"Mr. McCool is conducting a riot, sir."

The tavern, on the second level, was a large room with a low ceiling. Humanoid robots tended bar and served drinks. It was rarely crowded, except after formal duels in the courtyard outside, but it had attracted a number of sellouts looking for a quiet place to talk.

Evidently it had also attracted McCool, who had put down several whiskeys. When a sellout had approached him to ask for more information about the Pattern, McCool had replied, "It is the greatest, most soul-devouring abomination humanity has ever suffered. If you do not fight it with all your mind and strength, you are a traitor to the DNA in every cell of your wretched body."

"That's not what your shipmate Alex Macintosh says," the sellout had protested, and McCool had grinned and kicked the sellout in the crotch. She had doubled up, and he struck her again, with the edge of his hand to her exposed neck.

Alex could scarcely stand to watch the recording of the next few minutes. With an expression of seraphic tranquillity on his lined face, McCool had disabled eight attackers and two robots. A genuine pre-Contact antique Budweiser neon sign was so much broken glass tubing, and the mahogany bar had been kicked in.

"I brought that sign all the way from Pittsburgh," Balthasar lamented, "and the bar came out of a hotel in Kinshasa. Is he crazy?"

"He's a Violent, but he doesn't practice much," California said.

"Why should he? The son of a bitch is just about perfect." The platform master fumed as they watched two security robots, at a safe distance, fire knockout darts into McCool's backside. The old man toppled over onto his last victim.

"They're bringing him up here," Balthasar said. "When he wakes up, he better have a good story."

"He's going back to *Wuthering Heights* at once," Alex said. "The old bugger's probably lost us the war."

A few minutes later the robots hauled McCool into the living room. He was coming to already and gazed with detached interest at the cuffs on his wrists and ankles. They were not linked to one another, but any sudden or intense exertion would cause them to paralyze him.

"What the hell do you mean, starting a riot in my tavern?" Balthasar bellowed.

"And against a bunch of sellouts!" Alex added. "Liam, you've blown our deception. Someone's sure to be talking to the gryphons about this, and then—and then—" He imagined some unknown beam reaching across space and disabling *Wuthering Heights* just as his shuttle had been.

McCool blinked amiably at them. "I appear to have offended you somehow. Please accept my apologies."

"He's drunk," California said.

"Doesn't he neutralize the stuff?" Balthasar asked.

"The whole purpose of alcohol, my friend, is not to be neutralized. May I sit down?"

"No!" Alex barked. "Balthasar, I'm very sorry. When he's not drunk, he's fine. He came up with the whole idea of the supermind. But sometimes—"

"Alex." McCool grinned fondly at him. "My advocate. I am in your debt."

Alex growled and turned to Balthasar. "Can you sober him up and put him on a sled back to my ship?"

"With pleasure."

"We'll go with him. Now we'd better talk to your friends really fast, Balthasar. I don't know what the Chaiar will do, but they're sure to do something."

McCool was very much himself again by the time they boarded the sled for the twenty-kilometer hop to *Wuthering Heights*. Brilliant sunlight, falling through the transparent canopy, made him seem more wrinkled than he really was. He sat erect in his chair, watching Eros fall away against the dazzling backdrop of Venus's clouds.

"The trouble with alcohol," he said calmly, "is that it blurs the experience of the divine. In the right mood I can feel divinity as well as the person I'm communing with. But drunk—I might as well be watching it happen on korshak. Or television."

"You've cost us time, Liam."

"Some. Perhaps too much, but we'll have to let the gryphons be the judge of that."

"Why? Why did you get drunk?"

The old man truned and looked into his eyes. "Too much time in the Database. Too much time. Young people can take a lot more of it. But that last dive was a very bad one, Alex. Very bad." He stared ahead through the sled canopy at the rapidly approaching white sphere and black cylinder of *Wuthering Heights*. "For a while I was afraid I might lose my way back. And I was—afraid. Really afraid. In the Database you can't find God. You can't experience violence. It's like being in a kind of empty hell."

"Well, you're out of it now," California said cheerfully. "And if you don't get a chance to experience violence in the next couple of days, I'll be surprised."

McCool smiled slightly, then shook with a silent laugh.

"She's *still* in the dive?" Alex echoed, gaping up at Victor. The gryphon nodded.

"We went looking for information on the Chaiar. We found it, but somehow I lost her. Finally I decided she must have surfaced without me, but when I ended the dive, I found she was still in the Database."

Alex, California, and McCool ran from the terrace to the dive room, Victor right behind them. On the bed, Rik lay unmoving. The red dive patch on her forehead seemed grotesquely bright against the grayness of her skin. Her breath came in short gasps.

"How long has she been under?" California asked.

"About two and a half hours."

"Emily!" Alex shouted. "Can you bring her out?"

"Don't be silly," the computer replied. "I'm not designed for diving. If she's lost in the Database, she'll have to find her own way out, or someone will have to go in after her."

McCool shouldered past Alex and stretched out on the bed. He already had a dive patch in his hand, and he smiled at Alex and California as he pressed it to his forehead. A moment later his eyes closed, and he seemed to fall into a deep sleep.

Alex slammed his hand against the wall in frustration. "He's going to hurt himself. Now we've got two problems."

"It was a sensible thing to do," Victor said. "They went diving before, and Liam will know the path she took. She was interested in Chaiar history and biology; I suspect she found what she was looking for."

"I should have gone," Alex answered. "He's right. You can get too old for diving no matter how young you look. I'm going in after them."

"Then so am I," California said.

Alex touched her arm and shook his head. "Stay in touch with the merge. We should be getting dozens of new people in the next hour or so. I won't be under more than forty minutes or so, anyway." He fished another dive patch out of a drawer in the base of the bed and shoved McCool closer to Rik. Stretching out, he looked up for a second at California and Victor and then pressed the patch to his forehead.

He seemed to be falling through a universe of black dots in white space. Looked at one way, the dots were arrayed in countless parallel lines in all directions; looked at another way, they formed swirls, spirals, clumps, and enigmatic fractal patterns. Distance was meaningless.

The Database roared and squealed and rumbled; it stank and tasted of sugar and salt and stomach acid; it rasped across the skin of his buttocks and prickled on his face and glided like velvet over his hand. It turned hot and cold, bright and dim, as he fell. He reoriented himself, and the sensation of falling turned to one of rising. As always, he automatically looked at himself and shivered to find himself invisible.

He looked for landmarks and blazes. No one knew how simply thinking could create them, but without that property the Database would have been only an impenetrable hallucination. Early divers had used words and phrases, but with increased experience they had adopted symbols like those of the trolls. Alex moved quickly through the early blazes until he found the path he was looking for. A string of dots turned blue against a red background: a blaze he had used from his first dive. He moved toward it, through it, and turned to the next blaze. That one was olfactory, a scent of roses; the third was the sensation of a mild electric shock on one of his invisible hands.

He turned the wrong way and found himself caught up in what seemed like an enormous multicolored spiral: the genome of a small, unintelligent relative of trolls. Moving upward and backward, he returned to the black and white world and moved in search of the next blaze. What had Rik said her blaze was? A yellow flower. Some divers left blazes that were easy to identify, but others were as enigmatic as the Database itself. Even after three centuries of diving by millions of people, the blazes and the trails they marked were few and scattered; many ended in dead ends where information lay hidden behind locks without keys.

Endlessly changing sensory impressions swept over him as he soared and plunged through the Database: the scent of tomato leaves, a hiss like surf leaving a pebbly beach, an eye-watering stink. Then he got a glimpse of a gryphon and plunged through it. A long way beyond it was the yellow flower, and beside it was a small image of an Irish wolfhound. McCool had made it that far also. He pushed on. He sensed someone's presence not far away: One of the many mysteries of the Database was how disembodied minds could detect one another and communicate there.

—Liam!—he called. —Rik!—

—Here,— came a reply. He turned right without knowing why the call had come from that direction. Two more false turns gave him glimpses of ancient Makhshuar, the gryphons' home world: a shallow lagoon in winter, with hundreds of gryphons sleeping under the ice and a female gryphon dancing at night in the light of the planet's huge Marslike moon.

Then he knew he was in the presence of his friends, though he could not see them.

—She doesn't want to come back,—McCool said. His voice was barely audible over a rapid snapping noise.

—Rik, come with us,—Alex said.—It's dangerous to stay here too long.—

—Soon. Soon.—

—Now. Can you sense me?—

—Yes.—

—I'm moving back the way we came. Stay close.—He put down a blaze, a small image of Heathcliff.—We'll come back soon. Come on. Come on. The gryphons are going to attack soon. We need you, Rik. Come on.—

—Soon. Just a little longer.—

He felt helpless against that faint reply. Then he sensed someone else, a mind he had not expected. It was close by but different from anyone he had ever dived with before. Fear swirled around him.

—Now. Quickly!—

Reluctantly she followed. He made her sing so he could tell how far behind she was lagging. McCool sang, too. Every little while Alex left another blaze, always Heathcliff, until he reached Rik's flower and McCool's wolfhound.

—We're almost back. Keep singing.—Alex felt sharp needles stab at his nonexistent flesh but kept going. The strange mind was far away, but he was still aware of it. He wanted very much to get to the surface.

They were back at the entry point, a dot in the whiteness that expanded into a glowing, deafening kaleidoscope of blazes, and an instant later the dive room was around them once more.

Alex shuddered and groped across McCool to pull the dive patch from Rik's forehead. Then he rolled back, grunting and dizzy, and tried to find his own patch. Other hands—California's?—removed it. He blinked, squinted, and saw her looking down at him.

"Alex, Alex—I nearly went down after you myself. You were gone over an hour."

He stroked her arm sleepily. "That long? Mmm. See how Rik and Liam are." He felt more than dizzy. The dive room seemed less real than the Database. He absently took his and Rik's patches and put them on Emily's little reader beside the bed.

"Thank you, dear. I'll consider what you've found and pass it on to the molmacs."

"Good. Good." Then he shook his head and laughed sleepily. "I don't know if you need to bother telling them."

"Why not?"

"I think they were already there with us."

Sixteen:

Alex dragged himself upstairs to his bedroom and went to sleep. He woke with muted sunlight glowing through the curtains and California beside him. She lay dozing, her body warm, and he felt surprised to be pleased. Never had he wakened next to a lover before; the lack of privacy, the vulnerability would once have been disgusting. For a moment he worried that the invasion and its aftermath had subtly damaged his character. But the solid reality of her, after the sustained hallucination of the Database, reassured and comforted him. They made love silently and intensely and then for a while lay serene in each other's arms.

"Open the curtains," Alex mumbled, and dazzling sunlight filled the room. "Ugh. Filter it down a little, please, Emily."

The windows darkened until the sunlight was no brighter than a summer day on Earth. Alex stretched and yawned and kissed California.

"I'm glad you were here. How are Rik and Liam?"

"Rik's still asleep. Liam's out in the gardens somewhere, sitting under a tree."

"Where's Victor?"

"Up in your office, talking to the machine-shop molmacs. He says he's found another new weapon in what Rik brought back yesterday."

"She's a natural diver, isn't she? I hope it's something the Chaiar don't know about—but we were right in the middle of a Chaiar data region."

"An old one, remember. They don't use the Database much anymore. Come on, get up. I'm hungry."

They had breakfast on the terrace, gazing out at the yellow-cream clouds of Venus that filled almost half the dome. Eros, looking surprisingly large, glinted against the clouds a few kilometers distant. High up, Lord White-head circled patiently.

Alex and California ate doughnuts while Emily passed on some messages: Carson was setting up the equipment for a shardana bubble, as were many other grounders; the molmac net was up to eighty-six persons and growing at the rate of four per hour; the Venusian sellouts were leaving Eros and the other platforms, heading for the safety of their estates; and the Chaiar were interrogating Emily on the meaning of McCool's outburst in the tavern.

"They definitely suspect something," Emily said. "I had to cook up a story about Liam's alcoholism, but I don't think they believed it. Alcoholism isn't part of the Pattern."

Alex washed his doughnut down with a mouthful of coffee. "When the sellouts find out about the molmac merge and the shardana bubbles, they'll warn the gryphons at once. If they can black out korshak around Venus, we'll be right back where we started."

"Nonsense," Emily replied briskly. "The narrowcasters shouldn't be affected at all. But if the gryphons *think* we're blacked out, so much the better."

California laughed. "Emily, are you warwired too? You seem to be having a good time."

"Not as good a time as our furry friend Heathcliff," she replied, managing to convey prim disapproval.

The Labrador came bounding up out of the gardens, dripping wet. He shook himself and flopped onto the floor of the terrace, grinning and panting. If he had overheard Emily's remark, he gave no sign of it.

—The water's really good today. But I think you should go see Liam. He's sitting on a bench out in the rockery, muttering to himself. He seems very unhappy.—

—All right. How does the molmac merge look to you?—

—Confusing. When I talk to Lord Whitehead's mol-macs, I never know who's going to answer. Sometimes it's someone else's molmacs, somewhere down on Venus.—

—If they confuse you, what would they do to me?— Alex answered.

He and California walked down into the gardens with Heathcliff tagging along. The shrubs and flowers were ex-uberantly healthy, lifting their leaves to the light of the sun and the clouds of Venus. A family of wood ducks escorted them down a slow moving stream under a line of willows, then turned back. Heathcliff ignored them.

The gravel path curved around a marsh and climbed into a secluded area behind a boxwood hedge. On the far side alpine flowers grew in tiny clusters of color among sharp-edged rocks Alex had collected from Luna, Mars, and the asteroids. On a bench carved from one of the larger rocks, McCool sat staring angrily at nothing.

Alex and California sat down beside him. The rockery was close to the edge of the estate, where the lines of kuldi-force pseudogravity curved the most, so the bench felt as if it were tilted; they all had to lean a little to keep their balance. Just beyond the rockery and the hedge was the dome; the clouds of Venus seemed very close.

"What's the matter, Liam?" Alex asked.

McCool's eyes swung to meet his. Alex felt alarm at the sadness and loneliness he saw.

"Too many dives," McCool said hoarsely. "Go down there too many times and you realize how hopelessly lost we all are. How old is First Stone—two million years, three million? Or Parakar? And all their knowledge is just a small part of the Database. We're like ants in a library. The best we can do is chew up a page or two to line our nests and leave our scent on some of the shelves."

"We're not ants, we're human beings," Alex said quietly. "We have to do what we can with the Database and not judge ourselves by other species."

"Human beings." McCool smiled without humor. "We used to call ourselves *Homo sapiens*, wise man, but no one's used that term much since Contact. We were wise men, happily destroying our world, but now that someone else even wiser is doing it, most of us are surrendering. And if we do resist, all we can do is to jump up and down, and hoot, and throw our own shit at the gryphons. We ought to call ourselves *Tyrannopithecus abjectus*, the miserable tyrant ape."

Alex smiled faintly and glanced at California. She looked worried. For a Violent like McCool to lose heart was alarming; after all, he had rejoiced in the prospect of battle with the Chaiar, labeled them sure losers and inspired Alex and California to resist rather than merely run and hide.

"Are you unhappy because we might lose? Then we'll just join God that much sooner," Alex said.

"If there is a God. I told you before—in the Database God doesn't exist. Entropy doesn't exist. You just fall into an endless fractal spiral, and the order keeps changing but it's still ... order." McCool's lips twitched in a kind of smile. "I believe I'm suffering a crisis of faith."

California put her arm around his shoulders. "Would you like to duel, Liam? Buttons off? Maybe you just need a wound or two."

He shook his head. "Thank you, dear, but I'd better work this out on my own."

"What about your own molmacs?" Alex suggested. "They ought to be able to cure your depression in a second."

"Do *you* let them control your emotions?" the old man said.

"No," Alex admitted. "Well, we'll keep you out of the Database from now on. Victor says he wants to go diving with Rik, anyway, so we'll try that."

"We're going to need you, Liam." California's dark eyes were serious. "Maybe sooner than we think."

He patted her hand and smiled. "It's good to be in the presence of friends. I'd forgotten how good. Even a tyrant ape needs company, especially a tyrant in exile."

The three walked together back to the house, while Venus seemed to rise to the top of the dome: *Wuthering Heights* was slowly turning, pivoting so that its nose pointed directly toward the planet. The terminator appeared, a fuzzy line between day and night. As the ship orbited over Venus's nightside, the light in the gardens dimmed. The clouds were darker but still visible as a gray blur like moonlit clouds on Earth. Lightning flickered restlessly, triggering photochemical reactions in the planet's upper atmosphere that suffused it with the "ashen light" of the Venusian night.

Looking up, Alex said, "I think I begin to see why the Venusians don't want to terraform."

"Indeed," McCool grunted.

—Alex.—It was Victor on the comlink, sending widely enough so that California and McCool received him also.

—What is it?—

—The pro-Chaiar Venusians have learned about the merge. Three of them have sent messages to Earth to warn them.—

—Well, we knew it had to happen. How many people in the merge so far?—

—Ninety-one. The three sellouts were offered the narrowcaster plans also, so the Chaiar will know we have that, too.—

—Have any other spacers picked up the narrowcaster from the Database yet?—California asked.

—No. But that last dive turned up some very useful information. I'm having some equipment built to exploit it. And I want to go diving again soon with Rik.—

—Excuse me for interrupting,—Emily said, using com-link rather than voice.—I think the sellouts are starting a war against us and the resisters. We're under attack by sixteen missiles, and another eight are headed for Eros. I count four cloudcastles rising into the upper atmosphere, and I assume they're going to attack us with missiles or beamers.

—In addition, robot spacecraft are landing on three of the comet nuclei orbiting Venus. I believe the sellouts intend to drop them out of orbit onto the surface.—

Alex looked at California and McCool. "Sixteen missiles are a lot. Care to help me fight them?"

"I'd love to!" California whispered.

McCool hesitated. Then he smiled, and Alex saw a familiar glint in the old man's eye.

"Come on, you tyrant ape," Alex said. "Show 'em you can throw shit farther than anyone else."

"While jumping up and down and hooting," McCool grunted. "All right, Mr. Macintosh, give me a range."

They fought from chairs on the terrace as korshak images popped into existence and out again. Alex controlled the ship's forward defenses while California guarded the flanks and McCool, the tail. Missiles leapt out at *Wuthering Heights* from the dimly glowing clouds below or from orbiting spacecraft halfway around Venus. Alex sent his own missiles out and listened proudly to their war cries as they raced to destroy themselves against the attackers. McCool used his beamers with skill born of over two centuries of warfare; California was almost as quick.

As the ship crossed the terminator back into daylight, Victor came out onto the terrace. He stood silently beside

Alex until the first wave of missiles had been dealt with and the second was still safely out of range.

"Excuse me," the gryphon said, "but we now have a new weapon you may wish to apply."

Alex looked up cheerfully, his eyes still full of the afterimages of exploding missiles. "Come up with something else, Victor? What is it this time?"

"A kuldi-field dissipator."

"A what?"

"It's a tightly focused kuldi beam that breaks up any kuldi field it encounters. The molmacs have built dissipators into three of the ship's beamers. They'll work quite well against missiles, but even better against cloudcastles."

California crowed. "Let's try it out. Can you give me a target, Victor?"

"A cloudcastle now over Beta Regio is the source of six of the missiles sent against us. Will that be suitable?"

"Absolutely."

A korshak screen appeared, showing the surface of Venus with the atmosphere stripped away. Magnified and foreshortened, the yellow-black plains seemed to race past. The screen locked onto a cloudcastle and paused.

"It's the *Kansas City*," Victor said quietly. "The proprietor is a woman named Phoebe O'Hara. She's one of the three sellouts who warned the Chaiar about us."

Even as he spoke, four more missiles lifted from the cloudcastle. It was circular, about two kilometers in diameter and sealed under a flat dome. Within, most of the cloudcastle residence area was forested. The lower hull of the cloudcastle was sulfur-crusted, showing glints of silver amid the yellow streaks.

"Take out the missiles first," Alex suggested. California nodded, focusing on the aiming circle that appeared in the image. She moved it onto one of the missiles, sent an inaudible comlink command, and watched the target tumble and slow.

"That's easy," she said, and quickly knocked out the remaining three. Then she turned to the cloudcastle. The aiming circle locked on.

Without warning, the cloudcastle began to fall. It fell slowly at first, then rapidly, then slowly again as it reached denser air below the clouds. Jets of vapor burst viscously from breaches in the hull and hung, Alex thought, like strands of spiders' silk in the thick air. About thirty seconds after being struck, the cloudcastle dome collapsed and the whole structure exploded. Long tentacles of superheated smoke spread from the nucleus, slowly twisting in the thickening atmosphere.

"My goodness," McCool said softly. "What was the range on that, Emily?"

"A bit over eight thousand kilometers."

"Praise God from whom all blessings flow," the old man said. "I assume you found this wonderful device in the Database."

"Yes. Along with a shield for the dissipater as well."

"Good!" Alex blurted. "I wouldn't like to be the target."

"What about knocking out kuldi generators?" California asked.

"Very difficult," Victor said. "The beam interacts with the field, but any solid matter can block it. If we were struck by a dissipator, we would lose our gravity but not our power. A cloudcastle uses kuldi for power, not gravity. The *Kansas City* was destroyed by heat and pressure, not by the beam."

"So it's not useful against, say, a grounder estate," McCool said.

"No. I wish I could find the beamer that the Chaiar used to shoot down Alex's shuttle. The principle must be similar."

"Keep looking," California said, stroking the golden fur of the gryphon's arm. "Meanwhile, let's find some more targets."

In the next ten minutes they destroyed the second wave of missiles, four more cloudcastles, and a spacecraft at a distance of fourteen thousand kilometers. Balthasar called to ask what they were using and demanded the plans at once. Eros had taken two hits, both at the opposite end from the residence sphere; the satellite was engulfed in a swarm of micron-sized dust particles from the vaporized rock.

The attacks ceased. Alex, California, and McCool got up, stretched, and called for something to eat. Suddenly a new korshak image appeared on the terrace: a tall, sallow man in a book-lined room. He was wearing a glowsuit turned down low to a dark violet.

"Who's that?" Alex said.

"It's a narrowcaster image," Victor said. "I suspect we have another recruit."

"Wait a minute," California said. "He's looking right at us, but with no reaction."

"No wonder," Emily broke in, her voice seeming to come from a tall azalea in a full bloom. "It's Richard Abogado. He's a resident of Olympus Mons, on Mars."

"Hello," the image said. "This is Richard Abogado. There's a seventeen-minute time delay between Mars and Venus now, so please don't expect normal conversation. But I found this remarkable invention in the Database yesterday, and I want to learn more about it. Please respond."

Alex looked at California and grinned. "If we can merge with the Martians, we'll be on our way."

Beside the image of Abogado appeared another: Dwu-liu Carson, sitting beside his swimming pool and looking furious.

"I have a problem, my friends," he said. "The sellouts have managed to drop three comet nuclei out of orbit. They're coming down in two hours, and one of them is headed straight for me."

Seventeen:

The other two nuclei were aimed at the estates of Naznin Kelly in Ishtar Terra and Melissa Alvarez on Hathor Mons. Both were among the early members of the narrowcaster net; they soon reported in to say they had no intention of evacuating.

"We'll find out if your shardana bubbles really work," Naznin Kelly said to Alex. She was a magnificent brunette with an all-over dermograph that made her look like a golden idol.

"The bubbles will work," Alex promised her. "But just to make sure, we're going to try beams and missiles on the nuclei. They're too big to destroy, but we may be able to deflect them."

For the next hour he, Balthasar, and several other members of the net kept up a steady barrage on the nuclei as they dropped toward the dazzling haze of Venus. Alex watched ten of his missiles crash into the nucleus aimed at Carson; each vanished in a flare of white against the red-black surface of the nucleus. However, its mass was too great for nonfusion warheads. Emily predicted that the missiles had shortened the trajectory of the nucleus by only five or six kilometers; it would strike on the floor of Diana Chasma rather than directly onto Carson's estate.

"Use the beamers, too," Alex commanded.

"Pointless," Emily said calmly. "Besides, the converts are starting to shoot again. We need to defend ourselves."

The whole planet seemed to have gone crazy. Scores of cloudcastles, ground estates, and orbiting spacecraft were firing at one another—most simply to register opinions, but some to kill their targets. Alex, California, and McCool fought steadily and calmly. *Wuthering Heights* took over a hundred missiles and beams in half an hour, and Eros almost as many. Emily reported sixty resisters and almost two hundred converts engaged in combat. Alex, California, and McCool were too busy defending the spacecraft to keep track of the falling nuclei. The dissipators worked well at neutralizing the missiles, but the ship's energy reserves were barely adequate to maintain shield fields against beamers.

The korshak image of Naznin Kelly reappeared. "I'm buttoning up," she said. "Wish me luck."

Melissa Alvarez was next, a two-meter-tall woman who wore only a tiger-stripe dermograph and orange hair cascading to her hips. "I'm going to take a direct hit," she announced calmly.

"You'll be fine," California promised.

Like Carson's estate, those of the two women were built into cliffs with extensive views, but they were narrower and deeper, with most of their structures underground. Alex asked Emily to give him permanent korshak contact with all three estates while he continued to run the defense of *Wuthering Heights*.

The battles between converts and resisters seemed to be tapering off, as if both sides wanted to see the outcome of the comet strikes. A resister's cloudcastle took a multiple missile strike and broke up over Lakshmi Planum, not far from Naznin Kelly's estate. Balthasar scored a direct beamer hit on a convert's shuttle, destroying it within a few kilometers of its cloudcastle destination. But most of the other combatants paused, tracking the comet nuclei through their last few minutes.

Each comet was a roughly cylindrical mass about two kilometers across and ten to fifteen long, the property of some Venusian who had used it as a source of water and minerals. Now the nuclei were trailing thick yellow-brown clouds, steam mixed with the organics that gave them their color. Alex and the others aboard *Wuthering Heights* watched the nuclei curve around the nightside, dropping fast as their trails glowed brilliantly against the ashen light.

The nuclei were back on the dayside; from orbit, they were invisible to the naked eye, though their trails made hairline yellow streaks against the clouds.

"I'm closing up," Carson called. He was halfway up his atrium, looking out at the slow-moving lava at the bottom of Diana Chasma. Alex watched over Carson's shoulder via korshak, enjoying the view much more than he had in person. In the far distance, the air suddenly rippled; it was not another mirage but the cessation of the endless, sluggish wind of the surface. The atmosphere around Khanshoiar was trapped within a bubble.

"Thirty seconds," Carson said, watching a korshak image of the falling nucleus aimed at him. The atmosphere had been edited out of the image, so he and Alex saw only the explosive destruction of the surface of the nucleus. Friction with the upper atmosphere had burned away only a thin layer; the nucleus was skidding through the lower air, both insulated and lubricated by its own steam. Just before it struck, it broke into two unequal chunks.

The orange sky over Diana Chasma flashed an intense, featureless white. Almost at once the light dimmed and reddened, while thick tentacles of steam shot over and around the shardana bubble. The steam itself was invisible, superheated to almost five times the boiling point of water, but the organics it carried were a glowing orange. The air darkened rapidly as vaporized soil, rock, and lava erupted in a lightning-wrapped cloud. In ten seconds the sky over Diana Chasma was black yet filled with twinkling sparks of red and white: droplets of melted rock, burning like stars. The lava flowing at the base of the cliffs made a dim orange river; lightning flared constantly, illuminating a sky of twisting, rising clouds.

"Well, well. I'd forgotten I wouldn't hear anything," Dwuliu Carson said conversationally. "Makes it a little anti-climactic, doesn't it?"

"Be glad," Alex answered.

"It certainly looks better from space than it does here," Carson added, glancing at one of his own korshak screens.

Alex looked up through the dome. In the center of the planet's dayside three dark spots widened, gaining sharpness with every second as they rose through the dense atmosphere toward space. Shock waves from each strike were clearly visible, breaking up the familiar Y-shaped cloud pattern.

Naznin and Melissa were laughing and cheering. The nucleus aimed at Naznin's estate had fallen short by over forty kilometers. Ejecta from the strike had traveled almost fifteen kilometers before reaching the shardana bubble and flowing in unpredictable directions. Iceberg-size fragments were glancing off the surface of the bubble and piling up all around it. They burst violently and repeatedly in the shocked, superheated atmosphere.

Melissa had indeed taken a direct hit, and as the nucleus had struck, it had deflected from the nonspace surface of the bubble. Traveling almost straight up, it rose through the cloud decks above a column of steam and organic sludge. Within twenty seconds the nucleus was over a hundred kilometers high; it broke up, exploding into a monstrous red-black flower whose petals extended for hundreds of kilometers before sinking back toward the surface. Then it began to drift, drawn westward by the endless winds, until it formed a lengthening black scar across the planet's face.

"When are you going to turn your bubbles off?" Alex asked the grounders.

"Not for a while," Melissa answered. "Chunks of the nuclei will be coming down around us for at least an hour. Besides, the temperature at the strike points has gone up and down by a couple of hundred degrees."

Alex confirmed that with a glance at a readout: at each strike point, the compressed atmosphere had heated far beyond a thousand degrees; then, as the shattered cometary ice had absorbed that heat in vaporizing, the air temperature had fallen to just above six hundred.

"So if we pop our bubbles," Dwuliu Carson said, "all the atmosphere inside it will rise and we'll be in the middle of a real cyclone. At ninety atmospheres, I don't think we'd survive it."

"He's right," Naznin said. "Besides, if we just sit tight we'll worry the sellouts. By the way, are you still shooting it out up there?"

"It's died down," Alex said. Glowing numbers in the korshak screens showed no beamers active, and only ten missiles en route to targets. Eight convert grounders had been killed, but no resisters; in fact, two of the converts had been killed by overpressures from the comet strikes against their opponents. Nineteen convert cloudcastles had crashed, along with twelve owned by resisters; their ruins lay bubbling and melting on the rolling plains of Atalanta and on the harsh slopes of Maxwell Montes. Alex thought of the fall of *Munshaour*. The bottom of the Pacific was a gentler grave than any Venus could offer.

Others had died in space. Xanadu, a platform whose proprietor had been a convert, had suffered severe beam damage. It tumbled slowly through space, occasionally venting air or liquid through breaches in its residence sphere. No one was transmitting from it. Two converts had died in their shuttles; three orbiting steamships had taken direct missile hits in their residence spheres and were considered destroyed.

"We've got to end this," Alex said to McCool. "Every ally we lose means millions of molmac computers lost as well."

"I agree." The old man locked onto an incoming missile and destroyed it. "Let's get on regular korshak and see if we can start negotiations."

Korshak broadcasts were a jumble. Converts were frantically comparing damage in crude codes and trying to persuade neutrals to join them. The news from the cuckoos on Earth, however, did not help the convert cause. With equal cheer, they announced the peaceful takeover of Luna and the fact that deaths from allergies to gryphon toxins had risen to just over three million.

"The Pattern," John F. Kennedy said gravely, "is testing humanity."

He was standing in his office, as he had on the first morning of the invasion, wearing a light gray suit of antique cut. The decor of the office no longer appealed to Alex. "Three centuries of chaos have weakened our species," the cuckoo went on, "but we will emerge stronger than ever after this. Earthborn humanity has grown lazy and self-indulgent, insulating itself from reality. Now reality, the Pattern, has asserted itself. Only those humans who recognize and accept the Pattern will survive to reproduce a new generation—a new species. I have no regrets about those who are unable to meet the demands of the Pattern except by leaving it. They are making room for those who can. We estimate that the human population will be a hundred million within thirty years, and a billion in forty. By then, of course, many of us will be serving the Pattern in other solar systems. In a century, humanity will be established from one end of the Net to the other. In a thousand years, we will span the galaxy, serving the Pattern along with countless other species."

"What a disgusting idea," California said, but Alex saw a hint of wistfulness in her dark eyes. The memory of the Pattern's simple, deceptive beauty was still strong. "Alex, turn him off and call the converts."

Alex did so with relief. Kennedy and many of the other cuckoos made him nervous. He knew they were only imitations of their namesakes, yet they seemed even more real. They were not simply icons, colorized and computer-enhanced from ancient films and tapes; they were full korshak images, as vivid as the one of himself that was now going out to thousands of Venusians.

"This is Alexander Macintosh of the steamship *Wuthering Heights*," he said. "I urge everyone to cease fire at once. We're wasting lives." He paused. Would that persuade anyone? Was he dealing with *Homo sapiens* or with *Tyrannopithecus*? "We're destroying ourselves to no point. I want to call a cease-fire. If anyone wants to convert to the gryphons, go ahead; I won't attack you. All I ask is that you not attack anyone who wants to resist the invasion."

An angry man materialized in front of him, wearing a wispy red beard and the ornate uniform of a twenty-first-century Afrikaner general.

"You're even dumber than you look, Macintosh! The Pattern *wants* us to wipe you out, just like the molmacs on Earth are getting rid of all the resisters and weaklings."

"What about the converts who get killed by us?" Alex answered, but the image had vanished.

Emily's voice emanated from the terrace coffee table. "We've lost ordinary korshak, Alex. It looks as if the gryphons have blacked out Venus."

Other korshak screens hung in the air around the terrace, showing the views from Khanshoiar and the other bombarded estates. Alex gaped at them for a moment and then jumped to his feet. He grabbed California by the shoulders and hugged her.

"Hey!" she complained. "What's this all about?"

"They don't know how to black out narrowcasting! All they've done is blind their allies." He released her and howled with delight, his face lifted to the blotched, blackening face of Venus. "We're going to beat them! We're going to beat them!"

Without korshak, the converts could not continue the fight. A few launched missiles blindly, achieving nothing. The Venusian War, having lasted about three hours, was over.

That afternoon Alex convened a conference of the surviving resisters. They appeared to be sitting in a Greek theater on a sunny afternoon in ancient Attica, with the image of the current speaker appearing on the stage. It was an unusual group, Alex thought: seventy-nine Venusians, most of them flamboyantly dressed and dermographed, twelve visiting spacers, Richard Abogado and eight other Martians, and the residents of *Wuthering Heights*.

"First," Alex said, "we should break up into subconferences. Can we have reports in two minutes on the following: adequacy of individual defenses, extent of molmac merge, likely recruits among the neutrals, development of the merge on Mars and possible expansion to Jupiter and beyond, projections of likely gryphon strategy, any new Database discoveries."

The answers came back in much less than two minutes, and Alex winked at California and McCool when the data hung glowing on korshak screens before them. The others in the illusory Greek theater also shifted excitedly and murmured to one another.

The war had badly depleted everyone's arsenals, but molmacs were growing new missiles and beamer cells. Within two or three days everyone would be back to fighting strength and in a position to destroy every convert estate unless the gryphons lifted the korshak blackout.

Lord Whitehead—or his wild molmacs—reported that the merge was complete so far but would require exponentially more molmac computers.

—We are already the most powerful computer array in human history.—Lord Whitehead told them via comlink. Alex was pleased but unsurprised by the eagle's improved grasp of English.—So far we have spent most of our time in testing certain theoretical constraints on our capabilities and in exploring the Database. It is clear to us that we cannot expect the Chaiar to remain outside the Database for much longer. They already understand the source of the narrowcaster and the kuldi-field dissipater. They probably realize that enough information on Chaiar genetics and culture is available to give us further advantages. If they understand the access we may acquire to other parts of the Database, they are certain to take steps to forestall us.—

"What kind of steps?" Alex asked.

—Certainly a direct assault on Venus, one that would

attempt to wipe out all resisters. More significantly, the Chaiar may also attempt to gain control of the Database.—

Dwuliu Carson instantly materialized on the stage. "You can't gain *control* of the Database. All you can do is move around in it, and leave blazes, and move a little data around."

—We are certain it is possible to deny at least parts of the Database to others.—

"And if the Chaiar deny it to us?" California asked.

—We are acquiring relatively powerful intellectual capabilities,—Lord Whitehead replied.—Given time, we could undoubtedly develop practical countermeasures to force the Chaiar out of the solar system. However, we do not have time. Therefore, we must seek countermeasures in the Database.—

One of the floaters, a hard-faced man with Japanese features, took the stage. "How do you know the Database has anything really effective?"

—The Chaiar are not one of the more sophisticated species in the Net. We estimate that their key physical discoveries, such as rapid interstellar travel and steerable shardana bubbles, have been made by at least two other Net species, and perhaps as many as four. The relevant data are likely to be accessible once we understand the means by which they have been encoded in the Database.—

The meeting sank into silence. Everyone stared at the eagle, who appeared to be perched on the limb of a dead fir.

"Lord Whitehead," McCool said. "I certainly won't quarrel with your reasoning, which I'm sure is quite beyond our powers—as it's supposed to be. But I must question your conclusion. If some of the Net species have already invented starflight, *why aren't they here?*"

—We don't want to speculate on the motives of species that are by definition far more capable than we. The point is that we must maintain our access to the Database, and if possible keep the Chaiar out of it. To do so we require far more molmacs as well as a great many capable human divers.—

"Why humans?" several people asked at once.

—Some are better at making associations than we are. Eventually we may acquire a similar capability, but until then we will need humans like Fredrika Aalstrom.—

Alex glanced at Rik. She had slept through most of the battle and still seemed detached from the discussion.

—Victor is also very capable,—the eagle continued. —He has suggested a joint dive with Rik. We think it is a good idea.—

"I'll be glad to go whenever you like," Rik said. She looked at Victor, and the gryphon lifted a hand in assent.

—We have another problem, however. The merge has begun on Mars and will soon spread into the asteroids and beyond.—

Everyone looked at the images of Abogado and the other Martians, who were sitting patiently and waiting for the beginning of the conference to reach them.

—Time delays are inevitable in a merge on this scale, but we would like to minimize them. Therefore, we suggest that *Wuthering Heights* leave Venus for a point approximately midway between here and Mars. By the time we take up station, the number of Martian molmacs may be greater than those here on Venus. Each planet will have to work independently to some extent, with *Wuthering Heights* acting as a clearinghouse.—

Alex felt alarm. Orbiting Venus, with images of allies all around, he felt relatively secure. Out in space, somewhere in the orbit of Earth and Habrakha, the ship would be isolated. It was an irrational reaction, he knew. The Chaiar could attack here quite as easily as anywhere else and probably would before long.

"That raises a question," he said. "If we're attacked, we have the means to protect ourselves now by creating shardana bubbles. But a spacecraft would have to go into a complete bubble, and korshak doesn't transmit through bubbles. We'd have lost contact with Dwuliu and Naznin and Melissa if they'd formed complete bubbles."

—This will be a difficulty,—Lord Whitehead agreed. —But we don't foresee the Chaiar maintaining a constant bombardment of *Wuthering Heights* or anyone else. Intermittent use of shardana will be a nuisance, but a tolerable one.—

The conference went on with squabbles about recruiting neutrals and even halfhearted converts. Everyone agreed that the gryphons would soon launch a serious attack on Venus, one that would probably require shardana bubbles for survival. That posed problems for the floaters.

Their cloudcastles were not designed for spaceflight, but as soon as they were completely enclosed in a bubble, they would be free of Venus's gravity and would fall away from the planet into space. Lord Whitehead advised them to start growing space shuttles at once if they did not already possess them and to prepare for a switch to a spacefaring life.

—At least temporarily,—the eagle said.—Several dozen comet nuclei are still in orbit here. Especially if you share nuclei, everyone should be able to obtain adequate resources for several years' life in space.—

"If we wanted to be vacuum suckers, we'd have grown spacecraft already," one floater muttered. Beside him, a grounder snorted contemptuously. Alex saw a quarrel impending and moved to stop it.

"I suggest we pause for an hour to give our Martian friends a chance to take part. Thank you all for your help so far."

The Greek theater vanished, and Alex found himself back on the terrace overlooking the gardens, with California, McCool, Victor, and Rik sitting nearby.

"So far, so good?" he asked.

"I think so," Victor answered. "The war could have been much worse. If the Chaiar realize their mistake and restore korshak, the converts could start fighting again. But I think they'll be glad of a truce and some time to think. The resisters are pleased to have an edge, so their morale is high."

"What if the gryphons try something much worse?" California asked. "They could just give up on Venus and blow us all to bits, including the converts."

"Perhaps." Victor snapped the cartilage behind his beak, a sign of thoughtfulness or anxiety. "I think we can count on them to underestimate the problem we pose. They have gained control of the vast majority of humanity. The spacers are few and scattered. The Chaiar will understand the importance of narrowcasting, and they will start using the Database, but they will feel less urgency than we do about it. We should encourage them to believe that we are not a real threat."

"And if they do think we're a threat?"

"They may well destroy Venus."

Alex looked out through the dome. The black clouds formed by the comet strikes were trailing west in blurred triangles across the face of the planet. For all its terrible hostility to life, Venus had shown itself defenseless even against the limited power of humans; the Chaiar would have no trouble stripping its clouds and turning its surface to a sea of lava. Any Venusians who survived inside shardana bubbles could be safely left to rot.

He sighed and stood up. "Let's reconvene the conference. I want to hear what the Martians have to say."

A korshak screen appeared before him: the image of a woman in a simple white blouse, seated at a bare desk. Behind her was a window overlooking a broad plain under a pale overcast: the view of Los Angeles from the ramparts of Mordor.

"Hello, Alex," Lydia said. "I hate these interplanetary conversations, but I need to talk to you."

Eighteen:

She looked as cool and poised as ever, her thick blond hair pulled back into a simple ponytail, but Alex saw weariness in his mother's eyes.

"Mother!" he blurted. "I'm glad to see you."

Of course she did not respond. The signal from Earth, after all, was several minutes old.

"This little device is supposed to send a tight korshak signal," Lydia said. "And it came with a tag of Heathcliff at this setting, so I assume you planted it in the Database. If it works, I should be talking to you now, but I have no idea where you are. I'll leave the channel open for a reply. Just don't try to convert me."

Alex reflected on Victor's foresight. The gryphon had inserted a tag that Alex's friends would easily recognize but that would mean nothing to strangers like Dwuliu Carson, who had at first assumed Alex was a missionary for the Pattern. If Carson had known the provenance of the narrowcaster, he might have assumed it was just another gryphon trick. Alex wondered how many nines there might be in Victor's intelligence grid.

"Emily, send a summary of what we've been doing straight to my mother's computer. And explain that we don't believe in the Pattern."

"Of course, dear."

"Emily's sending you the whole story about how we were converted to the Pattern and then deconverted. As far as we're concerned, the war is still on. We're orbiting Venus, but we're about to leave. The molmac net is all over Venus, and now Mars, and the molmacs want to even out the response times. I assume you and Mao Jian and Lyell want to get back into the molmac net, too."

He could not think of anything else to say and waited self-consciously while the korshak signal crawled at the

180

speed of light to Earth. Meanwhile Lydia sat at her desk, rearranging freesias in a vase. After what seemed like an eternity, she looked up, smiling, and listened to Alex's message.

"There you are! Venus? I should have guessed. And as soon as I saw Heathcliff in the Database, I suspected you'd gotten over that Pattern nonsense. Alex, I'm so glad. You look fine. Hi, California. And Liam, too. Liam, you need to get more sleep. You look dreadful. Well, you're getting my technical data—and I see I'm getting yours. Maybe it'll include something I can use. I'm also sending you a survey of the conditions here on Earth, Alex. You're not going to like it.

"I'm under bombardment, and so are Mao Jian and Lyell. The gryphons like to show us being attacked on their broadcasts. It's not really a problem for us, but it's destroying the regions around us. Nothing's left alive for a thousand kilometers downwind of Mordor. The gryphons are *bragging* about how many people are dying. Not to mention the trees and wildlife—even the floating forests are dying. They've got the gardens on Luna full of their damned flowers, and some of their converts are almost to Mars. I feel so—helpless. If Mao Jian and Lyell would just find this tight-beam device so I could talk to them! It's maddening to *sit* here with bombs popping off every few minutes. Tell me something to cheer me up."

McCool spoke. "Lydia, my dearest, why don't you grow a spaceship, put a bubble around it, and take off?"

Alex frowned. The idea made sense. At least the Chaiar would stop destroying the region around Mordor, and Lydia could continue her research in space, secure behind a shardana bubble. While they waited for the reply, Alex heard briefly from the Martians, who reported a sharp expansion of their molmac net and the imminent arrival of two steamships bearing missionaries.

Lydia's response came suddenly. "Grow a spaceship? Liam, you really do need more sleep. I can't grow anything big enough to hold my labs and factories. They reach all the way out to the edge of the bubble now, and thirty meters down. I've had to tear down most of the ruins to make room for them. And I'm growing molmac computers by the billions."

Overhead, Lord Whitehead uttered a shrill cry of aquiline rejoicing.

"So I'm more or less stuck here, and I expect Lyell and Mao Jian are in the same bind. Anyway, now that we can communicate and the molmac merge is working again, maybe we'll figure out some way to stop the gryphons."

Alex was hardly listening. He stared at California and McCool in amazement. "Billions of molmac computers?"

"And factories that stretch for fifty kilometers?" California added. "I—Alex, your machine shops look big, and they're not much bigger than this house."

Glowing green letters began to scroll beside Lydia's image, a detailed summary of her activities, and Alex's jaw dropped as he read them. He looked at California and Victor, who were sitting beside him.

"Your mother's been busy," California said.

"Steerable shardana bubbles," he whispered. "Emily, get this all into the merge. And tell the machine shops to get to work."

Lord Whitehead, soaring overhead, broke in with a comlink command. —Open a channel to Mordor's molmacs.—

"Do it," Alex told Emily.

"Lydia was always an ambitious woman," McCool murmured. "I suggest we reconvene our conference, with your mother in attendance."

But by the time the Greek theater was filled again, the conference had little purpose except to ratify the molmacs' agenda. Lord Whitehead, back in his illusory dead fir, told the humans what had been decided.

—We need *Wuthering Heights* to relocate near Earth and Habrakha at once. Lydia's molmacs are now ninety-two percent of the net, so they will be our central unit. Venus, Mercury, and Mars will supply help as necessary. Everyone in the molmac net will use Lydia's methods of computer replication to expand their capacities as rapidly as possible. The Martians will also act as a clearinghouse for Jupiter and Saturn.

—Our concerns now are to explore the Database and to deny it to the Chaiar. With Lydia's computing power, we should make much faster progress than we had expected. It seems likely that human converts will renew attacks on resisters and therefore on us. We will require strong defenses.—

"How are we going to stay in touch with the rest of the

merge?" Alex asked. "Every time the gryphons attack us, we'll have to form a bubble, and korshak doesn't travel through a complete bubble."

—It will be a nuisance for a while. When the Chaiar realize they can't harm you, they will leave you alone. Even if they do not, we must stay within a few light-seconds of Earth. *Wuthering Heights* will be defending Mordor and the other estates, and may be attacking Habrakha directly as well.—

"Ah." The thought of his little steamship attacking a planet full of gryphons made Alex feel dizzy. "I hope you know what you're doing."

—The alternatives offer much less acceptable outcomes.—

"Emily," Alex said aloud, "please prepare for a launch to Earth as soon as possible. Lord Whitehead will give you the parameters."

He looked around the illusory Greek theater, at the scores of images: men and women, some of them centuries older than he, who for various reasons had agreed to unite in a war. In an ordinary war, Alex thought, you tested yourself, one to one, against your opponent's wits and technology and ruthlessness. A social war was almost a contradiction in terms. How could you tell who was really better when so many variables came into play? And who would trouble to fight if the chance of glory was so compromised?

Wars had been different in the old days, and few of the Venusians had, like William Macintosh, survived the short and ugly era of old-style mass wars fought with Net technology. That made it even harder to understand why they now willingly took part in a similar enterprise. They had committed themselves, even at the price of exposure of their secret technologies, to a struggle whose only precedent was the nightmare of the twenty-first century—and this struggle was not against other backward and frightened humans but against a vastly superior civilization. To do so required a kind of courage that bordered on the perverse.

Dwuliu Carson was visible in one of the lower rows, his blond curls glinting in the Greek sunshine as he listened to continuing reports from his colleagues. Perhaps, Alex thought, people who lived in ninety atmospheres of superheated carbon dioxide and who had just been the target of a comet nucleus were the only kind who would go against the Chaiar.

The next morning, while barn swallows flashed through the air feeding on mosquitoes, Alex, Rik, and Victor sat drinking coffee on the terrace. Venus was over half a million kilometers astern, and narrowcaster transmissions already had a slight lag. For the moment the air around them contained no korshak screens; the only icons in sight were of a stegosaurus and a triceratops lumbering peacefully about the garden paths.

"The molmacs want a combined dive today," Victor said. "With Rik and me guiding them."

"Is that all right with both of you?"

Rik nodded and smiled. She seemed a little more reserved since her earlier dives, as if the experience had changed her, but she lacked the long stare and slack jaw of the addicted. "I'm looking forward to it."

"Did the molmacs say what they're looking for?" Alex asked.

Victor snapped his cartilage. "They want us to go into the archives of First Stone."

Alex laughed and then gaped at the gryphon. "They're serious? First Stone?"

"Yes."

First Stone: oldest civilization in the Net, millions of years old, whose contribution to the Database was said to be vast yet almost unexplored. Other species had built whole civilizations out of the few scraps they had deciphered from First Stone, but no one even knew what First Stones looked like. They continued to add to the Database, and they received everything from the other worlds of the Net, yet their current data were as baffling as their most ancient. Divers who explored First Stone data returned with only dreamlike memories of disjointed images or with no memory at all of their dives. Now the molmacs proposed to learn what had baffled even the trolls and gryphons.

"When?"

"Right away," Rik said.

The computers that stored the Database were relatively large, about the size and shape of a human hand. Instructions for building them had been the trolls' first gift to Earth, but the instructions had not clearly explained how the Database actually worked. The computers appeared to tap into a field of information and to permit users to enter that field directly. Users could download information into other computers' memories, move data around within the field, and contribute more data. Within some areas, new information from the Net poured in without stop: Data from the trolls still came in, thirty years old and showing no sign that they were about to be conquered by gryphons.

Understanding the data was usually impossible. Within the trolls' part of the Database, for example, was the Blue Desert: a region where the black dots turned blue, each a slightly different shade, and none of them were accessible. After three centuries of exploration, the Blue Desert was marked with countless blazes and tags; all were records of defeat. The trolls had never bothered to answer direct questions about it. Several other species' input was almost totally inaccessible, although some of it seemed to be repeated in trollish data.

But the wild molmacs could dive; Alex had felt them in the Database, and they had seemed quite at home there. He wondered why they still needed human assistants—and how they proposed to master the knowledge of First Stone.

Rik and Victor lay together on the diving bed, with Alex and California watching from the doorway. McCool had been invited to witness the dive also but had refused. The Database unnerved him now.

The gryphon made no gesture of farewell; he simply pressed the dive patch to his forehead and slumped into a trance. Rik waved and smiled, then sank into the dive.

For a long time the two divers lay unmoving. Then Rik reached out and took Victor's hand. Her breathing quickened.

—Something has gone wrong,— Lord Whitehead said in Alex's head. —We have lost contact with them. Alex, we need you to guide us back to them.—

"All right," he said, but he felt a tremor of unease.

The molmacs were with him from the moment the dive began. He sensed them like an unseen crowd at his back, their voices part of the murmur and thunder of the Database. They trailed him as he followed Victor's blazes: a glowing orange oval, a scent of jasmine, a tiny image of a jade frog that Alex recalled from his father's holarium on *Munshaour*.

The trail led directly into First Stone territory, where the black dots in white space seemed to shiver and spiral. Other blazes appeared here and there, but not many.

Experimentally, Alex turned to enter one of the dots that Victor had blazed. The roar of the Database ended instantly; he was aware of silence, darkness, and emptiness. Yet something was moving in it, something alive . . .

He recoiled into the even white glare and rumble. Impossible. The whole hallucination around him was simply a way of organizing data; nothing could *live* in there. Yet the sensation had been intensely real.

—Go on, go on,— the molmacs whispered behind him. —We still have far to go.—

The blazes went for a long time in the nondistance of the Database and then stopped. Alex turned, the molmacs always at his back. Everywhere was the same: black dots in white space, shimmering and half forming patterns and images. Victor and Rik had entered a dot, but which one?

For no conscious reason he turned again, chose one, and moved into it. The molmacs swarmed close behind him, humming like bees. They were all falling into an enormous green and blue spiral whose eddies burned purple and yellow and black, forming subspirals of red and white. It was like tumbling into a galaxy or a molecule. Alex tasted salt, felt himself weeping far away on the dive bed, and fell faster toward one of the subspirals while the molmacs' hum turned to a roar and a howl.

—Victor! Rik!— His call seemed thin and weak compared to the deep growl of the spiral and the yell of the molmacs. Nothing answered him except the scent of jasmine, and he followed it into a subspiral of swirling greens and browns that changed to whites and blues. Can we get back out of here? he wondered, seeing an orange oval drift past. The molmacs were shrieking. Alex found another subspiral, and another within that. Colors coiled around him with the sheen of oil on water. White noise crashed in from all sides.

—Alex. Alex, can you hear me?—

It was Rik's voice, faint but close. He turned, turned again, and saw a tiny jade frog suspended in the polychrome tumult.

—Yes. I'm here.— He reached out and felt her not as

flesh under his hand but as a presence. Close by was Victor.

—How did you find this place?— Alex asked.

—It found us. It wanted us here,— Rik answered. —I think the Database is alive.—

The shriek of the molmacs abruptly ended. —We can go, go, time to, time to leave, time, homeward, we, we understand, yes, go, we understand, guide us back, back, guide us.—

—Come on,— Alex commanded, and they lifted up into the spiral, climbing like invisible bubbles in a whirlpool or sinking like stones in an undersea avalanche. But the spirals flickered, vanished for fractions of a second, and were replaced by glimpses of stars above strange horizons, of long green leaves rustling in the wind at twilight, of simple flagstones formed into a path past blue moss and running water.

Then they were out of the dot and back in the greater Database. Alex turned and found the blazed trail. They hurried along it, the molmacs chattering behind them.

—Stop.—

They paused, obeying the molmacs' command. A dot beside them opened, expanding into a sphere of darkness. Alex felt panic. Was it the dark chamber he had blundered into before, the one where something alive silently waited forever? No, they had gone far past that point, but this space contained something similar. He felt it emerge, invisible, powerful, and circle them like some great predatory fish. The molmacs hummed and moaned.

—Go, go, it knows us now, go, knows us, go.—

Whatever it was, it had disappeared into the white space. Alex felt his body, far away on the bed, curl up self-protectively against Victor's furry side. Liam McCool had said that the Database was only order; now Alex knew otherwise. It could defend itself and those of its users who knew how to free the entities that slumbered there.

One of those entities was free now, prowling the white space. If it found gryphons or humans diving for the secrets of the Database, it would expel them.

He turned and pushed toward the next blaze, seeking the exit and the sanity of the ship while Victor and Rik followed close behind.

Nineteen:

Wuthering Heights drove straight through the inner system, across the orbit of Mercury, toward Earth. Its destination was as obvious as the long contrail that lazily curved away under pressure of sunlight, but the Chaiar did nothing to stop it.

Day after day Alex and the others watched events on Earth. The gryphons' own broadcast korshak had already lost interest in the millions of deaths and dealt instead with the settlement of cuckoos in the new cities. Most were young people with names like Vladimir Lenin, Wolfgang Mozart, and Murasaki Shikibu, all of them delighted to be building the Pattern on Earth. But the narrowcaster, linked to the ship's telescopes, gave them a detailed picture of the plagues and wars that scourged the planet.

No native humans at all were alive in Kantali Sho, the island continent once known as Australia. Two small cities, one on the west coast and the other on the east, held a few thousand cuckoos. The great estates that had once gleamed in the endless sun of Kantali Sho's inner deserts were empty; half were bombed-out ruins. The deserts were dark with the leaves of molmac plants.

Most of West and East America was wrapped in smoke; the forests of the north were burning in the oxygen-rich new atmosphere. McCool looked at the smoking ruins of Jasper House and shrugged.

"Most of the planet was a wasteland to begin with," he grunted. "I did what I could to make my own place green again. Someday I'll go back and do it properly."

California swore and raged when she saw Bikini. The cuckoos had bombed it, leaving a crater thirty meters deep where her reefhouse had been.

"They've killed Belinda!" Alex winced away from her as she leapt to her feet. He had never seen her so furious, so dangerous. The feral glint he often saw in her eyes was brighter and colder. "They'll suffer for that."

McCool, unimpressed with her anger, laughed. "Eight million people dead on Earth now, and you're unhappy about your housekeeper?"

"And what about Brian Boru?" she spat back.

"I don't think Brian has met God just yet. He'd have had the wits to get away from the estate, and if he didn't, Sanjuro would have sent him off. If he does die, I'll keep him *gezera ta oue*, held in memory, as you keep your little seal."

But they had little enough time to watch the sorrows of Earth. The molmacs kept them busy in dive after dive, deeper into First Stone's mysterious archives and into other regions of the Database where humans had rarely ventured. Much of what they retrieved was not intelligible to the humans, or even to Victor. Almost none of it went into Emily's memory banks; huge as they were, they were inadequate for the quantities of data the molmacs brought back. Instead the molmacs themselves stored the data, using a form of narrowcasting to transfer it.

"I don't like that—thing prowling around in the Database," Alex said to Victor one morning at breakfast after a dive.

"The watchdog?" The gryphon nodded and smiled, showing his small, sharp brown teeth. "It's unsettling but very helpful." The inhabitants of *Wuthering Heights* were the only persons in the solar system who could use the Database for the time being. The entity they had released was capable of driving out anyone it did not recognize. That meant the Chaiar and cuckoos and converts could not go diving.

"I'd be happier if it recognized our friends. They could go diving, too."

"The problem won't last long. It's a price worth paying."

"But the gryphons must have the narrowcaster by now. Plenty of converts learned about it. What if the gryphons black it out? Then we'll all be back where we started."

"A tight korshak beam can't be blacked out, only blocked in the line of sight. Actually, it should be helpful for them to have it. We may find the Chaiar more flexible if they can negotiate in private, without all their dependents listening in."

Alex's eyebrows rose. "Negotiate? What is there to negotiate?"

Victor uttered his metallic laugh, like a gong being softly struck. "We may be able to persuade them to leave us alone for a few days. Otherwise, if they attack us and we have to use a shardana bubble, communication will be hard for the molmacs."

"And what good will it do us if the Chaiar cooperate?"

The gryphon looked at him. "The molmacs believe they are very close to developing several new weapons. One is a family of deconversion molmacs for the Chaiar."

Alex thought for a moment. "Even if we could get the stuff to the gryphons, I don't know if it would work. They'll never stop believing in the Pattern."

Victor laughed again. "Because it is true?"

Memories of exuberant tranquillity rose in Alex's mind and were followed by sadness. "Because it ought to be true, and they wouldn't know how to live without it."

"Chaiar are good at phase transitions. We breathe air; we breathe water."

"Can you breathe vacuum? That's what it felt like when you deconverted us."

"I'm not worried about stressing them, Alex. The real problem will be getting the new molmacs into the ecosphere of Habrakha."

Alex looked into the gryphon's unreadable eyes. "You really mean it. You think we can change the gryphons? Make them give up the Pattern?"

"Yes. But that won't be enough. We will have to deconvert all the Chaiar and all the species they have conquered."

Alex put down his coffee mug on the mobile beside him hard enough to make the robot flinch. "That's absurd."

"Perhaps. But simply eliminating the immediate threat is pointless. The Chaiar will send another planet, and yet another if need be. If they can't conquer us, they will destroy us. One way or another they will eventually win. We are in the position of the natives of ancient Kantali Sho and America. We can win against individual invaders but not against their combined strength."

"Well, how are we supposed to overthrow an interstellar empire?"

The gryphon's dark eyes gleamed without expression. "I am still thinking about it. So are the molmacs. We may find answers sooner than you think. The merge is expanding very rapidly. Most of the neutrals on Venus and Mercury have joined us now."

"How did they get narrowcasters if the Database is closed?"

"By electromagnetism. For some purposes it is very effective. Meanwhile the Venusian converts are quiet. I think they expect the Chaiar to eliminate us without any help from them."

"What about the Mercurians? They seemed to be pretty doubtful about the Pattern."

"Most arc still neutral. About four thousand have agreed to merge. Only a few hundred are pro-Chaiar."

"Four thousand! That's wonderful." Something Victor had said now sank in. "You said most of the neutrals on Venus have joined us. How many?"

"One hundred and twenty-two thousand. We have another eighty thousand on Mars and about six thousand so far in the asteroids and the Jovian system. But Lydia's molmacs are still the largest single component of the merge."

Alex gaped at him. "How long has this been going on?"

"You slept for almost fourteen hours after your last dive. Most of the new merges have occurred in the last ten hours or so. Humans can be good at phase transitions also. We have so much support that a large fraction of the merge is dedicated to managing the data flow. Each planet is operating as a subsystem, with its own specialized assignments. Lord Whitehead is coordinating them."

"So the supermind is working out the way Liam said it would."

"Yes. But we appear to have very little time. I believe the Chaiar have decided to wipe out almost all native humans and replace them with cuckoos."

"What?"

"Eight million on Earth are dead now. Another million are sealed inside their estates, and the rest are suffering from the changes in the atmosphere. Almost no one is still alive in the new cities except cuckoos. In another six months Earth's original ecosystem will be destroyed."

Alex looked up at the dome, which showed a false sun in a false blue sky. At a silent comlink command it cleared, revealing two small, bright disks and a third still smaller, hanging in darkness.

"I don't like what this has done to me," he said quietly. "I started out just wanting to take care of myself, like any normal person. Then I worried about other people, like California and my parents. Then they killed my father, and I found I cared about him. Now they're killing everybody, and I'm angry about people I don't even know, people I probably wouldn't even like if I did know them. If feels ... unnatural. Almost the way the gryphons must feel, living all piled together in their cities."

The gryphon beside him said nothing.

Mao Jian and Lyell Bradley rejoined the merge a day later. At unpredictable intervals each rendered his shardana bubble transparent to radio and television, and Lydia managed to send them the details about the narrowcaster. Like her, they had grown a great many molmac computers during their seclusion, but each had pursued his own interests with them.

While nuclear weapons had rained down around him in the mountains of Mexico, Mao Jian had developed a missile whose drive and warhead were the same: a carefully unbalanced V-tap. In the microsecond of detonation it released about two hundred megatons from the virtual field within a sphere five centimeters in diameter. Each missile was about the length of Mao Jian's index finger and could in theory attain a speed of three thousand kilometers per second.

Lyell Bradley meanwhile had designed new molmac computers; they were fewer than Lydia's but more powerful. He seemed less concerned about them than about explaining to California what had happened to her mother just after the invasion.

"We went back to her place," he explained, rubbing the port-wine stain on his cheek. "She was more upset about your leaving than she admitted, and a little scared also. I tried to encourage her to get to work on her defenses, but I guess I wasn't very, uh, persuasive. Anyway, she hasn't fought a serious war in ages, and I think her factories weren't really adequate. She probably thought so, too. Finally she decided to pause and told me to leave. So I left." He looked uncomfortable. "Now I wish I'd made her come here with me."

"Don't feel bad," California said. "Mother always does things her own way. She couldn't stand being somebody's guest for more than a day or two, and she'd have driven you crazy. She's probably better off where she is."

When her words reached Earth a few seconds later, Bradley looked unconvinced. "I hope so. But not many people are still alive in Japan these days."

"Well, Mother's not alive—she's paused. You'd have to give her a direct hit with one of Mao's new missiles to hurt her."

"Oh, I don't know. The missiles they're using on us are pretty good."

Alex, looking at Earth from a distance of just a few million kilometers, could see what Bradley meant. The cuckoos were steadily bombing all three shardana bubbles. The Indian Ocean around Free Acres, Bradley's estate, was dead—a boiling radioactive soup. Poisoned clouds drifted far eastward; even some floating forests were dying from the fallout. Mordor and Castillo Paricutín stood amid similar devastation. The fallout from southern California had killed everything in a broad belt reaching clear to Florida, while central Mexico was equally dead and the islands of the Caribbean were dying.

"How long can you take the bombardment?" he asked Bradley and Mao Jian.

"Indefinitely," the warmaker answered. "The generators for our shardana bubbles are V-taps like nothing you've ever seen before."

"But eventually the insides of the bubbles will be too hot to live in."

Mao Jian smiled ferociously when Alex's objection reached him. "About thirty thousand years. A lot longer if we want to live like Venusians."

"What about the world around you? How long will it last at this rate?"

Lyell Bradley nodded somberly. "Not as long as we will. What isn't poisoned will end up growing those molmac plants. Our estates are virtually all that's left of the original ecosystem."

"Not that that means much," Mao Jian growled. "We've really made a mess of this planet in the last hundred years or so. Outside the estates, it was already a desert."

Thinking about the old pre-Contact films and holograms, Alex realized that Mao Jian was right. The world then had been green almost everywhere. Great jungles had stretched across the ancient nations of Brazil and Zaire, where now laterite desert stretched orange and wrinkled like scar tissue from burns. Even the barren slopes of the Giuliu Tuo, the Rocky Mountains, had been thickly forested, and the seas had teemed with fish and whales. The whole world had looked like someone's estate; then it had been gouged and seared to make fifteen million little domed paradises.

"The gryphons don't seem to care what they do to it," he said, "as long as they keep your heads down."

"I know," Bradley said. He looked very unhappy. "I don't know what we can do, unless the molmacs find something soon."

Earth and Habrakha loomed large and bright in the dome; *Wuthering Heights* was only two light-seconds away. The gryphons' world was blue and white and dark green; Earth was turning gray and dun. The continents lay blurred under a haze of smoke. The cuckoos were using meteorography to divert the fallout of ash and acid rain from the burning forests, so each new city stood out with strange clarity.

It was late afternoon; Alex, California, and Victor sat in the living room talking about the latest bad news from Earth. Rik was on a dive, and McCool had gone for a swim with Heathcliff.

Emily's voice sounded silently in Alex's head. —I have a message coming in from the Chaiar.—

He looked at California and Victor. "The gryphons are calling. Shall I talk to them?"

"Yes," California said at once. "But just you. Don't show them anything but yourself."

"Fair enough. Emily, have you got that?"

"Yes, dear."

A wall of holograms vanished, replaced by the korshak image of a great room whose stone walls rose to form an arch overhead. Alex remembered the living room in his father's house. This room's floor was tiled in blue and gray, forming patterns that reminded Alex of the Database. The room seemed dark; a few pale beams fell from unseen windows high up, illuminating two seated figures.

One was John F. Kennedy, dressed in a blue cloak of a type fashionable fifty years before. He looked gaunt and angry, older than he had appeared a few weeks earlier on Alex's birthday.

Beside him, and much larger, sat a male gryphon. His black fur was silvered, and his nasal horn had spread up around his eyes and over his forehead: signs of age but as artificial as McCool's wrinkles. The gryphon wore an open-weave garment like a white fishnet, covering his long torso without concealing his osmotic membrane. Unlike Kennedy, the gryphon seemed relaxed.

"I believe I'm speaking with Alexander Macintosh," Kennedy said.

"You are." Facing the cuckoo and the gryphon, Alex felt himself, his self-awareness, concentrating in a point just behind his eyes: a warning of rage struggling to break free.

"I am John F. Kennedy. The Chaiar with me is Tsaunghok. He represents a group called the Explicators. They analyze the workings of the Pattern. You could say they're the government. Tsaunghok wants to know why you have broken away from the Pattern."

Alex said nothing at first, while California and Victor watched him. Then: "Does anyone ever leave the Pattern?"

"In a sense you're right, of course. But you're resisting the will of the Explicators. You've led others to resist, and you've fought and killed people who have recognized the Pattern. Many people have died because of you."

Alex's laugh was an angry bark. "High praise, coming from you."

Kennedy looked pained for a moment. "You're also associated with the three resisters in the shardana bubbles. They're causing serious damage to Earth."

So Victor had been right: The Chaiar wanted to bargain. "The damage will stop when you quit bombing them."

"The damage would increase if we stopped. You are engaging in forbidden communication, and you have somehow closed off the Database. None of these things will really hinder the Pattern, but they make our work needlessly difficult."

"You didn't call just to complain. Get to the point."

"You were part of the Pattern once, and you can be again. Explain your actions, and we may be able to restore you to harmony. If you do not explain, we will destroy your ship and your allies."

"That threat failed to work on my father. It won't work on me."

Kennedy's tension suddenly seemed to evaporate; he flashed a dazzling smile.

"All right, then, Alex. Would you please tell me what you're up to? Just to satisfy my curiosity."

"I'm traveling around the solar system, visiting friends."

"And fighting wars."

"When they're forced on me. Let me ask you a question, John. What will happen if you kill off all the native humans on Earth? Will you abandon the invasion?"

"We don't expect many more Earthborns to die. In any case, we'll have the population up well over fifteen million again within a few years. The terraforming is going well, so in a couple of decades you won't even know these difficulties ever took place."

"Except that native humans like me won't be able to breathe the air, and your molmacs may still be fatal."

"That issue is out of my hands."

"Then I won't waste my breath about it. You say you want to know what I'm doing. If I did tell you, what would you give me in return?"

"That would depend on what you told us. If you wanted to observe what's happening on Earth, we might give you a day or two in exchange for access to the Database. If you wanted to try to interfere with the terraforming or attack our new cities, of course we would give you nothing."

"Well, I intend to go into orbit around Earth and to communicate with my mother and friends. I have no intention of attacking your new cities or your spacecraft unless I am myself attacked."

"If you reopen the Database, we will give you forty-eight hours. After that, if you have not broken the terms, we will allow you to depart Earth orbit in peace."

"I'm not in a position to reopen the Database."

Kennedy looked unhappy again. "You're not lying, but you're not telling us everything."

"Nor are you. If the Database is that important to you, I'm sorry."

"I presume you are searching the Database for information to use against us."

Alex did not answer. They would get enough of a reply from analysis of his nonverbal responses.

"If you find it convenient to search while in Earth orbit, we will have to inconvenience you. You have four hours. Either change your mind about the Database or change your trajectory. Otherwise we will destroy your ship."

—Try to stall them,— Victor said over the comlink. —Every hour is valuable.—

Alex was shocked, first by Victor's use of the comlink and then by what seemed to be advice to bargain in bad faith. His first impulse was to reject Kennedy's demand and invite him to do his worst. That was how William Macintosh would have reacted. Alex reflected that his father had indeed reacted that way and had shown the folly of it. Victor's suggestion made sense.

"I'll give you my answer in four hours."

Again they sat in the Greek theater, squinting in false sunlight. Rik had come up early from her dive; McCool sat beside her. Dwuliu Carson, Richard Abogado, and scores of other spacers crowded the illusory seats, while Lord Whitehead perched on a dead tree on the hillside beside the theater. On either side of the podium on the stage, korshak screens poured out images and data.

This time the audience also included Lydia Korolyeva, Mao Jian, and Lyell Bradley. They sat together in the front row next to Alex and California, showing no sign of anxiety or impatience as the time lag between planets stretched out the meeting.

Alex had opened the meeting by explaining the Chaiar's offer and asking for advice. While the message went out to Venus, Mercury, and the outer planets, he talked with Lydia and the others on Earth.

"The molmacs scarcely bother to talk to us," Lydia said. "They seem to be on the edge of a breakthrough— maybe several."

"Are they still talking about a way to deconvert the gryphons?" Rik asked. "All my dives seem to relate to gryphon molecular biology."

"Mine are into shardana physics and things I don't even begin to understand," California said. "But none of it seems to relate to the gryphons—just First Stone and a couple of other species I never even heard of before."

"Lord Whitehead," Alex said. "Can you explain what the molmacs are looking for and how much longer they're going to need?"

—No.—

"Do you mean you can't or you won't?"

—Won't. You are in contact with the Chaiar. What you know, they may learn.—

"Who's fighting this war, anyway?" Alex snapped. "If we can't even be trusted—"

"He's right, Alex," California said. "That's why I didn't want them to see anyone but you. The more they see of us, the more they can deduce about what we're doing."

"In fact, Emily ought to transmit an icon of you when you talk to them again," Rik said. "A fuzzy icon."

His indignation faded. The women made sense. Of course humans had the right and obligation to fight duels and wars with only indirect aid from computers, but this was not really fighting yet—it was just the maneuvering, the foundation of deception and ruse every combat required. Still, it made him uneasy that so much of the preparation for war was concealed from him and his human allies.

Was it concealed from Victor as well? He looked at the gryphon, whose short golden fur gleamed brightly in the sunshine.

"How much do you know about what's going on? Do you have a sense of what the molmacs are doing?"

"A fairly good sense. But they're right to keep their progress secret for now."

California leaned toward the gryphon. "Given what you know, Victor, should we offer to let them back into the Database? Will forty-eight hours be enough time for the molmacs to develop something solid?"

"I think they will need more time than that."

Around them the spacers had received Alex's opening message and had caucused briefly. Dwuliu Carson appeared at the podium, dressed in a black luminar tightsuit.

"We and our molmacs think you should reject their offer, Alex. It's a nuisance that we can't get into the Database either, but we understand why. Our molmacs are happy with the material you've been sending by narrowcaster, so tell the gryphons they don't have a deal."

Richard Abogado replaced Carson at the podium. "We

agree. I'm worried that if the gryphons get back into the Database, they'll figure out a way to keep us out of it for good."

"Good, but consider this," Alex replied. "If we're attacked and we go into a bubble, we'll lose contact with everyone. Korshak doesn't go through a complete shardana bubble. If we tune it to transmit TV, they'll jam us. So as long as the attack goes on, we'll be blind, deaf, and mute. That means we'll need someone else to take over the coordination of data flow for as long as we're sealed off. Any suggestions?"

It felt odd asking advice of other people instead of simply doing what one felt like doing. How had the ancients ever fought wars like that—or kept the peace?

—It doesn't matter, —Lord Whitehead said over the comlink. —We have adequate resources for the time being to enable us to function as independent subsystems. If you must go into a complete bubble, you can tune it to very narrow optical wavelengths and randomly vary them. That will allow you to monitor events and to send short messages via laser to Venus and Mars.—

"Emily, can you handle that?"

"Of course, dear." Emily's voice seemed to come out of thin air just above their heads.

"This is going to be like no war I ever heard of," Alex said. While he waited for the signal to reach the planets, he asked Lord Whitehead what needed to be done in the next three hours.

—Dives.—

—But we're certain to be attacked soon. I've got to be ready for combat.—

—Dives. You must dive. Time is short.—

Alex looked at California, Victor, and the others sitting in the theater and felt something like dread.

Twenty:

Dizzily, Alex swung his feet over the edge of the dive platform and stood up. The dive was fading from memory like a strange dream. "How much time do we have left?" he asked hoarsely.

"Thirty-three minutes," Emily replied out of nowhere.

California was pulling the dive patch from her forehead and standing up as well. He reached out and took her hand.

"We have to get ready. Come on."

Arms around each other, they lurched down the hall and into the living room. Fred Astaire and Ginger Rogers were dancing across the polished marble floor again. Oblivious to the icons, Victor, Rik, and McCool spoke quietly to korshak images of Lydia, Mao Jian, and Lyell Bradley.

"Just in time," McCool said. "The gryphons are dropping a bomb or photon probe on the bubbles about every ten seconds."

"It was easier to take when we couldn't see what was happening outside," Lyell said. He looked wretched.

"They've destroyed all of southern California and half of Mexico," Lydia said. "The fallout from here is lethal all the way to the Mississippi. Assuming anyone's left to be killed by now."

"Where are the bombs coming from?" McCool asked.

"Robot factories all over the planet. The gryphons' molmacs are producing a nuclear missile every thirty seconds. Mao Jian's little missiles could do something, but he'd be destroyed the moment he detuned his bubble to launch them."

"So all we can do," California said, "is sit tight until our molmacs come up with something so we can fight back."

"Not quite," Lydia said. "The gryphons understand us

pretty well, but maybe not well enough. They think they can blackmail us by threatening to kill our planet. It's not going to work." She paused. "Alex, we are going to do something. It's going to be terrible, and I hope you're not angry with us about it."

"You will *not* kill yourselves!" Alex roared. "The molmacs won't allow you."

His mother's smile was sad. "No, we won't kill ourselves. But not much else will survive. We're closing our bubbles." She reached out, as if to touch Alex's face. "Good-bye for now, dear. I'll talk to you soon, I hope. If not, we'll hold each other in memory."

The transmission broke off. Alex stared at California, not sure he had actually heard what his mother had said. Before he could speak, Emily announced a message from Habrakha.

"Put it through," he murmured. "Send them a bad icon of me."

John F. Kennedy had exchanged his blue cloak for a black and white luminar tightsuit. He stood in the same dim room, one hand on the back of the chair he had previously sat in. A few steps away, Tsaunghok sat unmoving.

"Hello, Alex," Kennedy said. "May I have your answer?"

"Emily, seal off the ship."

The room darkened instantly; then the lights came up. California threw her arms around his neck and kissed him.

"Come outside," McCool said gently.

They all walked out onto the terrace, with Victor looming behind them. Beyond the dome was blackness relieved only by a distant cluster of tiny lights.

Alex looked at it and groaned. "Don't tell me we've got another steamship inside the bubble!"

"No, you dunderhead." California laughed without pleasure. "That's the reflection of *Wuthering Heights* on the inside of the bubble, thirty or forty kilometers away."

"Get back inside, dears," Emily said out of nowhere. "It's not safe out here."

Obediently, they went back into the living room. Alex was just as glad. The thought of being enclosed in a bubble made him uncomfortable, though he could not understand why it might be dangerous to stand on his own terrace.

"Just in time," Emily said. "You were very wise to

close us off, dear. I've kept a little window open. The bubble's transparent up in part of the ultraviolet, so I can see something of what's going on, and we just had a dreadful hit by some kind of beamer. If you'd stayed outside, you'd have had a nasty burn and maybe even a touch of snow blindness. I hate to think what it would have done to us without the bubble."

"Are they still shooting?" McCool asked.

"Not at the moment. Now, dear, we're falling out of the solar system. Would you like to set a course and speed?"

"Put us between Earth and Habrakha," Alex said. "If the molmacs come up with something, we should be as close as possible."

"Of course, dear. I can give you a rather poor image from the UV window if you like."

"Please." A korshak screen sprang to life in midair. A fuzzy, recolored image of Earth appeared, with Habrakha like a ghost image beyond it. "I'm afraid that's the best I can do," Emily apologized.

"It's fine, Emily. Just keep it centered on Earth. On West America if you can."

Alex reached out for California's hand. "Do you understand what my mother and Mao Jian and Lyell are going to do?"

She nodded, her dark eyes wide. "They're going to wreck Earth."

None of them spoke more than a few words. Emily summoned Lord Whitehead. The eagle perched on a chandelier and looked down at the screen. Rik and McCool sat together on a couch, close to Alex and California. Heathcliff lay on the floor, thumping his tail nervously.

"Lord Whitehead," Alex said, "does this have to be done?"

—They can stay within their bubbles indefinitely. But the ecosphere of Earth is close to collapse. A few more hours of bombing would leave the planet uninhabitable, except for the cuckoos' cities. Even they would have to be sealed off. The longer your mother and the others stay on the surface, the worse the damage. When we defeat the gryphons, we will be able to rebuild the surface if it does not suffer much more harm.—

The screen showed West America from the ocean to the Hakitan Tuo—the Sierra Nevadas, William Macintosh had always called them. The region around Lydia's bubble was black and orange, a burning landscape whose flames were intense enough to blaze through dense clouds of smoke and dust. The flash of a photon probe twinkled painfully.

"Increase the magnification, please," Alex ordered.

"The image will blur badly if I do."

"Then widen the window. Give us some visible spectrum."

"If they beam us again, dear, we could all be blinded. Including me."

"Randomize it—do anything you like, but give us a clear image."

The computer obeyed, and suddenly they were looking down at Mordor from an apparent height of fifty kilometers. Emily enriched the image based on the random millisecond glimpses she allowed herself. The hemisphere of the bubble was hard to see; it reflected the smoke and dust around it. The screen went black.

"What's the matter?" Alex demanded.

"Another nuclear strike, dear. I blocked out the image until the light intensity drops a bit. I'll edit out the cloud, too."

Before Alex could answer, the image returned. The terrain of Los Angeles was unrecognizable, a scorched wasteland on all sides. But from the southern reaches of the San Fernando Valley to somewhere south of Westwood, the shardana bubble still held. It was fully opaque, a curved mirror of the devastation around it. Alex imagined the bubble far below the surface, gradually extending its rim through kilometer after kilometer of rock until it became a complete sphere and everything within it was severed from Earth's gravity—

Without warning, the boundary of the bubble revealed itself in a thin, curving curtain of glowing red, a curtain that rose rapidly into the tormented atmosphere. Its mirror image rose beside it, curving up the reflective surface of the bubble.

"She's cut loose," McCool. "Praise God."

The bubble, a single curved plane of nonspace, extended twenty-five kilometers into the crust of the planet, where the rock was red-hot and rivers of magma slowly flowed. The image seemed to blur as Mordor, free of gravity, lifted into space at a thousand kilometers per hour.

Where it had been was a hemispherical pit fifty kilometers wide and twenty-five kilometers deep.

The atmosphere had been compressed and sundered by the passage of Mordor; now it crashed back into the wake of the bubble. The shock waves were clearly visible from space, rippling across West America and the ocean. They would be powerful enough to topple the remaining forests, to shatter estate domes, to trigger hurricanes.

Air whirled into the pit, dragging with it dust, rock, and debris from many kilometers away. Everything that touched the glowing stone of the pit became heated and rose in a violent pillar of red and orange fire. More air rushed in, colliding with the pillar in a ring of tornadoes that rose and merged with the superheated air climbing through the stratosphere. The burning pillar darkened and spread into a vast mushroom cloud that pulsed with lightning.

On the west the bubble had intersected the coastline at the crumbling cliffs of Santa Monica. There the rim of the pit began to slide. Layers of stone hundreds of meters thick collapsed toward the glowing bottom, but only the largest chunks could keep falling through the turbulently rising air. The rest, like hailstones in a thunderhead, rose, fell, and rose once more.

Through a gap that rapidly spread from a few meters to five kilometers or more, the Pacific Ocean burst into the pit and began to fall toward the glowing rock far below. But it could not fall far. The hurricane of inrushing air lifted millions of tons of water into the burning pillar, where it flashed into steam and exploded.

The shock was too strong even for the pillar of fire. Superheated steam cut across the pit, blowing hundreds of cubic kilometers of air, dust, and rock eastward toward the poisoned deserts. Emily could no longer reconstitute the image of the terrain beneath the cloud; Alex and the others saw only the boiling, glowing chaos of a vast *nuee ardente*. Something like that burning cloud had rolled down the sides of Vesuvius to destroy Pompeii and Herculaneum, and something like it had destroyed St. Pierre on the island of Martinique. But this cloud rapidly spread until it was moving on a front over two hundred kilometers wide.

To the west, the shock held back the inrushing ocean for a few seconds; then it fell once more, only to rise again in a still greater explosion. Insulated by its own heat, the bottom of the pit glowed dully through the haze of debris that whirled in from all sides and then blew out again with each detonation of steam.

"Emily." Alex's lips moved, but it was a moment before he could speak. "Show us Mao Jian's estate."

The mountains of central Mexico, shattered by hundreds of nuclear bombs and photon probes, lay under a thick cloud of burning dust much like the one burying Los Angeles. The walls of the pit were collapsing rapidly, changing the perfect circle into a growing, irregular oval as whole ranges of hills slid twenty-five kilometers down and then, shattered into rubble, shot into the roaring air again. Enormous canyons, themselves several kilometers deep, extended in all directions from the rim of the pit.

"And Lyell's."

The Indian Ocean was on Earth's nightside, but moonlight reflected brilliantly on the white plume of condensing steam high in the stratosphere. Free Acres, Lyell Bradley's estate, had been surrounded by water, which poured in from all sides before vaporizing and rising to the edge of space.

With light enhancement, Emily could show the flooded coasts of Madagascar and Africa; soon the tsunamis would strike Sri Lanka and the Indian subcontinent. The lights of a cuckoo city glowed where Colombo had once stood; soon it would disappear, Alex realized. The waves would circle the world many times before they calmed. He wondered what would happen when they struck West America and forced still more water down into the pit where Mordor had been.

Rik was leaning against McCool, one hand to her face. The old man looked dazed. California put her arms around Alex's shoulder and held him while she shivered. Only Lord Whitehead and Victor seemed unmoved.

"That's enough," Alex said thickly. The korshak screen vanished.

"Emily, please give me a projection of the consequences."

"Of course, dear. The atmosphere will become almost opaque within ten days. Several million tons of dust have already been injected into the upper atmosphere, and that should continue for months or years. Fires are burning all over the planet because of lightning strikes, and the hukhung plants are providing a great deal of fuel, so the dust is mixing with a lot of smoke. Of course, the extra oxygen in the atmosphere is helping things along. In thirty-six hours the air temperature under the clouds will drop by fifteen to twenty degrees. In ten to twenty days the whole planet will be twenty-five to forty degrees colder than it now is."

"That means the northern hemisphere will be below zero—and it's summer there," California said.

"Yes, dear. The southern hemisphere won't be quite as cold because of the oceans, but Argentina and southern Africa will still be awfully chilly, I'm afraid. I wish I could tell you when conditions will normalize, but I'd only be guessing. The craters will induce much more volcanism all around them, and that means even more dust in the atmosphere."

"So Earth is going to freeze," McCool said quietly.

"Oh, in some places, Liam," the computer answered. "The oceans will stabilize temperature to some extent. But I really have no idea what will happen once the craters in West America and the Indian Ocean fill up with seawater. Sea levels will sink a little, of course, and with more land surface exposed we'll see a sharper drop in air temperatures." Glowing green numerals and graphs hung in the air for a few seconds. "But we'll also have some very hot water in the craters, and that should help warm the air."

"But the craters won't stay that deep," California said. "They're already collapsing."

"In five or ten years they won't be more than ten kilometers deep, I should think. And the crust will rise around and under them. Between volcanism and collapse of the crater walls, they'll be almost back to normal in a few thousand years."

"So Earth is going to be buried under a mix of dust and ice," Alex said. "Almost nothing on the surface is going to survive."

"Some of the domed estates and the cuckoo cities should do all right," Emily answered. "As long as their kuldi generators keep working, it hardly matters whether they're on the surface or a kilometer underground."

Alex paced restlessly around the living room. "Give us a look at Earth again, please."

It was far worse than the image of Venus under the

comet strikes. The clouds streaming away eastward from Mordor and Castillo Paricutín were dark gray, shot through with sparks of red and flaring with lightning. Much of West America was invisible beneath the rapidly spreading dust, and the Mexican cloud had reached well out into the gulf. On Earth's nightside the lights of the cuckoos' city on Sri Lanka were gone. The coastlines of India seemed subtly different: The first waves from the Maldives were reaching far inland, while new ones, hundreds of meters high, crashed down on the drowned shores.

"I've had to edit out most of the water vapor," Emily apologized. "The whole Indian Ocean is simply covered in clouds, and it's raining very, very hard all the way from Africa to central India."

"Are you tracking the shardana bubbles?" Alex asked.

"Oh, yes. Mordor and Castillo Paricutín are heading for Habrakha, too. Free Acres is circling Earth."

Alex wondered what kind of strategy the three of them had devised. Or had the molmacs devised it?

"Lord Whitehead," he said, "what are the molmacs doing? We're all moving toward Habrakha, but what do we do when we get there?"

The eagle groomed himself. —We are working on several possibilities. Be patient.—

"*Patient?*" He kicked over a small round coffee table; a mobile rolled forward to set it up again and then retreated, probably, Alex thought furiously, because Emily had ordered it to. "I want to fight a war, not be patient! We've just seen Earth destroyed. Isn't it about time you damned molmacs actually *did* something besides give orders? I want to blow a hole in Habrakha, poison the gryphons—anything!"

—Keep on our present course, Alex,— the eagle answered calmly. —Everything will work out. Meanwhile, we could use some more dives.—

Without a word, Alex took California's hand. "Come on," he said. "At least in the Database *they* have to follow *us.*"

The dive was brief, a plunge into yet another corner of the great white space. The watchdog had circled, recognized them, and vanished. The molmacs, buzzing behind them, had seemed pleased with whatever information Alex and California had found.

They were back on the dive platform, peeling off their dive patches. "Let's go for a swim," Alex said wearily. "Not in the ponds—in the pool downstairs."

Much of the basement of the house was a single room, filled with a pool more like a stretch of tropical river; in a series of tight curves, it stretched for almost three hundred meters, lined with reeds and bamboo. The bottom was fine blue-gray gravel mined from Luna; springs rose here and there, stirring the gravel. Countless fish darted through the crystalline water: neon tetras gleaming red and blue, glowlights with bright orange stripes, gouramis reflecting gold, orange, and white, transparent glass catfish. Water plants rippled in the current, and frogs chirped and croaked in the reeds.

A false sun blazed overhead in a cloud-dappled sky. Naked, Alex and California swam and drifted on the current. Where the water shallowed over fine white sand, he waded out and sat, arms on knees, on a grassy bank. California sat beside him. Her olive skin and black hair glittered with thousands of droplets.

"Something's gone wrong," Alex said.

"I know. We're supposed to do the fighting, but the molmacs have taken over."

He sighed. "Liam said to build a supermind, and it just sounded like a big computer. I never thought it would decide things for itself. It's—maybe it'll even make a deal with the gryphons. It doesn't seem to care a lot about us. Did you ever look at holos of ancient China?"

"Sometimes."

"Fishermen on the rivers used to train birds called cormorants to catch fish. They'd put rings around the birds' throats so they couldn't swallow what they caught. I'm starting to feel like that. We dive for the molmacs, but they keep what we catch." He remembered that cormorants, like most birds, were extinct, but he did not mention it.

California leaned against him, warm and comforting. He put his arm around her and wondered why physical presence had ever made him nervous.

"Now we're literally flying blind," he went on. "Maybe they'll find some new weapon, and maybe they won't. And maybe the gryphons will figure out a way to punch a hole in our bubble." He drove his bare heel irritably into the sand. "I'm going to have to take the buttons off and show the molmacs we're still in charge."

"Good," California said. "But let's do it right. All the humans together, and Victor."

"All right. Emily, would you ask Liam and Rik and Victor to meet us in the living room in about ten minutes?"

The computer's voice seemed to come out of a lily pad. "I'm sorry, dear, but Victor wants you to stay where you are for the time being."

"What? Emily, don't be silly. Just pass the message and send a mobile to pick us up."

"Dear, you and California are to stay at the pool until Victor tells me you can come up."

He looked at California. "Emily, this is Alex. I'm *ordering* you to send a mobile to pick us up. I'm *ordering* you to bring Liam and Rik—"

"Well, I'm evidently not making myself clear," Emily said sharply. "Victor has taken charge of this ship. I obey his orders now, not yours, dear. Now, please enjoy yourselves and don't worry about a thing. If you get hungry, the pantry down there is full."

Through his surprise Alex felt something else, something more important: If he responded wrongly, he would be just another childish proprietor throwing tantrums at his life-support systems.

"Emily, let me talk to Victor."

"He's much too busy, but he told me he'd speak to you in a little while."

"All right, Emily. That'll be all, thank you."

"You're welcome, dear."

Alex gripped California's hand and ran with her toward the nearest door. It led up to the main floor of the house, and it was firmly shut. He gritted his teeth, remembering his father's fondness for old-fashioned "appropriate technology" like doorknobs.

"There's an elevator at the far side of the pool," he said. They ran down winding paths among the reeds while the false sun shone down and the frogs croaked. The elevator doors were shut and would not respond to commands.

—Victor! Liam! Rik, Heathcliff! Get us out of here!— California's comlink cry was sudden and shocking, but Alex realized it was necessary.

—I'm locked in my room,— McCool answered.
—What's going on? Where's Alex?—

—I'm with California at the pool. Rik?—

—I think she's on another dive. Do I have your permission, Alex, to knock down this door?—

—If you can. But Victor seems to have taken over the ship. If you get out, you'll have to deal with him.—

—I'll deal with him, all right.— For a few seconds McCool was silent. Then: —You built this place too well. I can't even scratch the paint.—

—Be silent.—

The command had come from Victor. Alex responded instantly.

—Victor, I order you to release us all. This is my ship.—

—My name is not Victor. I am Bhrukang, a Chaiar and part of the Pattern. We are on our way to Habrakha.—

Twenty-one:

If they had ever had a hope of winning, Alex thought, it was gone forever. Perhaps McCool's idea of a computer supermind might have worked, but the gryphon had been involved in it from the beginning—subverting it, turning it to the purposes of the Chaiar.

Victor had been wise to give them enough rope. The spacers' alliance and the molmač merge had been a demonstration of just how well humanity could resist the Chaiar: a demonstration controlled and guided by a Chaiar at every point.

"We should have thought about Rik," he muttered.

"I know," California said. "Give a cuckoo the chance, and it'll go to its own species. But Victor's so—human. He deconverted us. He found the narrowcaster."

"Well, we were fooled. But now it's buttons off."

"What do you mean?"

"We can't win, but maybe we can make life a little harder for them. Come on."

He led her back toward the knobless door they had tried a moment before. On the way he listened to his comlink and heard only white noise. Tentatively, Alex tried to communicate with California, right beside him, but the hiss only intensified. He felt a mixture of admiration and despair: If Victor could jam comlinks, he understood them better than humans did.

The door was set in a wall, a little over two meters high and seemingly of brick, which ran all around the room. Above it was the illusion of a sunny sky. Alex ran his fingers along the wall, feeling the smooth fome that the wall was really made of. About a meter to the right of the door he found a small button and pressed it. A panel swung open, revealing a dark space within the wall.

"Ventilation shaft," Alex explained. "It'll be tight, but it'll get us out of here."

"What's the plan?"

"Emily's got a manual panel up in my office. If we can get to it, maybe I can override Victor and take the ship back. If that works, we'll head for the Neptune Belt or deep space."

"And if it doesn't? How do you know Emily isn't listening to us right now?"

Alex smiled. "I don't. Come on."

He clambered up and into the shaft. Once inside, he could brace himself easily against the walls. California followed.

Warm air rose from far below, ruffling their hair. Light falling through the open panel let them see where they were going for a couple of meters; after that the darkness was almost absolute. The shaft walls were smooth but not slick, enabling them to slide easily upward.

The ventilation system laid itself out in his imagination. This shaft ran up through the mobiles' garage, past the auxiliary kuldi generator, and past the dive room and then branched out to the various rooms on the second floor. The main shaft continued upward, branching again on the third floor and eventually opening into his office on the fourth.

As they climbed, Alex remembered sulking about his father's advice to soundproof every room in the house. "Your systems will be noisy at best, Alex After a few months in space, a squeaky hinge or a hum in the korshak will drive you mad." Alex had obeyed his father if only to end the nagging, and he rejoiced that he had. The thumps and scrapes they made seemed noisy, but Alex knew they could not be heard just a few centimeters away.

Or would it matter? Emily could well be tracking them, reporting to Victor every few seconds. Alex could only hope that both the computer and the gryphon were distracted by the ship's normal demands.

They had to be up at the level of the dive room. Was Rik still in there, obediently retrieving some new scrap of data? How would she react when she learned the truth?

Higher still: the bedroom floor. McCool might still be trying to kick down his door, but no sound reached the shaft. The third floor: studios, the dueling pit, recreation rooms. The air seemed very warm, and sweat was soaking through his shirt and shorts. He could hear California's breath coming a little harder.

The fourth floor: his office. He rehearsed what he would have to do—the sequence of keys to hit, the commands that would override Victor's. Emily might well sound an alarm the instant she saw him move to the keyboard. What would his fallback response be?

He ran quickly through a few possibilities: A dash to the shuttle would be pointless since it, too, was trapped inside the bubble. If they could reach the drive unit, they might be able to blow the ship up. Barricading themselves in the machine shops might buy them enough time to build a weapon of some sort. None of them made any sense. If he could not wrest back control of the ship through the keyboard, he would have to kill Victor.

With a single quick shove, he pushed the access panel open and leapt into the office. In three strides he crossed the room, put his hands on the keyboard, and began to tap it. California was right behind him, her breath loud in his ear.

"No good," he muttered. The keyboard failed to come to life, no korshak screen materialized, and Emily did not respond. "Quick, downstairs."

The carpeted stairway did not betray their footsteps. To Alex the house seemed strangely silent and menacing and no longer his. Later on he might relax with a burst of sorrow and anger, but for the moment his warwiring kept him focused.

The door to the dueling pit was open, and inside all was in order: the foils, epees, and sabers neatly racked, jackets and masks hanging on pegs, and framed holos of Alex and California glowing on the walls.

"We'll have to try to kill him," Alex murmured softly.

"With swords?"

"I know, I know. It's ridiculous fighting for a steamship with these things, but what else do we have?"

She took down her favorite foil, sliced it through the air, and checked the charge dial in the pommel. Then she pulled off the button, exposing a tip so sharp and narrow that it was hard to see.

Alex chose a saber and peeled off the blunting strip that ran from guard to tip. Beneath it was an edge of fome-carbon composite that tapered to a thickness of little more than one molecule. It was capable of slicing through a meter-thick log. Like California's foil, the saber also carried a shocker; even a stray tap with it could knock out an opponent. Alex wondered how well it would work against a gryphon.

"Spares?" he asked.

California shook her head. "We won't have time to draw twice. Now we've got to find him."

"On the main floor. In the living room or the dive room."

"Are you all right? You're sweating."

"I'm fine—just upset. You?"

California shrugged. She, too, seemed tired and sweaty. Alex reminded himself that not long ago they had surfaced from a dive. He wondered if her ears were ringing as his were.

They made their way downstairs again, past the wide hall onto which the bedrooms opened. Alex paused for a moment at McCool's door, pressing a hand against it, but felt nothing. If McCool was still trying to get out, the door was resisting his best efforts.

Rik's room was open and empty. They moved down the wide stairs to the living room, Alex a few steps ahead of California. If Victor immobilized his first opponent, the second might have time to attack.

"Hello, Alex. California. Come in."

The gryphon's deep, resonant voice showed no human emotion; it never had. Alex reached the bottom of the stairs and saw Victor sitting in his usual chair, his legs oddly crossed, his dark eyes unreadable as always. The gryphon was wearing a black T-shirt and shorts much like Alex's. His short golden fur gleamed in lamplight.

Alex sprang from the last step, saber up, and collapsed onto the carpet. The sword, falling from his fingers, sliced deeply into an overstuffed armchair.

Every muscle in his body seemed to be in spasm, knotting and cramping. He tried to draw breath but could only gasp silently and ineffectually. After what seemed like a very long time, California sprawled across him. He felt her shivering against his back, heard her panting for air.

"Your molmacs have flooded your bodies with lactic acid," Victor said. "It will wear off quickly."

Out of the corner of his eye Alex saw mobiles glide over the carpet, delicately withdrawing his saber from the chair and plucking California's foil out of the floor. He almost felt like laughing despite the agony that filled his body: a bold charge, with swords drawn, when the enemy was not only within the gates but within the blood. Even the molmac computers in their bodies were part of the merge, obedient to the will of the billions of other components of the supermind. And the supermind was obedient to the will of a gryphon.

"We are now approaching Habrakha," Victor said. "Emily is already sending them a message. Once the Chaiar receive it, I will detune the bubble and we will take the shuttle down to the surface of Habrakha."

Alex forced his jaws and tongue to work: "Taking—us?"

"Yes. It's clear that the Chaiar do not fully understand human psychology and culture. Your behavior wasn't prepared for. I think they'll learn a great deal from you."

"Convert—us—again?"

"I doubt it. You do have genuine molmac antibodies that would keep you from converting. In fact, we will have to keep you all in a sealed environment to prevent allergic reactions. That seems to be the cause of the die-off on Earth, by the way. Many people's molmacs considered ours to be an infection and overreacted. Again, a unique human response."

The cramps were easing slightly, enough to enable him to slide out from under California and ease her into a more comfortable position on the carpet. Her teeth were clenched, and tears gleamed on her cheeks.

"Get me up," she demanded. "Get me up."

Painfully, Alex pulled himself to his hands and knees, slid an arm under her shoulders, and lifted her. She locked her arms around his neck and let him pull her to her feet. They swayed together, exhausted, until Alex guided them both to a long couch. Not until they were sitting did he taste blood and realize that he had bitten deeply into the inside of his cheek.

"You might as well kill us," Alex said hoarsely. "Kill us now. Because if we ever get a chance, we'll destroy you, Victor."

"Your own molmacs will prevent that. Please, Alex, understand that you are simply two more parts of the Pattern. You had your parts to play, and you still do. But the parts have changed."

Emily's voice came from somewhere overhead. "Bhrukang, dear, we have a reply from Habrakha."

"We'll take it here, Emily."

Once more they looked into the high, dim room. John F. Kennedy was gone; Tsaunghok and three other gryphons stood motionless, looking at them. Tsaunghok spoke in his own language, and Victor replied—a little hesitantly, Alex thought. One of the other gryphons spoke up, and Victor answered again. The gryphons raised their hands, palm out, in some kind of salute. Then the korshak images vanished.

"The Explicators have accepted us. Emily, you may completely detune the bubble and resume normal drive. Please take up station ten thousand kilometers sunward of Habrakha and ask Charlotte to get ready for a flight."

"Of course, dear. Will everyone be going?"

"Yes, Alex, California, Liam, Rik, and I will all be going."

Alex leaned against California, drawing comfort from her presence. He kissed her, tasting the salt of her sweat and tears. She saw blood on his lips and gently touched his face.

"You're hurt."

"Doesn't matter. Be fine in a minute." Ignoring the gryphon, he stroked her long black hair and closed his eyes. "Not much of a fight. At least we registered our opinion."

"Yes."

Victor looked at them. "I hope you understand that your molmacs will stop you every time you try to resist."

"Yes," Alex said. Then he looked at the gryphon. "You said we were all going. What about Lord Whitehead?"

"Lord Whitehead is dead. The wild molmacs resisted, so I had no choice. I regret it."

"He was so beautiful," California whispered. "You'll have to clone him, Victor."

"Perhaps."

"What's going to happen to my mother and Mao and Lyell?"

"I don't know. They're maintaining their positions. If they detune their bubbles, they'll be destroyed. Would you like to see what Earth looks like now?"

"No," he muttered.

"I can give you an estimate of the dead."

"No."

"As you please. Emily is packing for you. I'm going to

be busy for the next while. Would you like to go upstairs to rest until it's time to leave?"

"We might as well," California said.

"Rik is just coming up from a dive. Perhaps you should explain to her what's happened."

"All right," Alex said. He and California rose awkwardly to their feet and tottered arm in arm out of the living room down the hall. Rik was just sitting up, her dive patch pressed to Emily's reader beside the platform. She smiled and then saw their expressions.

"What's wrong?"

"The gryphons have won," California said. "Come on upstairs. We'll explain."

The explanation did not take long. Alex could see sweat break out on Rik's forehead as they climbed the stairs and walked into his bedroom. He remembered the warning symptoms he and California had felt before their attempted assault on Victor. "Don't try anything," he warned her. "Your own molmacs will stop you. It's not pleasant."

Rik sat heavily in a rocking chair. "Does that mean we can't even talk about anything?"

"We can talk," he said. "Unless we start plotting against Victor."

"Did Victor explain what he meant about the wild molmacs resisting?" Rik asked. "I thought they were all merged into the supermind with everyone else's."

"So did I," Alex answered. "But they must have managed to hold on to some independence. Fat lot of good it did them. Poor Lord Whitehead—he was just their host, after all."

"So now the only resistance is the bubbles."

California sprawled across Alex's bed, ignoring the mobiles that were quietly removing clothes from his closets. "If you can even call it that. The instant they detune and start shooting, the gryphons will pulverize them. If they're smart, they'll give up and leave the solar system."

Alex, standing by the windows, looked down at the gardens and sadly shook his head. "Mother would never do that, and Mao Jian's a warmaker. Lyell might pause himself and head for the stars, but he knows the odds against survival." Then he raised a hand to his face in silent horror.

"Maybe the molmacs are already in control inside the

bubbles. They were part of the merge until they closed off completely. Victor could have planted some kind of virus."

"Then why haven't they detuned the bubbles and destroyed the three of them?" Rik asked.

"They wouldn't need to detune the bubbles," Alex said.

A tall figure entered the doorway: McCool. He was dressed in spotless white trousers and a loose black shirt, and he looked truly old. He walked in a little unsteadily and settled into an armchair.

"I take it we've suffered a reverse," he said with an attempt at a grin. "When I couldn't get out of my room, I tried to blast my way out, and the next thing I knew I was all doubled up and God was inside my every limb and organ."

Alex explained what had happened. McCool listened with interest.

"Very resourceful of you to get into the ventilation shaft. Too bad Victor or Bhrukang or whatever he calls himself must have foreseen something like that. But he's good at foresight, isn't he?"

"Better than we are," Alex growled. He felt a brief impulse to rationalize, to say that defeat had been inevitable when resistance was left to a handful of young people with few resources. But something stubborn in him refused to admit it. Maybe Lydia and the others were still safe, after all, and planning a counterblow. Maybe on Habrakha the Chaiar would reveal some unexpected weakness, and maybe he could work out some way to defeat his internal guardians.

The mobiles had finished packing without once consulting them: Emily would have told them what to take and what to leave. Alex walked restlessly about the room, working out the last of the cramps. Strange to think that he would probably never see that room, that house, that ship again.

"Heathcliff."

"What?" California said.

"I've got to say good-bye to him." His comlink still carried only white noise. He went out into the hall and down the stairs more slowly and awkwardly than he had a few minutes earlier. The others followed him. "Victor, where's Heathcliff? I've got to say good-bye."

The gryphon had not moved from his chair. "I believe he's in the gardens, Alex. Please be quick. Charlotte will be ready for launch in about twenty minutes."

All four of them went out onto the terrace and down the wide flagstoned steps into the gardens. The dome overhead was clear; Habrakha loomed close, with Luna beyond it. Earth was a mottled gray and white hemisphere just above the horizon of the gardens. Part of its nightside was visible, blotched with glowing red dots that must have been enormous fires burning straight through the pall of smoke and dust.

Alex pulled his eyes back to the garden. It looked consolingly normal, with sunlight pouring warmly in from low over the boundary hedges. A mallard and his mate lifted quacking from a pond; barn swallows, their bronze breasts gleaming in the sun, swooped and circled. A breeze stirred the long branches of a willow tree and made the tulips nod.

"Heathcliff?" Alex shouted for the dog but got no reply. It was odd when Heathcliff had always been as close as the comlink.

The Labrador came walking slowly up a path from his favorite pond. But he was not wet; he seemed despondent, barely able to wag his tail. Alex squatted and rubbed the dog's silky ears.

"You can't even talk to us," Alex muttered. "I'm sorry, Heathcliff. I wish we could take you with us, but you still have to look after this place." And all its traitor molmacs, he thought bitterly. "Did Victor change you the way he did Emily?"

The dog growled.

"Too bad, it would've been kinder. Well, you still have a job to do. I know you'll do it well."

The others all patted Heathcliff, who whimpered and licked them. Then Victor's voice carried like a gong across the gardens from the terrace:

"It's time to go."

Slowly they returned down a gravel path, Heathcliff whimpering and growling at Alex's side. McCool slapped at himself. "I wish Victor joy of your mosquitoes," he said.

"I should've brought in more swallows and martins."

"Or left them all out of your ecology," the old man said. Mosquitoes danced around Alex's head; he waved them away. They had been an amusing eccentricity once, when he had been young and governed by his whims. Now they were only an ironic comment on his triviality. Humanity had enjoyed its Net-given powers by reverting to childishness, and it had learned how fatal it was to remain children.

Twenty-two:

    Wuthering Heights had a new master, yet everything ran as before. They took the elevator down from the residence sphere and then glided in free fall down the tunnel to the shuttle hangar. The robots in the workshops along the way still chirped their greetings, and Charlotte welcomed her passengers as always with fresh bread and cookies.

    But she spoke chiefly to Bhrukang and asked after Alex as if he were merely a guest. He answered her briefly and civilly and wished his comlink worked. How did he do it? he wanted to demand of her and Emily. You're mine, mine—how did he steal you from me?

    They took their seats; korshak screens sprang into existence. If the blackout still functioned on what was left of Earth, *Wuthering Heights* had been exempted from it. Alex watched the red-black surface of the comet nucleus fall away as the shuttle launched and then saw four gryphon shuttles approaching to escort them to Habrakha. The iridescent white ships gleamed against the blackness of space.

    Bhrukang regarded the screens with his usual calm; Alex supposed he was communicating with the escort via comlink or some completely different means. He showed no interest in his passengers.

    Alex looked away from the screens, down at the worn Oriental carpet. It was a relief in a way to have no further responsibility. Perhaps the war might go on, perhaps the spacers would cobble together some kind of resistance; it was no longer his concern. He could not even contemplate an attack on Bhrukang. In a strange sense he was freer than he had been as proprietor of *Wuthering Heights* and leader of an alliance. Then he had had to consider consequences before acting; now someone else took that burden and he could simply relax and observe events.

The flight was uneventful. They ate sandwiches, drank coffee or tea, and watched Habrakha grow larger on the screens. No one said much. The escort shuttles stayed on station, two ahead and two astern.

Thirty minutes out from Habrakha, one of the leading escorts vanished in a dazzling flash. Then the other one exploded.

Bhrukang tensed; Alex heard the gryphon's nose cartilage click sharply. A new screen appeared, showing two bubbles reflecting the clouds and continents of Habrakha.

"We're under attack," Bhrukang said quietly. "It appears Mao Jian has found a way to launch his V-tap missiles through his bubble."

McCool laughed. "What do you mean, *we're* under attack? You're the target, not us."

Alex looked at California. She had said almost nothing since boarding the shuttle, but he saw that feral glint in her eye again.

"Two shuttles in two seconds," she murmured. "That's the best anyone's done yet."

Then the two following shuttles blew up. Bhrukang scarcely seemed to notice; he was evidently deep in communication with Charlotte or the gryphons on the surface. The images on the screens changed very little, but the orientation data changed rapidly and constantly: Charlotte was using evasive maneuvers, hurling herself randomly about.

The bubbles of Lydia and Mao Jian were closing fast, on a vector that would bring them alongside the shuttle within minutes. Bhrukang contemplated them for a time, then spoke.

"We will pass through Habrakha's bubble in three minutes."

"Assuming we're not vaporized by then," McCool murmured.

"If I must, I can create a bubble and tune it to Habrakha's resonance. That would take some time, however, and we are expected to land within the next half hour."

So he had even built a shardana generator into Charlotte. What else had he done? Alex wondered. What had he found in his Database dives that he had given to Emily without allowing her to share?

Abruptly, a new korshak screen appeared at the far end

of the dayroom: Mao Jian, looking cheerfully grim on a terrace of Castillo Paricutín. Lights burned somewhere above him; beyond was only darkness. Mao Jian might be sending korshak and firing missiles, but his bubble admitted no light.

"Alex, hello." The warmaker, plainly dressed in a dark cotton shirt and baggy jeans, waved a salute. "And everybody else. Mind telling me what's going on?"

"We are landing on Habrakha," Bhrukang said. "I have taken charge of *Wuthering Heights* and this shuttle. I suggest you surrender at once, Mao Jian."

"Alex, can you confirm what he says? You're not in charge?"

"It's true."

"Victor's gone over to the gryphons?"

"He calls himself Bhrukang now. Yes."

"So you're prisoners. Victor, you have thirty seconds to change course and return control of that ship to Alex Macintosh. Otherwise I will destroy it."

"It would take longer than thirty seconds to do so, Mao Jian. In fact, if you do not close off the hole in your bubble in less than ten seconds, one of our weapons will find it, and your estate will become uninhabitable."

Mao Jian's korshak screen vanished and was replaced by an image of his bubble, still matching the shuttle's course. Habrakha loomed closer. No screens showed hostile missiles, though Alex suspected that thousands of gryphon weapons were prowling outside the planet's bubble.

"We've passed through the shardana surface," Bhrukang said. "Mao Jian is dead. We inserted several photon probes through the aperture he put in his bubble."

A moment later, the image of Mao Jian's bubble disappeared in a flare of red and orange as it struck the surface of Habrakha's bubble. Colliding, they had exchanged energy: Mao Jian's had absorbed too much to hold and evaporated. The hemisphere of rock within, fifty kilometers across and twenty-five thick at the center, disintegrated on contact with the vastly larger bubble around Habrakha. The atmosphere and water held within Mao Jian's bubble spread outward in jets and filaments of white cloud. As they dissipated, a dull red starburst of shattered stone spread slowly across the black sky.

"The same will happen to your mother and Lyell if they try to open their bubbles," Bhrukang said calmly. "Each bubble is now surrounded by small missiles."

"My mother will probably assume something like that. I don't know if it'll stop her, though."

"I hope it does. I'm very fond of your mother."

Charlotte presented an image of Lydia's bubble, veering away with unbelievable speed, heading back toward Earth. She had evidently given up the fight.

"Poor Lydia," McCool said. "An admirable woman in all ways. She deserved better." He brightened. "Perhaps she'll crash herself into Earth. Not a bad way to join God and cause more trouble."

Better, Alex thought, than vanishing in a cloud of red-hot rocks as an entertainment for the gryphons.

He looked at his companions. McCool seemed poised and relaxed, sipping coffee from a china cup; Alex had half expected him to demand whiskey and get drunk. California had retreated within herself. Rik sat silently, a hand to her chin as she watched the lands and seas of Habrakha growing closer and clearer.

"Does it look like home?" Alex asked her.

"No. *Wuthering Heights* is home. The only one I ever had."

The descent from space was much like any other, with occasional patches of turbulence. Continents sprawled across the korshak screens, tan and green and blue; storms hung motionless over the great oceans. As the shuttle curved halfway around the planet, Earth rose over its horizon. It showed only cloud, gray, black, and white.

"It looks like Venus," California said. She touched Alex's arm as if seeking reassurance. "Maybe that's all we're really good at—messing up planets."

"Not as good as the gryphons. I wonder how Dwuliu Carson is, and all the others. Maybe their parts of the merge are still working."

California shook her head.

A few minutes later the shuttle glided over a tawny desert, crossed a shallow green sea, and descended swiftly toward a chain of large islands. The screens showed a complex network of roads linking compact cities of clustered gray towers. A city standing by a wide bay was their destination. The shuttle circled and dropped onto a landing platform at the top of a tower.

Alex sank deeper into his chair; the gravity was about the same as the .9g of *Wuthering Heights*, but now they were actually on the gryphons' world. They would have no chance of escape. The gryphons would keep them in a prison within a prison, feeding and amusing them while probing their minds for clues to the botched invasion. Eventually they would be of no further use, and the gryphons would dispense with them.

Bhrukang stood up, his fur slightly puffed out. "Welcome to Habrakha," he said.

"I hope you'll all be patient, dears," Charlotte said, projecting an image of herself standing on the Oriental carpet. "The gryphons would like to recycle the air in here a few times to acclimatize you to outside. It shouldn't take long."

Alex scratched absently at an itch on his neck while a light breeze blew through the dayroom. He wondered if their new quarters would give them an Earth-type atmosphere or the thin, overoxygenated air the gryphons liked. The air already had a faintly acrid scent, something like the smell of Bhrukang himself.

"All done," Charlotte said with a smile. "If everyone would leave by the main door, the gryphons are waiting for you."

"Good-bye, Charlotte," Alex said.

"Good-bye, dear."

Tears stung his eyes, and he felt himself flushing with helpless anger. Without even a struggle, he was walking away from everything: from his shuttle, from *Wuthering Heights*, from his mother, from humankind, from the dying Earth. Not even his body was his own anymore; he could kill neither his enemies nor himself.

Beyond the shuttle door was a small, dimly lit room furnished sparely with a few seats. As the gryphon and humans entered it, a doorway slid shut behind them and the room lurched slightly. Alex realized it must be a vehicle of some kind transporting them to their final destination.

A korshak screen glowed against one wall; the image of Tsaunghok appeared and spoke with Bhrukang for a few moments. Then the screen vanished. The vehicle tilted slightly as if descending a ramp and then leveled out again.

"A pity they didn't provide windows," McCool said. "We have no opportunity to be impressed by our masters' architecture."

"We are not trying to impress you," Bhrukang said. The vehicle halted without warning, and the door slid open to reveal a larger, somewhat brighter room with pale gray walls. It was furnished with four plain beds, a table, and four chairs.

"This is where you will stay for the time being," Bhrukang said. "Maybe I will see you again."

"Good-bye, Victor," Alex said.

"My name is Bhrukang. Good-bye."

The door slid shut. Alex turned and studied the room. It seemed needlessly small, no more than six meters by four, and was without ornament of any kind.

McCool settled onto a bed. "Very firm. We'll no doubt sleep well."

"It's like the place I grew up in," Rik said. "But that was bigger, and ten of us lived in it."

"Is there any way to look outside?" California asked.

"I'll see." Rik spoke in Chalar, her voice deep and resonant. At once, one of the short walls turned transparent. Sunlight flooded in.

Squinting in the glare, they walked up to the window and looked out. Below was a sheer drop of at least a hundred meters to what looked like a narrow strip of forest. Only thirty or forty meters away, another tower rose out of sight. Its smooth gray walls were broken in places by windows like the one they were looking through, but no gryphons were visible in them. To the right, they could glimpse a narrow sandy beach and sunlight glinting on green sea beneath a pale sky; to the left, other towers blocked the view.

"This must be Chon Sodhar," Rik said. "It means 'Green Gulf.' It's where the Explicators live."

Alex turned away and walked the length of the room. He felt like laughing at the sheer banality of it all: landing on a planet from another star and seeing only anonymous towers and a bare room. A door at the far end led into a small bathroom much like the ones that antiquarians installed in their estates: a shower, tub, sink, and toilet.

It was primitive but gave a shred of privacy. He closed the door, sat on the toilet seat, and put his face in his hands. A whole steamship could sometimes be too small for human groups; in this box, he and the others would go mad. Mao Jian had been lucky.

His hands came away damp; the cubicle was stuffy and

warm. Alex stood up and spoke to the sink. Nothing happened; he fiddled with the taps until water gushed from the faucets. Without hesitating, he cupped some in his hands and drank it. The taste was faintly sweet. If the gryphons had not sterilized it, too bad. He washed his face, enjoying the coldness.

McCool thumped on the door. "Come on, Alex. The Explicators want a word with us."

A korshak image filled much of the wall opposite the window: Tsaunghok and John F. Kennedy. The gryphon's fishnet tunic was yellow this time, and the cuckoo wore gray slacks and a dark blue pullover. Both were standing in the old-fashioned office Kennedy had used in his first message to Earth.

"Welcome to Habrakha," Kennedy said with a faint smile. "I'm sorry your facilities are so cramped. We didn't have much time to set up a quarantine for you. You'll move into your personal quarters in a few days."

No one said anything.

"Tsaunghok—and I—would like to discuss your resistance to the Pattern. Your motives, your methods. It's been most unusual. We think you can help us understand why so many people joined you."

"If you can help us understand why so many *didn't*," McCool said.

"And why you kept bombing the bubbles," California added.

Kennedy looked disappointed. "Anger now is meaningless. Please make yourselves comfortable. We have a great many questions for you."

The interrogation went on for hours. The gryphon and the cuckoo seemed interested in the most tedious details of Alex's childhood, of California's attitude to her dead father, of McCool's religion.

"Where is this getting us?" Alex finally objected.

Kennedy smiled faintly. "The Chaiar didn't come here on the spur of the moment, Alex. They studied everything they could about humanity, everything the trolls had recorded. They could see that humanity had behaved like most species after Contact. When you have the technology to do anything, you do whatever is deepest in you, whatever is truly in your soul. We humans are hierarchical apes; if we're outside the Pattern, we can't imagine a greater glory than being the leader of a baboon troop or the leader's mate. Before Contact, only a few could be leaders, with all the wealth and security they could want. But after Contact, everyone was rich. If you couldn't rule other people, you could rule your computers and house-keepers and icons.

"So you junked most of your social values and glorified individualism. Most of you died, and the survivors be-came even more egocentric, more anarchic. True?"

"That's one way to put it," Alex growled.

"The Chaiar expected to deal with you the way they dealt with the trolls—one at a time. And mostly that's what happened. People converted as individuals or re-sisted as individuals. But not you, and not California, and not Liam. You pooled your resources—and went out looking for more allies. You even included Bhrukang."

"Alas," McCool muttered.

"And yet nothing in your backgrounds really explains that behavior," Kennedy went on. "Liam is a self-indul-gent old fool who pretends to be a poet when humanity hasn't produced a real poet since Contact. He enjoys in-flicting pain on others under the pretense of religion. Cali-fornia is a typical spoiled brat who likes to show off her physical skills as a duelist and copulator. Your mother, Alex, calls herself a scientist but spends most of her time fighting wars against her colleagues. And you yourself are just another self-absorbed young man playing with toys like your steamship. All of you have spent your lives using technology for trivial, selfish purposes.

"Somehow, though, you transcended your limitations, assessed your resources, and launched the only real resis-tance the Chaiar have ever faced. Even if Bhrukang had not been there to help you, you would have accomplished a great deal. In fact, we still expect a difficult time dealing with your allies among the spacers."

"Good," Alex grunted.

Kennedy looked at him with amusement; Alex glared back.

"You know," Kennedy said, "we must seem like some of your ancient religious fanatics, always going on about the Pattern. But part of the Pattern is curiosity. We don't know everything, we'll never know everything, but the Pattern shows us where to look to learn more. Your resis-tance is a part of the Pattern, too, and one that can teach us all a great deal. That's why we want to learn from you."

"You are more ignorant than you know," McCool said.

"That is true of all intelligent organisms. Well, I see it's getting late. Let's pause for a few minutes. I'll send in some food for you."

A mobile arrived at the door, rolled in, and unfolded its back into an elegant dining table. Looking at roast pork in gravy, Alex realized it had surely come from a live animal and ate only a potato and some string beans. The others were even less interested in food, though McCool solemnly drank two beers in rapid succession.

Alex walked over to the window as Kennedy and Tsaunghok reappeared. A long path of light extended across the sea to the horizon, and above it was Earth. The clouds seemed thicker and darker than ever. Alex wondered how many still lived there, whether in estates or in cuckoo cities.

"Can you please turn down the heat a little?" Rik asked. Her blond hair hung limply across her shoulders, and her forehead gleamed with sweat.

"The temperature's only twenty degrees Celsius," Kennedy said, looking surprised.

"It must be hotter than that," California said. "We're all sweating."

Kennedy glanced at the gryphon beside him and then said, "We'll call a halt to the questions for the time being. I see you ate very little. Are you feeling ill?"

"Just hot," Rik said.

"We'll turn down the temperature."

McCool tossed his light cotton jacket over a chair and sprawled sweating on one of the beds. Rik fiddled with the controls of her tightsuit, increasing its ventilation. Alex stripped off his blue T-shirt, leaving only his shorts, and still felt hot; California unbuttoned her luminar blouse and pulled it out of the waistband of her pants.

"Hi, spoiled brat," Alex said.

"What *is* a spoiled brat?"

"I think brat is an old word for child."

"So he *was* insulting us. I thought I was going to explode when he said those things."

"I know. He was like one of those Starway School jerks, always brave on the other side of the korshak screen."

"Wouldn't have made any difference if he'd been here

in physical presence," California said angrily. "I'm still warwired, I'm still a duelist, but I wouldn't have dared react."

He nodded and hugged her. She was startlingly hot to the touch. The luminar blouse stuck to her sweaty back. "Maybe we are sick," he said. "The air feels colder, but I'm still burning up. And you're hot, too."

She looked intently at him, then turned to McCool and Rik. "I think Alex and I are running a fever. Are you?"

"I believe so," McCool said, and Rik nodded.

"Allergies?" Alex said.

"I wouldn't be affected," Rik said. "But we're all coming down with something."

The phrase struck Alex as quaintly archaic and wildly inappropriate for something that might kill them all. "We'd better ask for help."

McCool laughed painfully. "The gryphons aren't the most reliable physicians, are they?"

Another ancient term, Alex thought dizzily. Weren't physicians some kind of eighteenth-century shamans? Cured ailments with moxibustion? He sat on the edge of one of the beds and wiped sweat from his face. His head was beginning to hurt, and his arms and legs ached.

"I don't care what they are," he mumbled, stretching out on the bed and then drawing his knees up. "I feel awful."

Rik shouted something in Chaiar; nothing happened. Alex closed his eyes, then opened them and saw California sitting slumped on the next bed. He forced himself to get up and sit beside her.

"I'm sorry. You're sick, too." He put his arm around her again. Her olive complexion was flushed, and her eyes were too bright. "Kennedy's right—all I think about is myself. Come on, lie down and rest. Would you like a drink of water?"

Her lips, dry and cracked, brushed his cheek. "Mm-hm."

Alex lurched into the bathroom and came back with a metal tumbler full of cold, sweet water. California drank it thirstily, then sagged back onto the bed.

"I've got to get some sleep," she muttered.

Stubbornly, McCool still sat at the table, propping his head in his hands. Rik stood thumping her palm against the door, shouting hoarsely in Chaiar.

John F. Kennedy appeared. He looked tired and irritable. "We don't know what your problem is. Consult your molmacs. They may be able to tell you, and then we can act accordingly. I'll be back in ten minutes."

Alex rubbed his aching temples and collapsed back onto his bed. The thought of communicating directly with his molmacs was upsetting at best; now he would have to try to make sense of their babble while scarcely capable of thinking.

Triggering his comlink, he got silence instead of white noise. He chose the molmacs' channel, wishing Heathcliff had come along, and called.

—Alex Alex hello Alex hello hello sorry hello sorry.—

—What's wrong with me? What's wrong with the others?—

—Go to sleep go to go to sleep sleep rest go feel better sleep soon.—

His alarm overrode his drowsiness. Pushing himself up on one elbow, Alex saw McCool sprawled unconscious across the table, Rik curled up against the door, California sleeping while she breathed in quick gasps. He slumped down again, too exhausted to care what happened next.

The channel to the molmacs was still open, and his dreams were full of their countless murmurous voices. Even in sleep he was aware of pain; it reminded him of the ache he had felt after they had left for Venus, when the deconversion molmacs had seized them. That led in turn to dreams about the journey, about the glittering waterfalls in Dwuliu Carson's estate, and McCool brawling drunkenly in the tavern on Eros. He felt arms lifting him and called out for Victor; no one answered.

Then he slept deeply, without dreams, and woke in darkness. The comlink was still on but silent. Then a single voice, Lord Whitehead's voice, came to him:

—Alex, we need you.—

Twenty-three:

—Lord Whitehead? You're alive?— Alex did not open his eyes; he was sure he was still dreaming.

—We are not the eagle. We shared him on the floating island; now we share you.—

—How?—

—Mosquitoes.— Lord Whitehead's voice, the voice of the wild molmacs of the floating island, seemed dryly amused. —Some of them fed on the eagle's blood and took us as well. We guided them into your house. They hid in your luggage, in your clothes. They bit you and Liam and Rik and California.—

—Why? What are you trying to do?—

—Break the Pattern.—

Wild molmacs, Alex thought. Wild molmacs, living free on that floating island for years, surviving its alien chemistries, learning how to dull its poisons. They must have evolved in unexpected paths, developing an intelligence superior in some ways to the supermind of which they formed a part. They had even escaped Bhrukang's subversion of the supermind.

And for their own reasons they had decided to carry on the war. If humans were unavailable, mosquitoes would do.

—How?— he demanded.

—We know the Chaiar genome very well. We see the changes they have made in themselves. They have suppressed some of their deepest needs for the sake of the Pattern. We intend to restore those needs.—

—You're going to deconvert the gryphons?—

—Not all of them at once. For now we need only the Explicators.—

Alex opened his eyes. He lay naked on a wide bed something like a dive platform. A circular patch, shiny white, was stuck to the inside of his left elbow: a monitor of some kind, he supposed. He felt a dizzy terror; he was on the planet of the gryphons, plotting with their most dangerous enemies.

—Can they hear us? The gryphons?—

—Not now. We are communicating within your head. But if you try to communicate with the others, the gryphons will know it.—

—What do you want us to do?—

—For now, nothing. Wait. Look after each other.—

The comlink went silent. Alex sat up, shivering, and looked around.

The bed stood in a pool of dim yellow light. Three others, equally illuminated, stood nearby; around them was darkness. McCool, California, and Rik lay on the other beds, each apparently asleep.

"Hello!" Alex called out. His voice lost itself without echo in the darkness. "Liam, California, Rik—are you awake?"

They did not move. Cautiously, Alex swung his feet to the floor and stood up. His balance seemed uncertain; he swayed as he walked across a carpeted floor to McCool's bed.

The old man's forehead was cool to the touch. He stirred a little, then opened his eyes. "Where—"

"I don't know. How do you feel?"

"Better. You, too? They must have cured whatever infected us. Wish they hadn't."

The two men sat in the dim cone of light, talking quietly about nothing significant. Alex realized that the Chaiar were surely listening and recording. Even if they could not eavesdrop on an internal comlink, they could certainly follow ordinary conversation. He wondered if they could detect the slowly reviving hope he felt and the fear that was mixed with it.

The women woke a few minutes apart; Alex helped California sit up, while McCool looked after Rik.

"We're in a hospital," Rik said. "They must have decided we were really sick or they'd have treated us in that room. Some of my sisters had to go into the hospital."

"You had sisters?" California said.

"Clone sisters, thirty-two of us. Some of us didn't live." She took a deep breath through her nose. "It smells like a hospital. Thick air, almost as thick as Earth's." She began to cry. "I want to go home Alex, I want to go back to *Wuthering Heights*."

They all embraced her, consoling her.

Light suddenly glared at them, relatively bright in the gloom. It was a korshak image of Kennedy, standing again in that large and gloomy hall.

"Good morning," the cuckoo said. "I'm glad to see you're up. The medical systems reported you were feeling better."

"Let us out of here," California said.

Kennedy nodded and smiled. "Right away. We're just sending in a mobile with some clothes."

A door slid open in one of the walls, and a tall mobile rolled into the room. Its lights made the place seem smaller and duller, not a mysterious dungeon but an ordinary room.

The robot handed out tightsuits, all white and without ornament. When they were dressed, Kennedy spoke again. "If you board the mobile, it'll take you back to your quarters."

"What are you planning to do with us?" Alex asked.

"We're continuing the interrogation. You've been ill for two days. The Explicators are impatient to learn more about you."

Alex shrugged and stepped aboard the mobile. The others followed. It had no seats, only a narrow railed platform behind its cylindrical utility pod. Without warning, the mobile moved toward another wall, where a door opened for it. A swirl of warm air burst out with them: The room had been kept at the higher air pressure of Earth. Alex felt his ears pop.

They entered a long, arched hallway. The walls and ceiling seemed to be made of mottled gray stone incised with abstract repetitive patterns. A kind of twilight filled the hallway; the gryphons seemed to like dimness. Alex and California grimaced at each other, disliking the smell of the air.

At little more than walking pace, the mobile cruised down the hallway, paused, and turned right through a newly open door. Beyond was another hall, as long and sparsely ornamented as the first. Alex tried to memorize the carved patterns on the walls, thinking they might be useful landmarks if they found themselves free within the building. But after a few more doors and hallways, he abandoned the idea. The doors appeared to open only to signals from the mobile or its controlling computer, and escape from the building would be futile even if it were possible. For now they could only await events. He drew in a deep breath, trying to get enough oxygen out of the sour air.

At last a door opened into their original quarters. The window was functioning. Early morning light threw a narrow yellow stripe on the floor and part of one wall. As the mobile retreated and the door slid shut, air hissed in. The gryphons were at least trying to keep them comfortable.

"Home sweet home," McCool said. "I wonder when they're going to give us private quarters."

"I hope now that they won't," Alex said. "If we're split up, we may never see each other again."

California looked at him, horrified. "If they try it, I'll fight," she said. "Even if they pump me full of lactic acid again."

"Don't worry," he said, stroking her hair. "Don't worry."

Kennedy's image reappeared; this time several Explicators stood behind him, including Tsaunghok—and Bhrukang.

"We'll be monitoring your condition for a few more hours before we feed you," Kennedy said. "We were very alarmed at your illness, and we don't want to see a relapse."

Neither do we," California said. "It wasn't nice. If you can, we'd prefer synthesized food to something taken from a live animal."

"I'm sure that can be arranged. Now, the Explicators have some further questions. They still don't understand how you overcame your cultural conditioning enough to form an organized resistance group."

"Go ahead," Alex said.

"Bhrukang has suggested it was no coincidence that you all attended Alex's birthday party. He thinks that you may have shared some cultural values that put you at odds with the rest of humanity. Does this seem likely to you, Alex?"

"Maybe. My parents are—were—unusually conservative. They used Net technology, but they didn't care for a lot of the Net's values. The people who came to the party were old friends of my parents; obviously they shared my parents' beliefs."

"And your parents wished to put you in contact with like-minded people," Kennedy said. "That seems unusual in itself. Most human parents show no interest in their children's associations once they become fully adult."

"As I said, my parents were conservative."

Bhrukang raised a four-fingered hand and spoke briefly to the other gryphons. Kennedy listened defferentially, first to him and then to Tsaunghok, before turning back to Alex.

"Bhrukang suggests you are lying, or at least concealing part of the truth. He tells us we can't accurately judge your honesty unless we can monitor your pheromone output. So he's suggesting you be brought here, where he can smell you."

"That's ridiculous!" Alex snapped.

"Alex *is* telling the truth," California said. "Victor or Bhrukang, or whatever he likes to call himself, is crazy. Your computers ought to be able to tell when someone's lying."

Kennedy looked unimpressed. "The Explicators have learned to respect human capabilities," he said with a faint smile. "In any case, the mobile will be there at once. We will see you in a few minutes."

The mobile was equipped with seats, uncomfortable ones designed for gryphons. California sat next to Alex, with McCool and Rik just behind them.

"What is this pheromone nonsense?" Rik said. "Is it true?"

"Not as far as I know," Alex said. "Maybe Bhrukang knows more about us than we do."

The trip was longer this time and involved several trips in what seemed to be elevators. At one point the mobile emerged from the tower and carried them across a narrow bridge, hundreds of meters above the ground, into another tower. The view was brief but dizzying: scores of towers clustered between a placid green sea and snow-capped mountains under a deep blue sky.

Then they were inside again, rolling through still more monotonous corridors empty of other traffic. Alex suspected that the way had been cleared for them; the thin, sour air held the acrid smell of gryphons as well. A burst of irrational anxiety made him shiver. What if Lord Whitehead's molmacs could not overcome all the alien molmacs on the planet? He and the others might die as millions had on Earth.

He put the thought aside. They had more immediate problems to worry about. They were in the heart of the gryphons' world, approaching a concentration of power undreamable among humans. He hoped the molmacs would keep him calm; a single false move could destroy them all.

Without ceremony, the mobile entered the great hall. The passengers looked around, craning their necks at the vaulted ceiling high above. Light fell in narrow beams from high windows, illuminating patches of wall.

"Good morning." Kennedy's voice echoed there as it did not on korshak. The cuckoo stood on the edge of a cluster of gryphons, all much taller than he and all wearing fishnet tunics. Alex recognized Bhrukang at once. His golden fur seemed to glow in the dimness, where the others were brown or black.

"If you'd rather, you can remain seated on the mobile," Kennedy went on as the robot slowed to a gentle stop a few meters from the group.

"I'd rather stand," McCool said at once, stepping down to the flagstoned floor. The others followed him.

"As you wish. Are you ready to resume?"

"Yes," California said, "but Bhrukang doesn't know what he's talking about." Alex looked worriedly at her. Her voice was thick and muffled, as if the allergies were coming back. "You don't need pheromone analysis to tell if someone's lying. Any half-decent computer can do it from voice analysis and kinesthetics."

"I'm sorry to disagree, California," Bhrukang said. "Unlike most humans, I learned a great deal about human physiology and psychology during my years with Alex's father. Now, please answer the following question, Alex: What is your name?"

"My name is Alexander Macintosh." His throat seemed raspy; he was angry with himself for sounding querulous.

"And where were you born?"

"On my mother's estate, Mordor." He cleared his throat, then coughed. The cough triggered another. His nose began to tingle, and he sneezed. Watery mucus trickled down his lip. He sneezed again, violently and noisily.

"Are you feeling ill again?" Kennedy asked.

"A little. Sore throat."

Rik sneezed so hard that she bent at the waist. Then McCool's turn came. California coughed, laughed, and coughed again.

"We sound like a seal colony," she gasped. "I don't know what the matter is. Alex, are we getting allergies, after all?"

"I don't know," he said thickly. "I think so. I can hardly breathe." He sneezed again, tears running down his face.

"Get back on the mobile!" Kennedy commanded. "I'm sending you back to the hospital. Quickly!"

Obediently, they clambered back onto the mobile, which accelerated sharply. Still sneezing, Alex clung to California while McCool supported Rik. In seconds they were out of the great hall and back in the corridors.

Lights flashed amber and white in the corridor ceilings, and a low rumble filled the air: emergency warnings, Alex guessed. The mobile acquired an escort of two other robots, one ahead and one behind.

—Lord Whitehead,— Alex called.

Silence answered him. He wondered if the molmacs' attempted infection of the Explicators had actually succeeded. Perhaps not. They must have had to improvise when the opportunity arose to meet the Explicators face to face. And if it had succeeded, what difference would it make if they deconverted?

Abruptly they burst into the large, dark room with its four illuminated beds. Robots glided across the carpeted floor, plucking each person from the mobile's seats. Alex felt himself picked up and seemed to remember a dream in which it had happened before.

Lowered to a bed, he felt the robot's smooth fingers test his pulse, his electrofield, a hundred other vital signs. No doubt invisible and painless needles had already sampled his blood, as they must have done before. What had the gryphons made of the wild molmacs? Had they seemed like just more molecular clutter? And would they still seem innocent?

"Get away from me!" California shouted at her robot attendant; it ignored her. At last, however, they were left alone. Alex at once got up and sat on California's bed. McCool and Rik joined them.

"Did you notice something?" Rik said. "As soon as we

left the room, we stopped sneezing and coughing. Could we be allergic to the Explicators?"

"If only they were allergic to us," McCool said. "That was certainly an odd interview. Alex, what did you think of it?"

They had to be careful. The gryphons were listening, and their computers could indeed detect lies. "Amazing," he mumbled. "I've never seen anything like it." Then, changing the subject: "Rik, can you ask the robots for something to eat?"

Rik barked several phrases in Chaiar, and one of the robots responded briefly. "They're still worried about us," she said. "Maybe I should call Kennedy."

"That worrywart?" McCool scoffed. "If he's going to pack us off like this every time we sneeze, we're all in for a dull time here."

"Try him, anyway," California said. "I'm starving."

Rik called out, her voice echoing slightly in the darkness. Nothing happened. She called again.

The answer came over their comlinks: —Come quickly.—

They looked at one another in surprise. A door opened in a different wall, throwing gray light into the hospital room. The looming robots stood still and silent.

"Come on," Alex said. He took California's hand, and they ran for the door. McCool and Rik were close behind.

—Turn right.—

They obeyed and found themselves on a wide concourse, floored in a marblelike mottled gray fome. The far wall was an immense sheet of darkened glass. Overhead was yet another arched ceiling, scarcely visible in the gloom. The concourse was noisy with the splash of many fountains and the rumble of voices. Scores of gryphons and mobiles moved purposefully up and down the concourse; they paid no attention to the humans, who must have seemed to be just four more cuckoos.

Alex slowed to a brisk walk and muttered to California, "Did you get the message on your comlink?"

"Yes. What's going on?"

"I'm not sure." If Lord Whitehead was broadcasting over their comlinks, surely the gryphons were receiving the message also. They would react quickly and break up whatever plans the molmacs might have.

Unless the infection had set in almost at once and the

molmacs were in control of the Explicators. That seemed hard to believe, though Lord Whitehead had said the molmacs understood the gryphon genome very well.

—Turn right at the next corridor. Board the mobile waiting there.—

They walked slowly along the wall toward the mouth of the corridor. Alex glanced casually around, surprised at the bareness of the concourse. With all their resources, the gryphons seemed uninterested in ornamenting their cities. Or was this merely a collection of rough shacks, thrown together only to house a population on a mission to the wilderness?

They entered the corridor. Alex paused beside the mobile and took California's hand. "I don't know what's going to happen next. I—just want to say I love you and honor you."

She kissed him and stepped back to look at him, her eyes bright. "I knew from the start you were a lover and a fighter."

"Enough of this eloquence," McCool snapped. "The gryphons will begin to wonder what's going on. Come on, get aboard."

This mobile was designed to carry humans; they sank back into the seats, and it sped down the corridor, away from the concourse. This time they seemed to follow routes reserved for mobiles rather than foot traffic. The corridors were pitch-black, and the mobile did not use its lights. After a few minutes it emerged onto a bridge, crossed it to the neighboring tower, and entered an external elevator. They climbed rapidly to the top of the new building while the other towers seemed to drop away.

The elevator slowed and stopped. They were on a rooftop landing platform with nothing above them but cloudflecked sky. Luna, half-full, was overhead. To the east, the sea stretched to the horizon; Earth was just rising, looking to Alex like a sharp tooth of mottled gray and white. The nightside was blotched with red and orange, intense enough to show even at fifty thousand kilometers against a daytime sky.

Not far away, one of the gryphons' iridescent shuttles hovered just above the surface of the platform. A gangway led up into its belly.

—Board the ship, quickly.—

They clambered off the mobile while wind whipped

their hair and climbed the gangway. At the top was a small chamber, perhaps an air lock; after the gangway folded up into the hull, air hissed into the chamber for some time before an inner door slid open. Something like normal Earth air gusted in from a larger room beyond.

Alex went in first. He found himself in a long, semi-cylindrical room whose white walls glowed with korshak screens. Seats were scattered here and there around the room. At the far end, near the nose of the ship, five chairs faced a korshak image of the landing platform outside. Gryphons sat in each of them, taking no notice of the humans.

A chair swung round. In it sat a gryphon with golden fur.

"Hello, Alex. You can call me Victor again, if you wish."

Twenty-four:

Alex recognized other gryphons as they, too, turned around. They were the Explicators, as calm and impassive as before. Tsaunghok sat beside Victor, contemplating the humans without expression.

"Take your seats," Victor said, pointing to a cluster of chairs along one wall. "We're leaving at once."

Alex did not move. "Will you tell us what this is all about?"

"When we're on our way. Please sit, Alex."

As he obeyed, Alex tried calling Lord Whitehead's molmacs over the comlink.

—Do as Victor says and don't pester us.—

—Did you hear that?— Rik asked as she sat beside him.

—Yes.—

—This is very strange. I can't believe I'm in the same ship as the Explicators.— She looked around the cabin, obviously recognizing everything she saw, and then spoke out loud. "Brace yourselves. These ships are rougher than your shuttle."

A second later Alex felt himself pressed back hard into his seat. The korshak image beyond the gryphons turned a white-flecked blue and then darkened rapidly. Earth, a thick crescent of gray and black, swam into the image. The acceleration ceased, and gravity returned to Habrakha normal. Victor stood up and walked back to the humans.

"I'm glad you're all well," he said. "You've had a difficult time."

"What's this about, Victor?" Alex demanded coldly.

"We've begun to dismantle the Chaiar empire. You played your parts perfectly."

Alex glanced at the Explicators, who sat watching from

242

a distance. "The wild molmacs deconverted them, didn't they? Broke them out of the Pattern."

"Not exactly, though that will come in time. They've overridden the Pattern. The Explicators simply want to return to their birthponds on Makhshuar. They will do whatever they must to do so."

"Birthponds?" McCool repeated. "Do their birthponds even exist anymore?"

"I have no idea." Victor's thin brown lips, half-hidden under his beak, twitched as if smiling. "We will have to go to Makhshuar to find out."

No one said anything for a moment. Alex cleared his throat. "Are we going to Makhshuar in this shuttle?"

"No. We're taking Habrakha. The planet's flight control center is located on the equator—"

"Ta Parng," Rik interrupted, her eyes wide.

"Yes, the city of Ta Parng. We should be arriving in about fifteen minutes. The Explicators will order the . . . pilots to set a course for Kho An."

"But that's the trolls' planet," Alex said.

"Do you remember when I told you our only hope was to destroy the Pattern altogether? That is just what we are on our way to accomplish."

"Victor," California said, "did the molmacs deconvert you, too?"

"I was never converted. But I needed to make the Explicators think I had, and I could not include you in the deception; it is too easy to detect lies in humans."

"And it's not easy in gryphons?" McCool asked with a wry smile.

"Almost impossible. Especially when the Explicators were eager to believe that a legendary gryphon like Bhrukang was ready to join the Pattern."

"So you and the molmacs found a key to the gryphon genome in the Database," Alex said. "You built some kind of countermeasure, some special kind of molmac, and then you talked your way onto Habrakha. And you used us to infect the Explicators with the new molmacs."

"They were not happy at the thought of being in your physical presence," Victor said. "But they were eager to learn how you had come to resist them, and they were very afraid of being deceived."

"With good reason," Alex said.

"Victor," California said, "is Lord Whitehead really dead, then?"

"No. He's still on *Wuthering Heights*, in very good health."

"And can we go back to the ship?" Rik asked.

Victor looked at her for a moment before replying. "Perhaps. But first we must travel several thousand light-years."

Ta Parng was as compact as the other gryphon cities, a cluster of towers and domes on a high and windswept plateau. To the east, glaciers glinted on the slopes of jagged young mountains. The land lay bare and brown, dotted in places with scrubby gray vegetation. Alex wondered if it was native to the planet or had been introduced by the gryphons as part of their terraforming. His glimpses of the world only made him yearn for the lost greenness of Earth; even with much of its old beauty destroyed by ekata and other alien life-forms, it had been beautiful. Habrakha was not.

The shuttle landed atop one of the towers. Tsaunghok, who had said nothing during the flight, stood up and led the way out onto the landing platform. The other Explicators followed him, then Victor, and finally the humans.

Though the sun stood high in the equatorial sky, the air was chilly and much thinner even than that at sea level. Alex found himself panting by the time they reached a waiting mobile; the other humans were equally short of breath. The atmosphere might be slightly richer in oxygen than Earth's, but the lower air pressure made breathing difficult. Neither Victor nor the Explicators seemed to notice their distress.

The mobile lifted gently off the platform and descended at a steep angle among the surrounding towers. Alex looked out through the windows at the dizzying views and the air traffic that shot past them. For all that it was the creation of a long-established Net species, it seemed to him strangely old-fashioned, like the human cities of the twentieth century. The crowding could satisfy no need except that for physical presence, and the gryphons, like the ancient humans, had not troubled to make their cities sensually interesting. He reminded himself that every city on Habrakha was temporary. The gryphons considered the whole planet as only a means to an end.

Their destination was a large dome near the center of the city. Its surface was a glossy, reflective hemisphere, and for a moment Alex thought it must be under a shardana bubble. As they landed outside one of its entrances, he could see it was only some unfamiliar gryphon construction material in which the surrounding towers were distortedly reflected. The mobile glided inside and stopped.

They were in a single huge room, perhaps half a kilometer across. An arch of some black material, perhaps twenty meters thick, rose from the ground beside them, curved to the top of the dome, and descended on the far side. An identical arch intersected it at a ninety-degree angle. Beneath the black arches a number of low buildings were scattered almost at random. Lights burned at the corners of the buildings, leaving most of the enclosed space in darkness. The place was very quiet.

"This is the control center for interstellar flight," Victor said as they stepped from the mobile and approached a small group of gryphons. "Don't speak for now."

The apparent leader of the waiting gryphons was a female, taller even than Victor. She wore the usual fishnet tunic, but it glinted with shifting colors. As Tsaunghok approached her, she raised both four-fingered hands and lifted her chin. Her dark brown mane seemed to stand up. The three gryphons behind her spoke in a resonant chorus and repeated the female's gestures of salute. None seemed at all interested in the four humans.

Tsaunghok fluffed up his mane in reply and then spoke at length. The female listened, hands pressed against her brown osmotic membrane. When the Explicator had finished, she spoke in turn. Her eyes were fixed on the floor. Tsaunghok seemed to approve of her reply and ended the conversation with a single syllable like the note of a bell.

The female and two of her companions turned away and strode quickly toward one of the low buildings. The remaining gryphon escorted the Explicators and their party to a room built into the wall of the dome. Within, a dim light glowed over a few benches and a fountain splashing in the far corner.

The gryphons took seats on the benches, ignoring the humans. Alex looked at Rik, who led them to another bench.

As they sat down, she murmured to the others, "The pilot is very upset by Tsaunghok's orders. If he'd come alone, she'd have notified the others. But they're all here, so she has no one to appeal to."

"What happens now?" Alex whispered.

"I don't know." Rik looked worried. "They didn't tell us much about Ta Parng when I was growing up, but it makes me uncomfortable. This place took us from Tayas to Earth, and now Victor says we're going to Kho An. Maybe we'll never see *Wuthering Heights* again."

He touched her hand. "We will."

Yellow lights began to pulse in the ceiling, and a low rumble filled the air. An alarm of some kind, Alex thought, like the one that had gone off during their hasty return to the hospital. Had the pilot defied Tsaunghok, or was the alarm simply to alert the city that a journey was imminent?

Korshak screens appeared before the seated gryphons, but they presented nothing recognizable—only a complex and constantly shifting pattern of glowing blue lines and points that seemed to recede into infinity. As the rumble and blinking lights continued, the glowing korshak patterns changed color: to red, to orange, to yellow, to white. Then, without warning, they went black. The whole process had taken no more than five minutes.

The gryphons showed no response, though Alex thought he could hear the click of nasal cartilage. Victor stood up and walked over to the humans.

"We have left the solar system," he said quietly. "In ten hours we will arrive in the Kho An system. Until then we have nothing much to do."

"What will happen when we reach Kho An?" Alex asked.

"The Explicators have already begun production of deconversion molmacs for both gryphons and trolls. They will be launched through the shardana bubble at Kho An and the other inhabited regions of the system. We will tell the trolls that an attack from First Stone is imminent and that the missiles contain vital information for protecting themselves."

"Another lie," McCool murmured cheerfully.

"The first trolls and gryphons to be exposed to the molmacs will not appear to be changed in any way. The information in the missiles will be a pathway into the Database leading straight to a watchdog. By the time the trolls realize that they've been barred from the Database, the molmacs should be well dispersed and the deconverted trolls will know how to put the watchdog back in his kennel. We will do the same thing with the Ganigar and the Hie, the other species the gryphons have conquered. And then we will travel to the Tayas system and Makhshuar, and the Explicators will return at last to their birthponds."

"Why didn't you leave us where we were?" California asked him. "We're not much use here, unless you need us to sneeze on someone."

Victor's dark, unreadable eyes met hers. "This is a dangerous planet. If you are safe anywhere, it is here with me. If I had left you behind, you might have been destroyed."

"How?"

"By gryphons who realized the Explicators had been subverted. Or by humans. Many of them must be very frightened by what has happened."

"Are you frightened, Victor?" California asked.

"Only that we may not succeed."

A mobile rolled into the room with food for the gryphons, but none ate much. The humans got nothing but at least found a gryphon bathroom that served their purposes also. They slept on the carpeted floor, lulled by the splash of the fountain. The Explicators seemed to need no sleep; they sat without moving, contemplating the black korshak screen.

The rumble died away, but the yellow lights continued to flash. Alex woke from time to time, glimpsed the gryphons, and slept again.

California was shaking him. He sat up and saw her kneeling beside him. "Come on," she said softly.

She led him out of the room and through the tall gateway that the mobile had used to bring them there. A cold breeze stirred around them. Outside, the towers' windows glowed with lights.

"Look at the sky," she said.

Overhead was utter blackness. It was a night without a sun, he thought. The planet was moving inexplicably through a darkness deeper than intergalactic space. The glowing towers of Ta Parng looked transient and unreal.

The wind was colder, and the air seemed thinner than ever. Alex turned to go back inside when light blazed all around them.

A sun was high in the sky, brighter than Earth's. To the north, the narrow crescent of a planet glowed palely in the dark blue sky, rising from below the city skyline almost to the zenith. The sunlight felt surprisingly warm.

"We're here!" California said. "Look, that must be Kho An."

Despite the heat of the noon sun, Alex shivered. If Victor's plan failed, all the resources of the trolls and their gryphon masters would be turned against their world—and then, eventually, against what was left of humanity in the solar system. The gryphons of Tayas would decide that humans had no place in the Pattern and would grind them out of existence.

The dome was separated from its neighboring buildings by a narrow belt of some smooth material. Gryphons began to cross it from the towers, approaching the gate. California tugged at Alex's arm.

"Let's get back inside and find Victor."

The long black korshak screen showed a close-up of a troll who looked very much Bliokio, speaking in a rapid series of whistles and hoots. The gryphons in the room paid no attention. The pilot was back, speaking rapidly to Tsaunghok while Victor stood silently nearby. After some time she left, and the Explicator slumped back onto his bench. Victor turned to the humans.

"The journey has gone well. The missiles are launched. We will be on our way within a few more minutes. The next stop is the sun of the Hie."

Alex saw Kho An gleaming on the korshak screen, its great polar ocean flecked with clouds. It looked like any other korshak image he had ever seen of the planet.

"How many trolls are there now?" he asked.

"About six million. Forty million Chaiar live here as well, and a few thousand human cuckoos."

"I wonder how they'll respond to deconversion," Alex said.

"About as you did. It will be painful."

"And what will they do afterward?"

"That is for them to decide."

A thought belatedly occurred to Alex. "What about all the gryphons here on Habrakha? Aren't they going to realize what's going on?"

"Of course. Some of the missiles are spreading molmacs here, through the atmosphere and water. By the time we reach the Tayas system, this whole planet should be deconverted."

"What if some decide they don't want to deconvert? Will they fight back?"

"Perhaps. We did, after all."

"Victor, what if they do what my mother did to Earth? Suppose they destroy Habrakha?"

"Or just this city," McCool added.

"If they destroy Ta Parng, the shardana bubble will be detuned," said Victor.

"And then we and Kho An will break up," Rik said. She looked worried. "They might do it, Victor."

"I don't think the Chaiar will respond that strongly," Victor said.

"I don't mean the Chaiar. I mean the cuckoos."

A crowd of several hundred gryphons had gathered outside the entrance to the dome. They did not try to enter or to communicate with those inside; they simply stood and watched. Victor monitored them over korshak but seemed uninterested in them. He spoke occasionally to the Explicators, who replied briefly and resumed their silent contemplation of the korshak screen.

A mobile brought food for the humans: a kind of vegetable soup and a dense black bread. They ate it hungrily. Victor and the other gryphons ate nothing.

The room within the dome was full of korshak screens; images of trolls, cities, missiles, and gryphons flashed and vanished. Most of them went seemingly unnoticed by the Explicators, though Alex suspected the gryphons were sending out comlink messages.

The crowd outside the dome entrance was larger but still silent. "They're keeping an eye on them," McCool observed. "That's the fifth time they've turned up on korshak in the last couple of minutes. I wonder how well defended this place is."

"Probably not defended at all," Alex answered. "They'd have no need to."

"I don't think we need to fear being disabled by our molmacs if we attack a gryphon," McCool murmured with a faint smile. "We're warwired, except for Rik, and she still ought to be a formidable fighter."

"But would ordinary gryphons actually attack the Explicators?"

Rik spoke up before McCool could answer. "I doubt it. The Explicators define the Pattern. What they say often troubles humans and gryphons, especially gryphons, but it must be obeyed."

McCool grinned wolfishly at her. "Ah, but *is* it obeyed?"

"By gryphons. Not always by humans. The cuckoos don't always understand the Pattern, and sometimes they resist. Once, almost a hundred cuckoos mutinied. One of them said he understood the Pattern better than the Explicators, and the others followed him. They were all killed."

"And that's what Victor is worried about," Alex said. "That humans might try to save the Pattern."

Rik nodded. She looked unhappy.

The sun of Kho An crept toward the west, and the planet's vast crescent sank lower in the sky. During one of the brief checks on the crowd outside, Alex saw two gryphons suddenly collapse. Their companions turned to help them.

"The molmacs have reached them," Victor said. "And the first missiles are in the atmosphere of Kho An. We will be leaving within a few minutes."

The yellow lights began flashing again, and the rumble was much louder than before. Once again the screens glowed with lines and points while the Explicators sat patiently watching. When the screens went black, Victor turned away from them.

"We will reach the Hie system in six hours. But we face an immediate problem. You were right, Rik. The cuckoos are attacking us. They will be here in a few minutes."

Twenty-five:

"What can we do?" Alex asked Victor.

"Nothing. The Explicators have already summoned defenses. The humans have taken over seven shuttles, but we have a hundred times as many. The fight should be over in a few minutes."

They watched it on the screens. The seven shuttles had dispersed on courses carrying them all over the planet, yet all converged on Ta Parng. None responded to korshak messages.

"Why are they trying to get in close?" Alex asked Victor. "Remember how they shot us down from eight thousand kilometers?"

"This dome is much stronger than the hull of your shuttle. But I think they mean to assault us and take control without damaging the drive or the shardana generator."

"But they can't imagine they'll succeed," Rik said. "Look, the first one's destroyed already—and there goes the second. It's suicidal."

"Maybe they're just trying to make a point," California said.

"No." Rik shook his head. "We were never trained to do anything like that. Least of all by resisting the Explicators."

"Then it's a ruse," Alex said. "A distraction. The attack will come from here."

Victor said nothing, but Alex was sure the gryphon was issuing commands through his comlink. On the screens, shuttles continued to explode against the deep blackness of the sky.

Alex turned to McCool. "This place seems to have two main entrances, the one we came in and another one across the dome. Can you and Rik get to the far entrance and try to stop anyone coming through?"

"We have no weapons, you realize."

"You're a Violent, aren't you? And the cuckoos aren't likely to have anything serious."

McCool's eyes brightened. "Indeed. Rik, are you coming?"

Her eyes seemed very large in her pale face. "I'm coming."

Victor must have sent a comlink command, because a mobile appeared at the doorway almost at once. McCool and Rik boarded it and glided away across the floor of the dome.

Alex and California went to the other entrance. It was a simple archway without a door; the gryphons needed no protection against weather when they could control it.

Outside, the crowd had disappeared. The plaza was lit by scattered lamps and the lights of the nearby towers. Perhaps three dozen gryphons lay or sat on the pavement, breathing heavily, while five or six others knelt beside them to try to give help. As Alex watched, two of the helpers also collapsed. They lay shuddering, hands pressed to their osmotic membranes.

Mobiles suddenly rolled out from three different buildings across the pavement. There were five of them, all crowded with humans in multicolored tightsuits. Alex looked for weapons but saw none; the attackers were trying to defend the Pattern with their bare hands.

And their robots. The mobiles, suspended centimeters above the pavement on their kuldi fields, accelerated straight at the dome entrance. One mobile struck a sitting gryphon and knocked her rolling across the pavement.

"Back!" Alex shouted, pulling California away from the entrance and back to the doorway of the command center. The five mobiles jolted to a halt and spilled a cluster of grim-looking humans. Alex counted them: twenty-two, a few armed with metal rods or pipes, but most barehanded. They were young, tall, and beautiful.

As they swarmed into the doorway, California kicked out at the first, driving her bare heel deep into his stomach; he lurched back, then pressed on. The man beside him swung a pipe at California's head. She smashed the edge of her hand against his forearm; the radius cracked.

Beside her, Alex drove his stiffened fingers into the nearest man's throat, then threw a hard punch into a woman's face. She gasped and struck back with astonishing force. Alex stepped back, his jaw aching, and chopped at the woman's throat. It was no playful scrap: The cuckoos cared nothing for the rules of hand-to-hand dueling. The attackers used their weight of numbers to press forward. Alex struck out almost at random and felt himself hit and scratched by the cuckoos swarming around them.

Someone in the back of the crowd cried out in pain, and Alex glimpsed one of the mobiles battering into the cuckoos from behind. Victor must have gained control of it, but the effect was only to force the cuckoos farther into the doorway.

The woman he had been fighting was pressed close against him, trying to bring a knee up into his crotch. Her face turned a strange, mottled red; the glare of hatred in her eyes faded into surprise. She opened her mouth to cry out—

And liquefied.

The woman's tightsuit contained only a skeleton streaming with thick, red-black oily fluids. The corpse toppled sideways across another one, while one of the men California had been fighting managed a short scream before he too disintegrated.

Alex glanced at California and saw her white tightsuit splashed with glistening red and black. For an instant, seeing her looking at him with a horrified expression, he thought she, too, was about to die; then he realized that he was as drenched in human grease and blood as she.

The remaining attackers hesitated. Another one collapsed, his face dissolving, his flesh gushing from the arms and legs of his tightsuit.

Someone moaned and broke away, scrambling past the mobile that crowded the attackers into the doorway. The rest turned and followed; one stumbled, fell, and decomposed where he lay.

The dome was silent except for the fading echoes of running footsteps on the pavement outside. Alex stared at the red gleaming skeletons sprawled across the floor and found it hard to breathe. He turned to California, put out a bloodstained hand, and drew it back.

"It's all right, Alex," Victor said. The gryphon stood just inside the doorway; he put one hand on Alex's shoulder, the other on California's. "You can't hurt each other, or me."

Alex sagged against the frame of the doorway, staring down at the dark fluid staining his clothes and skin. "What—what was it?" he rasped.

"Toxins from the floating forest. The wild molmacs learned how to synthesize them and how to make humans immune to them. When they realized you were going to be attacked, they began to produce them in your bloodstreams. Every blow you took or gavé drove molmacs through your skin into your attackers'."

"And Liam and Rik?" California whispered.

"I've already explained to them by comlink. They're coming back. The fight was much worse at their gate."

Alex began to peel off his tightsuit. "Can you get this cleaned up?"

"Of course. The bodies will be cremated according to local custom. You'll want a shower."

He dropped his sticky garment on the floor. "Very much."

California stripped herself and reached out for Alex's bloodstained hand. Together they followed Victor to the bathroom they had used earlier. In a kind of shower stall they stood together while needles of hot water cleansed them. When the last of the destroyed flesh was gone, California hugged him and began to cry.

Liam and Rik came in a moment later; Alex thought for a moment they must have changed into red tightsuits before he realized that they, too, were naked. McCool nodded absently to them and stood for a long time under the nozzle of a spray. Rik knelt on the smooth, wet floor of the shower and then slumped over on her side while the needle spray gradually eroded the red-black crust. Still crying, California pulled away from Alex and went to help Rik.

Alex also sat on the floor, letting the shower pound on his head and shoulders. He edged over to Rik and California and leaned against them. McCool left his shower and sat down with the others, leaning against Rik's back.

"That was no epiphany," the old man said quietly, his voice echoing slightly off the wet walls. "God didn't touch them. Their entropy had nothing to do with divinity. We touched them."

"Just like the old horror shows," Alex said. "Marooned on a floating forest."

"But it is amazing," McCool went on, as if he had

'heard nothing. "Thinking molecules, capable of imposing order on chaos and then creating chaos again at will—with us as their instruments. We were masters, tyrant apes, and now we're utensils." He chuckled. "I thank God, whatever God may really be, that at least I have you companions with me."

Leaning wearily against California's back, Alex drew a deep breath. Instruments. He had felt that way on *Wuthering Heights* just before Victor had taken over the ship. The Chaiar had invaded humanity's world, but humanity had not really responded: The molecular machines had.

Well, and what of it? After all that humanity had learned in the last millennium, did it really expect to be master? It was enough, as Liam said, to have a lover, a companion to share the joys and horrors of life.

Something turned in his mind like a name almost remembered, a dream fading in the moment of awakening. He tried to grasp it, failed, and let it go. Perhaps it would come later. For now it was enough to try to blot out the memory of the woman's startled eyes.

They left the shower at last, dried and dressed in baggy shirts and trousers of black luminar, a fashion of several decades past and of course still in use among the cuckoos. In the control room the Explicators sat drowsing, their eyes closed and their great maned heads tilted forward. The doorway was clear; beyond it Alex could glimpse the empty gate to the outside.

"All the cuckoos who attacked us are now sealed in one of the towers," Victor said. "Tsaunghok spoke to them, and they promised not to interfere again. We expect to arrive in the Hie system in about an hour and then depart at once for Ganigar. In less than twelve hours we should be in the Tayas system."

"Do you really think we can deconvert the whole species?" Alex asked.

"Perhaps some will escape, but they won't be able to spread the Pattern. The deconverted will be immune, like you, and they'll pass their immunity on to the next generation."

"And what then?" McCool said. "Do we go back to what's left of the solar system?"

Victor, standing in the middle of the control room, looked over McCool's shoulder at the black korshak screen. "Maybe, Liam. But I think I will explore the Net and whatever lies beyond it. After all, it's only five thousand light-years across. Habrakha could cross it in a few weeks."

"What a thought," McCool murmured. "The whole galaxy. Worlds no one has ever seen, even on korshak. New species, new data."

Alex looked at California. "Wouldn't it be something, to go beyond the Net?"

"Some day," she said. The feral glint was gone from her eyes; he suspected he would never see it again. "First we have to bring Earth back to life."

He nodded. So did Rik and McCool. "How long do you think it would take?" Alex asked.

"Who cares?" McCool said with a hint of his old cheerfulness. "We'll have all the time in the world, won't we?"

The planet of the Hie was dry and mountainous; the gryphons had built their drab gray cities along the shores of its narrow seas. The false message about an invasion from First Stone went out, and then the missiles; then Habrakha vanished into nonspace again. The control room, like the whole planet, grew cold. Not much sunlight had fallen on Habrakha for many hours, and snow fell on the high plateau of Ta Parng.

The deconversion of the gryphons and cuckoos was proceeding rapidly. The dwindling numbers still clinging to the Pattern were disoriented and passive, obedient to the brief commands of the Explicators. The Explicators in turn were becoming impatient to reach the Tayas system and return to their birthponds on Makhshuar.

Halfway through their next jump, a korshak screen appeared. John F. Kennedy was looking out at them, his face haggard.

"Hello, Alex," he said in a whisper. "There won't be any more fighting. We're all out of the Pattern now. We're free. If this is freedom."

His image vanished.

Ganigar was a beautiful world of dark green continents and vast milky seas. Habrakha hung in its skies for a few hours, absorbing the heat of its sun, and then made the leap to Tayas.

The journey lasted almost sixteen hours, and once

again snow blew into the dome. The Explicators spoke for a time with Victor and then left in a mobile.

"They're going aboard the shuttle," Rik explained. "They thanked Victor for bringing them home. But the words also mean 'making them wise.' I wonder what they'll do when they finally deconvert completely."

"They are deconverted," Victor said, walking over to the humans. "But the urge to return is too strong to tamper with. Most of the other gryphons will begin to feel it also within a few days."

"Even yourself?" Alex asked.

"Yes. But my birthpond was on *Munshaour*."

Alex abruptly understood something of the sorrow hidden behind the gryphon's bony mask. He touched Victor's golden-furred arm, and as he did so he recalled the thought that had eluded him after the battle in the doorway.

"I know why we banded together to fight the gryphons," he said. "You changed us."

The other humans looked at him, surprised. Victor's eyes were unreadable.

"You grew up on *Munshaour*," Alex went on. "Father taught you about human history and biology and how to run the cloudcastle. You knew how everything worked, including the molmacs. When we came to *Munshaour* for my birthday, the robots served us molmac cocktails, the way they always did when people came from off planet, but these were special molmacs, weren't they?"

"Yes. They wired you into caring for one another again. The capacity had atrophied. Your culture had rejected it, and you were all dying. Even if the Chaiar had never come, in another century or two no humans would have been left."

"But the Chaiar did come," Alex said, "so we bonded together to fight them. But what about the others, all the people who joined the molmac merge? You didn't wire them."

"You were the catalyst. Humans longed for one another without knowing it, as gryphons long for their birthpond. Once they saw it was possible to bond together again, many did."

"What gave you the right to tamper with us?" McCool demanded angrily.

"You tampered with yourselves, Liam. You made your-selves into tyrant apes. I thought you would be happier as men and women."

Less than an hour later they walked outside into the darkness. Snow crunched underfoot and swirled in the glow of the lamps. Alex enjoyed the sting of cold on his face and hands; it reminded him of the snowy forest at the bottom of Dwuliu Carson's estate on Venus. The pilot was with them; she had deconverted during the first jump to Kho An and now obeyed Victor rather than the Explica-tors.

And then the sky turned white, a snow sky with a sun burning through it. Almost at once the overcast began to burn away, and the snow faded to a few flakes.

"There go the Explicators—and many others," Victor said. Gleaming in the sunlight, shuttles rose into the sky. Their contrails were thin and soon were erased by the dry winds of Habrakha.

"Not all of them are going to Makhshuar," the gryphon went on. "Some of them were born in space habitats and the other worlds of the Tayas system. They will spread the molmacs very quickly."

"Won't the gryphons who live here suspect something's gone wrong?" Alex said.

"The Explicators are seeking their birthponds. They will tell any lie to get there, and gryphons are very good liars." Victor turned to the pilot and spoke with her for a few moments. Then he said, "The shuttles are clear of the shardana bubble. Now it is time to take you home, to Earth."

Again Habrakha turned in the light of the Sun. On the landing platform on the tower a shuttle hovered; Earth was below the horizon, but Luna was near in the sky. A warm breeze blew, and thunderheads rose above the high plain of Ta Parng.

"Will you come back?" Alex asked. He and the other humans stood near the shuttle gangway with Victor and a few other gryphons. The korshak images of John F. Ken-nedy and several other cuckoos glowed nearby.

"Some day. I would like to see Earth as it once was and to show it to the Habrakhans." He nodded slightly toward

Kennedy. "And I will want to tell you about what we have found out there, at First Stone and Juhho and beyond."

"We'll want to hear it all." He put out his hand, grasped Victor's, and then reached out in an awkward embrace. "Thank you."

The gryphon's long, powerful arms tightened around him. The mask of horn brushed his forehead. "Build *Munshaour* again and I will come back."

The shuttle lifted off; in the cabin korshak screens, Ta Parng fell away until it was lost in a swirl of clouds. The curve of Habrakha's horizon lengthened. The shuttle passed through the shardana bubble, back into cislunar space.

Earth filled much of the main screen, a three-quarter disk of black and gray. Away from its glare, the sky was a thick web of contrails.

"Why all the travel?" Alex wondered. Rik spoke briefly to the shuttle's computer. Her eyes widened.

"They're spacecraft from all over the solar system, coming to Earth. They're going to rebuild it. And look— look, everyone!"

The korshak screen, at high magnification, showed two disks. One was green and brown: Mordor, its shardana bubble tuned to admit light. Not far away was Free Acres, Lyell Bradley's estate, holding the blue waters of the Maldive Islands. Passing across the disk of Mordor was a dark object: the steamship *Wuthering Heights*, in orbit around Earth.

Alex settled back in his chair, remembering how the face of Earth had looked when he had returned to it for his birthday. It had been beautiful then, and he had disliked it. Now it was in ruins, but it drew him as powerfully as the birthponds of Makhshuar had drawn the Explicators.

His life, he saw, was changed yet again: He faced centuries not of duels and coupling, of witty entertainments, but of endless work. With his mother and Lyell he would have to design new molmacs to feed on the poisonous mists that smothered the planet, new molmacs to precipitate the chemicals from its streams and oceans. With California and Rik he would have to explore the Database for the tools to restore the world. With McCool he would plant new forests like those of Jasper House. And with Lord Whitehead and the wild molmacs he would try to find a purpose when the work of renewing Earth was done.

What would it be? Repopulating the Earth would not take long, and the centuries stretched far beyond that simple task. Exploring the far reaches of the galaxy, finding new species? Perhaps. Perhaps humanity would ultimately merge with the supermind it had created, which would have goals he could only guess at.

Soon they would be docking with *Wuthering Heights*, and before that he would have to communicate with his mother and the rest of the alliance.

"Rik, ask the ship to try to contact Mordor, would you? My mother and I have a lot to talk about."

"Of course."

But before she could speak, another impulse struck him and he said, "And ask it to show us both worlds at once."

But Habrakha was already gone.

About the Author

Crawford Kilian was born in New York City in 1941 and grew up in California and Mexico. After graduating from Columbia University in 1962 he returned to California, served in the U.S. Army, and worked as a technical writer-editor at the Lawrence Berkeley Laboratory.

In 1967 he and his wife Alice moved to Vancouver, British Columbia, where he has taught English at Capilano College since 1968. In 1983 the Kilians taught English at the Guangzhou Institute of Foreign Languages in the People's Republic of China.

Crawford Kilian's writing includes several science-fiction novels, among them *The Empire of Time, Icequake, Eyas,* and *Lifter.* In addition, he has published children's books, an elementary social-studies text, and two nonfiction books—*School Wars: The Assault on B.C. Education* and *Go Do Some Great Thing: The Black Pioneers of British Columbia.* He is a regular columnist for the Vancouver *Province* newspaper.

The Kilians live in North Vancouver with their daughters, Anna and Margaret.